Praise for

"These days, for a variety of reasons, it's all too common for adults to ask: are the kids alright? Well, no worries. In Lewis Robinson's riveting new novel *The Islanders,* his eighteen-year-old protagonists are better than alright. They're brave and smart and decent and resourceful. Also, wildly entertaining. Reader, you'll enjoy every minute of their company."
—Richard Russo, Pulitzer Prize–winning author of *Empire Falls* and *Somebody's Fool*

"Robinson is at his expansive best, reaching into a fraught American moment while retaining his gift for creating endearing characters . . . I was enthralled from first page to last, and couldn't wait to get back to the island."
—Monica Wood, author of *When We Were the Kennedys, The One-in-a-Million Boy,* and *How to Read a Book*

"*The Islanders* is at once an engrossing story and a timely, urgent warning: What will happen when the one percent decide to pull up the rope ladder behind them?"
—Kate Christensen, author of *The Astral, The Last Cruise,* and *Welcome Home, Stranger*

Additional Praise for Lewis Robinson

"Accomplished . . . lean and sure-handed. [Robinson] is a keen observer of truths about place . . . and about people, too."
—*Boston Sunday Globe*

"With an impeccable sense of timing and razor-sharp depictions of character, Lewis Robinson takes the reader through incidents that are too intriguing to resist; funny, unexpected, and always oddly poignant, this storyteller has a voice that pulls you right in."
—Elizabth Strout, Pulitzer Prize–winning author of *Olive Kitteridge*

"Robinson is tremendously adept at building menace slowly, quietly, and the shocks as these stories unfold is one of their greatest pleasures."
—*Esquire*

"Robinson writes stories that feel like miniature novels, mostly because they make you desperate to know what will happen at the end. . . A great debut."
—*The Arizona Republic*

"In crisp, concise prose, Robinson probes unusual aspects of the human condition in this debut collection of stories with an edge that snags the reader's memory."
—*Booklist*

The Islanders

Alden Island

WHALEBACK ISLAND

Perimeter Trail

Ainsworth Trail

Gallowglass Trail

Osprey Cove

Osprey Cove Trail

Bridget Point

Big Rug

Bridget Point Trail

Airport

Old Shipyard Trail

Bayberry Trail

Obstacle Course

Tuckaway Island

Armory

Pliny's Trail

Pliny's Quarry

Old Shipyard

Kinnaird Golf Course

WILD Boat House

Athletic Association

Goliath Club House

The Channel

Clovis Point

Grunwald's Cabin

Other Fiction from Islandport Press

Just East of Nowhere
Scot Lehigh

Sunrise and the Real World
Martha Tod Dudman

Hard Line
Gerry Boyle

Silence
William Carpenter

This Time Might Be Different
Elaine Ford

Blue Summer
Jim Nichols

The Contest
James Hurley

The Sea Flower
Ruth Moore

The Islanders

A NOVEL

Lewis Robinson

ISLANDPORT PRESS

ISLANDPORT PRESS

Islandport Press
P.O. Box 10
Yarmouth, Maine 04096
www.islandportpress.com
info@islandportpress.com

First Edition: September 2024
Printed in the United States of America.

ISBN: 978-1-952143-92-2
Library of Congress Control Number: 2024940167

Dean L. Lunt | Editor-in-Chief, Publisher
Shannon M. Butler | Vice President
Emily A. Lunt | Book Designer
Marion F. Fearing | Assistant Editor
Cover Photo by Greg Rec, courtesy of *The Portland Press Herald*

To my mother
Mimo Gordon Riley
who showed me the way.

WHALEBACK
ISLAND

Perimeter Trail

Ainsworth Trail

Gallowglass Trail

Osprey Cove Trail

Big Rug

Ⓐ Ⓑ Ⓐ Ⓒ Ⓓ

Bridget Point Trail

Airport

Tuckaway
Island

Obstacle
Course

Old Shipyard Trail

Bayberry Trail

Armory

Pliny's Trail

Pliny's
Quarry

Old
Shipyard

Kinnaird
Golf Course

WILD
Boat House

Athletic
Association

Goliath Club House

The Channel

Grunwald's
Cabin

Clovis
Point

A - Drake
B - Cook
C - DaGama
D - Vancouver

1 - Erskine
2 - Kinnaird
3 - Brevard
4 - MacLean
5 - Abernathy
6 - Keith
7 - Bannerman
8 - Buchanan
9 - Boyd

WILD Huddle Groups

BRINKLEY HUDDLE
Luna - AK
Alexis - FL
Caleb - GA
Isaiah - ID
Luke - MI
Aaron - NY
Connor - OR
Makayla - CT

HENSHOFF HUDDLE
Cael - WV
Justin - KS
Sydney - NE
Everett - ND
Chloe - TN
Christian - WI
Ryan - WY
Logan - HI

MCCORKLE HUDDLE
Leah - AZ
Kelsi - IA
Mason - MT
Rylee - NM
Savannah - RI
Jordan - WA
Hunter - LA
Kyle - NC

GRUNEWALD HUDDLE
Bethany - AL
Aubrey - ME
Bianca - MO
Tess - MD
Sebastian - OH
Deshawn - UT
Walt - NH
Javier - CA

JANOWSKI HUDDLE
Feng - PA
Joshua - MA
Brian - NJ
Isabelle - MN
Jacob - NV
Olivia - SD
Kyra - VT
Matthew - VA
Mackenzie - DE

NASH HUDDLE
Cole - AR
Hailey - IN
Angel - KY
Faith - MS
Jack - OK
Adam - SC
Luis - TX
Aiden - CO
Zoe - IL

A thousand dreams within me softly burn . . .
—Arthur Rimbaud

The
Islanders

1. Next Summer We'll Have Sweet Jobs

Whaleback Island

I haven't forgotten any of it. The trailhead. My mother driving me there. I wanted her to leave right away because when she hugged me goodbye I almost cried. She said she believed in me and she loved me and I whispered *love you too* and she got back in our Mitsubishi.

At the gatehouse an older guy with a beard and sunglasses searched my pack for food, mirrors, drugs, alcohol, electronics, and weapons. He then pointed me toward the trail. I walked alone through umbrella ferns and spruce trees until the trail opened up to the ocean.

At the edge of the water sat a boathouse full of shellacked wooden rowboats on racks. On its door was a white sheet of paper addressing me and the others starting the program:

1. Three per skiff. Wear life vests.
2. The W.I.L.D. participant with the most experience rowing should row.
3. To reach the island pier row N/NE 21° across the channel.

Thirty yards out in the water, three kids my age wearing blood-orange vests flailed in a rowboat. They were laughing and rowing badly, zigzagging out into the choppier green water beyond the cove. Even now I can say with certainty I wasn't ready to get in a tippy boat and talk to people.

There were no neighboring houses. Just the ocean spreading out to a horizon dotted with islands. I lay down on the granite pier, closed my eyes, and waited for others to arrive.

As a way to recruit us, they told us we'd be of use. They said the program wouldn't cost us anything, and if we worked hard enough, they'd set us up with a job afterward. But in the moment I was thinking mostly about my mom driving back to New Hampshire all alone in the Mitsubishi. And everything else I was leaving behind.

That's when Aubrey and Tess showed up. Of course I didn't know their names yet. They were just two tall girls strapped into external-frame backpacks scuffing the dirt with their boots, walking up to the sheet of paper tacked to the door.

"Looks like we're rowing," Tess had said, thin black braids poking out from her knitted wool hat. She unshouldered her backpack and knelt down next to me. "You're our third," she said. Tess had a round, soft face, brown eyes, strong shoulders. With Tess—because of her confidence, her force-of-nature personality—it's hard to imagine a time when I didn't know her.

"10-4," I said.

Aubrey, standing beside Tess with messy brown hair covering her eyes, opened her pink palm, where she'd written the name *Aubrey* in black marker.

"That's all you'll get from her," said Tess. "Okay, buddy. Help us get one of these boats down."

Aubrey stayed silent and Tess said she could be the one to row. Stepping aboard and wedging our big backpacks between the seats made the boat see-saw, but we didn't flip. I offered to navigate from the stern of the boat. Aubrey, mantis-like and nearly six feet tall, folded herself up in the bow, keeping an eye on the compass to make sure we stuck to the twenty-one degrees N/NE course. I faced Tess but tried not to look at her. I kept my knees and feet together to accommodate her legs, which were braced against my seat.

At that point, I believed they had done something wrong to get picked for the program. That's what I thought the rules were:

We'd all been plucked from juvie or other dire circumstances and were going to be reconstituted, rehabbed, and rebranded by way of the leadership program.

And I thought this even though I myself hadn't really done anything wrong. For whatever reason, I just assumed what I'd done was much less serious than what others might have done. Tess leaned back to pull the oars through the water but they popped out of the oarlocks. She kept having to put them back in place. When we emerged from the cove, the wind frothed the green water and waves slammed the boat, spraying us again and again.

I wasn't worried we'd capsize and drown since I thought we were already being looked after. We'd entered the world of Club, and everything felt like it was going to be fine. Tess was making slow progress across the channel. Aubrey's tangled hair hung over the compass as she pointed to where we were supposed to go.

When Tess knocked into my knees with the overlapping handles of the oars, she didn't apologize, she just said, "Ship of fools."

"Yeah."

"That's us."

"Right?"

To get us to go where Aubrey was silently pointing, I told Tess: "pull harder with your left" or "a little more with your right." And she'd pull by leaning back and keeping her arms straight. Sometimes the wind filled up the hood of her jacket. She said, "Sure as hell beats cleaning motel rooms."

I remember really wanting to hear more about that, but not feeling comfortable enough to ask questions. She probably picked up on that . . . she said, "I worked a full shift yesterday. Someone left their dog behind. Can you fucking imagine? We tried calling the people, left messages, and then my boss let me bring the poor girl to a shelter."

In the open water the boat felt smaller, the three of us and our gear rolling from swell to swell.

"I had to drive like two hours to find a place that wouldn't kill her. I ended up halfway to Pennsylvania."

One of her oars landed wrong, spraying my face.

"Darlene. That's what her collar said. My boss was pissed I was gone so long. But that job's ancient history now. Now rub-a-dub-dub I'm here with you two."

I told her to pull a little harder on her right oar.

"How about you talk now, Walt. Since I'm doing the rowing."

I considered telling them about stealing my dad's keys—he was the head of maintenance at my school—and letting myself in to vandalize the art classroom, but I figured that would sound either insane or like I was trying to show off, so I just told them I'd worked for my uncle's landscaping company in Manchester over the summer.

"You get one of those riding mowers?" Tess asked.

"Fuck yeah I did."

"Nice."

We enjoyed ten or twelve oar strokes of silence.

Tess said, "Maybe next summer we'll have sweet jobs on the island."

"Maybe."

"That's part of the deal, right?"

"Not totally sure."

"I mean I guess they have to see what we're like."

"Right."

"The guy said working for the Club would set us up for life," Tess said.

"What guy?"

"The guy. I don't remember his name."

She was talking about Paul Brevard. He had strong feelings about what was best for us. He had strong feelings about a lot of things.

Tess tucked the oars underneath her legs and shook out her tired arms.

"He said if I didn't want to do college there'd be internships at one of the companies run by someone who comes out here in the summer. The guy used to work for the CIA, and he even said he could put a good word in for me if I did well in the program."

"Seems . . . I don't know . . . unlikely?"

"I know!"

"But honestly I don't know shit," I said, shrugging.

"What'd your guy tell you?"

I told her he'd been vague.

But what I didn't tell her was that I thought I'd been invited under special circumstances. I thought I'd been given preferential treatment. By now I know it's how everyone in the program felt. No one in the Club told us much on that first day.

2. Outside the Realm of Flimsy Plastic and Scams and Other Cheap Crap

Whaleback Island

A ubrey kept us on course, her scrunched-up face hovering above the compass, hair wildly blowing about, arm extending toward Whaleback Island as it grew larger and larger. Halfway across the bay, a lobster boat steamed by, white seagulls swirling above it, radio blasting Guns N' Roses. Tess had been rowing for nearly an hour so I offered to relieve her, but she wanted to finish the job.

Soon the water flattened out. The island blocked the wind. A shamrock-green golf course rose up from sun-bleached rocks. Tall-masted yachts were moored near an elaborate series of floats strung between square granite piers, parking spots for shiny fiberglass powerboats and several racks of kayaks. At the end of the dock was another shingled boathouse identical to the one we'd left from on the mainland. It seemed to hover above the water, with the same number of spots for boats. Hand painted on a single cedar shingle tacked above its entrance:

WHALEBACK ISLAND LEADERSHIP DETAIL

We drifted inside the island boathouse, dark and cool and smelling of oil and marine paint. We shouldered our packs, walked from the floats up a ramp to a wide circle of grass where a young, tan, blonde woman in a sun-visor and skirt sat in a golf cart, unloading children who sprinted toward the docks.

"Welcome, welcome! Good luck!" she said, beaming, then rolled silently forward, turning back up the hill, revealing a sign that had been obscured by her golf cart, another hand-painted shingle on a stake:

WILD—>

We walked up the dirt road through the Club property where adults milled about on the manicured fairways of the golf course, on the lawn bowling court, and on old single-speed bicycles. Some glided around in golf carts. A few long-limbed, shaggy-haired men with their skinny wives and daughters and sons played tennis in tight white clothes. Labor Day was their last chance to be on the island before jetting back to Boston or New York or wherever else. Everyone walked with a spring in their step, and their eyes were clear. Good sleep, fresh seafood, greens from their gardens. Ocean air.

We followed the WILD signs. I think we were all impressed by even the small details, the stone walls being sturdy, not too neat, lichen covered.

Aubrey ambled with purpose, head up, but totally inscrutable; her eyes were still hidden by her wind-tangled hair. Her silence was unnerving to me. When the trail narrowed and entered the woods, she tucked behind me, and Tess stayed in front. The trail was similar to the one we'd hiked on the mainland earlier—clean, healthy terrain—though here the trees were all evergreen, the stumps freshly cut, the path lined with woodchips. The spruce smell was so exaggerated it seemed pumped in. Everything felt outside the realm of flimsy plastic and scams and other cheap crap, and there were no cars. Whaleback Island was mostly just wood and rock.

We followed the signs away from the club to the WILD campus in the forest at the top of the island, on a hill where the trees had been chopped down to make room for five simple cedar-shingled salt-box buildings. The middle and tallest of them, three stories—the main building, labeled Big Rug—was flanked by four modest dormitories.

Tacked to each front door was a typed—by typewriter—list of names. My name wasn't on the first list—Drake—but fourteen others and I were on the list tacked to Cook, next door. I walked with Aubrey and Tess to the adjacent building, Vancouver, saw their names along with eight others on the list, and marveled at the thick white sheet of paper inflected with the typed names:

```
Bethany — Alabama
Hailey — Indiana
Aubrey — Maine
Bianca — Missouri
Alexis — Florida
Kelsi - Iowa
Tess — Maryland
Kyra — Vermont
Mackenzie - Delaware
Rylee - New Mexico
```

Aubrey and Tess entered their dorm without saying goodbye and the door swung shut. I didn't like that. All I could do was walk back to Cook, my heart pounding as I headed in past some ditched backpacks in the stairwell. From the second floor landing, I looked down the pine-planked hallway to an open door.

3. Her Word is Silence

Sebastian Corsetti was my roommate. We all called him just Corsetti, always. He was scrawny with ink-black hair cropped short, a red bandana on his forehead, big eyebrows. When I met him, he was splayed out on the twin bed near the door.

"Damn, finally, you're here!" he said, sitting up. "I grabbed this bunk, but you can have it if you want. My plan is to not be a dick."

That was my plan, too. I told him top bunk was fine.

"You know there are fifteen of us in this joint?" Corsetti said. "And fifteen in the joint next door. Twenty girls total, ten in Vancouver, ten in DaGama. You get recruited by Brevard? I got recruited by Brevard. I like that dude. You know if we'll ever see him again?"

I wasn't sure if I needed to answer any of his questions, but I said, "That's who recruited me, too."

Without elaboration, Corestti said, "He's made some pretty big promises, that guy."

He swung his legs over the side of his bed, hopped up, and put his hand out to me. I shook it. His skin was fish-belly pale. His Carhartt shorts hung low on his hips, and he zipped up his black hooded sweatshirt. It was a corner room, the sturdy bunk bed beside a single window, along with two simple wooden dressers, two chairs—untouched raw pine furniture. Simple and clean and the windows looked out at the nearby branches of the spruce trees. I sat down on the other bed, firm with a wool blanket.

He said, "Just so you know, there's no hot water in this building. No TV, not even a pay phone. And the shitter on our hall refills slow."

He gave me a water bottle because he said he had three of them. He shared his roasted cashews. He moved like a startled animal.

He'd arrived an hour before me, and in that hour he'd somehow managed to do some research by surveilling the building but also by talking to everyone he encountered. He'd gone to the tennis courts and chatted with the members there. He'd met the CEO of a company called Feldspar who described the island as the last frontier, the Club provided members with tennis balls, and dinner for us was going to be tacos. Also the island was two thousand acres, but until the building of the campus the only trees cut down had been along the coast, including, most notably, those used to construct the Islanders Club clubhouse, way back when, and the Club member–owned mansions, built even earlier, were also made from wood milled on the island. The houses were connected only by a series of trails. The island mail boat came and went once daily from Memorial Day until Labor Day. No Club boats ran regularly in the off season. Corsetti also met the wife of an insurance exec with two kids at Princeton who said she'd love to have him over for iced tea.

"She was weirdly hot," he said. "Let's go get some tacos."

Big Rug had three levels. WILD ate on the ground floor, which opened up to the hillside through a set of wide French doors. Inside, the furnishings were stark: a dozen or so large round wooden tables, simple straight-back chairs, shiny polyurethaned wooden floors. Evergreen forest bristled outside the windows. Two long straight serving tables, each with a bowl of apples, a stack of paper plates, a minaret of white Styrofoam cups, and a stainless-steel serving platter with hard taco shells and flour tortillas, metal bowls full of diced tomatoes, lettuce, ground meat, black olives, and salsa.

I was glad to have a roommate, someone to stand next to while surveying the scene. Half the tables were full, a quarter had some vacant seats, and another quarter were empty. Corsetti steered us toward an empty one, which was exactly how I'd operated as a student at St. Bartholomew's, and also at Central Lakes High School, after I'd been expelled from St. Bart's. I liked to sit alone and give others the choice to sit with me if they wanted.

One of the tables near the center was filled to capacity with huge, silent boys, all absolutely destroying their tacos. Another was packed with loud kids: talking, laughing, screaming. Everyone seemed to be dealing with their insecurities in their own way. I've always noticed this—when a group is newly formed, chaos reigns.

I spotted Tess. Far left, near the windows, looking out on the treetops sloping to the water, still wearing her wool hat. Aubrey was next to her in a chair, oddly still wearing her backpack. I told Corsetti I knew them, that I'd rowed over with them, and he headed for their table.

Tess looked up at me, jutted her chin and asked, "Where'd you go?"

Although they'd been the ones to ditch me, I started to mumble an apology until Tess said, "It's cool, it's cool."

Aubrey, hair snarled from the wind on the boat, raised her palm to Corsetti. The ink was more smudged but you could still make out her name.

"Got it," said Corsetti. "Hey, I got a question for you. Our first day and the only instructions we get are typed on a laminated sheet stapled to a fucking pole?"

Aubrey nodded.

"I guess it *is* what Brevard said it would be," said Corsetti.

I was dying to know more about the selection process. I thought I was different because I assumed Brevard hadn't sought me out. The way we'd met had felt coincidental.

Tess said, "He didn't tell me much. He told me I'd be on an island, but he didn't tell me—"

"—you'd have to row yourself there?" said Corsetti.

"No, he didn't," said Tess.

"Ha. These fuckers don't mess around," said Corsetti. "They're like, step up! Some kid comes out here from Ohio, never been in a boat before. Could have easily drowned. That's more than a goddamn trust fall."

Aubrey smiled; she seemed delighted by Corsetti's yammering. He pointed at her. "You don't talk?"

She kept smiling but held his gaze.

"Easy with the finger, man," said Tess. "She's not a dog."

"Hey, I'm just asking."

A track-meet horn blasted somewhere outside the building, and we were told to head upstairs for a meeting.

We gathered in a room with high ceilings, its south-facing wall all windows, and there was no furniture, only an oval rag rug of amazing size—perhaps fifty feet across. None of us knew what to do with ourselves. Tess and Aubrey and Corsetti and I pressed our noses to the wide windows, which looked out on an evergreen expanse sloping down to the distant gray-shingled roofs of a dozen mammoth houses along the shore. Beyond the houses: dark-blue velvety ocean stretching for miles to the horizon.

Someone whistled shrilly and yelled "circle up." A man with neatly combed blonde hair, a plaid flannel shirt, khaki shorts, and sandals walked out into the middle of the rug followed by four other adults, all wearing similar attire—spiffy, outdoorsy—who sat on the rug beside him, and then we all sat down.

The guy in charge looked to be about my mom's age. He paced amid the circle we'd created for him. His thin lips formed a gentle smile. He had a close shave, a manly jaw, and soft hair.

This was Davis Keith. Chairman of the Club's board of directors. He widened his eyes and asked those assembled to put every ounce of their heart into every task. He told us about his great-great-great-grandfather, Wallace Keith, who laid claim to the island in 1807 with a bunch of other "spitfire" Scots, including Hendrick Boyd, who'd married a local girl, Awanata.

He clearly loved this part of the island's history and kept repeating Awanata's name like he was vouching for the grace and beauty of Boyd's marriage to her. He said Awanata was strong and fierce and knew the woods. She could hunt and trap and forage. "Some say if she had lived at a different time, she would have been considered a witch, but here on the island, she was wild and free."

I can't say for sure what he was trying to express by saying that, but it reminded me of the way I'd felt in school after being fed a simple, happy version of a story obviously full of dirt and misery and death and innumerable horrifying mistakes.

Hendrick and Awanata, well, he told us they taught their kids self-reliance. They got their kids to forage and hunt. They trained their kids to be as tough as the crew of tooth-and-nail Scottish kids who worked for Hendrick. The Boyd kids and all other youth on the island became sharpshooters, archers, and slingshotters, competing against nearby islands in feats of strength and speed and agility. Acquiring these skills served an essential purpose—everyone on the island needed to learn that they were strong enough and fierce enough to protect a precious, beautiful place like this. "Ever since the revolution, America has been inventing itself," he said. "This island is one of those pockets of invention."

We in the Leadership Detail, he said, would be bringing the spirit of reinvention back. And the discipline that fostered it. Apparently, Hendrick Boyd and Awanata had raised their eight kids on the island, but it wasn't until the next generation or so that the island mansions were built.

The Club members were leaving the island on Labor Day, and we would have the place mostly to ourselves for the winter, when we'd be asked to reinvigorate the spirit of the island by reliving its past. Seemed like a lot, but I was open to it. I remember thinking as long as they kept feeding me enough, I'd be game for almost anything.

Davis Keith told us we'd be swimming each morning at dawn. And he told a story about growing up in Delaware. His father was a hardass, his mother was a drunk, he'd been held out of school by his dad one spring and asked to fell a huge dying oak tree in their yard. And he'd been given no instructions. This was before the internet. He had to figure it out on his own.

"I had a chainsaw and a shovel and one hundred feet of rope. My dad was working, and my mom was passed out upstairs. So, I made what I thought were the right cuts in the trunk of the tree, and the tree fell. It nearly fell on me but it didn't. It nearly fell on the house but it didn't. And then I cut up what I could of the tree and stacked it neatly, and when my old man got home, he beat me with his belt. I hadn't dug up the stump. So that's what I did for the next few days. And when all that work was done, he told me the tree hadn't been dying. He just didn't want me in school."

Davis Keith went on to describe the structure of the WILD program. The regimen for fall was devised by the instructors, and each instructor had been assigned a Huddle of eight or nine students. Six Huddles in all, co-ed, led by six instructors all trained by the military, all wartime veterans, all now island employees, caretakers and handymen and waitstaff. These instructors, they told us, deserved to be honored and appreciated.

Respect the island, respect everyone in WILD, and adhere to the goal of reinvigoration. "Your instructors will arbitrate that adherence," he said.

Corsetti leaned over and whispered, "I don't give a rat's ass about any of this and I'm fucking starving again."

There was no curfew, no specified time for lights out, there were no parietal rules. We were old enough to know how to take care of ourselves. After each assignment, they'd give us the next one. The assignments were not negotiable.

Davis Keith read the name of each instructor and their interns. Corsetti, Aubrey, Tess, four others, and I were in Dick Grunewald's Huddle. Grunewald seemed older than the other instructors, tall but stooped, dark eyebrows, shaved head, narrow shoulders, camo vest with a white T-shirt underneath. No warmth of spirit, even when he was laying eyes on us for the first time. He just seemed impatient. He was standing, but he told us to drop and give him ten pushups. When we were at seven or eight he joined us, and I noticed two of the fingers on his right hand, and his left pinkie, were cut off at the knuckle, calloused nubs. After we were done with our ten, he kept going. He did fifty.

Then he asked everyone in the circle to say their name, the state they were from, and the first word that came to mind. "Don't think, just say it." He pointed at me.

I said: "Walt. New Hampshire. Rug."

Corsetti said: "Sebastian. Ohio. Pizza."

And we went around the circle, everyone was game, no one paused for long, the tall kid from Utah, DeShawn, said "ocean" and then everyone else started saying nature words, like "tree" and "bird." We got to the only kid who hadn't spoken, Aubrey.

Grunewald said, "And?"

Aubrey looked at him without apology or a gesture of explanation.

"What's your word," asked Grunewald.

She stayed calm and didn't blink. She didn't look bothered. I'd spent the afternoon rowing over to the island with her, but I'd been too anxious about our arrival and not flipping the boat to notice her, to really look at her, her green eyes, her large forehead, her pointy chin.

Grunewald folded his arms on his camo vest, unfolded them to look at his watch, folded them again and said, "It'll be hard for you to be part of this program if you don't talk, Maine."

Corsetti said, "Want me to translate? Her name's Aubrey."

One of the other girls said to Aubrey in a southern accent, "Just say whatever."

Aubrey just sat still with that placid expression.

Corsetti said, "Can we just say her word is 'silence'?"

She seemed fine with this, but Grunewald said, "Maine can speak for herself. We'll just sit here until she does."

She didn't change the angle of her eyes. She scratched her arm. Color rose up on her neck. Maybe Grunewald's persistence was finally getting to her.

Other Huddles were being dismissed; Keith was offering directions to the banquet hall for Convocation which was to happen in a half hour near the golf course.

Grunewald said, "You're really wanting to make things hard on yourself, Maine?"

She stopped looking at him and looked down at the rug.

All the Huddles were gone except for ours. The cavernous room was empty. Purple glowed in the large windows.

"Okay, okay, for Chrissakes, fine," said Grunewald. "I don't understand you. And you seem not to understand me. Why are we doing this? I wish I knew what the fuck was in your mind. Is this a protest?"

Aubrey sat without moving for a few more breaths, staring down at the rug.

"I don't think she's protesting, sir," said Tess.

Aubrey then raised her thin palm to him, where her name was still smudged.

We all stayed quiet.

"Well, I say we go out for a run," said Grunewald. "That's a good way for us to communicate. You'll be late, and if anyone asks why, just tell them it's because your new friend here is stubborn and foolish. Okay, let's bring it in."

He stood and spread his arms out, and we linked up arm in arm, shoulder to shoulder, and he showed us how to put our heads together, skull against skull, all eight of us in the circle, looking down at the floor, and his baritone voice commanded us to close our eyes. He called out our state names, remembering all eight of them.

"Ohio."

"Maine."

"Maryland."

"California."

"Utah."

"New Hampshire."

"Missouri."

"Alabama."

Someone's hair was tickling my ears. I thought Grunewald was going to give us a rousing cheer, some inspirational words, but there was nothing, we just stood motionless like that with our eyes closed and our heads fused together, arms linked, until Grunewald whispered, "In Vietnam, this is what my platoon would do before a raid. That's how we showed each other the Lord saw us all as equals. I'm here to tell you, each of you is equal in the Lord's eyes."

During the upcoming weeks and months, it was clear we'd all have a chance to consider why we were there and how we would invent ourselves and what the Club might need from us. And whether or not we could meet that need.

Calmness spread through my body as I pressed my skull against theirs.

A few more ticks of silence and then Grunewald whispered, "Hey, Maine, you're in charge of your own life. Don't be a whiner. Show us you're bigger and better than whatever crap sandwich you were given. Now put on your running shoes. All of you. It's time for a healthy dose of the good kind of pain."

4. Cut Grass and Booze

G runewald ran beside the girl with the crooked teeth, Bianca, while the rest of us ran at a faster pace. When Grunewald whistled everyone had to circle back to him. This discouraged anyone—like Javier, the Californian, who was fast and didn't seem to get tired— from running too far ahead. Running far ahead was bad because you could get lost in the woods, you could end up on some Club member's property, but it was also bad because, as Grunewald said, we were just a bunch of assholes if we ran alone. Grunewald said he had plenty of work to do to teach us what it meant to be a Huddle.

That first time on the perimeter trail, out on the west side of the island where the path was tastefully cut into the side of a hill just above the Club member mansions, we could see the open ocean all the way to the horizon. We were up above the mansions, staring down at their shingled roofs and mulched gardens and covered swimming pools.

My legs felt limber, strong, tireless. I normally hated the tedium of running. But when we ran on that trail, I had to intuit what was coming, I couldn't plan my steps. I couldn't think, my feet had to think on their own, avoiding roots, jumping over fallen trees, guessing which rocks looked loose and which looked solid. A layer of warm sweat covered my body, and it felt fucking great. Wind blew off the ocean and my limbs pumped and only my fingers felt chilled. Crooked-teeth Bianca was behind me, as were Grunewald and Corsetti. The others were ahead of me; I could see Aubrey about twenty yards ahead, and the others occasionally circled back whenever Grunewald whistled. I remember not knowing if the massive houses we passed were monuments of hard work or dumb luck or sneaky wanton greed. Either way, I felt shy about meeting the strangers who owned them.

Bianca asked if she could puke. She was from Missouri and seemed trashy, which I didn't think of as a bad thing. Trashy actually meant knowledgeable. About sex, about drugs. Trashy meant tough, nihilistic, and perhaps a bit careless. She scared me and impressed me. Her hair was dyed blonde with an inch of black roots showing. She was Bethany's roommate, the one from Alabama. They'd been put together because they were both softball players. By the look of her, I'm sure Bethany could hit a softball out of most parks. In her old life I was one hundred percent sure Bianca dipped Skoal and played shortstop and had a sweet pop-up slide.

Grunewald responded to her by saying, "Why are you asking me?"

So she coughed up some bile and kept on running. That fall each of us, at some point, would end up puking on the perimeter trail. Even Javier, who Grunewald would force to run five perimeter trails in October as punishment for being so damn tireless and fast.

When we were completing the loop, Grunewald looked at his watch and said we didn't have time to change. Sweat-stained and hot-faced we were to head down the newly cut Bayberry trail to Convocation.

Corsetti and I caught up with Tess, who was telling Aubrey that she thought Grunewald was an asshole. Somehow the two had become instant friends, and I was jealous, but that's just the miraculous way some people operate.

The forest was dark and cool, and when the trail narrowed we walked single file and stayed quiet. Columns of light came down through gaps in the trees. The woods smelled of pine sap and bleached crab shells and skunk cabbage and mossy boulders. After about fifteen minutes of navigating through the stale cool air, over roots and rocks and wood chips, we saw the orange light of fire.

The Bayberry trail emptied out onto the eighteenth fairway, lush mossy green. No one was playing so we tromped right across it, toward the main clubhouse, where a hoard of Club members stood chatting beside tiki-torches. Spotting us, many of these Club members hunched over to place their drinks by their feet and applaud. They formed a channel through which they beckoned us to walk to the clubhouse. We'd seen the grounds from a distance earlier in the day, but being there atop the springy grass was thrilling. Faint light, the smell of cut grass and booze. The adults were loud, exuberant, definitely drunk. We'd done nothing to deserve their cheers. We'd agreed to come to the island, that's it. But these Club members were howling their approval, and they were much better dressed than us in our sweaty shorts and running shoes. The male Club members in pleated slacks and loafers, golf shirts. The women in wraparound skirts or long kilts and cardigan cable-knit sweaters. Their skin was pink or tan, and looked as though they'd recently bathed, perhaps they'd been playing tennis earlier, or they'd been out for a sunny hike around the island. I found out later most of them had no idea why we were there, except that we were part of a leadership program. A group of older women with freckled chests and gold jewelry beamed in a way that made me want to live up to their expectations. A few of the older gentlemen were wearing thin ties—identical thin blue ties, a Club staple—along with the same dark blazer with a coat of arms on the breast pocket.

We were the last to enter the clubhouse, and as we did, the two lines of Club members followed us in.

The room was the same size as Big Rug, but the heads of moose, deer, and cougar were mounted on the walls, along with a few full-body taxidermy mounts—bobcat, fisher, mink, beaver. There were leather couches on the periphery, four pool tables, a ping-pong table, a few dozen dining tables, a bar that ran nearly half the length of the room tended by four gentlemen in crimson vests. The door we'd entered abutted the golf course, but the French doors at the other end of the room opened up to a porch the size of a basketball court, held up by pillars over the granite shoreline, pennies of sunlight sparkling on the crashing waves.

I checked my running shoes to make sure I wasn't tracking in dirt or leaves from the woods. The other Huddles were dressed as sloppily as we were—basketball shorts, sweatshirts, jeans, windbreakers, track suits.

As I was filling out a name tag, someone grabbed a fistful of my T-shirt. I looked up and saw Aubrey. She pulled me toward the foyer, out of view, into a bathroom by the entrance. She got us both inside and locked the door. She swept the messy hair from her eyes and then for the first time looked fiercely at me. I was almost sure she was going to punch me in the face. Instead, she jabbed a hand in the pocket of her jeans and pulled out a pen and a small notebook. She crouched, placed the notebook on the floor, and wrote:

> *I can't stay. If Brevard or MacLean ask, tell them I'm sick.*

She closed the notebook and tucked it and the pen back in her jeans, opened the door, and slipped out of the building. Through the window I watched her pull the hood of her blue windbreaker over her head and cross the fairway toward the Bayberry trail. I wanted to be glad she'd entrusted me with her instructions, but I was mostly confused.

Everyone was making a big deal of our arrival, and the party was loud. I was sure Paul Brevard was there somewhere. I thought about what I would say if I were to run into him.

More crimson vests emerged from the kitchen with trays of food. Deviled eggs. Miniature hamburgers. Bite-size quiches. Shrimp cocktail. Beef-kabob skewers. Dumplings and dipping sauce.

One of the crimson vests who seemed a bit older, her lacquered dark hair in a tight bun like a ballerina, offered us a towering platter of chicken wings. She had it propped on a shoulder and passed me an Islanders Club napkin with a free hand.

Even though we'd had dinner earlier, we ate like starving dogs. The ballerina server smiled, all lipstick and eyeliner.

Corsetti said, "You want to just put that down here? Or can I hold it for you?"

"I'm fine," she said. "Have as much as you like. I'm not going anywhere."

"You work here full time?" Tess asked.

Another warm lipstick smile. "Yes, I do."

"I mean, do you live here?" asked Tess.

"For the summer," she said. "Going home tomorrow. Can I bring you some drinks?"

We placed our orders: chocolate milk, Coke, lemonade.

"Certainly. Help yourself to more wings and I'll be back with your refreshments."

The other kids in WILD were clumped together in the middle of the room, near the dining tables, stuffing their faces with food. Some Club members were beginning to mingle, introducing themselves, inviting us to join them at tables, which is when Paul Brevard marched toward us, looking healthy and relaxed, his salt-and-pepper hair wet and combed straight back, heather-gray golf shirt, broad shoulders.

"Welcome, folks! Terrific, terrific. Enjoying yourselves?"

With his mouth full of food, Corsetti blurted, "Yessir."

"The wrestler from Ohio! I remember you. How could I not. Are you happy so far?"

"Stoked," said Corsetti, wiping his mouth with his forearm.

It had been three months since I'd seen Paul Brevard. Aside from telling me a few general details about the WILD Program—its size, the basic approach, and that its campus was on an island—Brevard had also held court on other topics. I remember him asking me about my social life at the two high schools I'd attended, St. Bart's and Central Lakes Regional, but those questions were just an excuse for him to air his theories about the world. He said he was worried about the softness of our generation, but not about us.

"You're better than the others," he'd said.

He'd said he found recruits for the program by scouring the country for misfits, rule breakers, *smart* rule breakers. Defiant rule breakers with a purpose. No druggies. No fuckheads. Kids who had a decent sense of themselves. Kids who had no problem flipping the bird to inept leadership. Kids who'd failed in class because class was bureaucratic but who'd excelled in the gym or on the playing field or at being generally outspoken. Kids who could take a punch, land a punch. I had no idea if Brevard himself had done all this recruiting. He ran a hedge fund. He was used to delegating complicated tasks.

"As you might have suspected, in addition to being in charge of the whole program, I'm your Huddle sponsor," he said, extending a hand to DeShawn. "Paul Brevard." I wondered if Brevard wasn't used to this, shaking hands with someone who wasn't white or old.

He went around the Huddle shaking hands, and when he got to me, he pulled me an inch or two closer, setting me off balance. He winked, then pulled me in further with his meaty hand and whispered in my ear, "no preferential treatment for you, bud!" He looked up at the others and in a full-throated voice said, "Just here for the weekend, but so glad to see you all." He chugged half the wine in his glass. "This, well, it's an exciting project. We're all for it. Tell me, how do you like the island so far?"

We nodded and Corsetti said, "It's crazy."

"It is, isn't it? Tell me what you like about it so far. What strikes you."

"That golf course is insane," Corsetti said.

"We take good care of it."

"Actually, everything's fucking . . . well . . . it's amazing."

"The *Venus di Milo* of islands, I agree," Brevard said. "What else?"

Corsetti continued to be our spokesman. "People are nice."

"Ha! So true. I hope it's not too irritating. One thing I don't like is when people *congratulate* themselves for being members. Often they just stumbled into their good fortune."

Tess said, "Like we did."

"Well, I wouldn't say that. You're here for a better reason than most of us. Most of us were just born into it. You were chosen to be part of WILD. It's an honor. We need more of that. Belonging by way of merit. You'll make this place better."

"Is it true some of us might get fast-tracked to the CIA?" asked Corsetti.

"Well, the CIA isn't what it once was. You don't want to be in the CIA. Or the FBI."

"I'm not really saying I want to be in the CIA, I'm just saying I—"

Brevard raised his palm, signaling Corsetti to relax. He smiled, finished his wine, and pressed a hand to Corsetti's back. Brevard was an imposing presence, like a former professional athlete now calling a game on TV—strong bones and thick hair, smooth skin. I could tell he was comfortable discussing any topic that pleased him. "I like you, son. My friend Howie worked for the CIA for many years, and I truly believe you'd want nothing to do with it now."

The ballerina returned with a tray of drinks.

Brevard said, "You all don't want some wine?"

Tess came up for air from a deep sip of chocolate milk and said, "Sure, I'll have some wine."

"You're what, eighteen, nineteen? I think you can make these choices on your own," he said. "Meals up on the hill will be a bit more spartan, so let's have some wine now while we can. This is the first day of the rest of your life. You remember what Davis Keith said?"

"He said a lot," said Tess.

"What he said about your opportunity to reinvent yourself? Think about the island as your chance to do that. Out here, we're still safe from all the bullshit in the world. Dallas, can you refill this glass for me and grab that same Cab for these fine folks, but perhaps bring theirs in juice glasses. It's less obnoxious that way."

The waitress turned and, in a stage whisper, said to us, "Just so you know, my name is not Dallas. It's Jillian. We've known each other for decades and he calls me stripper names. Talk about obnoxious."

"You're a doll, Destiny. Thank you."

As she walked away, Brevard continued, "She's like my cousin by now. I met her when I was your age."

His face changed expression, showing some concern.

"Where's the other girl from your group? Aren't there eight of you?"

"Yeah, where's Aubrey?" asked Corsetti.

I remember really wanting to relay her message correctly. "She's not feeling well," I said.

"Send her our regards," Brevard said. "Let's go out on the porch. I have someone I want you to meet."

Brevard wore topsiders and khaki pants and that soft-looking golf shirt, and as he moved through the crowd, many of the Club members smiled at him, nodded in his direction, laughed, and said, "Paulie boy!" He bumped them with an elbow, asked them about tennis tomorrow or how long they were up for. He led us to the railing where a younger man, quite a bit shorter than Brevard, stood holding a cocktail. He had close-cropped hair, fashionable stubble, and a strong chin. He wore jeans and a V-neck sweater over a T-shirt.

"Joey!" Brevard boomed.

"Hey, old trout."

They hugged. Brevard gestured toward me and the others. "Folks, meet Joey MacLean."

"Welcome, friends," said MacLean. He flashed his shiny straight teeth. He was much younger than Brevard.

"This is one of the great American geniuses," said Brevard. "Can spot talent from a mile away. Runs a venture capital firm with exits that returned, what, over a billion dollars last year alone?"

"You think a number like that means anything to these amazing kids? Numbers are for boring middle-aged guys like us. Let's talk about the good stuff. How's your first day?"

"We already ran half-way around the island," said Corsetti.

Joey MacLean smiled and flexed.

"Bro, you're a billionaire?" asked Corsetti.

Again, Brevard clapped a hand on Corsetti's back and said, "Let's work on how we ask our questions."

"Ha, ha. That's fine," MacLean said. "Maybe you're interested in the numbers after all. And I appreciate that you're direct. That's what we brought you here for."

"What was your first job?" asked Corsetti. He had a way of moving too close to the person he was talking to, and while MacLean didn't seem to mind, Brevard said, "It's not a competition, son."

MacLean laughed. "I love it, Paul. Questions are great. First job? Working on a tuna boat. I learned patience and decisiveness. And how to play cards."

"You catch a lot of fish?" asked Corsetti.

"Tons."

"What were they, like, this big?" asked Corsetti, spreading his arms wide.

Everyone laughed, and Brevard said, "This kid will keep you honest."

"Way bigger, man!" MacLean said. "But then he lowered his voice to a whisper. "Most people in this room, they love the *idea* of a leadership program, but they have no fucking clue what it takes. I've had some rough and tumble days, just like you. I can already tell you guys have what it takes. And we love you and we want you to be part of our scene."

Jillian passed juice glasses of wine to me and the others.

"You're good at what you do, Crystal," Brevard said.

"You're shameless," said Jillian. The glass she handed Brevard was long stemmed and nearly full.

"Great pour," he said. "To Joey MacLean," raising his glass.

We all raised our glasses. MacLean said, "Congrats on getting here. Relish the work. Don't be afraid to succeed. *Be who you are.* That's who we want you to be. It's what I say to the companies

I invest in, and I'll say it to you. *Be who you are.* And I also say, *You're on our team!* And what I say to the bad guys is: *We're coming for you!* Ha!"

"Cheers," we all said. I drank half my wine in one sip and felt insatiably thirsty and excited.

MacLean downed the rest of his drink and said, "The history of this place is important, and it's almost completely ignored. We need more of what those kilt-wearing bastards had. Ingenuity. Toughness. Grit. You—all of you—have plenty to teach us."

"This guy!" said Brevard.

"Good party, man," said MacLean.

"What Joey MacLean won't tell you kids is that in the venture capital world, they keep track of a number. It's called the arrogance/accomplishment ratio. Obviously, the goal is to keep your number low. But you can get there two ways. You can do really well at your job, or you can be a super nice guy."

MacLean pounced on Brevard and in one quick move had him in a headlock. He was almost up on Brevard's back because he was so much shorter, and he had him immobilized. "Or you can do both, you big old buck! And your ratio approaches zero asymptotically!"

"Squeeze!" yelled Corsetti. "You got this! Don't let him reverse you!"

But MacLean released Brevard, and both men were flushed and smiling.

"You got to teach me a few wrestling moves, kid," Brevard said, smoothing his shirt out.

"Paulie, I'm gonna scoot. Need to meet a few of the other Huddles. Great seeing you all. Remember, be who you are."

"I'm on your team and we're coming for you!" said Corsetti.

"A-plus," MacLean said, pointing his big pink finger at Corsetti before slipping back through the crowd on the porch, disappearing inside.

"Joey's got the right amount of psycho in him," said Brevard.

I'd assumed the club members were going to be awkwardly stiff and formal. MacLean reminded me of some of the young coaches in my hockey league who were always super amped. Dressed for the part, wearing a suit and tie in a cold rink, gelled hair, but ready to go ballistic if something went wrong. They knew childhood was a violent time.

Jillian took her round serving tray and headed for the kitchen. Brevard said, "Bring back some more wings . . ."

". . . Bambi?" said Tess.

Jillian glared at Brevard and smacked him with tray. "You're teaching these kids your stupid game?"

"Sorry," said Tess. "I couldn't help it."

"I don't blame *you*, Sweetheart. It's Mr. Brevard's fault."

She slapped him again on the arm.

I chugged the rest of my wine—on that deck with an ocean view it tasted like grape juice. My tongue warmed and it was tough not to smile. The island felt supercharged, and I was happy to be there. Underneath us the white noise of waves crashed on the rocks.

Brevard pushed a hand through his well-groomed hair. "You know, the folks who were here when Keith and Boyd first showed up, Awanata and all the rest . . . for them, the word 'island' was a verb. It was like, 'to be an island.' That's what the word meant. A way to be, a thing to do, just like running or jumping or hunting or eating. Islanding. That makes sense, right? Like staking a claim. Standing up for what's in your heart. Standing out. Distinguishing yourself from the filth of the world. Islanding means living your own way, maybe even living forever."

We all laughed, not sure if he was totally serious. He was good at bullshitting, and it wasn't bad entertainment.

Brevard continued: "What's your take on Mr. Grunewald so far?"

"Cranky," said Tess.

"Ha, that's him. You'll be in good hands. He's got the right training, that's for sure. And he knows how rare a place this is, how important it is that it be cherished and protected. He's worked for

Joey MacLean and his family for twenty years. If MacLean can't pick 'em, I don't know who can. Grunewald is an analog man in a digital age. He's all about muscle and hard work." Then he cleared his throat, and said, "Last thing I want to say here and now is that your background no longer matters. Here on the island, you've got a fresh start. Clean slate. Now it's all about teaming up, making something special."

He looked over toward the pool tables. "Tiffany!" he yelled, getting Jillian's attention, raising his empty wine glass. "More!" Then he turned back to the group.

"Grunewald is a good one to offer lessons about allegiance and rising to a challenge. Rise to the challenge, and you could be Joey MacLean's protégé. That'd be nice, right? Help to make those billions? I'm not promising all of you will make it, but all of you have a chance. All of you have the potential to do great things for us and with us. Like MacLean said, don't be afraid to succeed."

Jillian arrived with the bottle, filled Brevard's glass, grinned at us, and Brevard said, "Top them off, too."

"Come on, Paul. Let's not get them into trouble," she said, with a no-nonsense side-jut of her hip.

"I'd take some more," said Tess. Jillian gave her half a glass, then raised her eyebrows, holding the wine bottle up for me. I was game.

There'd been such strictness at the mainland gate. They'd searched bags to make sure none of us had any contraband, but now we were getting offered multiple glasses of wine. I wanted to keep playing the part of someone familiar with a gathering like this. I drank my wine heartily. Brevard's body was angled toward Tess, laughing at her list of stripper names.

"Asia, Chyna, Paradise," she said.

"Mercedes," said Brevard, clinking her glass.

"Chastity."

"Charity."

"Sierra."

"Um . . . Bunny?" said Brevard.

"Borderline," said Tess. "I win."

Brevard laughed his baritone laugh while Tess not only finished her glass of wine but grabbed his and took a big gulp.

"How the heck do you know so many stripper names?" said Brevard, using his forearm to wipe his brow as though exhausted by the competition.

"I cleaned motel rooms," said Tess, staring him down. "And I have a good memory." She was still holding his wine. She took another big gulp. Brevard reached out for his glass and pulled it away from Tess's lips, mid sip.

She didn't skip a beat and said, "How do *you* know so many stripper names, sir?"

"I read a lot," he said, winking again. "All right. I'm going to sneak out of here before I cause any more damage." He finished the last of his wine. "Excellent meeting you fine people. I've got to head out a little early. It's better for me to get home before it gets dark. For future reference, my place is on Tuckaway, a little island right around the bend." He pointed toward the trees off the right side of the porch. "I've got a little putt-putt that I use to zip back and forth."

"A putt-putt?" asked Corsetti.

"A little outboard."

"Outboard?"

"A boat, kiddo. A motorboat. Listen, I'll be seeing you soon. The future of the island is bright. Be yourselves. We're counting on you." He tapped his enormous fist against my shoulder and walked down the stairs off the porch, heading across the eighteenth fairway.

5. Messages for the Pigeons

Whaleback Island

After the sun had gone down, after a leathery-faced man in a seersucker jacket gave us a short speech about the salt bond we all had as members of the community (salt at meals, salt in tears and sweat, salt from the morning swim), it became clear, because we didn't have flashlights, that a Club member needed to usher all fifty of us across the fairway to the trailhead. We didn't know the woman who led us, but she seemed plastered and friendly, and she giggled as she told us her heels were sinking into the grass. She used her flashlight to steer us unsteadily. When she got us to the trailhead, she said, "Best of luck, you adorable creatures," and she left. Little by little our eyes adjusted to the darkness with limited moonlight coming through the tree branches.

We had to take it slowly. I felt tipsy and wondered if Tess was even more drunk—she'd swigged two glasses and half of Brevard's. She grabbed Corsetti's hand to steady herself over the roots and rocks and said, "Don't get excited. I'm just not used to walking on this shit."

We proceeded that way: Corsetti first, then Tess, then me—and several clumsy steps into our hike I felt Tess reach back and grab the loose fabric on the front of my windbreaker. We were linked up in the darkness. Bianca and Bethany and DeShawn and Javier were somehow moving more quickly and had gotten well ahead of us, along with the other kids from WILD.

"What's a protégé?" asked Corsetti.

"Being under someone's wing," Tess said. "Like an assistant."

"Cool."

We moved quietly through the forest. The sound of the ocean in the distance, the strangeness of the welcome party, the gratitude for our presence on the island, the pitch black around us, all of it made me light-headed.

Only occasionally, at home, had I felt this excited about life. This happened when I was in charge of my own actions. And when I didn't feel in charge, at least I could retreat to my mental bubble and stay safely unharmed there, free to judge others when I couldn't stand to be part of the idiocy I often witnessed. Sometimes I'd go to the sand pit alone for hill sprints at dawn, the cold air filling my lungs, my face warming from the work, and from the sun's orange light on the walk home. I had no one to push me, which was fine. Tired legs, hunger, my warming body—all of it was my secret. That's when I could say to myself I believed in God, but that belief was personal and private and no one had to know. Stopping at Cumby's after one of these workouts, I'd grab juice from the cooler and tear open a little packet of salt from beside the hotdog machine and pour it into the juice. The cashier always seemed to have questions in his eyes about what I'd been up to, how I'd gotten sweaty. He might have thought I was some kind of freak, or he might not have seen me as any different from any of his customers. Either way, I reveled in the silence between us.

Tess, Corsetti, and I were moving slowly, still holding on to each other, when we saw a light up ahead, bouncing amid the trees: the headlamp strapped to Aubrey's brow. She whistled two notes, low then high, like the first two notes of "Heigh Ho, Heigh Ho, It's Off to Work We Go."

"Just in time!" said Tess.

We slow-walked our way through the inky forest, each of us holding onto the jacket of the person ahead, the beam from Aubrey's headlamp cast down at the terrain beneath our feet. We didn't say anything about Aubrey's decision to come all the way back to get us, or her decision to leave the party. It didn't matter. We were all together now.

In the quiet dark forest Tess told us about her uncle who kept homing pigeons on his rooftop in Baltimore, that she'd sometimes take the bus down to see him, and that they'd write messages on tiny scraps of paper, roll them up, put them in the little tubes attached to the birds, and send them out. They'd sit in the sun and drink tea and wait for the birds to return, and more often than not when they did—many hours later—the little notes were gone. Her uncle, she said, had not trained them in any fine-tuned way. What he did have success with was getting them to return, but as for where they went, he didn't ever really know. He didn't know who got those notes. She'd write dirty messages, roll them up before her uncle could see them, things like, "my boobs are growing" or "When can I dance naked for you?"

We laughed, and as we walked, we each made up messages that we'd send out with the pigeons.

Corsetti said, "I want to show you my junk."

"Aw, man, that's not very good," said Tess.

"You just said that thing about your tits?"

"Try again."

He seemed uncowed. He said, "Okay, how about: Let's meet on October 1 at noon in the ball pit of the McDonalds PlayPlace."

"Kind of long," Tess said, "but very, very romantic."

"I heard in Texas they found an anaconda in one of those."

When it was my turn, I took my time. They didn't care, they were patient. Finally, I said, "By being too sensitive I have wasted my life."

Aubrey laughed.

This was the first sound we'd heard from her, aside from the whistle. In the darkness, Tess said, "Deep, but sad. Romantic, too."

"It's from an Arthur Rimbaud poem," I told them, hardly believing I was admitting this, quoting from the book my mom had given me. "He wrote it in French, so I'm not sure if I've got the full meaning."

My hand was damp, gripping Aubrey's jacket. In my mind I returned to her laugh. Her laugh had sounded miraculous in those dark woods.

"You memorized that?" Corsetti asked. "What the hell does it mean?"

I understood his tone to be genuine, not critical. I said, "Maybe, like: don't think too much?"

"I like it," said Corsetti.

"It reminds me of another note I wrote for the pigeons," said Tess. "'Shut up and kiss me.'"

I assumed she was signaling her interest in having Corsetti kiss her. But I wasn't sure. And I was still so rattled by hearing Aubrey laugh.

As if in response, Corsetti whistled the two notes Aubrey had whistled earlier—"Heigh Ho." Tess whistled the notes as well. Then I did. And finally, Aubrey again. And these sounds made me happy.

Before we could propose any more pigeon messages, the trail opened up to the propane lights of the dorms, and we split off, unlatching from each other, Corsetti and I steering toward Cook, Aubrey, and Tess heading further uphill to Vancouver, Tess whispering "goodnight" without turning around.

6. Saltshaker's Son

About nine months before I met Tess and Aubrey and Corsetti, I was eating lunch in the St. Bart's cafetorium on the last day before winter break. It was the middle of hockey season, so I needed about four thousand calories a day, one-hundred eighty grams of protein, and I'd set myself up in front of two full plates of lasagna, another plate of fried chicken, steamed carrot slices, chocolate pudding, chocolate milk. That last meal before break was always a good one for peace and quiet, an ideal time to really pack it away. I'd just started the second plate of lasagna when Alessandra Shinwell stepped square in front of me holding a plate of lime Jell-o, slivering her eyes. She was a loud, unafraid girl with Cleopatra eye makeup and a pierced bellybutton. I'd known who she was all my life—she was the daughter of the art teacher—but it was just in the last few years that I decided I wanted to have sex with her, even though I'd never had sex, and I'd never talked to her.

"You can eat all that?" she asked.

I glanced down at the plates and nodded.

"That's inspiring," she said.

Her eyes were still squinting. Her brown bangs were a sharp fringe across her forehead. There was a shady hollow above her collar bone.

"You could take this act on the road," she said, sitting down across from me. "You could be a competitive eater. Train yourself to ignore your brain. Which is maybe what you already do? That's what *they* do, the guys you'll be competing against, the guys who eat fifty hotdogs. You know about that?"

I shook my head.

"Don't let me interrupt," she said. "Do your thing."

With her fork she stabbed a cube of Jell-o and set it on her tongue. She was the kind of person who didn't seem to worry about whether or not her socks matched, and she could laugh uproariously at other people's jokes, even lame ones. She existed as a cavalier force in our conservative school without being resented. She seemed to have better taste than everyone and yet she was still well liked because she wasn't an asshole. The other kind kids, they got trampled. But for Alessandra, because she was Ms. Shinwell's daughter, and because she was so effortlessly rebellious and attractive, kindness won her good favor. She was not kind to faculty members, including her mother, which boosted her standing among the students and made her kindness, especially toward the bottom-feeders, seem even more impressive. She was constantly in public battles with teachers, calling them out for their hypocrisy or their bias, and this never seemed whiney, it always felt justified and noble. She was the unofficial and unelected student spokesperson, a small loud girl who allowed her peers to feel, momentarily, like they had something on the adults.

I chewed a bite of lasagna.

"You're Saltshaker's son, right?"

Most kids called my dad Saltshaker because he spread salt and sand on all the icy pathways between school buildings by hand.

"He's a hard worker," she continued. Was she saying this because she really thought my dad worked hard, or did she just want to smooth over the fact she'd just called my dad Saltshaker? I'm pretty sure she was pretending she didn't know exactly who I was. She took a notebook out of her backpack and dropped it on the table beside my trays of food.

"Write something for me," she said.

I made a questioning face.

"Any sentence you like. I can analyze handwriting. I'm a graphologist."

"Why would I want my handwriting analyzed?"

"Self-knowledge," she said.

"Maybe I know what I need to know," I said. Apparently, I thought this was a good way to talk to someone I wanted to have sex with.

"Which probably means you don't know much. Hockey players are generally taciturn. Goalies especially. Crazy taciturn. Sometimes just crazy. You've heard that before, I'm sure."

It was something I'd heard. A lot. And disagreed with. But I wanted to keep the conversation going, so I wrote the sentence: *If you play hockey, you might as well win.* A quote from Martin Brodeur, former goalie of the Canadian national team, who'd surprised many with what he said during press conferences throughout his career.

"Deep."

"Not bad, right?" I felt oddly calm. Probably because the cafeteria was empty. Too often I was in a rush to get from class to class, from class to practice, from practice to study hall. Typically, I avoided talking to other kids. There were the guys on the hockey team, sure, but as the goalie, I was always separated from them, emotionally and physically. And I knew some kids were wary of me because of my dad's lowly role at the school, and because I was only there because of him, and because of hockey.

"You see the way the O's aren't complete circles?" she asked.

"That one is."

"Well, that one isn't."

"That one is, too."

"Don't lawyer me on this. I do actually know what I'm talking about."

"What does it mean?"

"People who don't complete their o's are prone to erratic behavior."

"It looks like I complete about half of my o's. What does that mean?"

"That you're sexually frustrated." She said this without smiling. She just stared me down. "You can see it in your p's, too. Not a big deal." She quickly switched gears. "See how angular your h's are? That means you're extremely smart, but prone to aggressive and potentially violent behavior. And that you have a high threshold for pain."

"For fuck's sake."

"Are you smart?"

I wasn't good at doing assignments if the rules weren't fair or productive. In my own mind I felt like a genius sometimes, and sometimes I just felt boring. I had no way of comparing this with what was going on in other people's brains. To this girl who'd ambushed me while I was happily eating, I said nothing.

"You seem smart," she said. "See the way you cross your t's? That suggests untapped potential. You seem fairly 'tapped' though. Like, the goalie thing. You're dialed in. I admire that. Why are you so quiet right now?"

"I'm thinking about what you're saying, and I don't have any reason to respond."

"Why don't I know you?" she asked.

"You do," I said. Given the circumstances it felt surprisingly easy to assert my opinions to her.

"Yeah, but you know what I mean. You're kind of known as someone who keeps to himself."

I said, "Why'd you ask me if I was Saltshaker's son?"

"You mean, why'd I call him Saltshaker?"

"No, why do you pretend you don't know who I am?"

"I was meaning for it to be a rhetorical question," she said.

"Really?"

"Do you have access to his keys?" she asked.

The normal rules didn't seem to apply to this moment. I was good at hockey and nothing else. It had taken me eighteen years to have this kind of conversation with someone I wanted to have sex with, even though I didn't really know what sex was, practically speaking. I felt grateful she'd been willing to come to my table and analyze my handwriting. I didn't believe her analysis, but what seemed genuine was her interest in considering what it felt like to be me.

"I know where he keeps them," I said.

"What time does he go to bed?"

"Around nine-thirty or ten."

"Meet me at eleven with his keys in the rhododendrons beside the main entrance," she said.

"Rhododendrons?"

"Those bushes next to the door, dude. Eleven."

7. Lockers

That night, after talking to Alessandra for the first time, I sat beside my dad in his warm Silverado with its plow lowered as he pulled out of the garage and into the storm, snow thick in the headlight beams. We crossed into the library parking lot and plowed back and forth like a mower across a lawn. I remember the red and yellow lights inside the cab reflecting on the lenses of my father's eyeglasses.

Earlier that night I'd asked him about the cold war developing between him and Mom, and every passing second in the truck offered Dad an opportunity to respond, but he didn't. We plowed the gym parking lot, and then admissions. Back and forth, back and forth. While I waited to hear what he had to say I began to wonder if the news would be related to having spent the weekend in the hospital six weeks earlier. Neither he nor my mom had told me anything about it, except that the surgery had been a success, a doctor had removed a few small sections of my father's lung. Apparently, he'd had a drainage tube sticking from his chest for a week after he'd gotten home, which had since been removed, and I was asked not to tell anyone at school about it—no one was to know my dad had been in the hospital.

We were on our third parking lot, the snow was still filling the air, when Dad said, "Okay, that's good."

"That's it?"

"That's it. For tonight."

"I thought you had something to tell me," I said.

He stopped the truck at the mouth of the lot, beside the library, before turning onto the main road. "I could but it's pretty difficult to explain."

"Try me."

"Okay," he said. He seemed impatient. "I love your mom. Do you understand that?"

"Okay."

"But even though I love her, I did something that hurt her."

"Why?

"It wasn't intentional."

We both stared out the windshield as the snow swirled outside. On the façade of the library, snow clung to the mortar between the bricks. I asked, "Was she upset you had to go to the hospital?"

"No," he said. "She's mad about . . . my friendship with someone."

"Someone?"

"Yes."

At that moment, despite great effort, the only occasion I could remember witnessing my father talking in a friendly way with another adult was the previous winter, when someone he'd served with—a guy he called Pop Rocks—had stayed in the house for the night.

"It's not right," Dad continued. "It never should have happened."

"What never should have happened?"

"I never should have become friends with her."

He took a pack of spearmint gum from his jacket pocket, unsleeved a piece, ripped it in half.

"Who? And when was this?"

Dad clicked off the wipers, popped the half-stick of gum in his mouth, offered me the other half. I refused it. The wind quieted but the snow was not letting up, sticking to the warm windshield.

"Here's the thing, Walt. Your mother and I haven't been seeing eye to eye for quite a while now. You and I both know how great your mom is but she's also a pain in the ass. Right?"

"She's not a pain in the ass," I said. I definitely wasn't the right audience for Dad's complaints.

He said, "Okay, well—you don't know her like I do."

"Maybe she's a pain in the ass to you because of your 'friendship with someone.'"

My mother worked full time at Brigham down in Boston as a psychiatric nurse and planned her schedule around my hockey games and practices and kept stats for me, but only because I'd asked her to, and had never once put pressure on me to join a team or anything else. She trusted me, listened to me, respected me. Dad was quiet now, so I asked, "Who's the friend?"

"It doesn't matter, Walt. It's over. Don't do what I've done. But remember you only have one life to live. If things aren't right—if your life is not turning out how you want it to—then do something to change it."

Dad liked making this kind of speech and it was his way of ending a conversation. He took his foot off the brake and the truck rolled forward, snow clinging to the windshield. When he clicked on the wipers, all we saw was sideways-blowing snow.

Dad being a stubborn prick made it easier for me to take his keys. I waited until he'd gone up to bed. Just as Alessandra had promised, she was waiting for me in the snowy bushes, and once I let us into the school, Alessandra led me first to the gym, where we toggled on the bright overhead lights, rolled a rack of balls to center court, took out a ball each, dribbled for a while, chucked up some shots. Neither of us was a basketball player but this was excellent, being where we shouldn't have been, the echo of the bouncing ball on the pristine varnished floor in the huge empty room. We went next to Father Gerard's office, took turns reclining in his chair. We then opened several classrooms, sat in the desks we'd sat in during school, and we sat in the teacher's chair, enjoying the feeling of being in that same space but being unseen. We didn't talk much, and Alessandra was making the decisions about where we went next. My body buzzed and my mind felt light and clear. She wore a long black parka and a baseball cap and so really all I could see of her was her mischievous eyes and her off-kilter smirk. After the classrooms we went back to the administrative offices, to Jane Callahan's desk—she was Father Gerard's secretary—and Alessandra found, at the back of a filing cabinet, a three-ring binder with a list of all the locker combinations. She held it up like a championship trophy.

"We now have access to every single item that every student in this school has chosen to hide."

I was excited, too, but it felt like a big leap. We only had the binder because I'd stolen my dad's keys. Alessandra seemed to pick up on my nervousness, and she said, "We don't need to take anything. We're not thieves."

I liked her use of "we."

We searched a whole bunch of lockers and found nothing of consequence. The first unusual item we found was a bottle of pills in Owen Langendorff's locker. Alessandra held up the orange container. *Depakene.* I learned later that this was anti-seizure medication.

Owen was a funny fat kid who got a little famous at school in the fall for the story he told about his second cousin sucking his dick over the summer. He got teased for being slow-moving and for being late for class, but he laughed at any joke told about him and was well liked for that very reason. When Alessandra put the pills back she said, "You know Owen's second cousin sucked his dick, and then kissed him and spat the spunk in his mouth and made him swallow it?"

I said, "Yeah" but I hadn't heard that second part.

"Owen's a good dude," she said.

"Yeah," I said, although I was thinking in that moment how little I knew about anyone.

"I mean, I still feel fine about searching his locker."

We checked five or six more lockers and found packs of gum, loose change, hair scrunchies, socks, headphones, a Whopper wrapper, more pills—lots of pills, mostly for ADHD and anxiety and depression—toothbrushes, notes from mom. We moved from locker to locker in a businesslike way. I was completely fascinated by each little universe we entered. We weren't talking a lot as we worked, but I felt an electrifying kinship with Alessandra. Would everyone find this fascinating, or did Alessandra and I have a special hunger? Maybe peeking into the private worlds of others was a common desire. I simply didn't know.

We'd checked the lockers of people she knew, until she asked me, unsolicited, if there was anyone's locker I wanted to pillage? A random name popped into my mind—Willis Lowe. A sophomore. Punched above his weight academically. Was in my Calculus class which was otherwise all seniors. I said his name.

"Who the fuck is that?" asked Alessandra, and I then felt I needed to offer a good reason that of all the people in the school, of all the kids whose lockers we hadn't yet opened, Willis Lowe was the top of my list.

"He's a genius," I said.

"Never heard his name," she said.

"Like, brilliant. Off the charts."

Alessandra spun the lock, chunked it open, then yanked on the door. What seemed like an entire load of laundry tumbled onto her. Shorts, T-shirts, pants, a parka. A few pairs of socks. As I bent down to pick up the clothes, Alessandra shined the light from her watch into the locker. She made a sound, an involuntary little hitch of breath. When I stood up, I saw what she saw. Inside was a clear bowl of water. A fish bowl. With a fish inside.

Again, our shoulders touched.

The fish wasn't moving. It just stayed suspended in the middle of the bowl like a grape in a cast of Jell-o. Alessandra had the light aimed at the side of the locker, so the beam wasn't too bright on the poor animal. It wasn't floating atop the water, so it was still alive, right? Alessandra and I stood there, staring at the fish, until finally the little guy moved its tail very gently. The fish coasted toward the light.

"Genius?" said Alessandra.

"I mean, he's good at math."

"Evil genius," said Alessandra.

"Should we free the fish?" I asked.

"That's not our place. But you should talk to this kid. *Willis Lowe?* He's a tenth grader? He should know better."

"I guess I could do that," I said, but I knew I'd never do such a thing. I did not think of myself as someone who could inspire others to change. I could take care of my own shit, sure. I was the winningest goalie in St. Bart's history and the goalie with the lowest career goals-against average in the state, but for as long as I'd played I knew I didn't want to be a leader. I didn't even want to be a person who said a single word in the locker room. I'd listen, absolutely. But my sport was all about action. I focused on keeping the puck out of the net. I just wasn't the type who could sling an arm around Willis Lowe and offer him life advice.

Again, Alessandra seemed to read the situation instantly and she said, "You know what? Fuck it. Let's take the fish."

"Totally," I said.

"Can you grab it?"

"Yup."

She stuffed the clothes back in and locked it up, and we walked back through the dark halls of the school.

"Let's do this again sometime," she said.

"Okay."

"I'll track you down after vacation."

She held the door open for me, and I walked into the cold night with the fishbowl in my arms, and said goodbye to her, for the time being, and began thinking about what I would tell my parents when asked where the fish had come from.

8. The Framed Candid Pictures of Smiling People
New Hampshire

T he week of school vacation, while Alessandra was in the Turks and Caicos, my father had a few more sections of his lung removed. My mom said to tell people who asked about my dad (and no one did) that he'd gone to Minnesota to visit his brother Gus. Again, despite how mad she was at my father, she wanted to make it clear that the lung condition, which I still didn't know much about, was not my father's fault. When he returned from the hospital with another tube in his chest, he went back to work, kept up with the plowing and the long list of maintenance jobs that were best done when school wasn't in session, waxing floors and steam-cleaning carpets. At home, my father was mum on the details of his conflict with my mother, and I wondered who the hell he could have possibly taken up with. This nearly broke my brain. It couldn't have been anyone at school. The options were few. Maybe it was the crazy-eyed cashier at Hannaford who always asked about the weird pickles he liked or Marcie at the dump, who seemed far too pretty to work there. Who else did he ever have contact with?

Even after the surgery my dad was working hard to keep things light and activity filled; he borrowed his cousin Trent's snow machines and we took them to the sandpit, which in theory could have been fun, but I'd never driven one before and the sled was louder and more throttle-responsive than I'd anticipated, and Dad, just days after his surgery, looked white-faced and uncomfortable, wincing, then forcing a smile when he pulled up beside me as my head pounded from the exhaust and noise.

There were only nine families who were given housing by the school, and they were spread out on the perimeter of campus. Although I knew where everyone lived, when school wasn't in session, there was no reason to see these people unless by mistake—if someone was out retrieving their mail or shoveling their front steps. The house where Alessandra and her mother lived was *not* a school-owned house, but it had once been owned by the school; they'd sold it in the seventies when they were short on cash. It had been the headmaster's house, three-stories tall with pillars. Father Gerard lived in a much more modest house, beside the rink. After snowmobiling, I had an hour or so before my mother was taking me to the roadhouse for dinner, so I went out for a walk in the dark, looping out past the library to the athletic fields, thinking about the recent attention Alessandra had been paying me, particularly our late-night locker rummaging, which had really plugged me in. I walked with long, confident strides. I hadn't even minded having to tell my mother about the divination of the goldfish, which I'd said was given to me by a friend. The night was cold and clear, my breath steamed. The snow from the storm was up to my knees so I kept to the walkways, which my father had somehow snowblown before sunrise.

I felt immune and invisible. I walked right over to Alessandra's house and stood amid the hedges beside the front door in the snow just below a window. The shades were drawn, but not all the way, so I could peer through the gap between the sill and the bottom of the shade. A streetlight on the other side of the building filled their kitchen with a wan orange light. The wrongness of what I was doing spread through my body like pinpricks. Or was it even wrong? I felt no fear of being caught. There were faculty and staff apartments nearby, some of which were still occupied during the Christmas vacation—plenty of folks were still around but I didn't care.

In the foreground was their living room—a modern sectional couch, a jade plant on a little wooden table, floor-to-ceiling bookshelves full of books and board games, a love seat, an orange cat sleeping beside another small table holding a ceramic sculpture: a pig, or maybe a whale. Nicer furniture than in my house, neat and tidy, no TV, lots of candid pictures of smiling people on the walls. That, above most other clues, made their place seem different. My mother had mentioned once that Sarah Shinwell came from money. The framed candid pictures of smiling people with mountains and sailboats and beaches throughout the house perhaps gave this away.

The double doorway to the kitchen was open and I could see a dark wooden table beside a window that housed another sprawling plant. I stood there, my muscles still warm from the walk, my breath rhythmically fogging the pane in front of me. I imagined myself inside the house, reclined on the couch, reading one of the books I'd plucked from the shelf, then resting the book on my chest, closing my eyes, and dreaming of time on the beach with Alessandra, where I was reclined on a towel beside her reading a different book I'd plucked from that same shelf and brought to Turks and Caicos. I was reading it aloud to her in a deep voice, not my own, and she was smiling.

The kitchen light blinked on. My heart careened. Sarah came into that far room holding a glass of red wine and set it down on the table, which made no sound. But very faintly, I could hear the music she'd switched on. I heard singing. I didn't recognize the song. I had a side view of her face. Maybe she and Alessandra were back from Turks and Caicos? She had wet-looking dark brown curly hair. She wore jeans and a red T-shirt and was barefoot. It looked balmy in there. I'd seen Sarah plenty in the halls. She often wore a paint-covered apron which kept her clothes clean when she was doing artistic things.

Now that I could see her through the window, images of her face reemerged in my mind. Her dark eyebrows, long thin nose. The crinkling of her eyes. Just her toes and the front pads of her feet were on the ground, beside the legs of the chair. Her arms were thin. She looked a hell of a lot like Alessandra. Similar face, different haircut. Why had I not noticed this before?

At school she presided over the student art studio, a room with enormous windows that could be raised and lowered by old fashioned pulleys within the jambs. The room faced west, dark in the morning—her beginning students huddled over the drawing tables, within pools of yellow light cast by table lamps—but by the afternoon, when the upperclassmen had open studio time, Sarah played classic rock at medium volume from waist-high fabric-covered brown speakers, sunlight poured through the floor-to-ceiling windows, and everyone seemed content and immersed in projects investigating their dreams. Clay sculptures of flying dogs. Mobiles of disembodied hands, legs, arms, and heads, balanced, spinning. Large canvas abstract oil paintings in which students were encouraged to revise their vision by painting over anything they didn't like.

If I had known any better, I would have spent time in the art room, and I probably would have loved Sarah Shinwell like everyone else. But I was afraid of the suspicions about me being confirmed: that I was a blunt instrument, a hockey goalie only, allowed admission to the school just because of my father's work unclogging toilets.

"Walt?" said a voice behind me. I froze and didn't want to face whoever it was. My gloved hand gripped the hedge. But when I heard the voice again it was an urgent whisper—my mother. "Get away from that window, please," she said.

I stood up, came back out to the walkway, quickly brushed the snow off my jeans, and walked with Mom back to our house. She hooked her arm through mine and said nothing, which I received as mercy.

9. The Horses' Heads

New Hampshire

When the waitress at the roadhouse brought a basket of warm rolls to our table, I grabbed one, ripped it open, put a pad of butter inside, and let it sit on my plate to melt. My mother said, "Looking through someone's windows, yeah . . . that . . . well, it's extreme. I don't want you doing that again."

"I didn't really see anything."

"Let's not tell your father."

"Yeah, let's not."

"You like Alessandra?"

"I'm just . . . trying to understand her better, if that makes any sense."

She didn't need to tell me that looking into someone else's windows was not a great way to better understand them. Instead, she said, "Your father gets sick, and he starts acting crazy. I don't want you taking notes from his playbook."

"Got it."

She'd received two calls from teachers in the nearby houses who'd seen me stationed there in the hedge. She told me this because she wanted me to know, to be aware of the information others had gathered about me. In her eyes, this didn't make my spying any worse, necessarily—it was wrong if I'd been seen, and it was wrong if I hadn't been seen. My mother was always clear about this: something wasn't wrong because you got caught; it was wrong because it was wrong. She didn't want to rub my nose in it, but she wanted me to have the knowledge I didn't have. I appreciated that about my mother. She was kind that way.

Since the New Year, my mom had been staying in the Great Blue Heron Motel on Route 28, a decision that deeply troubled my father, although at that point Dad knew not to complain about any choices she made. The Great Blue Heron was halfway to Boston, where she worked, and as soon as she moved there, she took on more hours, though she kept Wednesday afternoons free, which is when I often had hockey games. Neither of my parents talked in any explicit way about separation or divorce, but things seemed to be heading in that direction.

She ordered a cocktail, Johnny Walker and ginger ale. She said, "Your father is a fish who wants to breathe, walk around, play darts. Do you know what I mean by that?"

"No," I said. The butter had melted, and I ate the roll in two bites.

"He's out of his mind is what I mean. I'm not badmouthing him. In fact, I'm still fighting to stay in our marriage, and he is still screwing that other woman."

My mother didn't usually speak that way to me.

She took a small sip of her drink and said, "Sorry."

"No problem."

"Let's change things up, you and me. Your father, he won't change. But let's you and me, let's talk openly. Not only is he screwing another woman, but he has cancer. Did you know that?"

"Not exactly."

"Lung cancer," she said. "Which is not his fault."

"You've said that."

She had three more Johnny Walker and ginger ales before telling me about a poem she'd read with her poetry group that met on Thursday evenings, hosted by Dr. Charles. "Emily Dickinson," she said. "It ends with a line that I wrote down." She had her purse in her lap, and she started churning her hands inside it. She pulled out an ATM receipt. "Here. I think you'll like it."

Since then—'tis Centuries—and yet
Feels shorter than the Day
I first surmised the Horses' Heads
Were toward Eternity—

"Damn," I said. I liked the lines, even though I really needed to
know the context, and read the rest of the poem. And I would do
that later. But for now, the lines were something Mom and I could
focus on—the conversation had really been zigzagging. We'd talked
about her parents—my grandparents—who'd both died before I was
five, how proud they would have been of her, and how disappointed
they would have been in my father. (Did that count as badmouthing?) This led her to memories of playing basketball on the public
courts, how lousy she'd been, how much fun she'd had, and how
she'd stopped playing when she'd moved to Buffalo. "Though if we
hadn't moved to Buffalo, I wouldn't have been a hockey fan, and
you might not have played. God knows your father wouldn't have
given you the opportunity—it would have just been snowmobiling
and other crap like that."

"But he played hockey growing up."

"But that doesn't mean he'd want you to play."

"But then why would he want me to snowmobile?"

"Because he wants someone to do things with," she said. "But
fucking hell, he doesn't want to do things with me."

When she'd pulled that receipt with the lines of poetry on it
from her purse, I'd scooted around to her side of the table and we'd
studied the lines together. We could both picture the same thing, we
could both see those horses' heads, we could share that vision for a
minute, and that's what I'd wanted, that's what I needed more than
anything, and that's what my mother needed, too, and when we
were done looking at the receipt she handed it to me and I tucked
it in my pocket.

10. You Know That, Right?

By the time Alessandra returned from Turks and Caicos and school resumed, my curiosity about her had grown, particularly my curiosity about why she was curious about me. And I felt closer to her because I'd looked in her living room window. I hadn't cared about getting caught at the time, but now I was furiously afraid word of this weirdness would somehow get back to Alessandra or her mother.

On Thursday of that first week back, I'd come into the cafeteria at the usual time, right when it opened, and was sitting at the table closest to the stage, in the corner facing away from the room's entrance, moving in on my second cheeseburger. I was comfortable sitting alone as long as I didn't have to see people marching by. It was typically pretty easy to get a meal over within five to six minutes. On bite three of my second cheeseburger, though, Alessandra approached my empty table from the rear. I didn't have time to prepare. I looked up at her, blinking. Her eyebrows, her nose. She looked casually back at me, cocked her head as though she was working on a crossword puzzle, and said only, "Do you know about it?"

I continued to stare at her. My mouth was full. I'd stopped chewing.

"Hello?" she said. She waved a hand in front of my face. "Were you looking into our house because you know?"

I looked down, breathing through my nose. When I looked back up at her I commanded myself to be better than I'd been, to

chew my food and look her in the eye and convince her I wasn't the
dirtbag who'd looked through her windows—not that I was going
to lie to her—but I was going to try to replace the peeping-Tom
image with the image of the guy who'd suggested they look in Willis
Lowe's locker. I was again going to be that selfless guy who brought
the goldfish home. Every option—speaking, not speaking, chewing,
not chewing, making any facial movement—seemed awful.

But I swallowed, looked right at her and said, "That wasn't me."

"That *was* you," she said.

"I mean, that's not how I normally am."

"Those fries look good."

"Want some?"

She shook her head. "I just wanted to check with you about
whether or not you know."

"Know what?"

"Sounds like you don't know."

"Why didn't your mom go to Turks and Caicos?"

"I went with my dad. He lives in New York. He's an asshole,
but we have fun together sometimes."

"How is he an asshole?"

"We don't agree about anything. Seriously. He's like a cartoon
version of a selfish greedy prick. Sorry. And he cheated on my mom.
But, you know, he's still my dad. And if we're just doing something
together, like walking in the woods or snorkeling or whatever, he's
decent company."

She knew I'd been looking through the windows of her house and
she didn't seem mad or weirded out. She actually seemed willing to
stand there and talk to me, and she wasn't looking for an opportunity
to leave. I considered confiding in her, telling her my dad had also
cheated on my mom. But instead of doing that—I didn't want to
betray my mom's trust—I just asked her, "Can we go back? Into
the school? At night?"

"I can't," she said.

"Okay," I said, heart pounding.

"I mean I can't tonight."

"Okay."

"But I could tomorrow."

"Nice."

"Eleven tomorrow," she said in a casual, friendly way, holding onto the lapels of her jacket. "I gotta get to Chemistry," she said. "Later, man. Psyched for our plan."

She took about four steps from my table before returning.

"I do have a boyfriend. You know that, right?"

"I don't, but sure, that makes sense."

"I mean, whatever, just want to be clear."

"Okay," I said, reflexively. She left and my whole body felt full of light.

11. It Felt Natural

That first morning on Whaleback Island, Corsetti and I left the dorm together at one minute past six to sprint down the trail to Bridget Point. We were late because the night before I'd inadvertently kicked my sneakers under the bed, and it took a while for me to find them. Two Drake boys were right behind us. In the dark forest it was just our breath and quiet footfalls. The spruce and pine branches were trimmed on either side, and above our heads the canopy shrouded the trail. The newly cut woodchips were just bright enough to follow. As the path rose and fell, curved around boulders and through thicker stands of trees, I felt fast and strong running right behind Corsetti. It wasn't long before we heard the cries of seagulls and the voices of the other boys. We emerged onto the bleached granite shoreline. I bumped into Corsetti, and the Drake boys bumped into me. The sun hadn't yet risen but shone bright on the wide rock at the edge of the stone beach. Three instructors I didn't know were waiting for us, and in an aluminum skiff floating in the cove was Grunewald, seated, pale tired face under a khaki bucket hat, looking on.

The instructor known only as Janowski said "six thirteen" and began to count numbers. There were twenty-eight of us present, which meant that two of us weren't yet there. A minute later the last two Drake boys stumbled onto the rock, smiling and unbothered: a stocky black-haired boy with a dimpled chin, in just a swimsuit, and Cole Watson, aka Arkansas, wearing a Superman T-shirt, also barefoot.

Janowski said, "Very close. Six-fifteen. You could have gotten here quicker if you'd worn something on your feet." He then turned to Grunewald in the aluminum skiff and yelled, "That's everyone." Grunewald leaned back and pulled hard, just two swift strokes to bring him further away from the shore to make room for the swimmers.

The three instructors sat down to unlace their sneakers, pulled off their socks, T-shirts, and shorts, dropping them in a limp pile atop their sneakers. They descended bare-assed and single-file down the stone steps and continued across the rock beach toward the water. Nash and McCorkle both looked like runners, lithe and boney, and Janowski was thicker in the chest and hairy like a dog. Everyone kicked off their shoes, pulled off their T-shirts, and followed. About half the boys walked toward the water naked, the other half, myself included, kept our suits on.

The instructors were fifteen yards out, treading water, watching us inch our way in. Nash told everyone to completely submerge. When the water was halfway up my thighs my toes were already numb. A taller wave rolled toward me and came up into my shorts; I dove into the pinching, suffocating coldness, then breached back up, and the air felt insanely warm. Everything in the world was brighter and sharper, my skin felt tight on my slippery body, and my heartbeat was up in my ears. Just above the ocean horizon the orange sun lit everyone up, and we were quiet as we treaded gingerly on the egg-sized rocks, holding our arms out for balance.

I felt an odd relief swimming with strangers. I'd heard people sleep best in large groups, full bunk rooms snoring in unison, and this was probably true of swimming, too. I felt strong and ready for the day making my way out of the water.

Towels hadn't been on the pack list, so we followed our instructors' example, wiping off our limbs, putting our clothes back on our damp bodies without complaint. We circled up as a group before leaving Bridget Point.

McCorkle told us that if we swam without suits, we'd warm up more quickly afterward. It sounds weird, that an adult was telling us teenagers to swim naked, but it wasn't. He also told us to grab tea or coffee in the galley while Janowski Huddle prepared breakfast. And finally, he said, "Each day, morning swim starts at sunrise. Keep track of the time. Stick together, support each other, embrace the privilege of being here. You've been chosen for this, so do your part."

12. I Almost Killed Someone With My Bare Hands

Whaleback Island

The second night in Cook, we gathered in Billy Feng's room for cards. Feng wanted to teach us Bridge, which I was immediately intrigued by—especially the ways you could signal to your partner in the bidding process—but Corsetti and DeShawn were impatient, saying it would take months to learn the old-lady game. So Feng taught us Texas Hold'em instead. Some knew the basics from what they'd seen on TV, but Feng answered the questions from the others clearly and concisely, helping everyone understand which hands might fare well in a group of eight.

We didn't have money, but Corsetti came up with the idea of Cook Cash. He tore some white lined notebook paper into little pieces, wrote 'CC' on every one, and gave each player twenty.

We stayed up late, probably too late, but we couldn't help it—there were no adults in the building, those propane lights were glowing, and we didn't yet know how rigorous our days would get. We sank ourselves into the night, learning the rankings of hands, figuring out when to bet, when to bluff, how the blinds worked. Like Feng, Corsetti was from what they called the shitbelt—Feng was from Pittsburgh, Corsetti from Cleveland. Corsetti asked Feng about the sports teams he liked, and then veered quickly to more personal questions, about what kind of school Feng went to and how he ended up coming all the way to Maine to be at WILD, which was a topic Corsetti and I had covered in only a general way. Feng said he'd heard about the opportunity from his track coach.

"Is your dad a doctor?" asked Joshua Dellahunt, aka Massachusetts or Mass. He was probably six-foot-five with spiky blond hair. He sat next to another football player, Mason Rowell, who had a dark birthmark on his right cheek, and wide meaty hands. He kept his elbows planted on either side of his pile of Cook Cash.

"What? No," said Feng as he dealt.

I hadn't yet folded. No one had. The value of Cook Cash was completely abstract.

"Scientist?" asked Mass.

"What the fuck are you asking me that for?" asked Feng. "Bet's to you, Corsetti."

Corsetti raised two. Everyone stayed in.

Feng turned over the last card, a four of diamonds, got the next round of betting going, then said, "Maybe you don't know any poor Asian people?"

"Ha," said Mass. "Fuck off."

"What country do you think I'm from?"

"Korea?"

"The United States," said Feng.

"Originally?"

"Born in Pittsburgh," said Feng.

"Adopted?"

"Nope," said Feng. "My parents were born in Pittsburgh. My grandparents are Chinese. But you know what? I'm done with those people. They have no idea where I am right now."

"Right on," said Mass.

"Dude, I'd kill for some Chinese food," said Mason.

"I'd be happy to make you some," said Feng.

Mason didn't seem to comprehend Feng's sarcasm, and Feng raised the bet five Cook Cash, and one by one everyone tossed their paper on the pile.

"You fools don't know what you're doing," he said. "I have a flush. Play the game like the Cook Cash is actually worth something." Mass and Corsetti and I all folded. When the final shared card was turned up, Feng raised the pot another five Cooks, and Mason folded, too. "I can't beat a flush."

"This is all mine," said Feng, scooping up the paper scraps.

"Diamond flush with what high card?" asked Mass.

Feng turned over his cards. He had nothing.

"You said you had a flush!" roared Mass.

"That's how the game works," said Feng. "You're supposed to lie."

"There should be a rule against that shit," said Mass.

"There should be a rule against you being an idiot," said Feng.

Mass stood up, towering over Feng, but Mason Rowell held him back. Mass sat back down and said, "You know I could end you."

"Congratulations for being large," said Feng.

Mass glared at him, still flushed from the commotion.

"So," said Feng, calmly. "What was the trouble you douchebags got into to land here in the first place?"

"Trouble?" asked Mass.

"I mean, what'd you do? I know what *I* did."

I dealt the next hand. Mass peeked at his cards, careful to guard them from view, and said, "Oh yeah? What was it?"

"I asked you first," said Feng.

"I didn't do anything," said Mass.

"You were just born fucked up," said Corsetti.

"You didn't have to fuck up to come here," said Mass.

"I got thrown out of my school for stealing," said Feng.

"What'd you steal?" said Mass.

"You can get kicked out for stealing?" asked Corsetti. "I'll raise five."

"You didn't know that because you're from Cleveland," said Feng. "Raise five."

"You can have Cleveland," said Corsetti. "I'm never going back there. I'm the only Corsetti left, so fuck 'em. I'm writing my own history from here on out. What'd you steal, Feng?"

"A car," said Feng.

"Nice," said Mason.

"The principal's car," said Feng.

"Ha," said Corsetti.

"What did *you* do, man?" asked Feng.

"Me?" asked Corsetti. "I didn't do shit."

"No?"

"I guess they might say it's because I knifed my wrestling coach, but—"

"I'll go out on a limb and say that's probably what it was," said Feng.

"How about you, Walt?"

"You knifed him?" I was surprised Corsetti hadn't yet told me about his wrestling coach.

Corsetti said, "I didn't kill him, if that's what you're asking."

Feng asked, "Yeah, what was it, Walt? What got you in?"

"Yeah, man. Who'd you fucking knife?" said Mason.

Poker games are all about lying and I didn't want to say anything about my personal connection to Paul Brevard. I didn't want to tell them about vandalizing the art room, which they'd see as silly. I stayed quiet and thought about the Club, the gold-broached moms, the golf-shirted dads, the tan barefoot kids, the luxurious mansions, and why they'd want to invite a bunch of fuckups to their island. It seemed like a bad idea. Or maybe they just wanted kids who weren't scared to break the rules.

I said, "I almost killed someone with my bare hands." This was true. But it lacked context. To give them context I'd have to tell them about Alessandra, which I didn't want to do, and her boyfriend.

Mason laughed, but he was the only one. He stopped laughing and everyone focused on their cards.

"Nice, Walt," said Feng.

"That's a lie," said Mason.

"Deal the cards," said Corsetti. "Or I'll knife you."

13. You Can Be Part of This

Whaleback Island

By one in the morning Feng had everyone's Cook Cash and there was nothing else to do but sleep. The next morning, Feng took it upon himself to wake the dorm up by dinging his coffee cup and singing, "Drop your cocks and grab your socks."

It felt like only a few minutes had passed since we'd all been sitting around that table flinging cards. Corsetti and I groped for our sneakers. It wasn't until we were jogging in the woods, squinting to make our way down the dark trail, that I felt myself actually wake up. I tripped on a root and somehow kept my body from crashing into a spruce tree.

When we arrived at the granite beach, some kids were jogging in place to stay warm, others were doing jumping jacks. It wasn't freezing, but the shadows held the damp chill of nighttime, and everyone knew we'd soon be plunging into the water.

Nash was in the middle of a headcount, and he pointed at Corsetti and me, yelling to Grunewald, who was in a small rowboat in the water: "twenty-seven, twenty-eight!"

Grunewald had his camo vest on, and his oar tips hovered above the calm surface of the water. A gentle swell made his little boat rise and fall. A wave shushed onto the stone beach. "Are we missing the same two that were late yesterday?" Grunewald shouted.

"We're here," said the barefoot kid, Cole Watson.

Nash glanced at his watch. "All I know is we're missing two. And they've got less than a minute. Which is a minute more than everyone had yesterday, with the days getting shorter."

A warm purple glow came into the faraway trees on the mainland.

Mason and Mass lumbered out of the forest and onto the rocks, red-cheeked and breathing heavily. Mason chuckled and said, "Are we late?"

"Eighteen past the hour," shouted Grunewald from the skiff. "A reasonable time to arrive for a morning swim, but unfortunately, not the time we asked you to be here. Do you know what time we asked you to be here?"

"Yes," said Mason.

"Yeah," said Mass.

"And what time was that?" shouted Grunewald.

"Six-seventeen," said Mason and Mass, in unison.

"Correct. At least you know what time you were supposed to be here, though *knowing it* doesn't really matter much in the end."

"I couldn't find my socks," said Mass.

Grunewald let this excuse hang in the air before shouting from his boat, "Oh. But it looks like you *did* find them after all."

"Yup," said Mass.

"But even that didn't help you much, now, did it?"

A beat of silence, and then Mass said, "What?"

"Finding your socks. That didn't help you much?"

"I . . . well, I guess not."

"And you, turkey cunt? What's your excuse? What's that on your face?"

"Birthmark," said Mason.

"Is that your excuse?" shouted Grunewald

"No," said Mason.

"Well?"

Mason shrugged.

"Use your big-boy words, son."

"No excuse."

"Okay, good. No excuse. Just fucked it up. Fumbled the ball. Do you two know where we are?"

Another long beat of silence. Then Mason asked, "Sir?"

"Where are we. Either of you can answer."

"Whaleback Island," said Mass.

"That's right," said Grunewald. He dipped his right oar into the water, pulled once, which turned the bow of his boat toward shore. In three pulls with both oars, he was nosing onto the stone beach. "We're on Whaleback Island. Come down here to the boat, please."

Mason and Mass glanced at each other, stepped down from the wide granite shelf onto the smaller stones of the beach, and walked gingerly across the uneven stones to Grunewald in the aluminum skiff as it pinged and scratched against the rocks. As Nash undressed, he said to the boys, "You two will be the first to swim today, so prepare yourselves."

We all stayed up at the edge of the woods and there was no talking among us. Nash pulled the bow of Grunewald's skiff onto the rocks. Grunewald stepped ashore, and said to Mason and Mass, and the rest of us: "We're in a place that was settled long ago, and they had big plans. A place where intention and determination were and are important. This shit is real, boys. What we're asking you to be a part of, it's real. Now is the time to open your fucking eyes. Now is the time to seize your opportunity, got it? They're telling you they want you. They're telling you: you can be part of this. They told me that twenty years ago and without them I'd probably be dead. Seriously. What I have in my life, being part of this place, fucking hell, I'm the luckiest man on earth. But I had to pay attention, right? I had to jump when they told me to jump. And I'm telling you right now, they're giving you that option, and it's real, and you better fucking wake up or it'll be gone, and you'll be back in your shitty little lives, okay?"

An osprey wheeled overhead, cried at us, landed in a nest at the top of a spruce tree. Many of us nodded at Grunewald. I remember thinking I didn't want to go back to my shitty little life.

He said again, "Okay?"

"Okay!" we called out to him.

Then Grunewald pointed at Mason and said, "Him." Nash and Janowski each grabbed one of Mason's arms, and led him into the water up to his waist.

"Get him facing the other men," said Grunewald. Nash and Janowski turned him toward the woods. Mason was clowning a reaction to the cold water, pushing his breath through clenched teeth.

Grunewald put his hand on top of Mason's head and lowered it into the water while Nash and Janowski held his arms.

At first some of us cheered, thinking he was just getting dunked, but then Grunewald used both hands to keep Mason's head underwater. The kid was fighting hard to get his head up for air. He flailed as the instructors held him under, and obviously we stopped cheering.

Mass, taller than all of us and mostly muscle, stood nearby on shore, naked, his back to the group. It seemed he wasn't going to intervene. He just stood there watching like everyone else for thirty, forty seconds. I think a lot of us wanted to yell, wanted to ask him to stop, but no one said anything.

Mason's legs thrashed in the water. Mass took a few steps toward Grunewald, then stopped. He must have thought better of it.

Mason was held under another ten or fifteen seconds—it may have even been less but it seemed like forever—before Grunewald released him and he surged out of the water, red-faced and wild eyed, pulling air into his lungs. Mason then staggered to the rocks. Janowski and Nash came out of the water, too, but only to grab Mass and haul him in, and they did to him what they'd done to Mason, who was now sitting on the rocks as though he'd just swum across from the mainland.

It was pretty fucking awful to watch. We were all quiet. I remember really feeling my heart beating in my chest and my blood pumping through my body.

When it was over, Mason and Mass returned to the granite shelf where everyone else was standing.

"Let's go, men," said Nash. "Time to swim."

That time, we all went in naked. The surroundings were wild and unfettered, no houses in view. We were all kinds of body types— wiry wrestlers, football-playing giant boys, thin-calfed cross-country runners, bow-legged soccer players.

In the water, I felt like an ocean creature sliding through the deep, and when I stepped back onto the rocks, I felt reborn. I remember feeling glad to be on the island, to be getting a chance to prove myself.

Once we were all among the instructors again, clothed, ready to walk up the trail, Janowski had us huddle up. It was a big huddle, but the instructors had us mash in together like a football team in prayer.

He said, "We don't ever want to have to do that again. You're on our side. We're on your side. We're all together. Let's all follow the rules. We all follow the rules, we'll get to where we need to be. Restoring the spirit, protecting this place, making it ours."

14. You Need to Practice Being a Person
New Hampshire

My father went to sleep early, around nine-thirty, and I waited until ten-thirty. to creep downstairs and grab the main-building keychain from the hook in the mudroom closet, slip into my parka, and flip the hood up, stepping out the side door and into the night. I jogged to the snow-covered track, ran half a lap in my boots just to calm myself down, my breath steaming up toward the sky and stars. I wanted to let myself into the gym early to burn off more energy but instead I walked into town, making sure not to be seen, lapped the Cumberland Farms, outdated Christmas lights over the gas pumps, and returned. I got to the bushes ten minutes early and Alessandra, also in a parka with a fur-fringed hood, showed up two minutes later. She was early, too.

She raised her gloved hand. I thought she wanted a high five, so I raised mine, but instead she grabbed my hand and pulled me in for a bro hug, her chest against mine, her arm patting my back, her face beside mine. After that I fumbled for the keys, and as I opened the door I could see how jazzed up she was—we both quickly unlaced our boots and sprinted in our socks down to the gym to shoot hoops like last time and again we were hopeless at scoring baskets, but this time we shared a ball and passed it back and forth and took turns missing shots and running the full length of the court. After a while Alessandra took a break and we went to the drinking fountain and each splashed water on our faces, left the gym, and jogged the halls in the dark—from the gym down past all the trophy cases to the stairs up to the English classrooms and the admissions department and then back downstairs to the science wing. Every time we passed a glowing exit sign, I jumped up to smack it. *Clang!* And Alessandra leapt up and could just barely nick it with a finger. After our second lap she said she was tired, and she stopped outside the girls' locker room.

"Have you been in here before?"

"No," I said.

"Want to check it out?"

I wanted to say no right away, which seemed like the correct answer, but then I remembered I was a new person with Alessandra; I was not the kid who kept to himself on the hockey team, who was ashamed to masturbate but still did, so was often ashamed. I wasn't the kid who got embarrassed on behalf of others who were acting foolishly, and I wasn't the kid who could only talk in a true and genuine way with my mother, and I wasn't the kid who didn't want other students to know I actually did well in math. I wasn't the kid nominated by his eleventh grade English teacher, Mrs. Faber, for the work I'd done on an essay I'd written about a trip I'd taken to Quebec with my father in the school's pickup truck during which we'd been mistaken for locals on several occasions. I didn't think the essay had any real point and so declined the nomination because being nominated would have meant others would read it. No. I didn't have to be that kid with Alessandra.

"Yeah, totally," I said. And it worked. She lit right up. She wanted to show me this place I'd never seen.

My body moved without thinking, unlocked the door, and held it open for her, which was something I was sure I'd never done for a person my own age. And we were in.

I felt like someone who'd just been told I had six weeks to live, but for whom heaven existed for sure after death. I could have glorious and unstructured days with which I would do exactly what I wanted, without fear.

The room was more maze-like than the boys' locker room, but it had the same moldy-shower smell, with the additional odd smell of syrup. The lockers were stacked two high, floor to ceiling, with benches in between. Everything was painted a mustard yellow. There were a few stray towels on the benches, just like there often were in the boys' locker room. Alessandra showed me her locker. She spun the lock.

"Here's a combination you actually know," I said, which I'd normally think was a dumb throw-away comment, the kind of comment someone who was brave would just blurt out—like I had—without worrying too much about whether or not it would land.

"That I do, that I do," she said, wriggling out of her coat, letting it fall off her shoulders and onto the bench, opening up the locker door.

Hanging on the hook—two gray St. Bartholomew T-shirts, school issued. Folded neatly in the bottom of the locker, two white towels. The neatness and spareness of the locker was a delightful surprise. A loud, brash, beautiful, popular, rebellious person could, and maybe even likely *would,* have a neat locker, and this was new and somehow electrifying information.

The neatness of her locker didn't prepare me for what happened next. She pulled a notebook out of the back of the locker, behind the towels, and handed it to me. "Here's a peek into my weird brain," she said. I held it in my hands. I turned it over; the binding was soft; the notebook had been opened and closed many times by Alessandra herself. She was looking for something else in the locker, reaching into its dark corners. And while she did this she finally said, "You can look in it."

My fingers looked foreign to me, pink and soft, holding her notebook. I lowered the hood of my sweatshirt, opened the cover, focused my eyes on the words at the top of the page written in careful, rounded letters: *The War of 1812 . . . what was Madison thinking?* The rest of the page, the rest of all the pages, were filled with her doodling. I sank into these little drawings, trying to make sense of the patterns; I considered the state of mind she'd been in when she'd created them, the spirals and cupcakes and faces, the dogs and camels, the swords and battle axes, the flowers, the horned monsters, the frogs and salamanders, the trees and endless unidentifiable patterns and shapes, wondering if there was some code she wanted me to decipher, if there might be some connection, first, between these drawings and the War of 1812. Then I figured these delightful and precise scribblings welled from deeper places, they were drawings that marked a singular impulse at a specific moment. If I wasn't the son of the head of maintenance but instead the son of the art teacher, maybe these would have been my doodles. Alessandra's doodles represented a series of private moments, moments that were long gone, and that I had no access to, a fact which momentarily saddened me, until I remembered she was right there beside me.

She'd found what she was looking for. A plastic sandwich bag with a joint in it.

She looked over my shoulder to see what page I was on.

"What do you think?" she asked.

"I love it," I said, no hesitation, no fear.

"Look at that crazy camel," she said, proudly. "He's like . . . eat my hump, haters!"

She looked at me and seemed to be sizing me up in a way that normally might have provoked a fight in the locker room, but I gave Alessandra the benefit of the doubt. She held the bag with the joint in it up to me and said, "This is weed."

I nodded.

"Maybe you're not into this kind of thing."

I shrugged. I'd never tried any kind of drug. I'd been drunk three times in my life: once when I sucked down beer after beer as a way to avoid conversation in Kevvy Brockhouse's basement after we won our second state championship; once at a St. Bart's faculty Christmas party, when people gathered around Father Gerard's piano to sing, while in an adjacent room I drank seven or eight abandoned half cups of eggnog; once at the end of a day in which my English teacher, Mr. Delp, had said to the assembled class: "We're not leaving this classroom until McNamara says something smart," and I'd said nothing, not because Shirley Jackson's *The Lottery* had been boring or meaningless to me, but because I thought the story spoke for itself, and at the end of the fifty minutes Mr. Delp excused us anyway, didn't look at me as I left, but said "McNamara, you need to practice being a person." After my parents had gone to bed, I took an old, neglected bottle of peach schnapps from the back of the liquor cabinet down to the rope swing on the Headfield River, under the full moon, and drank most of the bottle, sang nursery rhymes at high volume, vomited, and returned to my bed and slept for twelve hours.

"No judgement," Alessandra said. "But I was thinking we'd smoke this together. If you wanted."

"I do," I said.

"You sure?" she asked.

"Yes."

She popped the joint in her mouth, dug around again in her locker to find a lighter. She lit the joint in a casual, practiced way that I found mesmerizing. The orange of the flame reflected in the wet of her eyes. She inhaled, held her breath, passed the cigarette to me, and I copied her. We handed it back and forth a few times and I willed myself not to cough. The smoke was dense and musky.

"Here, lie down," she said, sprawling face up on the wooden bench. I started to recline, and she said, "No, put your head up by mine."

We lay in opposite directions, facing the ceiling, the crowns of our heads nearly touching.

"I'm glad you don't know about that thing I asked you about yesterday," she said. "And I'm not going to tell you what it was."

I still had no idea what she was talking about.

"I envy your ignorance on the subject," she said.

The flat hard bench felt oddly comfortable. The proximity of her head made my own head feel supercharged and warm.

"What's this supposed to feel like?"

"The weed? It's just, I don't know . . . a cozy cocoon. It's pretty mellow. Close your eyes."

"Why do you like it?" I asked. It felt amazing to speak so freely.

"What's not to like about a cozy cocoon?"

"Like a caterpillar?"

"Yeah."

"Caterpillar is a cool word. Caterpillar is a cool animal. Caterpillar caterpillar cool cool. Okay. I think I might feel it."

"Sweet. Happy to corrupt you."

"Thanks for coming up with this idea to break into school."

"It's not a break in if you've got the keys."

We talked about many things and about nothing at all. She told me a theory she had about Darius Coleman's bangs. She said the reason they were so plastered against his forehead was he was hiding a marble-sized divot in his skull up by his hairline that had been the result of a golfing accident. A club upside the head. Or a ball. Yes, a ball. The divot was ball shaped. He used hairspray to cover the ball-shaped divot. I asked her why she didn't like Darius. She said she liked him fine, she was just trying to tell his story. I said he didn't seem too bright. She said this was another reason the golf ball theory was likely correct. I asked her if he really did have a bump on his forehead and she said she had no idea, but it certainly seemed possible.

I liked the floating sensation. I kept my eyes closed.

She said, "Right?"

"Yeah," I said. "Cocoonish."

She chuckled. "I've got another thing I want to try," she said. I felt her standing up. I opened my eyes, and the room was bathed in warm light and my body felt pleasantly heavy. I stayed on the bench and then she was looming over me holding the two white towels from her locker.

"This is a little weird," she said. "But I'm feeling weird, and I think it's okay if we try this," she said.

Before that month, I'd only known her from a distance. She was adventuresome in a way I'd always envied.

"There are two rooms in the showers," she continued. "The showers have two rooms. Am I saying that right? Anyway, I want to take a shower. And I thought maybe you'd want to take a shower, too? There will be a wall between us. You don't have to, man. No sweat. I know I'm weird. You can just hang out here. But if you want to, you can."

I tried not to stand up too quickly. I knew I was going to take a shower, I knew it right away, and I didn't want to hide this from Alessandra, but I also thought I might stagger right into the row of lockers because of the floating sensation. I was used to group showers. The boys' locker room had two adjacent shower rooms, too. I was always one to take the empty room if it was available. But who was this person who was being asked by Alessandra Shinwell to shower nearby? Me. I was the guy she was asking. She had a boyfriend. He wasn't here. I was. I was sitting on the bench now. I was still myself despite the high. Despite the high, my reality was clicking along, film on a reel. I watched her walk fully clothed into the showers and around the tiled wall. Behind that tiled wall she was undressing. She had left a towel for me.

The person I'd known myself to be for most of my eighteen years would never have been asked to do this by the most powerful girl in the school. But what did that matter? The shower water shushed against the tile, and steam thickened the air. I stood and my feet felt stable on the ground.

And then there I was, naked, showering. The water thundered against my head. For some reason I didn't have a boner, and I was thankful for this—I was tethered to reality enough to know that having a boner, if for some reason she was about to charge around the corner fully clothed to laugh at me for falling for her trick, would have resulted in a heart attack or worse.

She started singing that song, "We Are Family." I knew the song. Everyone knew the song. So I joined in. Thoughts about Alessandra shaming me for falling for her joke evaporated. We were just two new friends, showering nearby, singing a song we both knew. She started clapping, too, and I joined this effort as well.

After she stopped singing, I heard her water turn off, so I quickly turned mine off too. I felt the quiet of the entire school. All but a few drips from her shower head and mine. Then I heard her say, in a small voice, "Hey, Walt, can I look at you?"

I felt blood coursing through my chest.

She continued, "I mean, in your towel."

"Okay," I said.

"Then we can get dressed and go home," she said. I heard her feet patting across the wet tile.

I was a big kid, and the little white towel just barely fit around my waist. I checked that the towel's gap exposed my thigh and nothing else.

She came around the corner wearing her towel up over her chest and tucked into her armpits, which meant that most of her white legs were exposed to me. She was holding her clothes in a ball against the part of the towel covering her stomach. I wasn't afraid to look at her while she looked at me. I was usually self-conscious about the patch of hair in the middle of my chest because only one other senior on my team had chest hair, but right then I didn't mind being seen. Her black hair wasn't tousled, it was straight back, wet against her head. And her eyes were wide open, unguarded.

We stood like that for maybe as long as a minute. Before she walked to her locker to change back into her clothes, all she said was, "Wow." And I didn't worry that I'd done something wrong. I didn't exactly know what she meant when she said "wow," but it was okay I didn't know. It seemed good, it seemed genuine, and I wasn't fucking up.

I dressed in the shower and when I emerged, I draped my towel on the edge of the hamper just as she had, and she held the door for me out of the locker room, and I held the door for her as we left the school. She initiated another bro hug. Again, I thanked her and didn't feel dumb about it. The world was sleeping as I walked home. Not a single light on in any of the buildings, only the streetlights on Route 83 bisecting campus. On any other day I lived for moments like this, snow squeak-crunching beneath my boots, sharp cold air moving in and out of my lungs, knowing I was on my own. But that night, there was someone else who knew the glory of what I'd just experienced.

15. Make These Acres Here a Little Better
Whaleback Island

At breakfast Tess told us a girl had been late to Osprey Cove, and she, too, had been held underwater by Henshoff and Brinkley, the two female instructors on duty.

Corsetti, in his black hoodie and shorts, shoveling granola into his mouth, said, "I'll tell you one thing: No one's going to be late tomorrow."

Tess had her braids wrapped up in a scarf atop her head, looking fully awake and ready for the day. "Wait—you think it's okay for them to do that?" she said.

I remember that morning Aubrey wasn't hiding her face, and the swim and the cold air had brought redness to her olive cheeks. She wore a sleek black track suit with red and orange racing stripes. She'd told us in a note she'd thrown the javelin for her school and seeing her dressed like this, I could imagine her heaving it with all her might.

Corsetti said, "I'm not saying that. I wouldn't do it if I was in charge. But I *will* say . . . we are more of a team now. That shit works."

Tess said, "Well, I mean, maybe."

"They want us to wake up, take this shit serious. They want us to know how lucky we are," said Corsetti.

"Okay, sure. I get it. It just seems—risky."

"Some risks are worth taking."

"Okay, I guess I'm okay with it, but fuck you anyway," said Tess, smiling, punching him in the arm.

The poker game with Feng had made me really wonder about the face value of any comment from any of us. But I liked what Corsetti was doing, asking us to take some abuse, get on board, work together, take things seriously, try hard, follow the rules, trust the opportunity we were being given.

"Here's another question for you," said Corsetti, raising his pointer finger. "You think if we put up with this shit, these guys are really going to give us jobs?"

"Damn I hope so," said Tess. "Maybe they'll start us in the mailroom."

"Mailroom? Then why all the goddamn exercise?" asked Corsetti.

"Maybe the exercise is just a test," said Tess.

"That's a test we'll pass," said Corsetti. "I'm just thinking . . . it's gotta be more than that. And I know for a fact I'll do better if it's not just a test. I'm going to act like they have big plans for us." He pushed the sleeves of his hoodie past his biceps. He pointed back and forth between Aubrey and Tess. "Bro, bro—you two write things down when you have a conversation in the dorm? How does that work?"

Aubrey didn't look up from her food as she pulled the elastic from her ponytail, combed her fingers through her wet hair, and let it hang down in front of her face again. Then she dug into her backpack and pulled out a little notebook and a pen, turned to a fresh page and wrote:

fuck off

Then she picked the wooden stirrer out of her coffee cup and started chewing on it. Tess laughed.

We cleared their plates, and Lisa Henshoff's Huddle loaded the bowls and spoons into the dishwasher just as the all-gather horn sounded. We bottle-necked into the staircase up to Big Rug.

Joey MacLean's boat was delayed so Grunewald ran the meeting. He asked us to sit in a circle, and if anyone had any questions—about anything—to stand and ask.

A red-headed Drake kid wearing a T-shirt advertising NORTH DAKOTA'S PREMIER BRAZILIAN JIU JITSU ACADEMY asked if there was a phone we could use to call home. Grunewald said no, we could write letters and Nash would bring them to the mainland once a week. Javier, the fast runner in our group, asked if we could ever exercise on our own. Grunewald said no. No for safety reasons but also no because everyone would be damn tired enough from the workouts they'd prescribe. A giant boy from Drake with a buzz cut and no neck asked about snacks for those who got hungry between meals and Grunewald said no snacks. Another giant boy from Drake asked what kind of jobs we were being groomed for.

"Groomed?"

"Yeah."

"You, my friend, aren't being groomed for shit," said Grunewald. "Who's Huddle are you in?"

"Janowski."

"Figures."

The hulking kid wore long nylon shorts and a white T-shirt stretched tight across his wide shoulders. He started to slowly lower himself back down onto the rug when Grunewald said, "You asked a question, didn't you?"

"Yes."

"Do you want to hear my answer?"

He nodded.

"Then why the hell are you sitting down?"

The large boy stood back up and tugged at the front of his T-shirt.

"The answer is: Work hard and be true to yourself," said Grunewald. "Because the Club will be true to you. The Club has been true to me for twenty years. I'm family to them. Act the part. Be a person who deserves respect. Right now, what they want you to do is get stronger and tougher. This place has a great history. Let's keep the island safe and sound. Keith and Awanata and their kids, those folks ate nails. You'll get there, you just have to put your time in. Be worthy and you'll get exactly what you deserve."

We heard the whine of a boat propeller.

Another football player stood to ask, "Can we save some of the food from mealtime for, like, later?"

"Sure," said Grunewald. "But you'll be punished for it."

The boy remained standing. "Like if I put an apple in my pocket?"

"I just told you the fucking rule."

"I'm sorry, sir. I didn't mean to. . . ."

"'Sorry' and 'I didn't mean to' don't get very far with me. Listen, follow directions."

Tess stood, adjusted her bunched up sweatpants and said, "What do you mean, keeping the island safe and sound?"

"I'd say that's fairly self-evident," said Grunewald.

"Um, no, not really."

"You feel secure?"

"How do you mean?"

"Completely safe. At all times."

"Pretty much, yes. I do feel safe out here," Tess said.

"Well, we want to keep it that way."

Someone else asked about visitation rules for the boys' and girls' dorms. Grunewald seemed to want to say no again but he said it had been decided that there would be no specific visitation hours. He said they had master keys for all the rooms, for safety reasons, and we couldn't just lock ourselves in our rooms to be obnoxious. He said we'd be tired in the evening, and we'd need to sleep.

Joey MacLean walked into the room, raising a fist, a baseball cap with its brim pulled down just above his eyebrows. "You guys are awesome. Good morning," he said, nodding toward Grunewald. He then turned to us with a smile. "I apologize for being late. Not always easy to get off the dock at Tuckaway when the wind's screaming from the north." He knelt down on the rug and smoothed his jeans. "Looks like we've started with the questions?"

Grunewald nodded and said, "We're all done."

"Are we?" he turned to the group once again and a number of hands shot up. "Well, maybe there are a few more questions."

Someone asked if anyone from the Club would be on the island during the fall and winter. He said no, just a few, like him and Brevard and the Huddle instructors. He said the others didn't know much about the specifics of the program, and he said it was fine to keep it that way. "Brevard and I want to give you lots of responsibility. The program, we'll get it right, then we'll share what we've done with the Club, and they'll get on board."

This didn't make much sense to me at the time; it makes more sense now. MacLean and Brevard had been given free rein to do what they wanted with us.

The same giant boy from earlier raised his hand and asked if snacks were possible. MacLean said: If you're working hard, sure. They could arrange for snacks. Javier asked if he could do workouts on his own. MacLean said sure, if there's time.

Grunewald stood and shot a look at Javier. "When this meeting wraps up, Grunewald Huddle will meet on the hill beneath DaGama dorm," he said, and marched out of the room.

Javier raised his hand again.

"Who gets recruited by the CIA?"

MacLean smiled. "You're all strong and capable, it's obvious. I know some of you have asked about working for the government. I think we can do better than that for you. I want to get you involved, helping us directly, and doing some big-ticket stuff for us out here and elsewhere."

In response the room filled with murmuring sounds.

"What else can I answer for you?" A few hands raised, and MacLean called on Feng, who was sitting just a few people over to my left. "You know the score of yesterday's Steelers game?

"Ha, ha. Nope. How'd you even know it was Monday?" asked MacLean.

"I keep track," Feng said.

"There's really no need. Consider yourself lucky that you don't know what's going on in the world for a while. You can just focus on the business at hand, right? Make these acres right here a little better. Find out how a place like this came to be."

He called on another kid, who said, "I don't have a question. Can I . . . how do I get in touch with my friends?"

"Sure. I get it. But you have friends here now," he said, and the air in the room changed a bit, the murmuring quieted, and it seemed to me that most people thought this was true. "Can I tell you a quick story before you go? Something truly miraculous happened last year on the Elk Basin River Ranch in Montana. It's a place owned by one of our Club members, a place with some of the best fly-fishing in the world. Crystal-clear air and water, heavenly stretches of forest and sky. Ride a horse for a day through that land and you won't see a soul. But there was a day last March during supper out there, all twenty-five guests were having a sit-down meal, just minding their own business on property they own, having had a glorious day of fishing and breathing that delicious air, when three pieces of shit—and I don't say that lightly—three *pieces of shit* came out from Bozeman and tried to take them all hostage. Tried to rob them and probably hurt them and get as much money from them as they could. Think about that. Think about the injustice. Can we have a moment to think about our Club members, our kind brothers and sisters, enjoying the fruits of their labors, getting ambushed like that, what that must have felt like?"

I was happy to close my eyes amid the quiet. MacLean's request seemed genuine. I tried to do what he was asking me to do. But I didn't actually think about those people I didn't know, nor the grave danger they'd been in. With my eyes closed I thought about Alessandra, what she was doing in college at that very moment.

Maybe she was in bed, reading. Maybe she was at play rehearsal, or smoking weed in the girls' locker room, or fucking her new boyfriend.

After twenty or thirty seconds MacLean said, "Thank you for thinking of my friends and what they went through."

Corsetti's hand shot up. "But what happened? Are they okay?"

"Thanks for asking, buddy. Yes, they're okay. They were saved by three ranch hands. Three simply awesome employees. They took matters into their own hands. And we will be forever grateful to them. I'll be glad to tell you more about them sometime soon. For now, though, I know you don't want to keep your Huddle leaders waiting."

After the meeting we gathered at the bottom of the hill beneath DaGama dorm, which was not really a hill at all, just the thirty-yard steep slope of dirt, littered with rocks and tree stumps, that had been cleared when the dorm had been built. Grunewald had put on clothing for exercise—an army green sweatshirt, and grey sweatpants cinched at the ankles—but he stayed on the porch. He held a whistle between his teeth, then let it drop on its cord to his chest and yelled, "Quiet!"

We'd been chatting, kicking rocks, waiting. Corsetti and Aubrey were sitting back-to-back on one of the larger stumps. We looked up the hill.

"On my whistle, I want each of you to run as fast as you can up to me," Grunewald yelled. "The last to touch the flagpole gets the belt."

"We get a belt?" asked Javier.

"I think he means you get whupped," said Corsetti.

"Line up behind that stump the mute girl is sitting on," yelled Grunewald.

We did as we were told, bumping into each other. He placed the whistle back in his mouth and blew. We couldn't sprint up the hill because of the boulders and the loose rock shards and the stumps and felled trees. But we could scramble, and we each cared deeply about not being last. Corsetti tried to hurdle a fallen tree—his sneakers slipped in the dirt, then caught on a branch and he fell—hard. I considered helping him up, but instead kept going, went the long way around the next group of fallen trees, scampered over a sheer patch of granite, and made it to the flagpole just after Aubrey and DeShawn and Javier. I turned around to watch the others come in—Tess, right behind me, then Bethany and Bianca. Finally, with a bleeding knee, spittle on his lips, Corsetti. He touched the flagpole, shrugged, scowled, looked around, and said, "I'm last? Fuck. I fell."

Grunewald snatched the long brown belt resting by his feet on the porch. "On your knees, son."

"You're actually going to hit him with that?" asked Tess.

"Yup," said Grunewald.

I felt panic rise in my chest. I raised my hand. "It was my fault he was last."

Grunewald turned calmly to me. "Great, you're next. Get down on your knees as well."

The others stood in a circle around Corsetti and me. Grunewald had us crouch down in the dirt. He asked us to raise up our sweatshirts to expose our backs to him.

"Fuck this," said Tess. "You can't do this."

"Why not?" asked Grunewald.

"This is a fucking leadership school, dude. You don't need to whip us."

"What do you propose," said Grunewald. He was looking fiercely at her, almost snarling.

"No proposal except you don't whip them."

"How about this," said Grunewald. "I'll give you all a choice. Either everyone gets the belt—every single one of you here—or only these two."

"We'll take the belt," said Corsetti.

"How about nobody gets the belt," said Tess.

"Not an option," said Grunewald.

"How about only I get the belt, and Walt whips me?" asked Corsetti.

"Ha, sure," Grunewald said. "Deal."

I didn't get a chance to voice my dissent, but Corsetti could tell. "It's fine," he said.

"I'm not going to whip you, man," I said.

"You don't whip him, everyone gets whipped," said Grunewald.

"I'll only whip you if you whip me back," I said to Corsetti. This got some laughs but I was perfectly serious.

Corsetti got it. "Right."

I stood up and took the belt from Grunewald, who was grinning. I hit Corsetti once—*crack*!—and saw a pink ribbon form just above Corsetti's hip. I heard Tess gasp. Later she told me Javier couldn't watch, and all he wanted to do was jump on Grunewald and strangle him.

"Nice, man. Good job," he said.

We swapped places. Corsetti swung the belt down on me. I felt a hot white sting, momentarily blurring my vision. I heard someone in our group—I think it was Bethany—quietly crying.

Afterwards, Grunewald put his belt back into the loops on his pants. "Okay, good job, folks. You're not a bunch of selfish jerks. And Ohio and New Hampshire can tell you, getting hit by a belt is not the end of the world. It's really not. You're fine. Give me a perimeter trail and you're done for the day."

After the run, we all gave each other hugs and things really weren't the same from that day on.

The next day when we woke to swim I saw a raised purple welt on Corsetti's back. Corsetti checked my back and said it looked the same.

After the swim and after breakfast, when we gathered with Grunewald to discuss the plan for the day, Tess said, "Were you actually going to whip them?"

"Of course not," said Grunewald.

"Why didn't you stop them from whipping each other?"

"Wasn't it fun to watch?"

We circled up in a wide spot beside some ferns and skunk cabbage, halfway down the Copperthwait trail. It had rained that night but the morning was bright and clear, almost warm.

"How can we trust that you're asking us to do the right stuff?" Tess asked.

"You can't," said Grunewald.

"Well, that's fucking insane," said Tess.

"Just know that it's all real," said Grunewald. "This place, what you do, how you do it, it's real. This is not a simulation. There are consequences."

"I'm fine with consequences," said Tess, "as long as I believe in who's making the rules."

I think we all were worried how he'd react to this.

"Believe in yourself, Maryland. That's the best lesson of all."

"It doesn't always work out if you believe in yourself," said Tess. "Shit happens."

"All the more reason to trust your own capacities. By the way, I told you exactly what was going to happen. It was a race, and the last one in got the belt."

"But you were lying. You weren't going to whip us."

"The last one in *did* get the belt."

"What's with the mindfuck, dude?"

"I want you to trust each other. I want you to know this all is real. I want you to come together. That's all. *Dude.*"

We followed him to the obstacle course. He pulled out his stopwatch. A mouse darted across the trail into the skunk cabbage, and a blur of birds—yellow finches, maybe—lit up through the spruce branches.

16. Can I Listen to Your Heart

New Hampshire

The night before my mother's fiftieth birthday, I brought her a cupcake and a toaster oven and brought them to the Great Blue Heron Motel. Aside from my mom's Corolla, there were no other cars in the plowed loop. I knocked on her door and through the curtains saw her light blink on, and I heard her say, quietly, "Walt?" Then the sound of the chain lock sliding, and the door opened.

She was fully dressed, and the bed was made but there was a dent in the pillow and a wrinkle in the bedspread, so I said, "Sorry to wake you."

"Stop looking at me like that," she said. "I'm fine. I really am. And I'm happy to see you." She hugged me and held me a little bit longer than usual. "You know how I know I'm fine? I have been lying there on that bed plotting to kill your father. I know I won't do it; he doesn't deserve to be let off that easy, but I think it's good for me to feel that rage. And direct it toward, you know, action."

"Sure," I said. "Seems healthy."

"Cutting the brake cables in his car might be the best approach," she said. "Because then there'd be a chance it would take her out, too."

Neither of my parents had told me anything about the woman my father had taken up with. Marcie at the dump still seemed like the only plausible option. "I thought he wasn't seeing that person anymore."

"Do you believe that?" my mom asked.

"Yes. And don't cut his brake cables please."

"Anyway," she said, running a hand through the back of her hair. "How are you holding up?"

I wanted the focus to be on her, it being her birthday and all, but I said, "I don't see him much," plopping down on the edge of the bed. This was true. The snow meant my father was out for longer hours. And it wasn't helping that he wasn't working at full speed. I had hockey—away games, lots of practice, team meals. "Sometimes I'm at the house when he comes back for a snack between plowing and shoveling. But when he comes back, I leave, which I think he likes."

"He doesn't like it when you leave," she said. "I can guarantee that."

"Well, whatever. He's relieved when he doesn't have to talk to me, even if he wants to."

She smoothed the bedspread and didn't say anything for a few seconds.

"You know," she said. "I think it's hurtful to him when you do that."

"You were just saying you wanted to cut his brake cables."

"I know. But we'll both really miss him when he's dead."

She walked over to the desk chair she'd positioned by the window, pulled a pack of Camel Lights from her jacket pocket, stuck one in her mouth, cracked open the window, lit the cigarette and took one deep pull, blew the smoke out the window, and stubbed out the barely smoked cigarette on a saucer on the table. She waved her hand by the window before closing it.

"Sorry."

"It's fine, Mom."

"I'm just so angry," she said.

"You should be."

"The fucking horse heads," she said.

"Yeah, the horse heads," I repeated.

"So, here's what. There is something I want to do, for real. I want to make him think I've found someone new. But I haven't.

I promise you; I am not romantically connected to this man. He's someone I work with. I'm just using him to show your father I haven't given up. Dr. Charles. Do you remember him? He's one of the shrinks at the hospital. And I will not ask you to back me up in this lie. You don't have to say anything to your father, okay?"

"I'm not really talking to him much, anyway."

"Well, you should. And you probably talk to him more than you think. And anyway, you won't be able to hide from your father for too long. Think about the next time he has surgery on his lungs. You won't ignore him then."

"Probably not."

She picked up the pack of cigarettes and turned it around in her hand. "Dr. Charles, he's become a friend of mine, we're in that poetry reading group together, we've gone paddling in his canoe a few times together on Miller's Pond, but I swear on my mother's grave he is not my boyfriend."

I'd met Dr. Charles before. He was stocky and short, maybe five-foot-six, with good skin and a great thick head of gray hair, and he was genuinely and self-deprecatingly funny.

"It's okay if he is, Mom."

"You stop that right now, Walt."

"I trust you."

"Okay, well, thank you. Dr. Charles is very kind. I think, but I'm not sure, that he's gay. Or asexual."

"That might make it harder to convince Dad he's your boyfriend."

"With every challenge you face in life, Walt, you've got to play the long game. Your father is blind to so much. I just want him to know I'm not finished with my life, just like he's not finished with his life. He's not going to kill me by throwing his own life away."

I had never heard my mother talk that way. There was a lot in the statement to wrangle with. I didn't feel up to the task, so I returned to the main reason I was there with her. "I have a present for you." I reached into my backpack, took out the Tupperware with the cupcake in it, and pulled out the toaster oven, still in its box, wrapped in light-blue paper.

She opened the present and tears sprang to her eyes.

"That's the sweetest thing, Walt. It's just the sweetest thing."

I set the cupcake on the table and borrowed her lighter to light the candle on top. I sang solo for her, badly off-key, and she started crying again. "These are only tears of joy, goddamn it," she said. She split the cupcake and gave me half.

"So, you're okay, sweetheart?" she asked.

"Yeah, I'm good. I'm kind of getting to know that girl Alessandra."

She looked at me then with wide-open eyes. "Oh, Walt."

"I think I might be becoming her fake boyfriend."

"Oh, Walt. I love you so much. You're never going to be anyone's fake anything."

When we hugged goodbye in the doorway I smelled the cigarette smoke in her hair, and over her shoulder saw her hairbrush, purse, phone, takeout menus, and channel guide arranged neatly on the desk beside the TV. She held onto me a little longer than I held on to her, which felt new.

Alessandra continued to be amazingly friendly to me both in public and in private, and while we didn't go back to the girls' locker room right away, she would seek me out during free periods—when, under normal circumstances, I'd be shouldering my backpack and hustling home—and the two of us played her favorite game, Scrabble, on the carpeted hallway outside the art classroom. To keep it somewhat even, she taught me about the two letter words—AA! GI! JO! KA! QI!—and I told her it seemed like cheating to use them, and she told me it would be fine if I didn't use them, though she would be most definitely using them, and my "refusal to cheat" would end up costing me, most likely, fifty points or more, and she already had a sizable advantage because of her prior experience and because she was a girl and therefore had a larger and more fully developed brain. When she spoke these words, I felt her fondness for me. And we were right there in the hallway in front of everyone who passed by. It was almost too much for my body to handle. I focused on the game, tried to block everything out. The wooden tiles on my tile rack. Assembling them into a word. It wasn't as though she never mentioned her boyfriend, she did, but when she did, she spoke of him in an annoyed way, like he was a narcissist who monitored his heart rate and caloric intake while all she wanted to do was play Scrabble.

At one point early in our second game in the hallway, Kevvy Brockhouse passed by us, said nothing, but caught my eyes and seemed to be saying *who-the-fuck-ARE-you?* I loved this and knew I'd be getting some questions in the locker room about playing a boardgame on the floor with a girl most on the hockey team considered stunning, but they wouldn't say this because she was a drama-clubber and didn't look exactly like a swimsuit model. Alessandra didn't seem to notice people were looking at us while we played. She didn't care. She told me about the horror movies she loved, the old-school ones. The entire *Halloween* franchise, for starters. *Friday the 13th, Nightmare on Elm Street,* too. Mike Myers, Jason, Freddy. I hadn't seen these movies. And why hadn't I? I'd been blind to so much.

Before we'd struck up our friendship, she'd been Lucy in our school play, *You're A Good Man Charlie Brown,* which I hadn't even attended because I had practice each of the nights the shows had been scheduled—such cultural events weren't on Coach Dunwoody's radar—and besides, I hadn't been awake to the upside of a high school musical before I started spending time with Alessandra. Hockey playoffs hadn't yet started when Alessandra suggested I attend the drama club's informational meeting about the spring production. She'd heard me say I was always a mess after the season ended—even when the season ended the way it had for the last three years, with a championship. She suggested I give myself something to focus on for the spring. Seemed like a decent strategy. I figured lighting or set design could be a good fit. Something behind the scenes. Alessandra knew she'd be cast in the play, a production of *Rosencrantz and Guildenstern Are Dead*, and the idea of turning her spotlight on and off—obviously I was fine with that.

The drama teacher, Mr. Sveta, was not used to having large athletic boys show interest in his productions. He stood from his chair when I showed up and immediately suggested I read for the part of Hamlet. Mr. Sveta, who wore a bow tie during the school day and a long-sleeve Arcade Fire concert T-shirt during drama club, assured me if I took the role, he could teach me everything I needed to know.

Alessandra piped up: "We're a little desperate. Some of us are already playing three parts." She was wearing a jean skirt and black leggings, leaning back in a plastic chair beside the long radiator beneath the windows.

"We're not desperate. We just want to share the joy of theater with you," said Mr. Sveta. The next day, though, posted on the cork board outside the cafeteria was the cast list. Mr. Sveta hadn't asked anyone else to read Hamlet's lines, and in *Rosencrantz and Guildenstern Are Dead*, Hamlet, it turns out, is a pretty minor part, but still, seeing this was shocking:

```
Hamlet_____Walt McNamara
```

I thought first about how this turn of events would please my mother and confuse my father.

For the two-week stretch when play practice coincided with hockey, I was busy, sure, and it gave me the chance to experience two ways of being. Hockey had always given me the feeling that I mattered, that what I did had an impact on others, especially as the team headed into playoffs. The persona of Drama Nobody, on the other hand, felt initially uncomfortable, but ultimately liberating. As a hockey star, there were few moments when I didn't shoulder the weight of the team. Play practice occasionally had some intensity—but what I loved was that when I wasn't on stage, when I wasn't worried about messing up in front of Alessandra, no one was watching me, no one cared what I did. Even when I *was* on stage, I disappeared.

The *St. Bart's Bugle* asked me to do a Q&A for their "spotlight" section. Their writer asked to meet during the thirty-minute dinner break at *Rosencrantz and Guildenstern* practice one evening. After Mr. Sveta shooed the actors out the auditorium doors into the main hallway for dinner break, Katie McPherson appeared, a freshman girl who could have passed as a fifth grader, braces sparkling in her miniature mouth. She set up two folding chairs in the hallway. The silver laptop resting on her legs dwarfed her. She greeted me and gestured toward the other seat.

During the first few questions, I was on autopilot. I'd been interviewed before by the *Bugle* and by the town paper, and even by the *Manchester Union-Leader* a few times. Katie had some good softballs for me. How did I prepare for games? How had I let in only three goals all season? What were my rituals? (I sipped from the water bottle atop my net right before any faceoff not in my zone; I tapped my own posts when the opposing goalie made a save.) When I'd started to play organized hockey as a six-year-old, I quickly realized those who are asked to play goalie often quit the sport, and those who choose to play goalie are stuck there forever and are a little bit crazy. Ask anyone who plays hockey, and they'll tell you this, even the goalies themselves. Was it being a goalie that made you crazy, or did only crazy people want the job? It hurt more to lose than it felt good to win, and a goalie is fueled by the avoidance of pain. There's no glory in stopping a shot—it's just your job.

I asked Katie, "Do you know who Martin Brodeur is?"

"I'm sorry, I don't."

"He plays for the New Jersey Devils and Team Canada. He's known for saying, 'If you play hockey, you might as well win.'"

"What does that mean to you?" she asked.

"Hockey is like life."

Katie kept her head down, slapping the keys. It seemed she was writing down twice what I was saying.

I had little conflict with my coach. Most of the problems I'd had with hockey were with teammates. Not so much my senior year, but when I was dominating as a freshman and sophomore, and there were older skaters who didn't respect me and thought they could treat me like a typical freshman or sophomore and not like the team's lynchpin, I was forced to correct that. During both seasons, I'd had to punch a senior teammate. Freshman year, it was Coleman Harris, a defenseman who blamed me for not stopping one of the seven breakaways that happened because of *Coleman Harris's* mistakes. I popped him in the nose, everyone pulled us apart, and that was the end of it. Sophomore year, there was a new twelfth-grader, Ryan O'Dell, who must not have heard the Coleman Harris story, and he, too, had gotten punched by me in the locker room between periods.

"Some goalies get coached," I said, as Katie typed, "but not me. I'm better on my own. Dunwoody gets this. He ignores me."

Just then, Alessandra walked through the auditorium doors, glanced over at me while wiggling into her leather jacket.

"Can I interrupt for a sec?" asked Alesssandra.

"No problem," said Katie.

"There's a prop on the top shelf in the bio classroom's closet and I need Walt's help reaching it."

I was confused about why this had to happen in the middle of my interview, but Alessandra grabbed my arm. She sprinted and I kept up. We took the sharp left turn toward the science wing, and once we were out of view, Alessandra stopped, and yanked on my arm to get me to stop, too.

"The bio classroom?" I asked, pointing feebly down the hall.

"Take off your shirt," she whispered.

"What?"

"Please?"

"Why?"

"I think it would be good for the scene we're about to practice. It'll give us both some energy."

I was new to the Drama Club. I trusted her. I took off my shirt.

"Can I listen to your heart?"

"Okay," I said.

She rested her head against my chest. I could feel my heart pounding against her ear. Her hair against my skin.

"Ba-dum-ba-dum-ba-dum-ba-dum-ba-dum," she said. Then she was quiet, and I could feel the same pattern with her ear and hair against my chest. I didn't put my arms around her.

She said, "Okay, I'm going to take your hand, here, and put it on my ass."

She did exactly what she said she was going to do. I had my hand on the seat of her pants and her ass felt warm and firm. My hand was there for about five seconds before she said, "Okay, let's run back."

I put on my shirt, and we sprinted back down the hall. When I took my seat next to Katie, she said, "All set?"

"All set."

"All right, next question. Aside from hockey, what do you like to do for fun?"

I was still catching my breath. "Scrabble."

She looked up at me, waiting to hear more.

"I've gotten into word games." I'd played Scrabble four times. I'd lost to Alessandra by these scores: 310-161, 352-149, 295-187, 332-202.

Katie thanked me for my time and left, and I considered catching up with everyone who'd gone to get subs at Romano's, but I scrapped this idea, unsure how soon I could handle seeing Alessandra again, having just had my hand on her ass. Had I felt the edge of her underwear through the fabric of her pants? Also, I didn't have much time. I'd packed myself dinner that morning, a plastic container full of pesto pasta I'd made myself. I went back inside the empty auditorium, nodded hello to Mr. Sveta who didn't acknowledge my presence because he was meditating or something. I checked my backpack for the pesto container but it wasn't there. Perhaps I'd left it on the counter at home. Packing dinner in addition to lunch was new to my routine.

Dinner break ended in ten minutes so I jogged home, slammed through the side door, scanned the cleared counter, checked the fridge, didn't see the pesto container, so I made myself a sloppy PB and J, ate it in three bites, put the knife in the dishwasher, saw an empty plastic container slick with pesto residue there—*Dad, you asshole!*—went upstairs to reapply my deodorant in case Alessandra asked me to take my shirt off again, didn't see my Speed Stick on the bureau, checked the bathroom, no luck, then heard a sound in my parents' room, and because my father would sometimes borrow my things without asking, which annoyed me, and because he'd eaten the pesto, I barreled into the bedroom.

A woman, naked, was sitting on top of my father, who was also naked, and whose chest tube dangled beside the woman's naked leg.

The woman was Sarah Shinwell.

I stood there for a very long half-second, then backed out and shut the door, calmly. Scorched on the back of my eyeballs was the naked profile of Alessandra's mother, including the side of one heavy-looking dark-nippled breast. Then her startled face as she turned to look at me. And their movements, in hyperspeed, terrified and embarrassed, grabbing sheets to cover themselves. And my father's flushed face as it transformed from concentrated focus to open-mouthed horror.

What I couldn't believe, then, or even now, looking back, was that despite how quickly I tried to flee the house, somehow my father got downstairs in his bathrobe before I could leave.

"Hold on there," said my dad, stepping in front of the door.

I reached for the doorknob and said, "Nope."

My dad pressed his back against the door, completely blocking me.

Hearing footsteps on the stairs, I said, "Get the fuck out of the way."

My father's face hardened, and he looked insanely mad. But then Sarah Shinwell came into the kitchen, fully dressed, with cheeks as red as my father's.

I looked back at my father, who seemed to have decided blocking the door was not the best plan.

I said, again: "Move."

"I'm so sorry," said Sarah Shinwell, hugging her arms to her chest, emitting a quick spike of laughter, as though she were about to say more, but didn't.

My dad stepped away from the door and lowered his gaze.

Before leaving I faced Dad and said, "You ate my pesto."

"Oh," said Sarah. "I'm so sorry. I was the one who ate that."

Dad raised his head and looked squarely at me, his hair spiked in places, flattened in others. "Which was my fault," he said.

I squeezed past them, pulled open the door, and tumbled out. I gulped the sharp cold air, mind on fire, started marching over to the auditorium. I'd left my backpack in the kitchen with my *Rosencrantz and Guildenstern Are Dead* script. I spun around and trudged back, crashing through the door.

Sarah said, "Oh!"

I stretched past them while trying unsuccessfully to avoid looking their way and grabbed my backpack. Dad took up his spot in front of the door again—he couldn't help himself—but this time I just moved toward it like a bull and Dad stepped aside.

As the door was closing Sarah said, "Remember, we're all human."

In the auditorium, Alessandra and Owen Pickarts—Guildenstern and Rosencrantz, respectively—were already on stage, waiting for me. Sveta had called promptly for the scene between the three of us. I leapt on stage and took my place in my chair. Guildenstern and Rosencrantz were visiting Hamlet's chambers, unsolicited. I cleared my throat. "My excellent good friends! How dost thou Guildenstern! Ah, Rosencrantz! Good lads!" I said, hugging them both. I squeezed

Alessandra fiercely. "How do you both?" I tried to cut myself off from my feelings but couldn't. At least I knew my lines. I wondered if I might black out. I couldn't really listen to what Alessandra or Owen were saying. The sounds from their mouths were garbled in my brain. At the end of the scene, my line was: "But my uncle father and my aunt mother are deceived."

Alessandra, as Guildenstern, said, "In what my dear lord?"

And I said, "I am but mad north-northwest. When the wind is southerly, I know a hawk from a handsaw."

Then the scene was over. The auditorium lights were still blinding me. When I turned away, I saw Alessandra squinting in my direction. She and Owen weren't leaving the stage, so I didn't, either. After a few beats of silence she said, "Holy shit, Walt. You acted the shit out of that."

Mr. Sveta stood up from his metal folding chair and applauded.

Instead of exiting behind the curtain, Alessandra hopped down off the front of the stage, and I followed. She gave me a tender hug, both arms.

"It worked," she whispered.

"I know," I said.

"We'll try that again before the next rehearsal," she whispered.

"I know about your mom and my dad."

"He finally told you?"

"Yeah," I said.

The kids in the next scene were taking their places. Sveta was already in a tizzy about some blocking adjustments.

"My mom's an idiot," she said. "I mean, seriously. What the hell's going on with those two? Sorry I couldn't let you know earlier. My mom told me it was your dad's call to tell you."

The chest tube dangling from my dad's body.

"We're not really talking much."

"I'm glad he told you, though."

More than ever, I felt unaccountable to everything in the world but Alessandra. "Can we break in again tonight?" I asked.

"Ah, shit. I can't. Not tonight."

"Okay," I said.

"You've got playoffs tomorrow, right? You should get some rest."

"Are you coming to the game?"

She took me by the arm and pulled me further from the stage to the back of the auditorium, where the only light came from the crack beneath the door to the kitchen.

"I'm sorry, Walt," she said, resting a hand on my chest briefly and then pulling it away. "I can't come to your game tomorrow, either. I'm heading to Williams for the night."

"Is that where—"

"The boyfriend. Yeah."

"Oh, that's fine. The game is . . . it should be a blowout. Turnersboro. They suck."

"I don't even really want to go see him. But he's like, dying over there."

"He's dying?"

"I mean, he's lonely."

"Gotcha."

"I totally like hanging out with you way more."

"Thanks," I said. The vibe had gone to shit. I didn't want to pout, I didn't want to storm off, but I was suddenly exhausted, and I knew—because of the calamity at my house—I'd be driving to the Great Blue Heron Motel to spend the night on a cot beside my mom's bed.

Sveta didn't need me for any more scenes that night.

"Travel safe," I said, and I gave Alessandra a bro hug and slipped out the side door.

17. Pepper, Tollefson, and Moorcroft

During those first three weeks on the island, we ran the obstacle course twice a day. We kept our bellies on the ground crawling under the low hurdles, then we'd scale a sheer wooden wall, climb a rope web, clear a trench by traversing a set of monkey bars. We got better and better at it. DeShawn could pull himself up and over the wall in one fluid motion. Javier and Corsetti wriggled across the dirt like they'd caught fire. I loved the way Bianca would grunt little puffs of air as she clutched and released the monkey bars. We'd all been athletes in our former lives, and we knew how to push ourselves, endure pain, work together.

Joey MacLean visited us twice. He wanted to tell us more about the three ranch hands who saved the day at the Elk Basin River Ranch in Montana. He wanted us to know the world was changing, and we'd never go back to the old way. You couldn't leave your doors unlocked anymore.

The ranch hands—they'd kept everyone safe. They'd received training.

"Does that kind of thing happen a lot in Montana?" asked Tess.

"Attempted kidnapping? No, not too often," said MacLean. "Especially with folks like Pepper, Tollefson, and Moorcroft at the ready. They can guard against the riffraff. Keep the outsiders out. You know what? People who follow the rules are the underdogs. We are the underdogs. You are the underdogs."

At the beginning of the fourth week, late September, MacLean and Grunewald brought us to the quarry on the south side, not far from some of the biggest mansions, and they assembled us near the edge of a sheer rock cliff in the rain. The granite quarries near my hometown were off-limits, cordoned off by barbed wire, but this one was wide open.

We wore our WILD oil-skin rain gear and peered over the edge, a forty-foot drop to the surface of the water. The tiny splashes of rain were mesmerizing. Grunewald said, "A good place to swim if it wasn't for the eels."

"Gross," said Tess.

"The eels aren't scared of you. They nip at your legs and arms," he continued.

"You swam here?" asked DeShawn, who never seemed to believe Grunewald existed before he'd started working with us.

"During instructor orientation," he said. "We had a few weeks here in July. Just the brass."

"Good times," said MacLean.

To get to the quarry we'd taken the Old Shipyard Trail to an offshoot I hadn't noticed before, marked by a tilted and weathered sign: PLINY'S. MacLean told us Albert Pliny had been enlisted by one of the Keith descendants to lead a team of stonecutters in the 1890s, when the demand for granite had been so high they would have been fools not to ship some of it down to Boston, New York, and Washington.

"So many great buildings in this country were built by Whaleback stone. And to get the stone off island, we have Albert Pliny to thank," said MacLean.

"Pliny was a buddy of my grandfather's," said Grunewald. "He ran a crew out here, did most of the work himself, and he died here. They'd skid the large blocks with horses. Bring them down to the barges at the main pier. Load them up and bring them to whoever needed them."

Javier asked how he died.

"California, there are about a thousand ways to die around this stuff," said Grunewald. "Where there's money to be made, there's also people dying."

"What's up, eels!" shouted Javier. His voice echoed on the quarry walls.

Bianca announced she was hungry. We all were.

Tess asked MacLean, "Do you treat him well?"

"Who?"

She pointed at Grunewald.

"I mean, he's your employee, right? Do you treat him well?"

"Of course," said MacLean. "He's family."

"Family who gets a paycheck," said Tess.

"True," said MacLean.

"I wouldn't be here if they didn't treat me well," said Grunewald.

The trail looped through the woods, sloping down to the place at water level where Pliny would skid the blocks.

"But come on, guys. Pliny was the one cutting rocks while the Club members were picnicking and raking in dough," said Tess. "And then Pliny got crushed by a block of granite."

"I don't know exactly how he died," said Grunewald. "He might have just drunk himself to death."

MacLean laughed. "They lived pretty hard back then."

Standing on the edge of the forty-foot drop, Grunewald kicked a flake of granite down into the quarry. We couldn't hear the splash because of the rain.

"All right. Here's what we want you to do. You have forty-five minutes to get everyone across the quarry," he said, pointing to the wet cliffs on the far side. "The only rules are that you can't go around on the trail, and you can't touch the water."

Bethany and Bianca, the quiet and strong softball players, were the first to say it was impossible. Bethany was sturdy with long blonde hair and long eyelashes. Bianca was a small muscular tomboy. When they scaled the obstacle course wall—the fifteen-footer—the first move, always, was to have Bianca climb up Bethany's back and stand on her shoulders.

"Forty-five minutes," Grunewald said, and he pulled a coil of rope and a knife from his backpack and handed them to DeShawn.

"What if we can't do it?" asked Javier.

"Listen," said MacLean. "Of course you can do it."

"But what if we can't?"

"Think of Pepper, Tollefson, and Moorcroft. Everyone might have died out there at Elk Basin if it hadn't been for them. And you know what? Those three now own part of the ranch. They are on the fucking deed, my friends."

"How would the guests have died?"

"The pieces of shit. The fucking drug addicts from Bozeman. The kidnappers. They could have had their way."

Bianca—who, along with being a softball player, had done time in juvie for pushing Fentanyl—asked, "what happened to the tweakers?"

"The tweakers?" asked MacLean.

"The meth heads. Junkies, whatever."

"They were taken care of," said MacLean.

"They died?"

"They died. And we started this program in honor of their death. Well, I should say, in honor of the people who killed them."

"Pepper, Tollefson, and Moorcroft," said Bianca.

"Exactly," said MacLean.

"That's fucked up."

"Can we get back to us, please?" asked Javier? "What happens if we can't get across?"

"The thing is, you *can* get across," said MacLean.

He pulled MacLean toward the trail and within seconds they'd jogged out of view.

Corsetti grabbed the rope from DeShawn, untied the coil, held one end and dropped the other end off the side of the cliff. It was long enough to reach the water below, but not much longer. "How the hell can this rope help us?"

"Let's use the knife to hijack a boat, get the hell back to the mainland," said Bianca.

From the far side of the quarry, we heard Grunewald yell, "Forty-four minutes!"

Rain pattered the hoods of our jackets. We stared at the staticky gray surface of water down below until Tess said, "That." She was pointing to the cable above us running from a tall wooden pole on our side of the quarry to a pole on the far side.

"Bingo," said Corsetti.

After a lot of arguing it was decided: I would climb the pole with a section of rope and then tie it in a loop around the cable. With the rain loud in my ears, I sat in that loop of rope and rocked my weight forward, scooting in six-inch increments, until I started sliding steadily along the cable. Above the middle of the quarry, my body shot through with adrenaline, I slowed to a stop. I tried scooting but I could only get an inch or so each time before sliding back.

"Twenty minutes!" yelled Grunewald.

"You're too fat, Walt!" yelled Corsetti.

"Muscle's heavier than fat," I could hear Bethany say.

I spent the last twenty minutes scooting forward and sliding back, the rope cutting into my legs.

"That's it, you're done," yelled Grunewald.

Everyone booed, and when they quieted, I heard Tess shout, "How do we get Walt down?"

Grunewald said, "Once you figure that out, we're meeting in DaGama classroom."

I knew how I'd get down. I had to grip the cable, pull myself up out of the loop, then let go, falling twenty or thirty feet down into the water. But I hated that plan.

"You okay, Walt?" yelled Corsetti.

"Just getting ready here," I shouted back.

"We love you, Walt!" yelled Tess.

The Huddle started cheering for me, whooping and clapping. I reached up to the cable and pulled myself up so I could step on the loop of rope and straighten my legs. As I prepared to jump, their cheers rose up again—"Walt! Walt! Walt!"—and my body imagined itself swimming in my rain gear and boots, which seemed awful.

I shook out my arms, gripped the cable with both hands and in a desperate move, stepped one foot out of the rope and hooked my ankle around the cable. I brought my other leg up so I could hug the cable, rain slapping my face.

"Walt! Walt! Walt!"

I thought about the ranch hands. Pepper, Tollefson, and Moorcroft. I didn't know much about them, but they'd saved the ranch. They'd killed the tweakers. They'd been trained by the ranch owners, and they'd taken matters into their own hands. Hearing the others on the far side of the quarry gave me enough strength to start inching forward, and once I got closer to the jagged cliff, all I wanted to do was keep myself from dashing my brains on the rocks below so I could be with my crew.

"Walt! Walt! Walt!"

They weren't letting up. Their cheers seemed to be getting louder, and I glanced over my shoulder and saw them running through the woods to get to the pole where I was headed. Aubrey whistled the first two notes from "Heigh Ho" and the others started whistling too.

I was past the cliff and over the trees. I released my left hand, shook it out, and hung from my right before inching further.

"You got it, brother!" yelled Corsetti, and then my right hand hit the pole. I'd made it.

I pressed my cheek against the wet wood. When I got to the ground, they hugged me, bouncing up and down all together, as though we'd actually passed Grunewald's test.

Next to DaGama dorm was DaGama classroom, a simple pine saltbox built atop one of the wide boulders there. Grunewald had arrived before us and started a fire, so by the time we all entered the tiny classroom, the room was hot and dry. Without saying anything to Grunewald we shed our wet rain gear and socks and spread them out by the stove, then sat down in long underwear at one of the tables, where Grunewald had spread out single sheets of paper and pens.

"Time to write home," he said.

"Walt made it across the cable," said Javier.

"Get a pen," said Grunewald.

"It was fucking awesome," said Tess.

"You lost," said Grunewald.

"You think you could make it across that cable?" asked Javier.

"Not relevant," said Grunewald.

"Doubt it," said Tess. "It was a beautiful thing. You missed out."

I couldn't tell if Grunewald cared. My body was still hollowed out from the stress and my hands were raw.

Grunewald had poured us cups of water. Once we were warm, the prospect of writing a letter home became appealing. Everyone picked up a pen.

There was so much I wanted to tell my mom.

"I'm dictating here," said Grunewald. "You'll write what I tell you to write."

Tess laughed.

Grunewald reached back and smacked Corsetti on the back of the head.

"You got something to say, Maryland?"

"Yeah," she said. "I do. Am I free to speak?"

"Of course."

"Of course I'm free to speak? You're not going to hit Corsetti again if I do?"

"Go ahead."

"Why would we write home if you're going to write the letter for us? What good would that letter be?"

Grunewald was also wearing only long underwear, and in the heat of the room he had more color than he usually did in his skeletal cheeks. Still, he looked waterlogged and tired. "I was joking."

Tess stared at him. We all stared at him. No one moved.

"Jiminy Christmas, write your goddamn letters. Remember? This is all real," he said, standing in front of the large plate-glass window looking out at the wet granite, dripping pine trees, and sheets of rain coming down into the gray ocean. The paper was appealingly thick, and it soaked up the ink from our roller-ball pens.

Aubrey sat next to me, and I couldn't help but glance at her paper. She'd written *Dear Mom* but nothing else. I turned back to my page and wrote:

> *Dear Mom,*
> *I would be kind of amazed if you got this letter but I hope you do. I miss you. I've liked what we've done out here so far. And I like my Huddle, which is what we call our group. We've all agreed to work hard. I just commandoed across a quarry on a cable. Our leader is a jerk, and we didn't make it across in time but I guess we learned that's okay. Are you picking me up at Christmas? I hope things at home are good. I love you.*
> *—Walt*

I sealed my letter in the cream-colored envelope Grunewald gave each of us with the return address "Islanders Club, Whaleback Island, Maine." Grunewald walked around the room collecting the sealed envelopes, stowing them in a plastic bag in his backpack.

"When do you think they'll get these?" asked Tess.

"I have no idea," said Grunewald. "Depends on how rough the seas are during the next few days. I might not even be able to send them. The important thing is you wrote them."

"For real?" said Tess.

"You have something to say, Maryland?"

"Please send my letter," said Tess.

Grunewald was looking out the window again, squinting into the fog.

"Sir? I want my mom to get my letter."

"Yeah, well, I want my mom to know my innermost thoughts, too, but she's long dead," said Grunewald.

"Wait. I don't really understand why—"

"You're your own person, now. Time to separate from your family and grow up."

"For fuck's sake. I'm out on an island in the middle of the ocean, sir. I think I'm doing pretty well at 'separating from the family.'"

"Not the end of the world if you don't stay in touch while you're out here."

"Then why did you have us write the letters?"

I assumed Grunewald would answer Tess's question, but he just turned away. He seemed far away, distracted. We sat in silence like that for a while, looking at the back of his head and beyond him, at the fog. Heat pumped from the stove; we were all red-cheeked and sweating now, and I felt light-headed. Somehow the feeling was luxurious. I wanted my mother to get my letter. I missed talking to her. I missed her opinions. I missed hearing about Dr. Charles, the new poems he'd introduced to her, the evenings she'd spent with her poetry group.

After a minute or two, Grunewald said, "I'll send them. But here's one thing I want you to know. Your education up until this point, school and what have you, it's been fake. It's a pretend version of preparing you for a pretend future. What we're doing out here is as real as it gets. You've got to know you're capable of greatness. Like in Montana, the ranch hands. They did their job. Someone tried to come to their place and take their stuff. So the ranch hands did what they'd been trained to do. They ended the threat. They didn't fuck up. And now they own the place."

Our socks had dried, and our rain gear was filmy and hot. We suited up. Grunewald took us back to the obstacle course, and within minutes we were soaked and cold again, and it was as though our time in the classroom had been a dream.

18. That Wasn't Me

New Hampshire

The news about my dad and Sarah Shinwell had been well known months before I'd found out, which got me reconsidering interactions I'd had with teachers and coaches during that time. Ray McNamara, the stoic unknowable head of maintenance, was hooking up with the wealthy, kooky art teacher. It was premium, grade-A, platinum gossip. Sarah Shinwell was known by everyone. Even I knew plenty about her, and I'd never taken her class.

Her studio door was always open. She liked asking earnest questions. What made the news especially delicious for the community was that no one thought Saltshaker capable. People must have been wondering how the hell it had happened. Who had even heard Ray McNamara's voice? Maybe he'd muttered something to them, once, about a clogged toilet or a broken window.

The puck dropped at four in the afternoon. Time jumped around during games. Next thing I knew I was deep in the second period, no pucks passed me. Not even a single close call. I was intuiting the angles, not needing to check the pipes with my stick. From the glow of the lights and the angle of the rafters and the joints between the boards, I knew exactly where I was on the sheet. *Rosencrantz and Guildenstern Are Dead* and every other micro-distraction was obliterated from my head. I felt ten times my normal size, the net tiny behind me. Turnersboro's moves and shots came at me in slow motion. Everything mapped out in my brain. In one play they broke out of their zone with three zipped tape-to-tape passes, resulting in a breakaway—the quick tenth grader I'd been hearing about, Ethan Montgomery—and as he accelerated, carving the ice, striding over the blue line past our last defender, Kevvy Brockhouse, black-helmeted Ethan Montgomery pushed the puck out in front of his stick and looked up. Looked straight at me. I charged out of my goal, sprinting directly at the kid, and I lunged with my stick and poked the puck back between his legs. The stands went nuts. I retreated to my goalmouth exhilarated, not because of the cheers—I was indifferent to the crowd—but because I'd timed the poke check perfectly. Perfectly. Not much is perfect. That poke check was. I wasn't yet much of a fan of poetry, but it was like the end of that Dickinson poem: the Horses' Heads, there they were again. Toward Eternity. Little Montgomery went sprawling. The whole play had lasted about two seconds, everything so bright and sharp, the electric white of the ice, the wet vulcanized rubber puck, the *scritch scritch scritch* of his quickening strides.

I loved a physical game. Everyone amped and hitting hard. Most of the time, the hitting had nothing to do with me; I stayed in front of the goal like one of those fuzzy-headed guards at Buckingham Palace. But if anyone came near me, they got decked. This never took me out of my game; I'd hit them, and my vision would brighten.

The only thoughts outside of the realm of Turnersboro's attack that entered my orbit were little self-assuring reminders that I was staying focused, doing my job, not troubled by dark thoughts that had nothing to do with the task at hand. I wasn't thinking about Alessandra's pretty, yet-to-be-named boyfriend, and I definitely wasn't thinking about Sarah Shinwell's dark nipples or anything else I'd seen in my parents' bedroom less than twenty-four hours earlier. At the far end of the ice, Jalen Barman let a pass to the point go under his stick. Ethan Montgomery sprang to life again, *scritch scritch scritch*, probably guessing I would try the poke check again. Montgomery kept the puck on his stick. Meanwhile I was reading every stride, every scritch, and the unfortunate deke Montgomery tried—shot fake, right, left—was brutally obvious, no need to react, the backhand flip landed blocker side, and I deflected it so sharply and with such disgust that it flew behind the goal, as did Montgomery, slamming hard into the boards, which gave Kevvy Brockhouse time to catch up to the play, get the puck, and clear it out.

This time when the crowd bellowed, the sound angered me: It was the sound of unhappy adults hoping to escape their meaningless lives.

Playing Hamlet blipped into my brain. Somehow during the previous month I'd become an actor. I'd come alive by not trying at all, by just being myself.

Life seemed both easy and oppressively difficult.

Alessandra's ear had been on my chest. She reminded me about her boyfriend. The existence of that Williams football player was probably my fault. Maybe if I had been smoother in conversation, if I had masturbated less, if I had shaved my hairy face more often, if I'd had any other talent aside from hockey, she wouldn't have needed to travel to western Mass for sex.

The crowd quieted down. I returned to the breath within my mask, to the sweat in my glove and blocker, to a feeling of purity and cosmic surrender, everything balanced and peaceful. My slow-mo vision returned. My body moving without oversight.

The period ended. We returned to the locker room. When a game was going well, the Zamboni inched around the ice between periods. The droning of its engine coming through the turns filled my core with fuel. Everyone on my team knew not to fuck with me in the locker room, regardless of score. Coach Dunwoody churned through obvious feedback to everyone but me—"let's beat them to the puck" and "dump and chase" and "take shots if you got 'em." Coach knew better than to look anywhere near me.

The horn sounded, I slammed out of the locker room and led my team in sprinting a lap around the hardening ice. I set up shop in the goalmouth, scratched up the surface again, took a few warmup shots from Brockhouse before the whistle blew. The puck dropped at center ice, and I felt nearly as warm as I had at the end of the last period. Jalen Barman dumped the puck into Turnersboro's zone, and the whistle blew for a high stick. The skaters circled before the face-off at the other end of the ice. I stood from my crouch, grabbed my water bottle from atop the net, sipped, then spotted my father coming through the double doors into the rink. Beyond the Plexiglas, the old man walked in his black wool cap along the boards and tucked up into the back row of stands. The puck dropped, and Barman kept it in the Turnersboro zone. I returned to my vigilant crouch, feeling my father's eyes on me. Dad was always neutral about my games, never criticizing nor offering praise. Dad, fucker of art teachers, never clapped or cheered in the stands.

At the next whistle, a tripping penalty on St. Bart's best defenseman, Milo Kelly, gave me a surge of energy. I knew we'd be man-down for ninety seconds, and I'd be fielding more shots. As the ref waited for Milo to skate to the box, I stood again, grabbed my water bottle from on top of the net, and sipped—I wasn't thirsty but the ritual was automatic. During the sip, the rink doors opened again—Sarah Shinwell in a full-length parka, fur-lined hood, and suede boots. We locked eyes. Sweat slithered through my scalp. She smiled, raised a reluctant hand, then thought better of the wave—probably realizing I wasn't going to acknowledge her—and continued walking toward the stands.

My father peeked over at her. She saw this. I saw this. Dad and Sarah pretended not to see each other. She tucked herself into a different part of the bleachers. Next stoppage of play, an off-sides call on Turnersboro, Brockhouse slid the puck to the ref, fresh players came off the bench, I stood, grabbed my water bottle, and again, the doors opened. Mom. And behind her, the short, chunky, debonair Dr. Charles. It was a Thursday, when my mother always worked until six, but it was only five, maybe five-thirty. She took off her hat, reconsidered, put it back on. Had Dr. Charles, with his kind round-cheeked face and long mohair coat, ever set foot in the rink before? Probably not but fuck if I cared.

The puck dropped. Turnersboro won the face-off, and their defense rifled the puck into our zone. I left the goal to settle the puck behind my net. My arms felt inexplicably weak. The puck went under my stick. One of their forwards slammed Brockhouse into the boards, won possession, brought the puck in front of my net as I tried to get into position, and dinked it past my left skate. Turnersboro skaters blurred in front, celebrating. I scooped the puck out of my goal and flung it out to center ice. I felt dizzy, nauseous. I looked again to the stands. My mother—her face pale and pinched in the cold—stood beside Dr. Charles high in the center bleachers. She, my father, and Sarah Shinwell were each in their own section. My vision tunneled; everyone in the stands looked like diligent soldiers in a war diorama. We were still on top by three goals, but my skates felt dull and slippery beneath me, and the weakness in my arms had traveled up into my shoulders and down into my legs. The ref dropped the puck at center ice; again, Turnersboro won the face-off, and again they dumped the puck into our goddamn zone. I stayed paralyzed in the crease. I let the puck zoom along the boards. My teammates must have sensed I was off-kilter; they were tentative, spooked. Three of the next seven shots by Turnersboro went right past me; I flinched, trying to react, but each time I was late. Coach called a time out so he could warm up the other goalie. I didn't move. I stayed in my crouch. Kevvy Brockhouse came out from the bench, tapped his stick against my pads and said, "Dude, dude, dude. Wake up. You okay?"

I knew I was being pulled by Coach, and this was the right move, but the short trip from the goal mouth to the bench would be absolutely brutal with everyone staring. Sarah Shinwell was probably making an attempt to show interest in me, telling those beside her what a great kid I was. And my mother, willing to be in the same rink as those assholes, had left work early just to humiliate herself.

Nat Finkel, my ninth-grade backup, glided out to replace me. I wanted to spare him the awkwardness of having to say something, which was probably well prepped ahead of time—"Tough luck,

Walt" or "They got lucky" or, worst of all, "Sorry"—so instead of skating to the bench I headed in the other direction, to the boards by the bleachers. I took off my helmet. I pitched my head back to get the hair out of my eyes. The rink was silent. No one knew why I was skating *away* from the bench. In my loudest voice I yelled, "THE FUCKING HORSES' HEADS!"

To everyone but my mom, what I said was insane, but I didn't care. I flung my helmet down to the other end of the ice, ripped off my jersey and my neck guard and chest protector and chucked them as high in the air as I could. I glided to the door in the boards closest to the exit, tromped to the locker room, took off the rest of my pads for the last time and showered alone.

That night I couldn't sleep. I went downstairs, ate some cereal, popped in the VHS tape of *Halloween*, stopped watching just after the killer strangled a dog, finally drifted off around three and woke up a few hours later. Everything in the world around me was shimmering too brightly. I wanted to go back to sleep. I didn't want to talk to anyone. An hour before classes started, I put on my clothes, ate more cereal, and zombied over to the main building.

I went right to Sarah Shinwell's art room. The door, as always, was open, though at seven in the morning no one was there, only the smell of pencil shavings, paint, gummy erasers. The ceilings seemed higher. Easels ringed the perimeter, as did a cork board wall full of drawings of vegetables and fruit and candles and teacups. In the far corner was the only desk in the room, hers, burdened by a few manila interdepartmental envelopes, a framed photo of Alessandra (fifth grade, razor thin, sitting in a pile of orange leaves), a little brass Buddha, and a set of car keys.

Sarah would sometimes dress up as Frida Kahlo or Mary Cassatt during class and stay in character for critique. She'd hold a buzzer in her hand that emitted the "wrong answer" sound of a game show, and if any of her students ever said anything negative about anyone else's work, if there were comments that could be construed as inhibiting, or nullifying, or overly prescriptive, if a critique got personal or nasty, she would neg these comments with the buzzer. Her classroom was a place of free-wheeling expression. Leaving her car keys out was consistent with this approach.

My plan was to take these keys to the faculty lot. I'd steal her Subaru, drive it down to the public landing, leave it in neutral on the boat launch, and watch it roll down into the intertidal zone. But I heard someone humming outside the classroom in the cavernous hallway, and when it got louder I crouched down behind her desk.

Sarah came into the room, flipping the lights on, still humming, lowering her backpack beside the door. I heard her take a few more steps. And stop. Could she see me? I inched my head forward: She wore boots and jeans as well as a skirt. She said, "Oh! Hello?"

I had no choice but to stand with my back to her, lean over the radiator, and try to escape through a window into the courtyard, but the window didn't budge.

"That one's painted shut," she said.

I sidestepped to the next window, raised it with ease, swung a leg out, then the other, and dropped down into the crusty snow just a few feet beneath. As I jogged across the courtyard, Sarah said, "Thank you for visiting my classroom, Walt. Come back any time."

I jogged all the way around the science building, looped to the back entrance of the main school building, then down the empty hall into the library, where I could hide until first period. I sat at one of the tables with a public desktop computer and caught my breath, closed my eyes. My mom was ballistic, and now I knew why. Sarah Shinwell was cluelessly nice and generous and also a narcissistic vampire.

I thought about this for a few minutes. I decided to log into the computer and send my mom an email. This was when email was new. I remember liking it early on because it was less immediate than a phone call. Atop my unread inbox was a brand-new message from Sarah Shinwell. The subject heading was, GOOD TO SEE YOU TODAY!

I felt my whole body get cold. I clicked open her message.

> *Dear Walt,*
> *What a delight to find you in my art room this morning.*
> *I was sorry you had to leave, but of course I understand.*
> *Won't you come again? Let's chat sometime—I would*
> *really like that.*
> *Fondly,*
> *Sarah*

This got my heart pounding again. I composed a quick reply.

> *Eat shit and die, homewrecker!*

I deleted that and tried again.

> *Your politeness is irritating and it seems totally fake.*

I backspaced over that and wrote:

> *I apologize for sneaking around in your room. I won't*
> *do it again.*

Why apologize? What I ended up writing and sending was this:

> *That wasn't me.*

19. Squid Eaters

On Whaleback Island in early October, sharp frigid wind blew from the north. We all gathered outside Big Rug on the damp grass beside the granite slab in hats, gloves, and parkas to talk about Thoreau's *The Maine Woods*.

MacLean, in a fleece hoodie, held a cardboard box full of heart-rate monitors he wanted us to wear on our wrists.

"Okay," Janowski shouted. "While Mr. MacLean passes out the wrist bands, I want to hear your thoughts on Thoreau."

Silence.

"This is good stuff, people. Am I wrong?"

Maybe two or three heads nodded, max. I'd liked the book, but I didn't nod. I'd been shocked by how searingly true the book seemed. Thoreau speculated about the possibility of the moose becoming extinct, and it had gotten me wondering what it would be like for future generations if those awkward breathy beasts existed only as fossils. I imagined a moment in the future when we'd depend on artists to reconstruct the moose's inconceivable face.

Joey MacLean said, "*Alabama?*"

Bethany raised her hand. He strode over to her and tightened a monitor to her left wrist.

"Okay, first question," said Janowski. "Just to make sure we're all on the same page. What state does this story take place in?"

"Maine," said one of the giant boys.

"Correct," said Janowski. We'd been swimming naked with Janowski in the icy water just hours earlier. We'd learned to sprint in and out of the ocean on the round rocks, submerging for an instant. It woke us up better than coffee.

Joey MacLean was calling us out by state name. He used the last hole to fit the monitor on Alaska's slender wrist.

Janowski pulled one arm to his chest, then the other, stretching his shoulders,

"And what's the name of the big mountain in Maine that he climbs?"

DeShawn sighed and said, "Katahdin."

"Good," said Janowski. "We're on a roll. Okay, here's another one." He flipped through the pages, stopped on one randomly.

"*Arizona!*" said Joey MacLean. "*Arkansas!*"

Janowski drew his finger down the page, and asked, "What's the name of the falls after Pockwockamus Falls that the expedition needs to carry their boats around?"

A breeze took up in the trees. Some looked in their books. Others, like me, just stared blankly at Janowski.

Earlier in the day Grunewald had added another two feet to the obstacle-course wall. We'd approached it just like the ten-foot wall, with Bianca climbing up Bethany's back. We'd gotten everyone up and over the wall in less than two minutes. It had been several weeks since we'd failed one of Grunewald's tests. We all felt strong and capable and worthy.

Everyone started leafing through the book to find the answer.

"*California!*" MacLean said.

Javier, sitting on the grass, held up his wrist.

"*Colorado!*"

"Someone's got to know the answer," said Janowski.

There were about fifty different lakes and waterfalls mentioned in those early pages, each with a long Wabanaki name. Janowski was asking us an idiotic question, but there *was* an answer.

"*Connecticut!*"

"I'll give you a hint," said Janowski. "Starts with a K."

Janowski had been a grunt in Vietnam like Grunewald, and since then he'd been a helper on the island. He painted boats and was greenskeeper of the golf course. I don't know exactly what it was about *The Maine Woods* that Janowski loved, but I bet it was something about how nature should be experienced in the foulest of weather, so that when it clears, you can really appreciate it.

"Give up?"

"Delaware!"

From a month on the island what I knew about our Huddle, and the other Huddles, was that we weren't going to give up. So finding an answer to this dumb question became a competition. The girl with dirt smudges on her face sitting next to me said to no one in particular, "Say it again? The falls after Wocka-pocka-what?"

While we looked for the answer, Grunewald came out of the woods in his wool sweater, camo vest, rain pants, and bucket hat. He kicked a twig with his boot, skittering it across the large flat granite slab. "How much more time do you need here, Dale?"

"Florida!"

"We're just getting started," said Janowski.

"Georgia!"

"What's he teaching you?" asked Grunewald.

After a few seconds of silence Tess said, "Mr. Grunewald, do you know the name of the falls they get to after Wocka-pocka-wocka?"

"Hawaii!"

"Let's go do some pushups," said Grunewald. "Did you read the book?"

"Idaho!"

Many of us nodded. Grunewald said, "They've read it, Dale. You don't need to quiz them about it."

We weren't sure how offensive Grunewald's statement was to Janowski. Joey MacLean kept on handing out the heart monitors.

"Illinois!"

"I'll dismiss them when they're done, Dick," said Janowski. "Where do you want your Huddle to meet you?"

"My Huddle is coming with me right now," he said. "Let's get going, freaks."

"Indiana!"

I'd gotten conflicting instructions from my parents on how to interact with my teachers. My dad had been in the Marines before getting his job at St. Bart's, and he respected most chains of command. When I was little, he'd say to me most mornings before school, "Do what your teachers say." A good, clear directive. In middle school I showed signs of restlessness. My mom told me she thought seventh and eighth grade boys should be put to work on farms. She said it was fine if I didn't want to do the worksheets I was asked to complete. She told me I was clever enough to be fine without school.

I glanced at Tess, who seemed to be waiting to see what Aubrey would do, but Aubrey was looking down at her lap, perhaps embarrassed by the conflict between the two instructors. DeShawn elbowed me and turned to Janowski. Then it seemed we were all looking at Janowski, waiting for his instructions.

"Thanks. We need to finish up our discussion," he said.

"Iowa!"

"You're not having a discussion. We have important shit to do," barked Grunewald, and he waved for us to follow him.

"Kansas!"

Janowski said, "Joey, don't you think some Thoreau would do these kids some good?"

"What I can say with confidence is that you all look strong, fast, and fit," MacLean said. "A team of thoroughbreds."

"He's saying we should keep up with our training," said Grunewald. "Okay, folks, let's go."

"Or maybe he's saying we can afford some rest and contemplation," said Janowski.

MacLean had a wide handsome face, thick brown hair, a stocky frame with gym-built legs and arms. He looked apologetically at Janowski. "It's up to each Huddle leader."

I remember not loving his use of the word *thoroughbreds*.

"Right," said Grunewald. "Up and at 'em."

"Let's call it a win that they've at least read the book. But before you go, Grunewald, let me offer a few thoughts," MacLean said. "Thoreau was the one who lived in that cabin for a while, right?"

"That's a different book," said Janowski.

"Right, right. But when he was in that cabin, wasn't his mom bringing him lunch every day?"

"He was on his own," said Janowski.

"Well, look. I'm sure he's got lessons to teach us about life in Massachusetts," MacLean said. "But we're in Maine. Let's try to learn from the folks who lived here on Whaleback a hundred years before Thoreau ate his mom's sandwiches. Did you know Whaleback had the best freshwater wells in the entire bay because our people chipped away down beneath the bedrock? Did you know our fur stocks were the best in the entire region—we traded with the French and English—because there were no better hunters and trappers around? Did you know the people of Whaleback suffered many raids, beat back all attackers, because we were the best in a fight? Did you know our ancestors faced significant health scares, had to make considerable sacrifices, just to ensure the community as a whole could persist and thrive? This land has its own story. A lot of blood and sweat in this soil. *Islanders*. That's what they were. *Islanders*. That's what we are."

"Yeah, fuck Thoreau," said Grunewald.

Everyone cheered. Janowski couldn't help but offer a tight-lipped smile. Grunewald waved his Huddle toward the trail.

"Hold up," MacLean said, "Grab these before you go."

We gathered around him and told him where we were from: *Utah, New Hampshire, Ohio, Missouri, Maryland.* He handed us the remaining monitors.

MacLean gave Aubrey her monitor and said, "*Maine.*" She kept her eyes focused on the ground.

Corsetti said, "Be ready, they're coming for you!"

"No joke," said MacLean. "Be ready."

"Oh, I'm fucking ready," said Corsetti, grinning.

"Are you?" A switch seemed to flip in MacLean. He looked angry. "Hold up. Sit back down, everyone."

We sat.

"I actually need to know," said MacLean. "Are we ready?"

Many of us nodded, but I'm guessing those who nodded didn't know why.

"Look at this place," he said, and he pointed out toward the treetops and the ocean below. "This place is fucking *yours*. We want you here. Forget your before-lives. Forget the shit you've endured. Forget it all. You," he said, pointing at Mass. "Joshua. What did it feel like when you had your head under the water. When they held you down in the icy water, and you couldn't breathe?"

He just stared fiercely back at MacLean.

"It didn't feel good, did it."

He shook his head.

"We don't want to have to do that again. But we want you to operate within that understanding. Suffocation is what we all face— even me—if we don't stick together. What would have happened to Boyd and Awanata and their tough-as-nails kids if they hadn't stuck together?"

"They would have been fucked," said Grunewald.

"That's right," said MacLean. "Don't be fucked, okay? We need you. And we have your backs."

Then he let us leave. We were twenty yards down the trail when we heard Janowski yell, "Kat-ep-skon-e-gan!"

Corsetti yelled back through the trees, "Fuck Thoreau!"

Grunewald told us to grab an extra warm layer from the dorms and to meet him at the Chapel at ten-thirty.

It had rained for several days but now the clouds were gathering and lifting, and a sharp wind was pulling the dampness from the forest. Tess had brought the map from her room, and we found our way to the northeastern quarter of the island, most of the way down the Old Shipyard trail, to a clearing amid a grove of hardwoods. The rain had darkened the trunks of the trees and left a glossy mat of reds and oranges and yellows beneath our sneakers. A weathered wooden sign was attached to a maple with a single silver screw, painted with white letters like the other trail markers: CHAPEL. But there was no building, just large blocks of lichen-covered granite settled into the ground forming a rectangle, the foundation of a structure that had perhaps burned or just been leveled by weather. DeShawn checked the time: 10:28.

Grunewald appeared in full yellow rain suit—oilskins, he called them—having come from the other direction on the Old Shipyard trail. He had a black strap around his neck with a shiny disc at its center.

He sat down with us in the Chapel. During the early weeks on the island, we'd wince when he spoke and look away, but now we met his eyes.

He said, "Today we're going out on a boat. If anyone is prone to get sick, tell me now. If anyone is afraid, tell me now."

We were quiet until Tess spoke, "What's that thing on your neck?"

"Security blanket," he said.

"How so?"

"I've got one on my camo vest, too. See that button in the middle? I press that, it sends a distress signal. It's for expeditions. All right, heathens. Let's head out."

We marched with him single file another quarter mile to the place where the trail ended: a cedar-shingled building surrounded by spicy-smelling bay bushes. The sun had emerged from the pillowy clouds. An Islanders Club flag atop the boathouse snapped in the wind. Moored in the middle of the cove were three sailboats, two wooden masts each. Grunewald moved slowly, saying nothing, wanting us to gather information with our eyes. We walked down the pier to the ramp onto the floats.

"Who likes to row," asked Grunewald.

Tess and Javier raised their hands.

"California," he said. "You row. We need a man to row."

"That's ridiculous," said Tess.

"You're strong for a girl, Maryland," Grunewald said to Tess, untying the rowboat. "But California could kill you with his bare hands. And he's not even that big."

"We're talking about rowing a boat," said Tess. "And by the way, you asked 'who likes to row?'"

He ignored her and handed the rope to Javier, who ferried us out in groups of four, and by the time we were all aboard, Grunewald had DeShawn and me raising both sails and was keeping the boat pointed into the wind so it wouldn't start sailing before we were ready. He said, "This boat was built by the grandson of Wallace Keith. He modeled the design after the whaleboats they used in *Moby Dick*."

"The grandson of Awanata, too," said Tess.

"Yes," said Grunewald.

Once he'd secured the rowboat to the mooring, he yelled at DeShawn to grab the bottom of the sail and push it up into the wind, which steered the bow of the boat out toward the mouth of the cove. Then he yelled at Bethany to grab the coiled line by her feet and yank hard. Within seconds we were silently picking up speed. I'd never been sailing, and the feeling was counterintuitive—the stiff breeze, blowing toward us, was somehow pulling our boat through the water.

Grunewald, to his credit, let us do the work to keep the boat moving, even though we were doing it wrong. He let us bumble around. He sat beside the long wooden pole used to steer the boat, called the tiller, and ordered Bianca—who was clearly terrified—to sometimes push the pole away from her body, or pull it toward her, to keep us on course.

When Grunewald screamed "Trim!" that meant the boat was tilted too far in one direction, and he wanted someone to move to the other side of the boat. I got confused when he screamed "Trim the mainsail!" since that meant Javier needed to pull the line so the sail would tuck closer to the boat.

Aubrey was assigned the job of quartermaster, the person who would prepare lunch whenever Grunewald allowed us to eat, so at first, she was just responsible for not letting anyone step on the canvas bag of food. Grunewald let us make mistakes, but he also yelled incessantly during those first ten or fifteen minutes, until Bianca figured out she could pick a point in the distance, a rise in the trees on a faraway island, and steer toward it. Her terror subsided, and it got quiet on the boat again. For the first second or two of silence I realized the boat was operating as it was supposed to, it was tilted at just the right angle, the sails hauled in to maximize speed. We started breathing again and looking around. We were slicing through the waves, water kissing the bow and racing along the side of the boat, the canvas sails were drum tight, the sun was bright and warm on our faces, though the October wind was cold. Achieving that speed without a motor felt like a miracle. Grunewald said we were going eight knots, roughly the same as eight miles an hour, but if someone had told me we were going fifty I would have believed it. And it was quiet. Grunewald wasn't yelling, and everyone was at rest in our assignments. The little pieces of fabric that signaled the wind direction were flapping, and the water shushed against the hull of the boat.

"New Hampshire!" Grunewald yelled. "We need a bow watch!"

"Where is it?" I yelled back.

"You! *You* are the bow watch! Sit on the bow and watch. Watch for rocks, or lobster traps, or Russian submarines. Shout back to us about anything you see."

The boat was roughly thirty feet long, no cabin, no place to hide—just bench seats called thwarts, and metal wires keeping the masts in place, and ropes with various unknown purposes strewn about. I wobbled, crouched low, and climbed over my Huddle mates who seemed as dumbstruck as I was by the magic of the wind-powered machine.

I sat astride the bow, my legs hanging down toward the waves. My sneakers got wet from the spray, so I took them off, and my socks, too, stowing them behind me, and rolled up my sweatpants. I'd been on a horse once and being raised and lowered by the undulating swells reminded me of horseback riding, but what consumed me was the mesmerizing pattern of waves we were slicing through. I thought about the fathoms beneath the gunmetal-blue surface and things swimming beneath us. I yelled back to Grunewald. "How deep out here?"

"Three or four hundred feet, New Hampshire, but stay vigilant!"

A football field straight down. I'd only been in ponds and lakes in New Hampshire.

We changed direction again and again—each time, Grunewald would yell "Ready about!" and we were told to respond, in deafening unity, "READY!" And then he would bark a rapid-fire series of commands: "Tiller toward me! Hold the main sheet . . . now release it! Duck! Trim the sheet!" None of us really understood what was happening, but we understood what he was telling us to do, the small action each of us was responsible for when we changed direction. As bow watch all I had to do was make sure I didn't pitch overboard as the boat tilted in a new direction and survey the seascape to make sure we weren't headed for rocks.

After one of these tacks, I readjusted my seating, blinked, scanned the horizon, and saw not far in front of the bow a slippery blue orb rotating above the swells. As the orb rotated, it exposed a hooked triangle, a fin—so sharp and shark-like, it hit me in the torso like an electric fence. I couldn't speak right away. Then: "TWELVE O'CLOCK! GRUNEWALD! TWELVE O'CLOCK!"

I turned back into the cockpit and saw Grunewald jump atop a thwart and bend his body around the sail, eyes blazing toward the horizon.

"Whataya got, New Hampshire?"

"Shark!"

"Rub your eyes and look again, New Hampshire!"

Some of the others started shrieking, and I could hear them all fumbling around behind me.

I hungrily scanned the water. The waves were wrinkles and triangles. But then, clear and closer: the same animal rounded its topside out of the water. And beside it, another one, mirroring the first. Synchronized swimmers.

"Pilots!" yelled Grunewald.

"What?"

"Squid eaters! Moby Dick and fucking Shamu! Those are whales, New Hampshire, and we're just about on top of them!"

The boat zagged and I grabbed the mast to avoid falling in. Grunewald yelled, "Hold your course, Missouri! You don't need to avoid them! They'll avoid us! Look at those bastards! God love 'em!"

We whooped and screamed along with Grunewald. The whales didn't come up for air again, but that sound, the whoosh of their breath, stayed with me. I'll take that memory to my grave.

20. Signs of Tucker

New Hampshire

While swimming halfheartedly through my calculus homework during seventh period study hall at St. Bart's, I heard the chuffing of shoes on the nearby carpet. I started to turn, and Alessandra was already crouching down beside my desk, inches away, eye to eye. She was so close I couldn't see anything but her soft face—nose and mouth and neck so close I couldn't make sense of them. The smell of mint and coconut. The individual hairs. She pulled back, offered me a fist bump and said, "Holy shit. I heard about the game."

"Um, thanks."

"So, hockey's over now."

"Yeah. Probably forever."

"You'll play in college though?"

"I have no idea." And I didn't. I'd gotten interest from a few schools, but New Hampshire was small potatoes, and the story of my meltdown would make its way to all the coaches I'd been ignoring. I asked her when she'd gotten back from Williams.

"This morning. And, ugh, Tucker came back with me," she said, looking down. "He's here for the weekend. I don't know what I'm going to do with him."

She whispered, "*I think I need to break up with him.*"

I tried not to alter my expression as she explained that Tucker wanted more than she could handle. "Sorry to complain about this to you," she said. She changed the subject to her mom, who she said was having some kind of nervous breakdown.

"I think my dad's having a breakdown, too."

"It must be hard, being sick like that," she said.

I hadn't known she knew my dad was sick. "I honestly don't really know how he feels about it."

She was crouched beside me, her face toward the bright window, her brown eyes and eyebrows lit by the blue winter light. Looking at Alessandra up close made more sense to me than looking at her from a distance. It was like when she'd shown me her doodle notebook: I understood what it felt like to be her, to be looking out at the world through her eyes.

"Maybe you'll meet my dad sometime," she said. "He's a piece of work, too."

"Sure," I said. "I'd like that."

She was still crouching next to my desk, and she shifted her weight, put a hand on my arm for balance, held it there, continued staring at me. "I have a crazy idea."

"Yeah?"

"You should come watch me break up with Tucker."

To try to explain my actions from that point forward is difficult. I thought she was kidding. She told me she wasn't. She told me it was Tucker's fault for coming back with her from Williams in the first place, and that he'd treated her poorly, and that I could hide in the closet or behind the couch while she dumped him, and that I'd really be helping her. She argued that my presence in the room would ensure she wouldn't chicken out.

"I think you need to do this on your own," I said.

"He's not big or anything. He plays football, but he's one of the small guys. Free safety. Williams is just D-Three."

"Why does that matter?"

"Never mind. You're right. It's a dumb idea," she said.

Unfortunately, I focused on the fact that she actually wanted me to be there.

The plan was for me to come into Alessandra's unlocked house around seven, just after her mom left for book club, and before seven-thirty, when Alessandra and Tucker would be returning from Romano's with calzones.

I slipped through the front door at the appointed hour, into the mudroom, with its built-in bench, long row of winter boots, dozens of jackets on hooks, skis and snowshoes on the overhead racks. Beyond the mudroom there was that hallway chandelier and the smell of bread. The place was so different from my house, so messy and soft and comfortable. A piano. Golden light. Full bookshelves. Sprawling plants near each window. A whole tableful of opened mail and newspapers. Immaculate Persian rugs. I spotted the tan loveseat Alessandra had suggested I hide behind. I sat in the chair, sank right down into it, felt immediately immersed in the scene around me, like I could read all the books in the bookshelf, eat all my meals right there, grow old.

Back then, I didn't understand why Sarah Shinwell would teach art at St. Bart's, when she could have chosen to live off her savings, her trust fund, whatever it was.

A car door slammed shut. I heard Alessandra laugh sharply. I pulled myself out of the chair, saw there was no space between it and the wall, scooted it toward the middle of the room, which put a big wrinkle in the Persian rug, so I hefted the whole chair, bear-hugging it, wasn't able to see my feet because of the chair but tried to smooth out the rug, hoped I wasn't seen by Tucker through the window, eased the chair down but it landed with a thud, the door was opening, the space behind the chair looked too small but I dove into it, out of view.

The voices were loud now in the hallway. "How can you like that stuff?" asked Tucker.

"I just do," she said.

"Nasty."

I was breathing hard, but I just pressed my mouth against the upholstery. Someone turned on the tap, filled a glass.

"Man, I'm beat," Tucker said. "What do you want to watch?"

"I want to talk," she said.

There was a small gap between the loveseat and the couch, and I peered out in their direction: Alessandra's tiny, socked feet and Tucker's jeans, somewhere between the living room and the kitchen.

"When's she getting back," Tucker asked.

"It's usually around eight-thirty."

The cuffs of his jeans moved in closer to her socks. Silence. The sound of kissing.

"Let's stay downstairs," she said.

"Baby," he said.

They landed on the couch. They were now just inches away from my head.

"Hold on, hold on," she said.

"Are you okay?"

"I need to talk to you."

"Go ahead."

"I really think we should stop doing this."

"Stop doing what?"

"This. It's just, I have so much going on this semester, with the play, and—"

"Senior spring, baby. Don't worry. Let it all slide."

"No, I really want to just focus on this time I have with my mom before college and—"

Tucker started laughing. More movement on the couch.

"I'm serious," she said.

"I'm serious, too."

"Please, just listen to me. This doesn't have anything to do with you."

He laughed again, and she laughed. I wanted her to focus, finish the job.

"Put your shirt back on," she said.

I heard a belt buckle, more kissing.

"Tucker, listen."

He giggled. "I love you. You can't break up with me."

My heart banged in my chest and my face got hot.

More kissing sounds.

"Stop, Tucker. Come on."

"I'm serious. I love you," Tucker said again.

My muscles contracted and I started to move. I stood up. The chair rocked forward, landed hard.

Somehow Tucker flew to his feet, stumbled backwards in boxers, his pants partway down his wiry, hairy legs. Fists up, mouth open, insane with fear. I felt superhuman in my mission, though, and grabbed his arms and threw him onto the Persian rug.

Alessandra sat up on the couch, straightening her shirt.

Tucker scrambled back up to his feet, pulled his pants up, yelled, "Who the fuck?"

I went after him again, slapped his fists away, grabbed him around the chest and threw him back down onto the carpet. I felt ready for whatever would come next and said, in an even tone, "Apologize to her."

"Who are you?" Again, he got to his feet, turned to Alessandra and asked, "Who is this?"

She shrugged, tried to look surprised.

"Apologize," I said.

"For what?" asked Tucker.

A wave of heat surged through my body, and I punched Tucker hard in the nose. My fingers spiked with pain. Tucker staggered back, held his nose, looked at his hands, and took a step toward me. I punched him with all my strength, right in the nose again. Tucker hit the floor, squeezed his eyes shut, his flushed face smeared with blood from his nose, but he stood back up, yelled like a wild animal, came back at me, aimed a shoulder at my waist, and tried to tackle me. I spun and grabbed his arms, flung him again to the Persian rug, landed on top of him, and pinned his forearms with my knees.

"Stop!" yelled Alessandra.

I looked up at her. "Stop?"

"Fucking stop!" yelled Tucker.

I punched him again, point blank, Tucker's head snapping back and hitting the rug. "Apologize."

"I'm sorry, I'm sorry!" said Tucker, face messy with tears and blood.

I stood up, pulled Tucker to his feet, put him in a headlock, steered him to the door, through the mudroom, and outside.

"She broke up with you. Leave."

I slammed the door and turned to face Alessandra.

"You're just going to leave him out there? He's really hurt, isn't he?"

"He should be fine."

I picked up Tucker's shirt, opened the door, and tossed the shirt in the snow.

She moved past me to the window, pulled the curtains back, and scanned the yard and sidewalk for signs of Tucker. "Is he still there? That was fucking insane!"

"He wasn't listening to you."

"You jumped up like Mike Myers and tried to kill him."

"I did not try to kill him."

I was still queasy and light-headed with adrenaline. I walked back into the living room. Tucker pounded on the door. In her socked feet Alessandra ran to answer it.

"Don't let him in," I said.

I stood beside her in the mudroom, and we looked through the glass part of the door at Tucker. He had no coat, no boots. His nose was still bleeding, and his cheeks and eyes were red from crying. We could hear his muffled voice: "I called the cops. They're coming."

Alessandra grabbed me by the shirt and said, quietly and fiercely: "Go. Now, now, now. You need to go."

"Don't let him back in."

"Okay, okay. Go."

I stepped out of the door and Tucker gave me a wide berth as I passed him. I didn't look at the blood and tears on his face. I just walked calmly toward the street, then jogged, and, when as I was out of view, sprinted.

21. Eyes Open or Closed

Whaleback Island

Grunewald had us tack over to a calm channel of water separating a large island, Alden, from a chain of three smaller ones: Hay, Egg, and Pickett. Alden had a bold rocky shore leading immediately to dense pine forest, while the three smaller islands were mostly barren—wind-whipped sea grass, bleached crab and mussel shells scattered about the wide bird shit-covered rocks, a few scraggly spruce trees. He provided us with explicit and impatient instructions on how to lower the sails and then ordered me, DeShawn, Corsetti, and Javier to set up in the rowing stations. When Tess stepped in front of Corsetti and grabbed an oar for herself, Grunewald said, "Maryland, you're a stubborn pain in the ass." But he said nothing else as she began to row.

He had Bianca steer the boat toward the little stone beach on Pickett Island, brightly lit by noonday sun. I was still on bow watch, looking now for rocks just beneath the surface of the water. As we approached the island, I pointed at the swaying mops of brown-green seaweed growing atop boulders and Bianca maneuvered around them. Grunewald had us slow our rowing, and, as the boat neared shore, I put down my oar and hopped overboard into the shallows to guide the boat in safely, the frigid water numbing my legs. I pulled the boat a few feet up onto the shore with the help of an incoming swell. As soon as I did, the others started climbing up onto the bow and jumping down to the rocks.

"Do we need our jackets?" asked Corsetti.

"Up to you," said Grunewald.

"Our own deserted island!" yelled Javier.

"Can we eat lunch here?" asked Bianca, skinny in her tight T-shirt and jeans. What always calmed me was imagining everyone in our group in their mainland lives. I pictured Bianca leaping sideways on the infield grass, stretching for a ground ball, hopping to her feet, scowling with focus, gunning the ball to first, her off-center cap pulled down just above her eyes.

Aubrey was silent as she arranged the food. During especially quiet moments, I was always most curious about her and had a hard time making guesses about her past life, her reasons for not talking, how long she'd been that way.

"I suppose we could," said Grunewald.

Bethany walked past Bianca, right up to one of the huge stones at the high point of the beach and hugged it. "Solid ground," she said.

Aubrey was the last one to step ashore, grabbing the food bag, slinging it over her shoulder. She sat on the lichen-covered ledge just below the small stand of spruce trees and began pulling items out of the canvas food bag. A few apples, a block of unwrapped cheese, a sleeve of Saltines, a Swiss Army knife. She spread the bag flat, arranged the items atop the rough fabric and began cutting the apples and arranging the slices in a decorative semicircle.

I sat beside her, sun on our faces, feeling wind-whipped and hungry and reached for one of the apple slices. She slapped my hand. I tried to catch her eye to see how serious she was about guarding the food and saw the smirk—but still, I wasn't going to try again.

Corsetti, Bianca, and DeShawn scrambled to the top of a boulder at the far side of the little cove, another spot to rest and look out at the ocean. Others were up in the spruce trees or exploring the far side of the tiny island.

Grunewald hadn't yet come ashore; he was stowing life jackets, coiling lines. He heaved an anchor off the stern, and once it had settled on the bottom, he pulled the line taught. Then he yelled, "New Hampshire! Get down here."

I left Aubrey and went back to the boat, where Grunewald told me, "I don't want my hull to keep banging against these rocks. Once I get my weight aft, push me out into deeper water."

"10-4."

Grunewald moved nimbly from thwart to thwart and before stepping down into the cockpit he said, "Want your jacket?" He had his back to me, but he raised the red fleece in the air.

"No, I'm good."

"You're *good*? What the hell kind of answer is that?"

"I mean, no, thank you. I'm warm enough."

"Suit yourself," he said. He took the distress signal strap off his neck and tossed it to me. "You might need this. Wear it on your neck. Do not push the button unless someone dies, or someone is about to die. Broken bones don't count."

It was a rubber strap with a plastic clasp. "Couldn't we just yell out to you?"

"A captain stays with his boat. Push me out," he said, sitting down, putting his hand on the anchor line.

It didn't take much. With my hands on the bow of the boat, I felt the hull rumbling against the shore. I pushed it out into deeper water, leaving a stripe of green bottom paint on the rocks.

Grunewald pulled on the deep anchor line to get himself out even further, and he kept pulling until the anchor was aboard and he was out in the channel.

A flash of white emerged: the mainsail, flapping loudly before filling with wind. Grunewald was steering the boat toward Alden Island. He turned back toward us and yelled, "You're Islanders! Rely on each other! See you at oh-six-hundred tomorrow!"

I assumed he was joking. Only Tess had the presence of mind to yell out to him—"What? Hey, stop!"—but he'd already turned his back. When everyone else started yelling, Grunewald was far enough offshore that he surely didn't hear us. This was probably for the best. Hearing our squeals would only have made him happier.

Within seconds we were huddled around the food. Aubrey had already cut everything up into equal portions, displaying each little pile atop the canvas bag. It wasn't much.

"I wouldn't mind eating Grunewald's portion," said DeShawn.

"No, shit," said Tess. "We all want to eat that."

As Aubrey started to carve up Grunewald's cheese, reallotting it, Bianca pointed at me and said, "How about you take New Hampshire's cheese and split it up, too. He was the one who pushed Grunewald out into the channel."

"Yeah, and why are you wearing the distress signal? You work for him?" asked DeShawn.

I was still stunned Grunewald was gone. "He gave it to me. I had no idea he was leaving."

"Hey asshole, quote us some poetry," said Bianca. "Maybe we can eat that."

"Whoa, whoa, whoa," Tess said. "We'll be fine. Everyone gets the same amount."

"Yeah? Why are you making the decisions?" asked Bianca sharply.

No one else seemed to have a problem with Tess's leadership. We all started eating our piles, except for Bethany, still feeling queasy from her time in the boat, knees tucked up against her chest. She put her food in the zipper pocket of her windbreaker.

We chewed with the sun on our faces, sheltered from the wind by the curved shape of the cove. We hadn't started talking about how cold we'd be with no sleeping bags and only two jackets on a mostly barren island in October.

"I hope he capsizes and drowns," Javier said.

"But then who would know we're here?" said Bethany.

"Okay, I hope he gets back to Whaleback, tells someone where we are, and then falls in a well. How's that?"

"What is *wrong* with him?" asked Bethany.

"He just wants us to get stronger," said Corsetti. "Dude, this island is our training wheels."

"He gets off on torturing us," said Tess.

"Do you think he has a family?" asked Bethany.

"I'm sure he does," said DeShawn. "He probably likes torturing them, too."

It took us about three minutes to walk around the miniature island. Corsetti said he was dying of hunger, snapped off a branch of one of the six or seven spruce trees in the center of the island, peered at it, plucked off the green parts, and collected them in his left palm until Tess knocked the pile to the ground.

"Hell, no," she said.

"Hey! Brevard said I could," said Corsetti.

"Said you could what?" asked Tess.

"Eat, you know, trees and stuff."

"Brevard? He did not."

"Just yesterday he told me that."

"Yesterday?"

"I went and knocked on his door."

Tess punched him. "Yeah right."

Corsetti was quiet, so Tess said. "Wait, did you? Dude, his house is on its own little island."

"And?"

"So you just jet-skied over?"

"I swam."

Tess's smile faded. "You *swam*?"

"It's not far."

"And why exactly did you not tell us this?"

"Sorry."

"Fuck, man. That's messed up."

"He told me not to say I'd gone out there."

Corsetti explained that he'd swum out to show Brevard he was tough and willing to do anything. Brevard had told him to never swim out again, and to not tell anyone he'd taken such a risk. But Corsetti also said he thought Brevard was impressed.

Later, after the sun went down, we all walked back up to the most sheltered spot on the island, between the two largest trees, a little stretch of earth that we cleared of dead branches. Tess decided upon the sleeping arrangements. Corsetti and Javier on each end because they had jackets, and the rest of us in between, curled on our sides, a long line of spoons. Tess was right behind Corsetti, then Aubrey, then me, then Bianca, then DeShawn, then Bethany, then Javier. As the night went on, we seemed to compress even more—Corsetti and Javier both pushing toward the middle, sandwiching us. At first, I didn't care how cold my head and feet were. To be nestled behind Aubrey, to feel the movement of her breath against my chest, to feel even the slightest contact of my legs against her, to smell her dirty hair, which had probably not been grimy like this before and still smelled good, I felt like a space explorer zooming through the cosmos. Bianca clutched me tightly from behind, a combination of muscles and softness—she must have been freezing in just a T-shirt. Tess started to speculate about Grunewald's childhood, riffing, inventing his life story while we all spooned in the dark.

We knew he was raised in Maine, on the mainland not far from the island. Tess said of course he'd had a mean father, who whipped him if he showed signs of weakness or laziness, but she was also sure he'd had a cruel mother, who pretended to console him after he endured one of his father's beatings—she would smile, sweetly—but then she'd show her allegiance to her husband by stirring a teaspoon of dog shit into young Grunewald's oatmeal. He ate it without knowing, said Tess, it just lent to the sourness of his day. When he got to school he'd puke on the floor of the bathroom and then get beat up by the bigger stronger boys for making such a mess, and it wasn't until high school that he got his first gun, a pellet rifle, which he would use to shoot squirrels down from trees. His goal was always to maim them, get them on the ground, still alive, but to then take them hostage, cut off their hind legs, gouge out their eyes.

Then there was Vietnam, where his platoon hated him for his selfishness, his harsh assessments of others, his annoying habit of chewing loudly with his mouth open, but little by little Grunewald showed how ruthless he was in a fight, how willing he was to kill indiscriminately, how he didn't mind setting fire to villages full of innocent people, and they began to like him. They liked him even more when mortar fire blew off his fingers and he didn't complain. They liked that he was despicable and memorable, and the praise and respect he received ushered him to other opportunities to be mercenary and sadistic, like in this new job, being in charge of us.

As soon as Tess took a quick break in her storytelling, Bianca asked, "Can you imagine him fucking his wife?"

This elicited groans, much more than any other speculation about his wartime killing sprees.

"Are we sure he has a wife?" asked Bethany.

"He probably does. And he's probably good to her," said Corsetti. "Nothing he's done to us has been *that* bad."

"He wanted to whip us with a belt," said Bethany.

"But he didn't," said Corsetti. "We did the whipping."

"He didn't let us eat that one day," said DeShawn.

"We liked that," Corsetti said. "We could have gone to the dining hall, but we didn't."

"I bet he's got one of those curly-q dicks," said Bianca.

"All right, barf, I'm changing the subject," said Bethany, "what do you think this leadership camp is *really* about? What will they actually use us for?"

"I hope it's CIA," said Corsetti.

"It's not CIA," said DeShawn.

"Something political, maybe? But please make it not that. I'd fucking hate that," said Bianca, her breath warming the back of my neck.

"We're doing too many pushups to have it be something political," said Tess. "It's more like we're going to be their bouncers."

"That'd be fine," said DeShawn.

"They need bouncers?" asked Bianca.

"Everyone could use a bouncer," said Javier. "Personal security. A way to show off."

"I think the best way to show off is solo. Don't hire a bouncer," said Corsetti.

"I guess these guys don't want to do their own pushups," said Bianca.

"Maybe they're too old," said Bethany.

"Or too scared?" said Tess. "Too scared to not have bouncers. There's got to be a better word for bouncer."

"Protégé," I said.

"That's different," said Tess. "That's more like, student. But I see what you're saying."

"I think they want us to save the human race," Corsetti said. "They think everyone's too goddamn soft."

We listened to the waves for a minute before Tess spiraled off once again, dreaming up the story of poor Mrs. Grunewald. I don't think I ever really fell asleep. I felt my mind drift in and out of an awareness of Aubrey's warm body in front of me, Bianca's body behind me. Tess kept on telling stories in a quiet, convincing voice.

I was part of the group, and I was in line with them. I felt I was becoming more and more a part of the island. I was forgetting what it felt like to live at home, and that was fine with me. I really wanted this place, these people, to want me to stay.

The night was completely void of light—clouds must have rolled back in because there was no difference between what I could see with my eyes open or closed. Tess ended her Mrs. Grunewald story with a mention of the mailman Mrs. Grunewald would kiss sometimes in the basement, and we all wanted to know more about that mailman, but then Tess got quiet.

I thought of my dad and just like that, tears flowed from my eyes. I wasn't making any sound as I cried but Aubrey pulled my arms tighter around her, and she turned her head so that for a time my nose was touching her cheek, and I was sure she could feel my tears.

I felt Aubrey's body relax into sleep, which is when the air got very still, and the only sound we could hear was the ocean pushing its way up and down the stone beach.

22. Moss Nap

We woke up hearing the distant flapping of the boat's sails. We brushed off the lichen bits and pine needles and continued to hold on to each other. I clutched the sleeve of Aubrey's shirt as we stumbled down to the shoreline in the dawn light. It was calm enough that Grunewald could row the whale boat through the shallows all by himself, a headlamp lashed to his mast. He probably wanted this feat to seem impressive—sailing from Whaleback over to the channel, doing by himself in the dark what we'd done in the daylight with nine people—but everyone was too exhausted and cold to take much notice.

"New Hampshire," he yelled. "Catch my bow as I nose in."

I wanted to defy him, but I took off my boots and socks and stepped into the shallows to catch the boat. We were all quiet as we boarded except for Tess, who said, "I bet we slept better than you did."

"Oh yeah?" asked Grunewald.

"Yeah," said Tess. "You thought you were challenging us? That was a piece of cake. We were cozy and warm, and we ate a seven-course meal."

"Sticks, then rocks, more sticks, pinecones, a crab or two, dead seagull, and more rocks," said Grunewald.

Tess just laughed. And she wasn't really kidding—for all of us it was exhilarating to know that we could just lie down on the ground in October for the night on an island in the middle of the ocean and survive. This was not something we'd ever done. We felt cold and hungry, but our bodies were buzzing from having been wedged all together. This seemed to be part of the process of forgetting our former lives.

Grunewald had two thermoses—hot chocolate and coffee—along with plastic mugs and a bag of muffins. After we zipped up in the coats we'd left aboard, we raised the sails and got underway. Aubrey circulated the hot drinks and muffins. Grunewald didn't need to bark orders because we knew our jobs on the boat by then. He announced each turn and fine-tuned the steering by telling Bianca to push or pull, but otherwise, we all hunkered low in the boat, sipped our drinks and chewed our still-warm muffins. We watched the sun rise out of the ocean, giving shape to the swells.

Grunewald began yelling again once we were on the mooring, leading us step-by-step through the process of buttoning-up the boat. Once we were finally rowing back to the pier, I assumed we'd be given the rest of the day off after what we'd just been through, but Grunewald said, "We'll march up to the dorms to grab our sneakers, then we'll run the perimeter trail. Then swim. Then eat again."

We marched. We got our running clothes on. No one questioned this and it was comforting somehow. As usual, while we ran the perimeter trail, we could see the roofs of the mansions we passed on the back shore. But this time Grunewald had us stop and circle up beside a small garage we hadn't noticed, uphill from the trail, with a grass clearing in front. The plain rectangular building had an elegant painted sign over its door: ARMORY. Behind us were the sheer rock cliffs of the quarry.

Bianca said, "This is where they keep their suits of armor."

"Exactly right," said Grunewald.

"For real?" asked Bianca.

"No, idiot," Grunewald said. "It's where they keep the guns."

We waited to hear more, still catching our breath. I wasn't sure if I'd ever heard a grown man call a girl an idiot before. Grunewald had our attention now.

"The Club members like to hunt. Always have. And they shoot at targets. These are good skills to have, and they want you to learn them." He fished his keys from his pocket.

When Grunewald opened the door of the windowless building, the afternoon light spilled in, gracing a dozen or so shotguns with gleaming barrels and dark wooden stocks in vertical racks. We were all sweating and breathing heavily as we looked at the guns. We had no questions. I had no idea what the others felt about guns. I'd used a shotgun before for hunting ducks, unsuccessfully, with my dad. Grunewald seemed proud of the room, and proud to be connected to a club that had an armory, happy to be part of the rule-makers world.

In the corner beside the rack of shotguns was another rack containing a dozen semi-automatic assault rifles, barrels pointing up and stocks pointing down. I'd seen pictures of these, but that was the first time I'd seen one in real life. Dark gray, not shiny. Smaller than I imagined. Beside the assault rifles were two metal racks with eight handguns in each.

"This shit's for target practice?" Bianca asked.

We moved closer to this other rack of guns.

"For target practice, yes, while you still need to practice," said Grunwald. "And then they'll just be there. To be used if necessary."

The assault rifles and handguns, which looked like toys, came into better focus as everyone's eyes adjusted to the low light in the room. The starkness of the guns made the room feel sterile, cold, hollow.

After we ran, swam, and ate again, Grunewald brought us back to the Chapel. He had us sit on the granite blocks and said, "I've been chewing on what Joey MacLean told us about this place. I didn't know much of the history. It's not something folks have talked about in all the years I've been here. There are some good lessons he wants us to learn."

We nodded. Mostly we were just exhausted.

"I think we could use more time with Joey. Learn more of the stories of the island. Help you learn how exceptional this place is."

Grunewald told us to get some rest and, for the first time in weeks, there was a bit of warmth in the air, a sunny breeze sweeping through the trees. Just as everyone was starting to head back to their rooms, Aubrey tapped my shoulder, and when I turned, she held a finger up, raised her eyebrows without smiling, then ran to Vancouver. I waited for her to return, and I had no idea what she was going to get. She returned in seconds wearing a backpack. She motioned with her head toward the Old Shipyard trail, and I followed her. She took the offshoot toward Pliny's, which we'd traveled as a group only once when we'd gone to the quarry. Soon we were close to the granite cliffs, where we could see and hear the waves crashing on the back shore, and she looked back at me one more time before going off trail, away from the cliffs, through a grove of spruce trees to an open spot covered by green moss, stray twigs and pine needles. She knelt, shrugged out of her backpack, and unzipped it to reveal a dorm-issued blanket and pillow. She motioned for me to help her spread the blanket out on the moss and reclined with her back to me. I lay behind her. I put my arm around her and held onto her just like the night before, but this moss was much softer. Her hair was still damp with seawater.

When we woke after an hour or so, Aubrey sat up, reached for her backpack and brought out a pen and paper. She wrote:

> *My mom knew Joey MacLean. He invited her out to do some work for him. To help with the history thing, getting the island to remember its past.*

I looked at her, confused, hoping she'd write more. I watched her breathe, tiny downy hairs on her temple. Then she wrote:

> *After he had her out to the island a few times I came out too. Three or four times.*

I could tell it was hard for her to write this. She stopped and I put my hand on her arm.

I wanted you to know even though he told me not to tell anyone that I'd been out here before.

She ripped the page from the notebook and tore it into smaller pieces. Then she lifted a rock near the patch of moss, sprinkled the bits of paper on the ground, and covered them with the rock.

We ran back to the dorms, and I thought about how she'd spent time on Whaleback in the past, and how learning about it made me want to have spent time on Whaleback in the past too, to be more connected to the place like she was. But at that point I knew nothing about her mom, nothing really about the Club's impact on her family—but I was picking up on her concern, her tentativeness, the carefulness she felt was necessary when talking about MacLean and the others. Looking back now, I think she'd taken me out to the moss, and told me what she'd told me, because of our visit to the Armory to see all those guns.

That night we all gathered in Tess and Aubrey's room to talk about it. Shotguns were one thing, but handguns and semi-automatics launched our thoughts in a different direction. Their room was smaller than ours, but much more appealing. Somehow they'd managed to store more impractical belongings in their packs: a brown faux-fur rug that they'd placed between the beds, a poster of two monkeys in suits each pointing a banana as though it was a gun, overstuffed pillows on each bed, a collection of miniature figurines of Olympic athletes on the window sill—a pole-vaulter, a discus thrower, a slalom skier, a water-polo player, a sprinter. They were hand-painted and their faces evoked pride.

Dangling from the same sill were a pair of blue and white wampum earrings with silver shepherd hooks in the shape of little question marks.

Tess said to me, "Don't touch. Those are Aubrey's. Most of the cool stuff in here is hers."

Aubrey pointed at the rug.

"True, the rug's mine," said Tess. "Anyway, those guns? Pretty fucked up, right?"

Corsetti said, "Guns don't kill people, people kill people."

"Brilliant analysis, cave man."

"I mean, it's weird. Having all those guns on a pretty island," said Bethany.

"Right?"

Javier mimed spraying us all with automatic weapon gunfire.

"Did they have guns out at the ranch?" asked DeShawn.

"Of course they had guns," said Tess. "How else do you think they killed the meth heads?"

"They shot them?"

"Yeah."

"Jesus. That's intense."

We were all quiet for a few seconds. This time our moment of quiet for Pepper, Tollefson, and Moorcroft felt different.

I decided to speak up. Moments like this—when I felt compelled to speak and had things to say—had been happening more often.

"It's intense for sure. But I don't think it's scary. I really don't. They want us to protect them. It's a good sign, them letting us see those guns. It means they trust us. It means we belong. It means there's a real reason we're here."

23. Failing to Disappear

New Hampshire

Until I'd started hanging out with Alessandra, when I faced a decision, I'd do the quick math, weigh the costs against the benefits. In the end I usually stayed between the lines. Alessandra showed me the potential I had to be a reckless idiot. I honestly don't blame her for this.

I never found out if a patrol car had been sent over to Alessandra's house. Had I stayed at home, had I gone upstairs and looked from my bedroom window all the way across campus, I might have been able to see not only whether the cops had been called (they had) but I might also have gotten a sense of whether or not they'd be coming after me with assault charges (they didn't). But I went home only long enough to get the keys to the main building from the mud room closet, and once inside the school, I used a chair to shatter the glass of the trophy case nearest the science wing, and I used the 1973 baseball team's autographed bat from within that first case to smash the glass in all of the other trophy cases, as well as all of the windows in the art classroom. This happened while the cops were—or were not—talking to Alessandra and Tucker. All the smashing I did felt inevitable, it felt justified, it felt irreversible, and while it didn't feel exactly joyful, it felt gratifying. My arms didn't get tired.

I tried to be as honest as possible in my discipline committee hearing, but there was so much I couldn't explain. I knew they wanted to know why I'd done what I'd done. If I'd told them, they would have been more likely to go easy on me, regardless of the reason. But

I had no ability to discuss my mother's sadness. Or the confusing loyalty I felt to my father, despite hating him. I didn't want to tell the committee about my friendship with Alessandra—so I couldn't tell them about how the night I'd punched Tucker, I'd begun to question every aspect of that friendship, and why she was messing with me. After I'd put the bat back in its shattered case, I'd returned to Sarah Shinwell's classroom. Papers on her desk fluttered in the wind from the broken windows. I took a pen from her drawer and wrote on a scrap of paper on her desk:

"That wasn't me, either."

Since I said nothing to them, the case was open-and-shut: the maintenance man's son, who'd recently shouted an expletive while quitting the hockey team in the middle of a playoff game, whose grades had gone to shit, had vandalized the main school building, shattering four trophy cases with a chair and with one of the pieces of memorabilia therein, with which he'd also broken all of the windows in the art classroom. Because I was a psycho.

After all the particulars of the vandalism were presented, Father Gerard cleared his throat and asked, "Why?"

"I was upset."

"Could you tell us why?"

"It's very complicated and I can't explain it."

"Please try. We'd like to know."

"I'd rather not."

The committee didn't deliberate long. I got expelled. Everybody around the committee table looked at me as though I was being marched to the guillotine. I hadn't committed the vandalism to get kicked out of school, but once it was decided, I was fine with the outcome. They were saving me from the embarrassment of returning to St. Bart's and being talked about like I was a crazy person.

Before the committee adjourned, Father Gerard described me, gently, as having a "rage problem." I guess that was the price I paid for not telling them the whole story. I remember thinking I really wanted to tell him that the glass would be easy to replace.

The next day I wasn't allowed to enter the school building except to meet briefly with Mr. Sveta, to tell him that I wouldn't be able to act in *Rosencrantz and Guildenstern Are Dead*, and Sveta was kind, he said "You'll be hard to replace, Walt. Best of luck to you." He'd obviously heard a lot of the backstory by then.

I got no messages from Alessandra. She'd put her hand on my back when she'd told me to leave so she could attend to Tucker, and I was left with that memory: *Go. You need to go.*

Mom enrolled me at Central Lakes Regional High School where I sat in their classrooms like a ghost and daydreamed about the goings-on back at St. Bart's. The campus appeared in my mind like a museum diorama with little plastic trees, toy cars and buses in the roadways, soccer fields nubbed with fake grass, the students and teachers as ant-like creatures scurrying about. Nothing had changed. My absence made no impact. This was a shitty feeling, of course, but watching my mom in her efforts to move on, to create a new life for herself, and for me, helped me steel myself for what was to come next.

The day I started at Central Lakes, my mother took me out to dinner at the roadhouse and invited Dr. Charles along. He talked to me like an adult, told funny stories about his days as a bachelor resident in New York City. Up until then, he'd spent his entire life closeted in Kansas, and at dinner he somehow related that change to what I was going through, the liberating potential my release from the confines of hockey and St. Bart's would have. I didn't believe this, but I felt reassured to know my mom had a friend who was kind to her, and to me.

My dismissal was much harder on my father, who was still employed by the school. He'd call the secretary at the Central Lakes main office who would get messages to me—he'd double-check my return time; he'd ask what I wanted at the grocery store.

One night when he called me down for dinner, everything was ready, mom-style, roasted chicken and baked potato and broccoli. He didn't cook often, but he'd put some time into this meal. He'd even lit candles.

I thanked him and we dug in. After a few minutes of silence, I asked him if he still had the chest tube from the most recent surgery, and he said no, and his mouth stayed open partway as though he was going to say something more but he just inhaled, and we sat in silence.

After another bite, he said, "I'm going in for another surgery tomorrow—just a small one."

I asked no follow-up questions about the procedure because I knew I'd get no satisfying answers. But I did ask him if he was still involved with Sarah.

"That's not your concern."

"Fuck yes it is."

"Walt, I'm not discussing it."

"This affects me."

I could tell my father didn't know how to respond to what I'd said, and how I'd said it.

"One thing I will say, is that Sarah likes you and saw promise in you well before she and I got involved. Worth noting."

"Well, she's an idiot, then."

"She actually isn't."

"Anything else you want to correct me about?"

He took another bite and said, "I'm not sorry."

"Wonderful."

"I'm driving out to see your uncle Gus on Tuesday."

Gus lived in Minnesota, a two-day drive. I was baffled by this. The day after the surgery?

"School's letting me take a leave of absence. Looks like Phil Libby and his brother are going to fill in, which seems like a bad way to go, but that's their problem."

"Shouldn't you be taking it easy after the surgery?"

"I'll just be driving."

"How long will you be gone?"

"We'll see," he said.

"We'll see?"

"Seems like you need a little space. You can stay here, your mom can come back and stay in the house with you, you can get started at the new school."

"You could just take it easy here and I could help out," I said.

Dad raked his fork through his baked potato, not looking up, probably wanting to dispute this claim.

I broke the silence by saying, "But I guess you might as well change things up if you don't like how your life is going."

He glanced at me but continued raking his potato. "Right."

Did he not remember this as the advice he had offered me in the fall? More and more, the adults around me seemed misguided. After a few more bites I told him I wanted to go back to the motel to stay with my mother. Dad said, "I'm going to the hospital in the morning."

"Yeah, I know."

"Just stay here for the night."

My father was out of whack. He rarely asked for things he actually wanted.

"I left my homework at mom's," I said, which was a lie. I set my fork down and stood. He stood up, too. I said, "Aren't you supposed to avoid eating the night before a surgery?"

"It's fine."

"You should really listen to what they tell you to do."

"I've got it under control."

I nodded and walked out the door. I had no ride. I started walking. I knew I couldn't walk all the way to the motel. I considered calling my mother, asking if she would come pick me up, but after I left the house, I didn't want to go back. I wasn't sure if I was just going for a walk and would eventually go back to spend the night with my dad, or hitchhiking, or something else. I was confused and on autopilot, which had been happening a lot.

With my hands in my jacket pockets, I got into a limber rhythm—past the Irving gas station with flag pennants stretched from the corners of the building to the roof over the pumps. My dad seemed to want to disappear and explain nothing to no one. I considered what would happen if I died, which I knew would give the kids at St. Bart's and the kids I'd just met at Central Lakes a tiny thrill.

Chugging along in the cold, my breath steaming in and out of me, I passed the brick windowless Knights of Columbus Hall. I didn't fear death. Thoughts of death could overwhelm me at home in bed when my eyes were closed, but while I walked in the quiet streets of Headfield, there was something perfect about imagining that dark, endless hole. If I pitched myself off the Sanderton bridge and broke my neck, it'd just be lights out. The river was less than a mile outside town. Or I could just wait for an oncoming car, dash out into the road at the last minute, get flattened.

The likelihood of botching one of those violent options seemed high. As this occurred to me, I stepped off the salty shoulder into a snow-filled ditch.

My boots trudged through the snow, and soon it was up to my knees. In the dark I hooked an ankle on a branch and tumbled headfirst into the snowy brambles. I got the wind knocked from me and I scratched my face, but all I did was curl up.

Prone, enveloped in darkness and the soft, cold snow, everything but the sound of my breathing faded away. I closed my eyes. To be tough, to truly change things up when you didn't like how your life was going, you had to follow through. You had to be decisive. You couldn't mess it up. You couldn't go halfway.

Did I really have a high threshold for pain? Fuck I was cold.

I heard someone walking on the road. I was in the darkest part of the brambles, hidden by the snow all around me, so I was sure I was out of view.

But then I heard her voice. "Walt?"

It was Alessandra. I stayed quiet.

"Walt, I know you're in there." She was pushing her way through the deep snow, coming right toward me. "There you are." She dropped to her knees in the snow, then descended even further so she was lying right beside me. "Who are you hiding from?"

"How did you find me here?"

"When you walked by my house, I started following you."

A gust of wind blew through the tree branches above and a spray of snow landed on our cheeks. Our breath created a warm space between our faces. I couldn't see much, but I could see enough, and I felt myself getting angry.

"I go to Central Lakes now."

"I know."

"Would have been good to hear from you before I left."

"It would have been good to hear from *you* before you left."

"I think the ball was more in your court," I said.

"You did try to murder my boyfriend," she said.

"He's still your boyfriend?"

"No."

"Good."

"You know, he's not a bad guy."

I was not going to respond to that.

She continued, "That was so fucking crazy what you did."

The more time we spent in that quiet dark spot, the more of her face I could see, and the warmer I became. "I thought that's what I was there for."

"It's my fault," she said. "It was dumb of me."

"You're not a nice person."

"Says the guy who nearly killed my boyfriend."

"You're welcome."

"I think he told his friends at Williams a dog attacked him," she said.

I liked hearing that.

She continued, "I think you're right about me not being a nice person. But who is?"

"They're out there."

"Why are you here?"

"Why the fuck are *you* here?"

"I miss talking to you. Seriously, why are you here?"

"I'm trying to be alone."

"No, you're not."

"Hoping to disappear."

"Don't be an idiot."

"Fuck you."

She leaned her face toward me, and I pulled back, and she kept coming toward me, and my head couldn't move any further away and then she was kissing me. And I let her kiss me. My body felt like a waterbed, warm and fluid and uncontrollable, and Alessandra's mouth tasted like lying on your back in a field on a warm July night. And ChapStick. I was mad at her, but I loved what was happening. But she stopped and said, "Let's go home."

On the walk back to campus we didn't hold hands. She wanted to talk about *Rosencrantz and Guildenstern Are Dead* and Mr. Sveta, and she complained that I hadn't been around to play Scrabble with her in what felt like ages. When we reached her house she gave me a bro hug goodbye, friendly enough but with no reference to when we might talk again.

24. Swimming Dream

Whaleback Island

ate October, weeks after we were introduced to the guns, we set
up camp in the Chapel. Endless stars above us, no need for a
tarp. We lay our bags on the cold hard ground within the granite
foundation. The fire we'd built earlier had burned down to glowing
orange embers.

"All right, folks," said Grunewald. "Tonight, we'll be running
all-night duty again."

Throughout the month we'd regularly been sleeping outside
together as a group. During roughly half of these campouts Grunewald
had us keep watch in thirty-minute shifts, every four hours, all night.
The spot where we slept had to be encircled by trip wire.

Grunewald pointed at a canvas sack resting beside one of the
granite blocks, said "Missouri," and Bianca slithered out of her
sleeping bag and began to uncoil the wire.

"We are Islanders," said Tess.

"Goddamn right you are," Grunewald said.

"You can't fucking sneak attack us," said Tess. "We are the eyes
and ears of this place."

"That's right. I like it," said Grunewald.

"We're Islanders," said Tess.

"Preach," said Bianca.

"We're like Navy Seals," said Tess.

We always kept watch in the same order. I was fourth and Aubrey was fifth and we did our shift together. We stayed in our sleeping bags, sitting with our backs against the same spruce.

Since we first napped together on the moss, we'd returned to that same spot six times, always without others knowing. Being on watch together also gave us the chance to be quiet together, to breathe, to listen to the same things.

That night, a half-hour into our shift, Aubrey took out her notebook again. She kept her pen poised over the page and stared at the fire. Then she wrote:

> *My mom was the only family I had.*
> *I'm not supposed to tell anyone any of this.*
> *But after she died here*

I whispered, "She died here?"

> *She died here. On the island. The second summer she came out.*

Again, being as quiet as I could, putting my mouth right by her ear, I asked, "How did she die?"

Aubrey stared at the fire. Just as I was starting to regret asking her, she wrote:

> *Drowned. And I'm sure Joey felt responsible but he never said so. She had plenty of problems before he brought her out here, but she'd still be alive if she'd stayed on the mainland. Joey invited me here to make things right but of course he can't make things right.*

I put my arm around her, pulling her shoulder against mine. We kept staring at the fire. Then she ripped the page out, crawled over to the fire and tossed it in.

We stayed quiet after that. At probably two or three in the morning, leaning against the spruce tree, my arm still around her, the fire had turned to coals. My eyelids were heavy, and I nodded off.

I dreamed of swimming in warm water. Waves. Bobbing above the surface, looking for Aubrey, knowing she was somewhere there with me even though I couldn't see her.

When she elbowed me, I blinked and sat up. On the far side of the fire an animal was walking slowly into our camp, passing under the trip wire, weaving through our sleeping friends. I recognized it as a fox; it glanced over at us, then sat down on its haunches and stared. A minute passed, maybe more. Then it ambled out of our circle and back into the forest.

When the sun came up, I told everyone about the fox sighting and Aubrey nodded. Grunewald butted in to say what we'd seen was an arctic fox. The Club had brought them out to the island in the twenties to be hunted. They'd only brought a handful, and now the population was dangerously inbred, with mange and other diseases.

After we broke camp, instead of swimming at Bridget Point and Osprey Cove, Grunewald told us we'd run first and swim at the Old Shipyard after finishing the nine-mile perimeter trail. We completed the run within a few minutes of each other. We'd been working hard together for two months straight, and we'd become a single living organism, or at least it felt that way most of the time. Tess asked Grunewald if we could gather in a circle to check in and stretch before we swam, and he shrugged and said "two minutes," though Grunewald himself had no interest in circling up—he jogged out onto the dock, stripped naked, dove in, swam back to the ladder, climbed back onto the dock, pulled on his shorts, gathered the rest of his clothes, and jogged back up to our circle.

"We'll have morning chow in the cafe in fifteen minutes," he said. "Anyone who is late to the cafe, or who hasn't swum, gets the belt." He didn't actually mean this. He just said it as a reminder of our history together. We followed the rules. We did things the right way. He pulled his sweatshirt back on over his hairless torso and handed the distress signal to me. I clipped it around my neck.

He jogged off but we took our time, ambled our way up the hill until we heard Janowski's Huddle whooping their way across the fairway and down toward the docks. We had a good view of them from beside the Athletic Association porch, and we watched them pop off the floats into the water and swim their way out to the capsize drill, moored in the center of the cove. Watching them swim, I felt the cold creep through the center of my body, and we all started cheering for them. We liked competing against them, loved to beat them—but when we saw them from that distance, all we wanted was for them to show the higher-ups they were worthy of being here, because it would make us seem worthy too. But it was more than that. It wasn't just for selfish purposes that we wanted them to succeed. We knew them; we knew the struggles they'd had, and we hoped the best for them. We wouldn't have said it like that at the time, but it was the truth.

It was windy, and rain was starting to fall, which gave the whole cove a silvery hue, a sharpness, and the water looked alive as it roiled from the raindrops. We didn't know it at the time, but soon we'd learn the capsize drill involved flipping the boat, then righting it. That was all.

They all swam to one side of the boat, and maybe because of the weather, they were especially urgent in their movements. They pulled down on the gunwale at the same time, the far side of the boat heaved up out of the water, and the wind howled against the hull. The boat whipped upside down too quickly. Someone screamed. They were all up to their necks in the frigid water, so the sound of the scream wasn't loud, but it was terrifying to us—something had gone wrong.

Janowski's Huddle let go of the boat and circled up around one of the swimmers; even from up the hill we could see they were trying to get her nose and face above water. Her head was pitched down, and when they managed to pull her up, we saw it was Delaware—Bianca's friend who I met the first day.

We sprinted down to the floats; everyone except Corsetti, who went to Big Rug to look for any Club member who could help. He was the right person for this task, as he was the one who knew where the all-gather horn could be activated—by a switch in the broom closet on the ground floor. The rest of us got to the dock just as Feng and Mass were pulling Delaware out of the water. Blood seeped from a wound at the top of her head matting down her wet, red hair and washing down onto her face, which was white. Her eyes were closed. We couldn't tell right away if she was breathing. The all-gather horn was sounding, and once we had Delaware up on the float, we bunched up a towel to staunch the bleeding. She threw up, mostly seawater, which seemed like a good sign.

Corsetti and Joey MacLean came out of nowhere and sprinted down the ramp. Delaware was crying, also a good sign, but the towel was soaked with blood, and when we tried to get her to her feet, she wasn't able to stand on her own. Bianca was crying by then, too. She helped the others in Janowski's Huddle carry Delaware up the ramp. When they got to the edge of the golf course, they asked MacLean where they should take her, and he said to bring her into the Athletic Association where she could lie down. He'd send for Peter Abernathy, a doctor who happened to be on the island. We were relieved. She clearly needed a doctor. MacLean came with us through the double doors. Feng and Bianca each had one of Delaware's arms slung around their shoulders and her feet were dragging behind them. Arizona kept the towel pressed to her head. They planned to put her on one of the leather couches. MacLean wanted to avoid getting blood on it so we asked if they could put a couple of tablecloths down first.

MacLean left and came back in twenty minutes to say he'd been mistaken. Peter Abernathy had motored back to the mainland the day before. MacLean then checked to see if the bleeding had slowed, and it had. He asked Delaware if she knew where she was.

She answered Whaleback, and he said, "Man, you really got your bell rung." She nodded, and he said sometimes the cold water can make a wound bleed more.

Grunewald said, "Let's get the chopper, get her off the island."

Bianca said, "Yeah, man. The chopper."

"Let's see how she's doing in an hour, okay?" asked MacLean. And then, directly to Delaware, he repeated "Let's see how you're doing in a bit."

Again, Delaware nodded. Before we could say anything more, he left.

"I'm fine," Delaware said.

"Does your head hurt?" asked Grunewald.

"It's sore but it's fine."

Were we supposed to check her pupils? Keep her from sleeping? We weren't sure. Grunewald went looking for more bandages. I think we all felt more alone in that moment than we'd felt all fall.

25. I Think Tucker is Still Really Upset
New Hampshire

My dad was in Minnesota, and he hadn't told my mom about the latest surgery or the trip, so for the entire week I stayed on my own at home and drove the St. Bart's maintenance truck to and from Central Lakes High School.

I'd had plenty of time to think about how easy it was for Alessandra to get me to do what she wanted. The next time I saw her, I swore I would defend myself against her. I would ask her why she'd kissed me. I would ask her why she'd had me hide in the room when she broke up with Tucker. I would ask her what she actually thought of me.

On Friday, twenty minutes after I'd gotten home, there was a knock at the front door. It was Alessandra, smiling, and she leapt toward me and hugged me.

I immediately scrapped my plans.

"You are hard to track down!" she said. "And there haven't been any lights on over here for days."

"My dad's away."

"Oh, perfect," she said, and told me she wanted to make me dinner. She put a pot of water on the stove, and asked if she could see my room. In my room she asked if she could put on the Brodeur jersey I had tacked to the wall. "It's so cool."

I said yes. She matter-of-factly unbuttoned her shirt and shrugged it off—she was wearing a royal blue bra—and pulled the enormous jersey over her head. "Let's see if the water is boiling."

I followed her down the stairs.

"Where's the booze?" she asked.

"On top of the fridge."

Neither of my parents drank much but they kept a few bottles. Alessandra poured some screwdrivers using two sixteen-ounce jelly jars. When the water boiled, she dropped the pasta in. She gossiped about *Rosencrantz and Guildenstern*, telling me the show had been fine but not nearly as good as it could have been, then changed the subject abruptly.

"I think Tucker is still really upset," she said.

I took a big drink of my screwdriver.

She poured the hot water and pasta into a colander she'd set in the sink. She fished a stick of butter from the fridge, pinched off a third of the stick with her fingers and tossed it in the pot and dumped in the strained pasta. She shook salt on top. Stirred. Served us a heaping pile of noodles. She raised her screwdriver to me, and we clinked jelly jars. She sipped deeply, finishing half her glass, set it down, picked up her fork with her left hand, and said, "Walt?"

"Yeah."

"He's actually on his way over here right now."

"No he's not."

"I'm sorry, but he is." She chewed her pasta.

She really did think she was doing the right thing. I told her Tucker didn't know where I lived, and she said he did, because she'd told him. She'd told him where I lived because she'd also told him I'd kissed her, and apparently she'd told him that so he would stop calling her. But once she saw how mad he was, she figured it would be best for the three of us to get together to talk it all through. Clear the air.

"I don't need to clear the air."

We heard pounding on the front door.

"Open up!" yelled Tucker.

"For fuck's sake, this is your problem, not mine."

"Let's have our talk, get it over with," she said. She and I walked to the front door, and just before I pulled it open, we heard more fierce pounding.

"I know you're there!" he yelled.

I opened the heavy wooden door.

Tucker was flanked by two others, taller and wider than he was, in parkas and baseball hats.

With Alessandra behind me, all I could do was step out onto the stoop. Tucker and his friends had parked their truck with one wheel off the driveway, on the soft April lawn.

"All right. What do we need to talk about?"

The two taller ones grabbed me, one on each arm, pulling me out onto the wet grass. They tried throwing me down but couldn't get me to lose my footing, so they just held me while Tucker punched me, again and again and again, bright flashes in my brain, until my knees weakened, and the big guys let go.

I stayed home from school for three days. Alessandra stopped by twice and knocked on the side door while I hid upstairs. Late on that third day I got a call from my uncle Gus. Billiard balls clacked in the background.

"Your pops isn't doing too great," Gus said. "I thought maybe he'd just had too many chicken fingers."

I asked, "What happened?"

"I called an ambulance," he said.

"Where is he now?"

"At the hospital."

"And where are you?"

"Pool hall right around the corner from the hospital."

"Do they know what's wrong with him?"

"He has cancer," said Gus.

"I know that. What did you mean about the chicken fingers?"

"We thought he was having a heart attack, in addition to the cancer," he said. I hadn't been able to spend much time with my grandmother before she died, but I had endless curiosity about their upbringing, what generated their particular brand of low self-awareness and poor communication skills. What self-awareness I had, I'd gotten from my mom.

"Who's 'we'?" I asked.

"Me. Me and Ray."

"Okay. And it was confirmed? That he didn't have a heart attack?"

"Acid reflux, maybe. And cancer. Anyway, he's pretty sick. The doctor wants him to stay in the hospital here."

"I should probably come out there," I said.

In the background someone broke a rack of balls. Gus was silent on the line before saying, "Yeah. Sounds good."

St. Bart's still hadn't had the guts to retrieve my dad's work truck, so I took the plow off it, and because it was already full of fuel—my father thought it was irresponsible to keep a tank under three-fourths full—I knew all I had to do was throw a small overnight bag in the passenger seat and head south on the highway, and then west. Just before I did this, I dropped a short letter to my mom in the mail telling her what I was doing. I wasn't much of a letter writer usually, but I wanted my communication to be received by her after I was already out there. I told her I'd cleared it with my new teachers, which I hadn't, and I'd be back soon, though I really didn't know if that was true. The three days of school I'd already skipped that week hadn't raised any alarms. I planned to call them on Monday to check in and let them know I had a nasty flu.

I chugged most of a two-liter bottle of Dr. Pepper and drove through the night, stopping twice at stadium-bright truck stops to pee and splash water on my face. I'd never been further west than upstate New York. Being on the road like that, skipping school, beelining for Minnesota—it wasn't much fun. My stomach felt tight, and I didn't feel hungry for anything but Saltines and Fig Newtons.

When they'd beaten me up, I'd tried to stand too quickly, bloody and dazed on the soggy lawn in front of my house, only to fall down again. The punches had landed mostly on my head but somehow my whole body felt flattened. I heard crying. I thought the sound was coming from my own body but then I felt Alessandra's hand on my upper arm. She was sobbing. "Walt, what have they done to you?"

"Shit, shit, shit," I said.

She had helped me inside, got me to the sink where she tried to tend to my face, but I told her I needed to do it myself. I said, "No offense, but I think it's better if you go home."

I didn't want her to feel bad about this. I'd known what was going to happen when I stepped outside to talk to Tucker. I wanted Alessandra to remember the moment I'd done that, not all the blood. Again I asked her to leave, and she kissed me on the shoulder, told me she'd check up on me later, and went home.

I'd turned eighteen in January, and while I'd thought about death in the abstract plenty when I was little, on that overnight drive to Minnesota, with my jittery hands on the wheel and the green soybean fields blurring by in my periphery, I thought again about my own end of days, my body dissolving into the earth, becoming nothing, just as I'd been before I was born. Then my spirit would somehow rise from the soil like a bean sprout, taking a new form, knowing new things.

When I got to Gus's house, my dad's Chevy Malibu was parked in the brick driveway. I knocked on the door of Gus's split-level ranch, tried the knob and found it locked, then returned to the truck and lay down on the bench seat, covering my face with my hoodie, and slept.

26. Skritching of a Felt Tip Pen

The day after Delaware got hit on the head by the boat, our Huddle made plans at dinner to gather in Tess's room. We were weak and grumpy with hunger, so in the caf we loaded our plates with huge piles of rice and beans and ground beef and sour cream and stuffed our faces in silence. Tess and Aubrey wanted us to come to their room upstairs in Vancouver to read the next-day's assignment aloud, Book V of Marcus Aurelius's *Meditations*. Nash Huddle was on cleanup duty, so we just cleared our plates and followed the girls on the chip path in the dark to their dorm.

They never got Delaware off the island to have her checked out. No doctor saw her. She was back on her feet the next day, resumed activities, had a ring of gauze from the supply closet over the top of her head and under her chin for a few days, but that was the only care she got. We didn't get too upset about this at the time. We didn't really question it, we didn't know any better, and we probably didn't think we deserved anything other than what we got.

"Okay, everyone get comfortable. Who wants to read first?"

Again, we all sprawled out on the two beds, or on the faux-fur rug on the floor between them.

Bethany's round pink face appeared in the door crack. "Hey, y'all."

"Get your sweet can in here," said Tess.

"You know all we have out here for first aid is that closet in Big Rug with the pads and tampons?" asked Tess.

"Yeah, man. What if someone breaks their leg?" asked Corsetti. "Or gets the fucking plague?"

He was on his stomach at the end of Tess's bed. I sat on the faux-fur rug leaning against Aubrey's bed. Bethany sat beside Aubrey on her bed and pulled the flannel of her pajama sleeves up over her bandaged elbows. It was easy to imagine her gunning a baserunner down at second, her mask flung from her face. I recognized that quality in her. Softball catchers and hockey goalies are first cousins.

"The plague? You'd be royally screwed," said Tess.

"We do have a chopper," said Corsetti.

"Which they don't seem to want to use for us," said Tess. "Especially when a distress signal is really a camera."

That was the other thing that happened after we'd helped Delaware get out of the water. Tess took the distress signal off my neck, walked it back down to the dock and threw it into the cove. She said she thought it was a recording device and she didn't want to be spied on.

The only light in the room was a desk lamp on the little table between the two beds. We all smelled like sweat, pine, wet animal, dirt. It felt good to be together, not moving, at rest.

"We'll never know for sure," said Corsetti. "That strap's at the bottom of the fucking ocean."

"Better than on Walt's neck, creeping on us."

I felt defensiveness rise up in me again, and Tess seemed to sense this because she said, "I'm just messing with you, man. I know you didn't know it was a camera."

"We still need to ask Grunewald about it," said Corsetti.

"Why tell Grunewald?" said Tess. "He'd just tell us to shut the hell up, eat a shit sandwich, pray to God, and be a man."

"Okay, okay—assuming it was a camera . . . why? Why would they be filming us?"

"They're making their assessments, right? They're figuring out which of us should have the good jobs."

"But can't they just get that shit from Grunewald? And the other Huddle leaders?"

"How can they trust Grunewald?" said Tess. "They need first-hand evidence."

"They can't trust him?"

"He's not one of them."

"He *is* one of them. He's worked for them forever."

"But he didn't eat rocks out here in the 1800s or whatever."

"He's an Islander, we're Islanders, it's all good. We're good. They're looking out for us."

"They weren't looking out for Delaware."

"Delaware's fine."

Tess was sitting up on her bed and Corsetti grabbed her ankle and brought it to his mouth, baring his teeth. She squealed, ripped her leg out of his grasp, then jumped on his back.

"Uncle!" said Corsetti.

Bethany asked, "Hey, did y'all tell Bianca we're here?"

"Pretty sure she's with Delaware," said Tess, who climbed off Corsetti and returned to the head of her bed.

"That's good," said Corsetti. "Keep an eye on her."

"I thought you said she was fine."

"She'll be fine."

Bethany reclined on Aubrey's bed and stared at the ceiling. "By the way, do y'all know, I really don't want to leave here."

"Jesus, me neither," said Tess. "They think it's hard. It's not hard. Uncomfortable sometimes, but not hard. Really, it's not bad."

"That's because we're kicking ass," Corsetti said. "Grunewald won't admit it, but we must be ranking high on their lists. I think we're in good shape to be picked."

"The problem is, if it's not Grunewald making the call, then who knows?" said Tess.

"He'll hook us up. He knows we rule," said Corsetti.

"Sometimes it's hard to tell with him."

"If he doesn't hook us up," said Corsetti. "I'll slap his flat ass."

Tess laughed at this and hit him with one of her pillows. He put his hands over his face and said in a high-pitched voice, "No! Grunewald, don't hurt me!"

"Here's what I think," I said, and I was shocked when they all turned to me. "They need us. We should keep them thinking we need them. Make them wonder." I hadn't thought too much about these words as they emerged from me, but they felt true.

"Exactly," said Tess. "Let 'em think we need 'em."

"And we have to keep kicking ass," said Corsetti. "That'll help."

"Should we read?" I asked.

Aubrey picked up the pad from the bedside table and we listened to the sound of her skritching with a felt tip pen. She put the message in front of my face. and I read it aloud:

Let's not read that shit.

"My thoughts exactly," Bethany said.

"Walt's not filming us anymore so we can do whatever we want," said Tess.

"Ha," I said.

"Okay, I have a game," said Tess. "Let's go around the room and each say the part of your body you like the least."

"Sounds like a blast," said Corsetti.

"And then we go around the circle again and say something nice about someone else's body."

"What the fuck kind of game is that?" asked Corsetti.

"I just made it up."

"You start, then."

"I don't like my elbows," said Tess. "I have to moisturize the fuck out of them."

"Your elbows are better than my elbows," said Bethany, pointing her bandages at us.

"You've got a point," said Tess. "All right, Ohio, you're up."

"Obviously, my nose," said Corsetti. "It's a little in your face, right?"

"Your nose is cool," said Bethany. "It's, ah, you know, Roman. Don't y'all think?"

"Okay, hold on," said Tess. "And I'm asking this with love in my heart. Is the southern sweetness real? I mean, are you really that nice? Let's be honest."

"I like your elbows and I like his nose. Shoot me, y'all." Bethany smiled and folded her arms on her chest.

"You don't like my nose?" said Corsetti.

"Hey, your nose is great," said Tess. "I'm just like, trying to keep it real."

"Okay, you're up."

"My belly," said Bethany. "It's kind of, you know, *a lot.*"

"That's where you get your power," said Corsetti.

"Let her speak," said Tess.

"That is all," said Bethany, with a bow.

Tess said, "Aubs?"

Aubrey gave them a side eye and her cheeks flushed.

On the sailboat Aubrey had taken each of Grunewald's orders without hesitating. Each challenge got her focused and gung-ho. But this was a tougher assignment.

"Love you, Aubs," said Bethany.

"We'll come back to you," said Tess. "Take your time. You're up, Walt."

I thought about all the various ways I could answer the question. I appreciated the functional aspects of my body, everything that allowed me to be a goalie—my reflexes, my quickness, my dexterity, my pound-for-pound strength. But I had pet peeves, too. My legs-to-torso ratio was odd—for my height, I had shortish legs. They were also a little bowlegged, and a little pigeon toed. My knees and elbows seemed insane looking, although maybe I just hadn't looked at many other knees and elbows up close.

I pointed toward my face, drawing an imaginary circle. "My whole mug. Like, the way my chin sticks out. I think I've got too much of man-dog look."

"No dog about it," said Bethany. "You're all man. Don't y'all think?"

I stood up. "I need to pee."

"Walt's like, *I'm out!*" said Tess.

I walked out into the hall, dimly lit by the propane-fueled lights, and found my way down to the bathroom. I knocked lightly on the door, heard nothing, then opened it, and saw a brown-haired girl at one of the sinks brushing her teeth.

"Oh, shit, sorry," I said.

With a mouth full of toothpaste foam she said, "You can come on in."

I entered and felt weird standing beside her at an adjacent sink. It was awkward but I figured I'd wait until she was done.

"Don't mind me," she said, still brushing. "Have at it."

She nodded in the direction of the toilets.

I closed myself into a stall. I really needed to pee. It hadn't been an excuse to leave the room. Mid-stream I heard the girl leave, and seconds later, the door opened again. They stepped into the adjacent stall, started peeing and making exaggerated sounds of relief, moaning in ecstasy. Corsetti.

"Idiot," I said.

Corsetti laughed, flushed, and as we both emerged from the stalls he whispered, "Dude, you know I'm doing Tess?"

"Doing?"

He pumped his hips.

"Where?"

"That's seriously what you're asking? *Where?*"

"I don't know. What do you want me to say?"

"Who do you like, man?"

"No one," I said. "I mean—" and I stopped there.

"Aubrey, obviously."

"Obviously?"

"Yeah, man."

"We've been hanging out some."

"I knew it!"

"I mean, just napping."

Corsetti howled. "Napping is cool."

"Quiet!"

"There's nothing to be quiet about. We're Islanders, dude. We should all be naked constantly."

"We don't nap naked," I whispered.

"Try it out. You might like it."

When we got back to the room, Tess was sitting with crossed legs on the bed, bouncing. "Next round!"

"This is so middle school," said Corsetti.

"No, no, no," Tess said. "This is *important*."

"My nose is *important*," Corsetti said. "You have no idea what you're talking about."

"True. But anyway, my turn. I like Aubrey's ass."

Bethany laughed. Corsetti looked at me and widened his eyes.

Tess threw up her hands. "I'm an admirer of nice-looking human parts, what can I say? Her ass is nice. Your ass is nice, Aubs. Round and strong."

"I love Walt's balls," Corsetti said. "They're very classy and understated. Dignified. They cinch up when they're cold."

This time, Bethany was the only one who didn't laugh, until everyone was laughing and she started in.

"Okay, for real," said Corsetti. "I was going to say, Tess's eyes. You've got killer eyes, Tess. Like, mysterious and, you know, the windows to your soul."

"Okay, now we're talking," said Tess. "You were going to say that, or you are saying that?"

"I'm saying that."

"Thanks, man."

"My turn?" asked Bethany, combing her fingers through her own long blonde hair. "Tess's hair. I love your hair so much."

"Thank you, that's very white of you," said Tess, pulling one of her braids in front of her face, eying it closely. "But yeah, I like my hair, too. Anyone else want to talk about me?"

Aubrey pointed at me, then swung her feet up into the middle of the group and wiggled her toes. Her feet were long and thin. Bethany whistled.

"You like Walt's feet?"

Aubrey nodded.

"Okay, now this *is* important!" said Tess.

I looked down and remembered that thankfully, my shoes were on. The toes of my sneakers were pointed inward as usual, and I gently separated them.

"Let's take a look, man," said Tess.

"No," I said, feeling my face warm.

"Take 'em off! Take 'em off!" yelled Tess.

We heard pounding on the wall, then a muffled voice, "Can you keep it down, please?"

"Take 'em off! Take 'em off!" Tess yelled even louder.

"For fuck's sake," I said and started slowly unlacing my sneakers, and Tess whistled. "Okay, it's not my fault if they stink."

"Whose fault, then?" asked Tess.

"You're the one making me do this." I pulled off my gray wool socks, pulled my heels in toward my ass, and stared at my clammy white feet. Were they nice? I was immediately self-conscious about the brown wispy hair on each toe knuckle.

"Hmm," said Tess. "Not sure I get it."

Aubrey made the "ok" gesture with both hands.

"You're, like, into feet?"

Aubrey shook her head.

"You're just an admirer of *his* feet."

She put a finger on her nose. She shook the hair away from her eyes, picked up her pad and wrote:

Thin and strong, good arches. Second toe longer than the big toe.

"Thanks," I said. I had no idea these were admirable qualities.

"Okay, Walt," Tess said. "You're up."

Again, a million possibilities swam through my mind. I didn't want to unveil the obsessional way my brain worked, although maybe everyone's brain worked this way. I appreciated that Bethany had defended my face, so my first thought was to offer her a return compliment. I glanced quickly at her, sitting there in her flannel pjs, and I wanted to say something about her softball body, her strong legs, and powerful catcher's physique.

But then a prevailing thought emerged. To be perfectly honest, what I'd really appreciated was the specificity of Aubrey's description of my feet, it felt genuine and unfiltered, and so for a split second I closed my eyes and was transported to the moment earlier in the day when I'd been behind Aubrey on the trail, in a meditative zone, looking at the back of her shiny shorts and her long legs in running tights. And there'd been that night on the island when I'd been hugging her from behind and felt I was zooming through the universe, and there'd been the incredible deep-snoozing naps we'd been having, every chance we had, to hug with our eyes closed, my chest to her back, no bugs because of the cold.

But I blinked and said, "I like Tess's hair, too." I figured Corsetti would be okay with this.

"No, no, no. I'm calling bullshit on that," said Tess. "Sure, you like my hair. But Bethany already said that."

"Okay, Corsetti's balls," I said.

"We all do," said Tess. "But take this serious."

"Okay, well, I don't know . . . Aubrey's shorts," I said.

Tess and Corsetti screamed. Uncontrolled spit flew from Corsetti's mouth. Tess bounced on the bed, and Aubrey brushed the hair from her eyes, smiling.

"I've got some follow-up questions for you, man," said Tess.

"Um, I think we need to get back," I said, standing up and looking pleadingly at Corsetti, who was staring at Tess while bouncing beside her on her bed, grinning stupidly. I really needed to leave. Aubrey was smiling, but still, I was mortified, and I just needed to be alone.

"No, we don't," said Corsetti.

"Don't leave! We love you, Walt," said Tess. "I won't ask you any follow up questions about Aubrey's shorts, I promise."

"I'm actually really tired," I lied. "I should probably just read those pages and crash."

"Just sit back down," Tess said. "We'll read together."

The truth was, I wanted to stay in the room. I sat down, and when Corsetti started to read the beginning of Book V aloud, I felt relief, even though he stumbled over the words and seemed immediately bored:

> *In the morning, when you rise unwillingly, let this thought be present: I am rising to the work of a human being. Why then am I dissatisfied if I am going to do the thing for which I exist and for which I was brought into the world? Or have I been made for this, to lie under the blankets and keep myself warm? But this is more pleasant. Do you exist then to take your pleasure, and not at all for action and exertion? Do you not see the little plants, the little birds, the ants, the spiders, the bees working together to put in order their separate parts of the universe?"*

"Ha! Janowski thinks we're lazy!" said Tess.

"He doesn't know shit about us," said Corsetti. "We shouldn't have to read this."

"Fuck it, let's not," said Tess. "Grunewald won't care."

Bethany reached for the book and Corsetti handed it to her. She flipped through it, "Take charge of your life, yada yada."

"Janowski can suck my yams," said Corsetti.

"The Club wants *us* to jump out of bed, while they stay nice and cozy in their mansions."

"Those mansions are our mansions," said Bethany.

"These motherfuckers are scared," said Tess. "They're *scared* of something. They have everything, but they're still worried. It's kind of messed up."

"Well, having Janowski tell us to get out of bed won't help," said Bethany.

"True. But do you know what I'm saying?" asked Tess.

"They might just be delusional. They might be scared for no reason," said Bethany.

"For real," said Tess.

"Here's what I think. Suck the yam and suck it hard," said Corsetti.

Tess jumped on him, tickling him. She kissed his neck, then bit it. Aubrey wrote on her pad:

Get a room.

So Tess pounced on her, and Aubrey fended her off, then grabbed her pad again, and peeking through her tangled hair, wrote:

No more Janowski. Walt how about some Rambo

"I'm down with that," I said, hopping up and making for the door.

"You don't have it memorized?" asked Corsetti.

"I'll be right back."

"I'm timing you," said Tess.

I knew exactly where the book was in the room, the slim collection of Rimbaud's poetry my mother had given me. She and Dr. Charles had discussed that same book during poetry night, which kept my expectations low when I'd first started reading it. But as soon as I considered a few lines I got thinking about my mom's inner life, what she needed, what she'd been missing, how isolated she was, how colorful her dreams were. When she'd given me the book, despite my low expectations, I'd stayed up late reading it, trying to tease out her message to me, but I ended up just swimming around in its hallucinations.

What seemed to be happening between me and Aubrey made me run faster, and as I charged down the stairs and out into the frigid air, I remembered back to that day early in the fall when she'd laughed at the line I recited, "By being too sensitive I have wasted my life."

After getting the book, I tumbled back through their door, and Tess reported that the trip had taken me ninety-eight seconds.

"Okay," I said, glad to have the reading material in my hands, "Do you want a trippy one or a creepy one?"

"Creepy," said Tess.

Aubrey and Bethany nodded and Corsetti said, "Sure."

I read them "The Sleeper in the Valley":

> It is a green hollow where a stream gurgles,
> Crazily catching silver rags of itself on the grasses;
> Where the sun shines from the proud mountain:
> It is a little valley bubbling over with light.
> A young soldier, open-mouthed, bare-headed,
> With the nape of his neck bathed in cool blue cresses,
> Sleeps; he is stretched out on the grass, under the sky,
> Pale on his green bed where the light falls like rain.
> His feet in the yellow flags, he lies sleeping. Smiling as
> A sick child might smile, he is having a nap:
> Cradle him warmly, Nature: he is cold.
> No odor makes his nostrils quiver;
> He sleeps in the sun, his hand on his breast
> At peace. There are two red holes in his right side.

"That's the end?" asked Tess. "He's fucking dead?"

"That *is* creepy," said Bethany.

"Makes me want to go to sleep," said Corsetti, and he leaned back and rested his head on Tess's leg.

"It makes you want to be dead?" said Tess. She moved her hand over his eyes, closing his lids.

Aubrey held up her pad of paper.

Where the light falls like rain.

My whole body bristled.

We all stared at what Aubrey had written, and I knew we were all feeling powerful, like we might know more than anyone else on the island about the way life actually worked. I thought about Rimbaud at nineteen, brain on fire, hacking each page with a pen, trying to make sense of his vision, the words immortalized. Not long after he'd written that very poem, Rimbaud became a soldier and an arms dealer. When I first read the book, this autobiographical detail felt nonsensical, but in Tess and Aubrey's room that night, I absorbed this truth about Rimbaud and felt it in my bones.

After the lines of Rimbaud had settled in our minds, Bethany stood and announced she needed to sleep, and as she was giving hugs to Aubrey and Tess, Corsetti grabbed my arm and whispered in my ear, "Can me and Tess have our room?" Without thinking it through, feeling I needed to be a good roommate, I quickly nodded my agreement to this plan. Corsetti was euphoric in his rodent-like scrambling, first releasing my arm, then pouncing on Tess and whispering in her ear. He barely allowed her to grab her jacket before they both disappeared out through the door after Bethany.

Aubrey had her back to me and was switching off one of the lights.

"I should probably go," I said. I figured I could sleep in the common room, where the heater didn't work but there were always extra blankets.

She turned, stood beside her bed, and stared at me.

One propane light was still on in the corner, and the hair on my arms and legs stood on end. In the wind the tree branches were tapping the windowpanes. I still remember this moment, everything about it. Her snarled hair, the smudge of dirt on her left ear. Her left hand holding her right elbow. The tiniest movement of her eyebrows.

We stood close enough to each other that our noses were nearly touching. She pulled her sweater off, and as she started to wriggle out of her T-shirt, I unbuttoned my pants. Then we were still standing in front of each other but with most of our clothes peeled off and tossed aside. I already knew her body so well from training and resting with her when she kissed me. We kissed there standing up, and we pulled each other onto a bed that turned out to be even softer than moss, and we didn't feel embarrassed, though if we had, it would have been okay. That is how it's always been with Aubrey.

27. Have You Ever Had a Job?

W hen Aubrey woke me the next morning for kitchen duty, I
was deep in a dream about hang-gliding down the side of a
mountain. We scrambled into clothes and sneakers and made it
to the galley just in time. I was in heaven, and I was a mess. Aubrey
seemed to be sharing this feeling.

The radio was loud. Kitchen cleanup was the only time we
could listen to music. An old tuner sat on a high shelf beside the
spice rack. Two thick wires ran to speakers attached to the rafters
above our heads. Every song coming from that mess hall radio felt
like a transmission directly from the best kind of god. Just a simple
base-line thump, and the time-keeping of drums made my limbs
feel light. My vision sharpened. I sprayed plates and bowls in the
sink and passed them to Corsetti, who tucked them into the Hobart.

We rolled easily from "Legs" by Z.Z. Top to "Tom Sawyer"
by Rush to "More than a Feeling" by Boston. We screamed along
with each song.

DeShawn bumped me from my spot scrubbing plates to put his
head under the sink sprayer. He asked Tess to squirt some Dawn
into his hair, she promptly complied, and he furiously lathered up
and rinsed, knowing Grunewald would hate seeing this. DeShawn
finished, shook some water out of his black curly hair, wrapped it
in a dishtowel, and got back to work.

Cleaning up wasn't more than a fifteen-minute job, so we were
milking it, moving our sponges and scrubbies to the beat of the

songs. We'd heard these songs in bus depots, car mechanic waiting rooms, dentist offices, ice rinks, gas stations—and I'd heard them in my dad's work truck my whole life. It felt like we were immediate experts at clean-up duty.

Aubrey stood at the adjacent sink scrubbing pots. It could be argued that there were other things I should have been concerned about—the hole developing in the heel of one of my running shoes, or whether or not my letters were getting to my mom—but everything in my world that didn't concern Aubrey felt laughably inconsequential.

The lights flicked on and off. Grunewald charged his way through the double doors, the pale skin stretched taut over the bones of his face, dark circles beneath his eyes. He marched to the tuner and snapped off the music.

"Get that dishtowel off your head!" he yelled at DeShawn.

DeShawn removed the dishtowel.

"Line up!"

We lined up.

"Okay," he said, face irritably twisted. "I hear the neck strap ended up in the cove."

We blinked at Grunewald.

"It's actually my fault," said Tess. "I threw it in the water because I thought—"

"You did exactly what you should have done," yelled Grunewald, "It was a fucking camera. Why the fuck do they need to be monitoring you?"

"Maryland and Missouri," said Grunewald, hitting Corsetti with his canvas hat, a backhand to his shoulder. "I hear you two didn't swim. The club saw it on the cameras. They do *that* and they can't even get a kid to a hospital when she gets knocked out cold by the gunwale of a boat?"

We were all quiet until Tess asked, "Are there more cameras?"

Grunewald seemed to consider slapping Corsetti with his hat again, but he just folded his arms on his chest and looked at us like we were rats in his pantry. "I don't give a shit about the cameras, but yes. Yes, there are more cameras. And yes, they didn't tell me about the fucking cameras when they asked me to train you."

He hit Corsetti a second time.

"And quit bothering club members on Tuckaway, you hear me?"

"The cameras aren't our fault," said DeShawn.

"Is your hair wet?" yelled Grunewald.

"I was washing dishes," he said.

"You better not have used that faucet as a shower. Okay, follow me," said Grunewald. "All of you."

Each of the six bathrooms we cleaned had only two stalls. We were to scrub them one at a time on our hands and knees, sawing our toothbrushes over the grout between the tiles, around the sink fixtures, and inside the toilet bowls. Grunewald said this would give him time to think. He was pissed about the cameras, and he was pissed that he'd heard Corsetti had visited Brevard again, but most of all he was pissed that Delaware's injury hadn't been taken seriously.

We filled clear plastic cups with water and Comet. Grunewald ignored our complaints about the smell of the detergent, or the pee on the floor by the toilets. "For now, here's what we need to do: Don't bother the club members. Look out for your fellow WILDers. *Ductus Exemplo*, for chrissakes," he said.

Later, after Grunewald left, DeShawn said, "I don't think he's mad at us. I think he's mad at the Club."

"Yeah, no shit," said Tess. Then she got right in Corsetti's face and said, "What did he mean when he said you were bothering Club members?"

"Um, I probably should have told you," he said. "I went back to Brevard's house."

"Jesus fucking Christ. When?" asked Tess.

"Yesterday," he said. "Before dinner."

"You said you needed to take a shit. You swam out there again?"

She wasn't raising her voice, but she could get answers from Corsetti. She could handle him well.

"He told me again I shouldn't visit him," said Corsetti. "But I'm telling you, I think he thinks it's pretty fucking badass that I swim out."

Aubrey dropped her toothbrush on the tile and walked out of the bathroom. I started after her, but Tess grabbed my arm.

"Let her go, she's fine," Tess said to me, then turned to Corsetti. "What did you ask him?"

"About the guns," he said.

"Seriously, why would you not tell us about this? A second time!"

"I'm telling you."

"Well, tell me everything."

"Okay, okay, okay," Corsetti said. "I'm still kind of processing it."

"Dude, talk!" said Tess.

"Honestly, I think he was probably a little drunk. I talked to him about Delaware. I'm in total agreement with Grunewald. It's fucked up that they didn't take better care of her."

Tess just glared at him. "Well, good. And what did he say?"

"He told me not to worry about her."

"And what else did he say."

"He said I should be proud to have made it as far as I have and that he really liked what I'd done on the island this fall."

"And what else?"

"He said we'd all be doing combat training after Thanksgiving. We'll definitely be using the AR-15s and Glock 19s, and we'll be doing more hand-to-hand shit, 'combat simulations' is what he said—"

"He was telling you this in his house?" asked Tess. Now she was yelling.

"Yeah," whispered Corsetti.

"After you swam out there."

"Yeah."

"And you didn't tell me."

"You didn't tell any of us," said Javier.

"Fuck off!" yelled Corsetti. "I'm telling you everything now!"

"We *need* to know this."

"That's pretty much all he said. He wants us to do the combat training when most of the Club isn't here. It's going to be rad, right?"

"I like that they want us to learn how to use guns," said Javier.

I felt that way at the time, too, but our trust in them and our belief that they trusted us was no longer as solid.

"I won't keep any more secrets from you. Sorry guys." He looked toward the window, at the dark pane, and said, "I guess I should have told you."

"Yeah, man," said Tess, punching him in the arm. "We've got to stay together on this."

Later that morning we ran the perimeter trail in the rain, and Grunewald didn't seem to mind that we kept a slow and steady pace and stayed together in a tight group. I thought about the camera, that I'd had it on my neck during our overnight on the island. There wasn't anything the club could have learned from the video of us spooning in the pine needles, although I really didn't like that, in that moment when we'd felt so abandoned, we were under constant surveillance.

The message? You're Islanders, we trust you, but if you get hurt or if you show any kind of weakness, you're on your own.

My sneakers and socks were soaked but my legs felt limber and strong. What was even more troubling was that Grunewald seemed surprised and pissed about the cameras. What had Brevard said to him? I wasn't sure if we'd find out.

Swimming in the icy ocean in a cold steady rain got us eager to return to the caf on time for midday chow. We were back in our regular routine.

At our table, the eight of us ate quickly in silence, eager to refuel, not knowing when we'd next eat, not knowing what the next task might be. Aubrey sat across from me and was shoveling food into her mouth as fast as I was.

I still knew the Club needed us. That was at the front of my mind.

We finished inhaling our food. Tess asked, in a whisper, if we should check in with Grunewald about the guns, to make sure that he, too, thought the Club's decision to have us train with AR-15s seemed like a vote of confidence.

"No," whispered Corsetti. "Let's not push it. Let's take it as it comes."

That felt right.

As if on cue we heard Grunewald's whistle. "Idiots! Put your rain gear on!" He was wearing a new neck strap.

We suited up and he led us down the Copperthwait trail, an old trail we'd never traveled. We were a tight line of glossy-sheathed nineteen-year-olds trudging through the dark woods, slick roots and black mud beneath our feet.

"Sir, I've got to tie my shoe," said Tess, and she stopped, and Grunewald sucked his teeth in exasperation, and we stopped, but instead of kneeling down to tie her shoe Tess put a hand over the lens of Grunewald's neck camera and mouthed the word, "Why?"

He looked at her sternly. We were now all huddled up.

"This weather's fucking grim," said Grunewald, and he zipped up his orange rain jacket, covering the camera. Then he reached his other hand up into his jacket and unfastened the neck strap, unzipped his jacket, and—with the lens covered—folded the neck strap inside the jacket, and set it on the ground. He waved us down the trail about thirty yards. When we got there, he looked at Tess and said, "Maryland, for fuck's sake, have you ever had a job?"

"Yes," she said.

"Have you ever had a job you had to do things you didn't like to do?"

"Cleaning motel rooms."

"Okay, good. So . . . they told me to wear the goddamn camera. I don't like it. I don't want to do it. But I'm still trying to figure shit out. It's wait-and-see right now. Is that all right with you, Maryland? Do I have your goddamn permission?"

"Well—" Tess said.

"Do I?"

"Yes, sir."

"Now, fuck off."

We went back up the trail to retrieve the neck strap, then continued marching single file through the forest, rain dripping down on the hoods of our jackets.

Three minutes down the trail Grunewald stopped, unzipped his jacket, unbuckled the neck strap, set it on top of a trailside boulder, picked up a fist-sized rock from the ground, and brought it down atop the neck strap again and again, smashing it into oblivion.

"Okay, enough of this," Grunewald muttered to himself, and we all knew he'd done this for us.

Aubrey and I found a way to be alone together at least once every day. We had our spot on the moss by the quarry and that was always private, but after rain it was too wet and cold, and if we only had a twenty-minute break, it took too long to get there and back. Using one of our rooms wasn't ideal, not just because we'd have to negotiate with Tess and Corsetti, but because of the neighbors. When we tried Big Rug—which we thought would work, because it was used so infrequently—the room was so vast and empty, the ceilings so tall, we felt untethered and weightless, drifting through space. We went to Osprey Cove, where the girls swam, and we found a place for our blankets amid the trees near the rock from which the toughest girls jumped into the water. Once we were naked, Aubrey pushed me onto my back, her face just above mine, her eyes staring down at me or looking up at the ocean behind my head. That time—when it was over—she cried, and I didn't know if she was sad or happy or simply overwhelmed. She just collapsed on my chest, warm, and I didn't ask her. I just asked her if she was okay. And she squeezed me and gently nodded.

There were moments, too, when we kept our clothes on in her room, when I was able to ask her questions and she could respond with pen and paper. I wanted to know about her life in Maine. I wanted to know about her family, about track and field, about what it was like to be her before she'd gotten to Whaleback. She would answer me but not expansively. She seemed to like being asked but she didn't write much. She said she liked throwing the javelin. I asked her what she missed about it, and she wrote *right after you let go, before it lands* and I could see it in my mind, the tall girl who could throw things far, I could see her javelin whistling through the air.

I got the courage to ask her, "Have you ever talked?"

And she wrote immediately:

Yes.

"Will you ever talk again?"

Probably.

"Can I help you with that?"

No.

"Do you know why you don't talk?"

She put the pen down and turned away, lying back on her bed, looking up at the ceiling. I apologized but that didn't seem to be the right thing to say either.

The best place for us was the classroom where Grunewald had made us write letters. It had no lock on the door, and while it was unheated—we couldn't start the wood stove because the smoke coming from the chimney would have given us away—it was small enough that blankets kept us warm. And blankets made the wood floor more comfortable. After our second time in the classroom, I started telling her more about myself. I told her about my parents, how smart and funny my mother was, and how I'd retrieved my dad from Minnesota, brought him back for hospice.

"We had our problems," I told her. "He and I were really similar."

She looked at me then as though she was the one talking, as though she was saying *I am with you in this.* I had never felt that from anyone but my parents.

Grunewald told us as a Huddle we were to create a remote campsite before Thanksgiving, and because it was getting colder, he'd decided it was time to begin the task. We went to Big Rug to load up on provisions before we headed into the woods. Grunewald knew his way around the galley and the walk-in. He let us choose easily portable food for dinner. We packed crackers and peanut butter and carrots and sardines (which only Tess and Javier and Bethany liked) and headed out to the shipyard trail, where we walked single file through the cold drying forest, and then came back out into the crisp sunshine by the pier, where we gathered tools from a supply shed—bow saws, loppers, shovels, pick axes, machetes. The nasty weather of the previous few days had cleared out and the temperature had dipped. A frosting of ice clung to the seaweed where the waves lapped against the stone pilings of the wharf. Grunewald let us decide how best to split the load of tools and told us we'd be heading further along the main ridge of the island, past the dorms. He slung a coil of rope over his shoulder, zipped his jacket up, led the way.

Grunewald had us all circle up just out of sight of the dorms and he sent a scout—Javier—up to the school buildings to see if anyone had arrived since we'd left. Javier returned, having sprinted out and back, to announce—out of breath—that the coast was clear. It wasn't until we were bushwhacking in the thicket just west of the dorms that DeShawn asked why we didn't want to be seen, and Grunewald said, simply, "They fucked us. They fucked every one of us when they didn't tend to Delaware. We need to practice being on our own if that's how they're treating us."

"How do we practice that?" said DeShawn.

"We do what they're *not* doing. We work together as a group. We take care of each other," said Grunewald. Twenty yards into the thicket he tied one end of his rope to a sapling, and said, "Follow the rope. We cut the trail starting here."

"We have to bushwhack out to our own trail?"

"Yup. And each time we come through the thicket to the trail, we should go a different way or else the bushwhacking becomes the trail. Actually, you know what? Each one of you motherfuckers should bushwhack your own route to the start of the trail. That's the best way to stay hidden."

"That's fucking crazy," said DeShawn.

Grunewald ignored him and continued. "When you cut down the saplings, try not to leave much stump. Cut them flush to the ground. The trail can just wind around the bigger trees. We have the large bow saw to cut through the stout blowdowns, but if a tree is lying all the way on the ground, we can hop over the trunk. Got it?"

After he laid the rope, he came back and took up one of the bow saws, dropping to his knees to hack through a few small pines, tossing them to the side. The work was both easy and exhausting. Easy because it was obvious what needed to be done. Exhausting because the bow saws and hatchets didn't run on gas.

As the days accumulated, we talked more as a group in front of Grunewald. We peppered him with questions.

We asked him what he knew about Paul Brevard and Joey MacLean, and he said, "Powerful guys out here. On the mainland, too."

We asked him what they thought would happen during the rest of the winter.

"All you've got to worry about right now is your training. Trust your Huddle. If they're not looking out for you, you've got to look out for yourself."

We asked him if he thought it was fair for a group of people to have so many huge, beautiful houses. He told us to fuck off, of course it was fair.

We asked him why that ranch in Montana got attacked, and he said people with money everywhere had reason to be cautious. The old rules were changing. Some people work for their money, while other people steal it from the people who work.

I said the "work" done by some people is in fact just stealing. Tess agreed.

Grunewald asked if we were communists. We said maybe.

Tess said, "Do the people here on Whaleback think they'll get stolen from?"

He said probably.

"Even here in Maine they're worried?" I asked. It didn't make sense to me, especially when we were there in the pungent woods with our loppers and saws and the endless ocean in the distance.

"They want to be independent. They don't want to have to rely on anyone else. That's really what it means to be Islanders, right? No help. Solve your own problems."

"Or have a bunch of teenagers solve them for you," said Tess.

"Like I said, your job is just to worry about the stuff that's right there in front of your nose."

Bethany was down on the ground, trying to heave a rock out of the path. Grunewald grabbed a pickaxe and told her to step back. He wailed away at the soggy earth in front of the rock, digging a trench, spraying those nearby with dirt, missing his mark a few times and striking the rock, sending the smell of gun smoke into the air. He tossed the axe on the ground and plucked a shovel from where it rested against a tree, stuck it into the gap and leaned all his weight on the wooden handle—it seemed like it was going to snap—but he pried the rock slowly up out of the ground. Aubrey and I grabbed either side and flipped the rock down the slope, where it tumbled to rest against the sap-smeared trunk of a spruce. Without missing a beat, Grunewald looked up and said, "You're using that machete wrong, Corsetti."

Corsetti shrugged, handed Grunewald the handle of the massive knife, and stepped back. Aubrey and I were nearby, and we stepped back, too, remembering how Grunewald had wielded the pick axe. "Little swings," he said. "Flick your wrist. This beast is plenty sharp.

You don't have to be a home run hitter. Chip, chip, chip. It'll take a sapling down as quick as that bow saw, but you need to chip, chip, chip at it, don't use your shoulder much at all."

Then, in answer to no one in particular, Grunewald said, "I'm telling you right now, and I've been thinking about this a lot, they're asking you to trust them without knowing much. And they're asking you to trust them even though they're leaving you on your own out here. I've worked for them for a long time, and I've never felt as unsure about their motives than I am now. You have to decide for yourself what's right. You've got to follow your gut. It's the gut that God gave you."

We all heard him, and then we went back to hacking at the trees and bushes. We cut about twenty feet of trail each day. Grunewald didn't tell us how much further we had to go—he didn't want us bushwhacking beyond the trail we were cutting. When we were done with a section of trail, we just followed the rope. Grunewald said fast was bad, steady was good.

On the third day when Tess was finishing her midday sandwich, she asked, "What's going on with the other Huddles?"

He said Lisa and Dale were building campsites, too.

That morning, like the previous three mornings, in the brief period of time between the swim and morning chow, I jogged with Aubrey around the first bend of the Ainsworth trail, a trail no one used because it went to the houses on the north side of the island. Just after that first bend we stepped off the trail through the withering brown ferns to a bed of moss that felt like there was nothing beneath it but more moss; it was soft even with all our weight. Aubrey pulled four wool blankets from under the tarp in her backpack, which she spread out, two beneath us and two above. We kept our boots on and pulled our sweaters and shirts up enough to get our salty bellies together and take down our pants and underwear, and there seemed like nothing else in the world to live for. It didn't matter what else was going on around us. All that mattered was that we were there on that moss, just the two of us, half naked, kissing, pressing ourselves together. To keep the mess off the blankets, she'd grab me and help me shoot off into the ferns, and then she'd bring my hand down between her legs and show me what to do. When we were done, we'd pull our clothes back on and stay there, red faced and out of breath, not ready to return to the group, looking up into the canopy, watching the birds flit from branch to branch, or looking down at the moss together, following the path of a single ant. The first time this happened, I gave voice to the ant, imagining the mission she was on, giving her an Irish accent. On subsequent occasions, when we looked for her in the moss and couldn't find her, I could still find her voice: *havin' a whale of a time over here, a bit knackered but it's really, really grand . . .*

Grunewald worked us hard and he worked alongside us. We continued to plow our way along the ridge line, making progress each day. Some days we couldn't quite do twenty feet, because of the number of blowdowns in the way or the rocks we had to move. Some days it was only ten. And we didn't work all day; we'd hack out the trail until about four, having eaten our packed lunch in the woods. Then we'd run trails in the interior of the island—Bayberry, Old Shipyard, Pliny's—but we avoided the Club buildings, we avoided the mansions, we even avoided the dorms. We didn't see any Club members and we didn't see any other Huddles. We'd strung up a tarp about a hundred feet into the woods that kept our sleeping bags dry.

Grunewald still ran us just as hard, but he insisted we gather to talk more, and he'd stick around and listen in, heckle us, demean us, and threaten us. We were in wait-and-see mode. We were creating a trail that would lead to a campsite we could use throughout the winter. We were vigilant. We didn't know what was coming next, so we just stuck together. Grunewald stopped sharing his opinion about Club matters. He let us talk about whatever we wanted. Every three hours we spent on the trail was usually matched by an hour of what he called "crying," when we'd discuss what we'd learned about trail clearing, what we'd noticed in the forest, what we'd felt, what we feared, both generally and specifically. We'd debrief what had happened that day or earlier in the year, but our conversations—because he allowed us to speak our minds—often touched upon the experience of our past lives. It was in one of these conversations that I said I felt grateful I'd had the spring and summer to look after my father, to spend a good amount of time with him in his last days, and Grunewald surprised me by saying, "He must have appreciated that."

"I never could tell," I said. What I did know for sure was that my dad would have loved the trail-clearing project.

On the sixth day of our work in the woods, the air was dry and not excruciatingly cold. Around midday, Grunewald had us put down our tools at the base of a large boulder, a rock face that disappeared into the tree tops. He had us rake the ground beside the boulder, clearing it of pine needles, leaves, and branches. We sat in a tight circle on the cold hard ground.

"Okay, Javier and DeShawn, pass out sandwiches. Let's get some crying out of the way."

"I been thinking about my parents," said Bethany. Tears leaked from her eyes.

"I don't mean you have to *actually* cry," said Grunewald, chuckling.

Tess glared at him, "Let her be." She put her arm around Bethany. "You okay?"

"I'm fine," Bethany said. "I'm just feeling some regrets." She pushed her blonde hair away from her wet round cheeks. "Y'all know I used to have a problem stealing things?"

"Yeah, we know," said Tess.

"And I'm just thinking about that."

"Doesn't it all seem like a long time ago?" said Corsetti.

"Kinda," said Bethany.

"Why do you think about it?" asked DeShawn.

"It felt right to steal."

"I get that," said Corsetti.

"I pretty much always felt like such a mess except when I was taking something," said Bethany. "You know? Something from my mom's car or from a neighbor's house or from a store. I felt powerful, y'all."

"We love you," said Tess.

"We do," said Javier.

We sat in silence, chewing. I looked around at the rest of them, their eyes bright beneath the brims of their wool caps, wind-whipped chins above their zipped-up collars.

"You know what would hit the spot right now?" Bethany asked. "Cake."

"Cake!" said DeShawn. "I want some cake right the fuck now."

"Alabama, for fuck's sake, you can make cake," said Grunewald. "No Club members are here now, and the other Huddles are at their remote sites."

"You're saying we can make cake?" asked Corsetti.

"Knock yourself out," said Grunewald.

Corsetti said, "When Bethany asked you about cake the other morning you were like, 'I'm gonna make sure to murder anyone who talks about cake.'"

Grunewald said, "It's all about timing."

"Well, let's go make some cake," said DeShawn.

"Fuck no. We have shit to do," he said, and then didn't seem to understand why we were all laughing.

I was chewing my sandwich when I spotted the red rope tied to the base of a thin birch tree. I said, "Is that the end?"

"That is indeed the end of the rope," said Grunewald.

"Does that mean we're done with the trail?"

"We'll climb up this rock, take a look around, and I'll let you decide if this is our spot," said Grunewald.

We stuffed the rest of our sandwiches into our mouths, hopped to our feet, and followed Grunewald up the side of the giant rock, each of us careful to use the handholds and footholds he'd chosen, up above the treetops and into the wind and sunshine. I was in the middle of the pack. I still had a few moves to make before I could pull myself up onto the crest of the rock, but I could hear Tess and Bethany and DeShawn and the others cheering. The flat spot atop the boulder was just big enough for all nine of us to stand and marvel: a 360 degree, kaleidoscopic view of the island, its dense pine forest, the roofs of the dorms and Big Rug, the manicured-grass part of the island closest to the mainland, with the golf course and club houses, the mansions on the perimeter, and then, of course, the endless water with its white foam fringe at the shoreline but otherwise no interruption in the flat blue ocean. From that height, I couldn't quite make out the texture of the waves, but everything closer looked crisp and bright.

We were all pressed together in our parkas and Bethany said, "Thank you for bringing us here, sir." Her blonde hair was whipping about her round face in the swirling wind, so she tugged her black watch cap back on.

"You ripped the nuts off this project," said Grunewald. "We couldn't have done this without everyone's help."

Grunewald passed around a bag of chopped dried fruit he had in the pocket of his jacket.

Our cheeks and noses were cold as we looked out at the rocky contours of the island and the islands nearby, the vast sweep of the ocean, imagining the curve of the earth.

"Breathe this goddamn air, folks," said Grunewald.

"I could look at this view forever," said Bethany, her face bright red from the climb and the wind.

"Hard to believe there are any problems anywhere when you're in a spot like this," said Javier.

"Funny. I have the opposite reaction, kid. When I'm in a place like this, with evidence of God's creativity, I'm reminded of *why* there are problems in the world."

"Leave it to you, sir," said Tess.

"Well, come on, now. Giving a shit is a good thing."

"Who said I didn't give a shit?" said Javier.

"Well, what *I'm* saying is putting up a fight for what's good and beautiful is pretty much what life is all about."

"You guys are in agreement, then," said Bethany.

"We had about ten seconds of feels before you picked a fight, sir," said Tess.

"I'm trying to tell you something important," said Grunewald.

"What?" asked Tess. I could tell she was trying to soften her tone and actually listen.

Grunewald didn't speak right away. We smushed ourselves even closer together for warmth, the down of our coats compressing. I was mesmerized by the distant imperceptible movements of the water. I felt most alone when I considered the world was only real inside my own head. Feeling tired from the work, my face cold from the wind off the water, warm at my core from the bodies around me, I felt there was a group truth, a common way of seeing.

Grunewald must have been feeling this too because he said, "When I was eighteen in *Binh Duong* with my platoon, I was fighting for Uncle Sam, of course, but what got me through my days was protecting my buddies. I had to be self-reliant because I had to stay alive. I had to stay alive because I had to look out for my buddies. There's a difference between selfishness and self-reliance, and until you figure out that difference, you're not a man."

"Or a woman," said Tess.

Grunewald offered a gentle nod.

We stayed crammed together for another few minutes.

"So, this is our campsite?" said Javier. "At the base of this boulder?"

"Seems good," said Tess.

"And no one else in the world, or on the island, knows where the fuck we are," said Javier.

We climbed back down. Around the boulder the trees we needed to fell were mostly saplings. Grunewald said nothing, he just started hacking away, and we followed his lead. When we asked him a question, and he judged that we really needed guidance, he'd offer some. But mostly, he was just doing the work, and letting us make decisions on our own as a group.

The more we cleared, the more we could see the ridge line, the shape of forest around us, and what the future hideout might look like.

When it came to the framing of the lean-to, Grunewald was more directive, telling us where to saw, where to nail.

Javier and Bethany went to work unearthing the small roots just beneath the surface of the soil in the precise spot where we'd be sleeping in the lean-to.

We didn't know what the structure was supposed to look like ahead of time—but Grunewald knew, and piece by piece it was revealed to us. Once the frame was up, we stripped the saplings we'd felled and used them, wedged tightly together, for the roof. Javier and Bethany raked and smoothed the earthen floor.

"All right," said Grunewald. "Everyone lie down inside."

We piled in. We still had more to do, but he just wanted to double check the dimensions.

We lay on our backs, our heads away from the opening. After we'd tumbled into place on the dirt floor of the lean-to, Aubrey had stretched out beside me, the side of her arm and leg against mine. I felt her pinky finger, and then she hopped it over mine, interlocking them, and I saw the edge of her smile. Everyone was jostling into place, laughing; Javier log rolled himself down the whole row of bodies, over me and Aubrey, then wedged into a spot between Aubrey and Bethany. We all smelled like B.O. and soggy pine needles. Grunewald declared it a good fit, and we all climbed back out to finish the job.

That evening we finished the lean-to just as the woods were getting dark, and Grunewald asked us to stow all the tools under the overhang at the rear of the structure.

"Last thing I'll say today. This place really is for you. This whole fucking world is for you. It sounds corny, but you're the future. I hope that feels okay to you, because it's the truth, no matter what the

Club tells you." The November air felt thin and silver as it moved through the trees to our faces, and we slept like royalty.

28. Forest Take-Down

Whaleback Island

During the weeks before Thanksgiving, Aubrey and I made good use of the hour off between trail work and dinner, an hour when the sun was getting lower and lower in the sky, barely making its way into the bushy evergreens. One late afternoon during a rainstorm when we couldn't leave the lean-to for a nap in the woods, Aubrey handed me my rain gear and took my hand.

We jogged down the Bayberry Trail to an offshoot of the Old Shipyard Trail, and with the rain hammering our nylon jackets, we made our way to the biggest house I had ever seen up close. It had a pea stone gravel roundabout with a trellis covered in green vines leading to a maroon clay tennis court without a net. The back door was sheltered by a small roof supported by white pillars. Beside it a stone birdbath, and shrubs covered with cheesecloth. To the left of the back door was a row of windows looking out at the winterized gardens. Aubrey walked over to the middle window, and without hesitation, pressed her palms against the panes and slid it open. She climbed inside and I followed.

We took our boots off and I followed her past the sixteen-person dining table with its golden-framed paintings of sailboats on heavy seas, through the kitchen with its two sinks, two refrigerators, two gas stoves, copper pots hanging on hooks overhead, through another hallway to the foyer, up a wide staircase to a landing that led to six bedrooms, all of which had large windows looking out at the open ocean. Seeing the ocean from that landing, through the windows of the various bedrooms was like glancing at a river through the slats of a covered bridge.

She led me to another hallway, and another staircase, up to the third floor. In the far corner was a small room with a twin bed, a dormer with a window seat, and a roll-top desk. We sat side by side on the bed looking out at the rain falling on the ocean, the darkening sky. Aubrey reached into the pocket of her rain pants to retrieve her notebook, but she hesitated, her face crumpled, and she cried. Sobbed.

I put my arm around her and felt how her body shuddered with grief. I cried with her. I held her until she wiped her face and pulled out her notebook.

Joey MacLean said I could stay in this house whenever I wanted. It's the Buchanan's but they're only here like one week a year.

She glanced quickly up at me, her eyes glossy and full.

I miss my mom.

"I know you do," I said.

I should have listened to her more. She had things to tell me, but I ignored her because she was such a mess. Nothing she did made sense to me.

I wanted to say something about feeling the same way, that there was so much my father said to me that I either ignored or didn't take seriously. But I stayed quiet, I just squeezed her tighter, and she squeezed me, and then it was time to get back.

We retraced our steps through the house, out the window, and then raced up the offshoot of the Old Shipyard Trail, back to Bayberry, to the head of Copperthwait, where the Huddle was just assembling.

Grunewald said, "We're meeting at the airport at three for a field event against Janowski Huddle. Let me tell you right now,

Janowski and his kids, they're WILDers, so they're our brothers
and sisters, but they're the enemy for today, so of course they're a
bunch of candy-ass losers. Got it?"

"Candy-ass?" asked DeShawn.

"Losers. Can I hear you yell that, Bethany?"

"Candy-ass losers?" she said.

"It's not a question," Grunewald said. "Yell it like you're about
to get ambushed by someone who's gunning to cut your throat."

"Candy-ass losers!" she screamed.

"Better. How about you, Ohio?"

Corsetti barked "candy-ass losers" in a deep growl.

"Sound off, Maryland."

Tess had good pipes. "They're our brothers and sisters but today
they are CANDY-ASS LOSERS!" she screamed.

The airport was a clearing of trees amid the dense forest, a
shed, and a concrete helipad. At the far side of the clearing was
Janowski Huddle, in dark green rain gear, with red bandanas tied
around their upper arms. They hooted when we emerged from the
Ellesmere Trail. Grunewald started passing around blue bandanas,
which we tied to our arms.

"*CANDY-ASS MOTHERFUCKING LOSERS!*" screeched
Bianca.

"Well done," said Grunewald.

"Fuck you, cocksucker!" yelled someone in Janowski Huddle.

"All right, get in here," said Grunewald. We circled up. He took
a small tin from his pocket and finger-painted a black line beneath
each of our eyes. He had us push our hooded heads together like
we had on the first day.

"Humiliate these wimps," Grunewald said. "All of you are better
than their best. Take 'em out. No mercy."

"What are the rules?" asked Tess.

"Very basic. Forest Takedown. The team with the most bandanas
wins. You're out if either knee touches the ground. If your knee goes

down, they take your bandana. So you've gotta find a way to get them on the ground without getting on the ground yourself. Simple."

"What are the stakes?" asked Tess.

"If you've gotta ask, Maryland, that's a bad sign."

"Bragging rights?" said Javier.

"Rip their goddamn throats out," said Grunewald. "Janowski and I will be watching from the helipad."

We assembled shoulder to shoulder and looked across the field at our opponents, who were lined up in a similar way, staring back across the field, wearing the same Club-issued rain gear. Janowski Huddle had roughly the same range of sizes and body types in their ranks. I didn't know many of the Janowski kids, but Feng was among them, second from the left, arms folded, nodding his head. He was fast.

"I'll take the big girl," said Tess.

"I'll take Frankenstein. In the sunglasses," said Javier.

"You sure?" Corsetti asked. "Maybe DeShawn should get him."

"No, I'm good," said Javier.

"Let's *do* this," said Tess, and she started tromping across the soggy yellow grass toward them.

"Hold up, hold up," said DeShawn. "One more quick huddle."

Tess returned and we linked arms. DeShawn said it wasn't a great idea to just march straight across at them. That's what the redcoats did. Tess wanted to take them in the open field, but there were others who were better off going into the woods to hide and sneak attack.

"Let's do both," said Tess, staring over at Janowski Huddle. "Here we go."

"Hustle and heart on three."

"One, two, *HUSTLE AND HEART!*"

We hid in the brambles, behind lichen-covered blowdowns or large mossy rocks, but they found us, and we found them. After about an hour, those of us who'd relinquished our bandanas came back to the clearing and we counted. Seven to seven. There were only two competitors left: Mass on their team, Aubrey on ours. A layer of mist still lingered just above the grass. Mass was moving from tree to tree on the far side of the field, and Aubrey walked toward him, no hurry. All of us followed her, and as we passed Janowski and Grunewald on the helipad, Bethany gave them the bandanas.

"You think we're not keeping score?" asked Janowski.

Aubrey knew better than to walk into the forest looking for her target; she just stood about fifteen yards from the edge of the trees, knees slightly bent, ready for anything, rubbing her hands together to warm them.

"C'mon, Mass, you fucking caveman! We know you're in there!" yelled Tess.

"Mass is a sneaky bastard," Janowski said. "God love him."

"My money's on Maine," said Grunewald.

Mass poked his large white-blonde head out from behind a nearby tree. He said to Feng, "Who we got?"

"Just you and Maine."

Mass stepped out into plain sight. His rain gear was stretched tight across his wide chest, straining the buttons. He had a chiseled chin, smooth skin, a grown-out crew cut. "The mute girl?"

"Yeah, the mute girl," someone said.

He strode through the crowd, six-foot-five, and we cleared a path as he approached Aubrey, forming a wide circle around the last two competitors. Aubrey hunched her back, narrowed her eyes. She pulled the hood of her rain jacket down, shook her hair away from her eyes, then unbuttoned her jacket, shrugged it off her shoulders and handed it to Tess.

"I'm not going easy on you," said Mass.

Tess yelled, "Idiot! Neanderthal!"

Aubrey continued to stare, no change in her expression.

"How about you just take a knee, spare yourself the trouble?" Mass asked.

No acknowledgement from Aubrey's green eyes.

"You really can't talk?" he asked.

She started moving in a circular motion, which got him moving, too—they were facing each other, shifting slowly from foot to foot. "You're hot," he said. "I bet I could turn that scowl into a smile." Someone in Janowski's Huddle whistled, and someone else said, "Dang."

Mass said, "You been to Massachusetts before? You really should visit."

Without taking her eyes off him, she reached down into the grass and picked up a thick tree branch, about four feet long. She hefted it in both hands, raised it like a broad sword, sprinted toward him, cocked the branch, and swung it at the side of his body. Mass seemed shocked by this. He put his hands up by his face and the branch cracked into him, shattering, knocking him down. We erupted in cheers while Aubrey just stood there, stone-faced, and dropped what was left of the branch.

Grunewald grinned like a great northern pike, and said, "Howdy there, motherfuckers. Looks like we won."

29. Just Go

Out in Minnesota, I found my father in Room 214 of Maple Grove Hospital. The nurse at the desk told me it was okay to wake him. The white sheet was up to his neck, his face was thinner, there was some redness in his cheeks and nose, and whiskers on his chin. He never went a day without shaving. I put a hand on his knobby shoulder and kept it there until he opened his eyes. He said, "Oh, good. Grab my dopp kit."

I retrieved his dopp kit from the windowsill.

"And get that plastic basin from the bathroom and fill it with warm water."

When I brought it back to his bedside, he said, "You'll need a towel and a face cloth too."

"Did Gus tell you I was coming?" I asked.

He asked why I was asking that.

"Are you surprised I'm here?"

"No," he said, and he asked me to tuck some pillows behind his back, which I did. My father jutted his chin in the air.

"Are you comfortable?"

"Comfortable enough," he said.

I spread the towel out underneath his head and neck, and when I put the warm wet washcloth onto his face, he made a tiny sound of relief. I covered his forehead, eyes, cheeks, then pulled it down toward his neck, rewet the washcloth with the warm water, covered his face again, and he made the same little sound. When I uncovered his face,

Dad kept his eyes closed. His skin looked soft and less weathered. Without his glasses, he looked young, new to the world—his eyelids had a bluish tint. I told him I'd seen Gus.

He kept his eyes closed and said, "It's been a good visit. He's a good brother."

He had a mild rash on his chin—maybe from the last person who'd shaved him, or maybe from the chemo—so I was gentle with the shaving cream and the first few pulls of the blue plastic razor. I used my off hand to pull the skin taut in the tough-to-shave places under his nose and along his jawbone.

I said, "Dad, you shouldn't have driven out here."

My father said, "My clothes are in that little locker."

"You need to take better care of yourself."

"You got kicked out of school. And what are those bruises on your face? Seems like you should take your own advice."

"Maybe so," I said. I was angry and embarrassed, but I didn't want to act defensively.

"Watch the door for nurses."

He was so skinny and weak it took him a while to get his pants and shirt on. I kept to my post. The nurses were tapping at their computers. The man in the hospital bed next to my father's, near the window, was snoring.

I asked him if he was getting discharged.

"Yeah, I'm going with you," he said.

"The doctor discharged you?"

"It's fine, it's fine," he said. "Grab all those pillows and some of those blankets." I did, and we went the long way around to avoid the nurses' station, and within ten minutes I was setting the pillows down in the footwell behind the bench seat of the St. Bart's truck, as instructed.

"This seems like a fucking idiotic thing to be doing," I said.

"Are you with me or not?"

"I'm with you."

My dad lay on top of them and pulled the blanket over himself, and I asked, "What about the Malibu?"

My dad said, "It's fine, it's fine," although his voice was quieter, coming from the footwell. I asked him if we were going to see Gus before driving back to New Hampshire, and he said, even fainter this time, "Just go."

30. We Are the Winning Team

Whaleback Island

DeShawn and Javier ran to Grunewald and put him up on their shoulders, and because their shoulders weren't the same height, Grunewald was canted askew, but the rest of us reached him and joined the effort before he could tumble to the ground. He was soggy and boney and heavier than he looked. I took over for Javier, and we kept him up on our shoulders as we marched back across the field. Tess and Bethany led the way, strutting in front, while Janowski Huddle watched, laughing at us for acting like fools, but really they wanted to be the ones acting like fools.

We marched all the way across the field and back into the woods, out of view. Beside a dead fallen pine tree, its roots a vertical tangle ten feet in the air, Grunewald said, "Let me down, let me down!" and once he had his boots in the dirt, he opened his arms to his Huddle.

"They said it couldn't be done, with a group of talentless degenerates such as yourselves."

"Ooh-ra," said Javier.

"Ooh-ra, indeed," said Grunewald. "You've achieved something here today. The occasion should be duly noted. Who here is wet?"

We all raised our hands.

"Who here is cold?"

Again, everyone.

"All right, fall in," he said, and he headed off down the trail, and we followed, single file. He led us down the hill to the dorms, where he had us grab our swimsuits and asked us to meet him in two minutes at the head of the Bayberry trail, which lead to the eighteenth fairway. It was probably thirty-five degrees out. We marched across the overgrown soggy grass, still green, the damp wind off the ocean blasting our exposed skin, swimsuits poking out of our jacket pockets. Since we were no longer sprinting around the airport field, or carrying Grunewald around on our shoulders, the icy air was slowing us down, sapping our energy, and no one was talking.

He steered us to the left of the main clubhouse, to a brick building with a modest sign over the door: WHALEBACK ATHLETIC ASSOCIATION. He patted the snap pocket on the left side of his coat, found his keys, and we mashed together for warmth as he unlocked the door. Aubrey's face was near mine, and I felt her breath.

Among the lobby's white marble floors and brown leather armchairs and couches, Grunewald told us to head into the respective locker rooms and change into swimsuits.

The men's locker room had brightly shellacked benches beside chestnut lockers and white-and-blue checkered tile floors. The accommodations in the dorms were nice, fine, simple, but the aesthetic here was godly, pearlescent, a cool-clean narcotic. My whole body relaxed.

When we reassembled in the lobby, the girls were already there, all of us now in our bathing suits. Grunewald was wearing a neoprene wetsuit top.

Tess said, "No fair. Why do you get to wear that?"

"'Cause I'm fucking older than you. Almost fifty years closer to death. Now zip me up."

He turned around and Tess grabbed the long zipper tail and pulled it up toward the back of Grunewald's neck.

"Start running in place," he said.

We faced him and started quietly jogging.

I started to feel pinpricks of sweat in my hair.

"All right, jumping jacks," said Grunewald. "And repeat after me: '*We are the winning team!*'"

"*WE ARE THE WINNING TEAM!*"

"*This is what we scream!*"

"THIS IS WHAT WE SCREAM!"

Grunewald hesitated. We continued our jumping jacks until he thought of the next line. *"Janowski is a wimp!"*

"JANOWSKI IS A WIMP!"

We kept moving in rhythm as Grunewald struggled to think of the next line. Then Javier yelled, *"Grunewald is a pimp!"*

"GRUNEWALD IS A PIMP!"

Grunewald said, *"Sound off!"*

He'd given us numbers and we shouted them in order. I was four. Aubrey was five. She didn't say her number out loud, but she clapped five times, rapid fire.

We continued to do pushups and sit-ups and burpees and squats for twenty minutes, and were all pink cheeked again when Grunewald looked at his watch and said, "Follow me." Barefoot we jogged with him to the back door of the Athletic Association building. He propped it open with a chair, and we followed him down the stone walkway to the adjacent pier, with a ramp down to the floats. The air was icy, but we were still warm from the indoor exercise. We circled up and continued to jog in place.

"One more team challenge, then we'll really be able to celebrate," Grunewald said. "Listen up. We have ten minutes from the time we jump in the water to be climbing back up that ladder."

He pointed toward the middle of the little cove where a boat just like the one we'd sailed was moored—except it had no mast and no rigging. Just the bowl of a boat resting lightly atop the waves. We all knew immediately we were being asked to do the same thing that Janowski's Huddle had been asked to do a month ago, when Delaware had gotten clocked on the head.

"No one can get a job with the Club unless you pass. It's doable. And if anyone gets hurt, which you won't, I'll personally fire up the chopper and get you to shore." We were all listening carefully, and his voice was loud and urgent: "No fucking around. Ten goddamn minutes."

From the side of the float, he plucked a plastic thermometer tied to a string up out of the water and squinted, drops rolling off its plastic casing. "All right, we've got forty-eight degrees. So we definitely fail the island test if we're not all out of the water in ten minutes. But also, we'll probably croak. So let's do this right."

"Agreed," said DeShawn.

"You going to keep the wetsuit on?" asked Javier.

"You got a problem?" asked Grunewald.

"Yes, yes, please wear the wetsuit," said Bethany.

"Yeah, don't take off that wetsuit," said Corsetti.

"Club says each Huddle is in charge of its own shit. So go ahead, unzip me, Maryland."

This seemed like a bad idea, but I said nothing.

"Whatever you say, dude," said Tess.

She pulled the zipper down, and he shrugged out of the neoprene as Tess pulled it off him. Grunewald was thin and strong for his age. Without hesitation he dove into the icy water off the floats. His head popped up like a harbor seal.

"Okay, my balls are in my throat," he said with shallow breath, treading water. "Let's get going." One by one we splashed in. My lungs shrank and my whole body felt like a cramping muscle. Once we were in, Grunewald yelled, "Sound off!"

"One!"

"Two!"

"Three!"

"Four!"

Aubrey slapped her wet hands together five times, her face oddly joyful, wet hair flat against her head, large green eyes wide open. Blue-tinged lips.

"Six!"

"Seven!"

"Eight!"

We swam out to the boat, gripped the gunwales on either side. "Now get in," he said. His voice even lighter now. He was just a few feet away, treading water, as we wiggled ourselves up into the boat's cockpit.

"All right now, everyone get on to the starboard side," he rasped. We banged into each other like bowling pins. "Starboard, starboard. Where Utah is, you fucks."

With all eight of us on one side of the boat, it began tipping over, but it wasn't until the next direction—"Now stand up on the rail"—that the other side of the boat slid so far out of the water that it was directly above head.

Grunewald said, "Now . . . grab . . . the port side . . . that's the other side you miserable cocksuckers . . . when the boat flips."

The bottom of the boat swiveled further, darkening the water, like a dome quickly covering us up. We all pushed ourselves away from the rail at the last second to avoid getting hit. The boat completely turtled, and I heard splashing on all sides.

"Sound off!" Grunewald sputtered.

I said my number and Aubrey clapped. Then quiet.

"WHO'S SIX! . . . WHO'S SIX! . . . WHO'S SIX!," screamed DeShawn.

"Javier," sputtered Bethany. We could hear him, a muffled cry beneath the capsized boat.

Grunewald grunted and upended himself like a dolphin and we watched his blurry body disappear beneath the boat.

He hauled Javier out—bear-hugging him from behind, his stubby blanched fingers clamped around Javier's slick chest—and when their heads came above the surface, Javier spat water and continued shouting. "FUUUUUUUCK!"

Grunewald coughed and spat.

Javier started swimming toward the float.

"Javier, we need you," said Tess. "We fail without you."

Grunewald's chin was beneath the surface. Water sluiced off his slippery head, and he looked even more gaunt and pale and cadaverous than usual. His wide black eyes showed he wanted to speak but couldn't. The cold had chilled his brain. He muttered a feeble "hey" again. This was somehow enough to get Javier to turn around, and we cheered him on as best we could through our numbing lips.

"START . . . TELLING . . . ME . . . WHAT . . . TO . . . DO!" Javier screamed.

"I . . . this . . . boat . . . ," sputtered Grunewald.

DeShawn tried climbing up the overturned boat, his long-out-stretched fingers slipping on the bottom paint.

"How long have we been in the water?" asked Tess.

"Mah," said Grunewald. His eyes seemed to be losing their focus.

I felt my heart beating beneath my thin cold skin. We all started shouting, raking our fingers on the hull of the boat, one by one we tried scuttling up its side, no one able to get purchase.

"Fuck, fuck, fuck," yelled Bethany.

"We're cooked," said DeShawn.

Aubrey clapped her hands fiercely together, then grabbed the side of the boat. We followed. We needed guidance, we needed it fast, and Aubrey was offering it. We all put one or both hands on the slippery hull of the turtled boat. She was pressing down on the side of the boat, so we pressed down, too. As the far side of the boat started coming out of the water, Aubrey grabbed the thin piece of wood that ran down the center of the boat's bottom. So we all grabbed it and hung on, and the boat continued to slowly and miraculously turn through the icy water. Once the boat flipped, we all pulled ourselves up and tumbled inside, clutching each other: taut cold slippery bodies, an involuntary group hug, like iron shavings leaping to a magnet. My chest pressed against Aubrey's back, and I could feel her heart thumping. DeShawn and Bethany were wedged against me, and they could probably feel my heart, too.

At some point Grunewald had flailed his way back to the Athletic Association float. His bald head was resting against the ladder, one of his mangled hands was raised, propped on a higher ladder rung, keeping him afloat.

Corsetti dove in first, and one by one the rest of us followed, swimming toward Grunewald. Tess was the strongest swimmer among us and when she reached the float, she launched herself up out of the water without the help of the ladder, and from the float, she tried to pull him up by grabbing him under the armpits. He grunted and barely moved. Corsetti and I were next on the dock, then DeShawn and Aubrey. With two of us on each armpit we hauled Grunewald up out of the water, his legs slowly kicking, and when we got him on the floats, his pink feet on the wooden planks, he pushed us away, and staggered toward the ramp. His swimsuit hung low on his boney hips.

"Grab him!" said Tess.

Once we got him back into the middle of our group and pressed our bodies against his, he growled, his watery blue eyes blinking in anger, and he managed a few rubber-mouthed words—"stop" and "no" and "go"—which only got us all to press more tightly against his zombie movements, and DeShawn and Corsetti were giggling nervously, which got the rest of us giggling, and this laughing and shivering, as a blob of flesh on the floats, must have accelerated the warming process for Grunewald, because it wasn't long before he managed to say, "Let . . . go of me . . . assholes . . . go . . . inside!"

We carried him toward the building. He resisted at first, slowly flailing his legs, but then he succumbed to the care, one arm around Corsetti and the other around DeShawn. Bethany and I each had a cold solid leg, and we got him up the ramp and across the pier and back into the Athletic Association building, which didn't seem so cold anymore, and once inside Grunewald started giving us directions—"left!" "straight!" "left!"—soon we were all in the men's shower room. We lowered him down onto his feet and he stared at us, disoriented but trusting. And we all stared back, hunched shoulders, shivering, numb toes splayed on the cold tile. He padded over to one of the fancy chrome fixtures, and with one of his gnarled hands he opened it up, testing the temperature, then folded his arms on his chest.

DeShawn opened up one of the other fixtures, putting his flat palm into the stream of water. "Ow. Fucking ice."

We let the water run. Grunewald stood there, inscrutably.

"You want us to take cold showers?" asked DeShawn.

Grunewald said nothing. He moved his gaze up to the ceiling, and we looked up there, too. Satin brickwork of white tile.

Bethany and Aubrey and Tess and Bianca huddled together, shivering, their toes probably stinging with regained feeling just like mine.

DeShawn piped up. "Wait a second. I feel something." He kept his open palm in the jet of water. "Fuck yeah, fuck yeah, fuck yeah!"

Tess jumped over to Grunewald's fixture and she and Grunewald both felt the water. "Maybe you're not the sadist we thought you were after all."

We each rushed to a showerhead of our own, turned them all on, and within a few minutes, we were pillowed in a dense cloud of steam. Pummeling water pressure. Glorious warmth that filled my head—my eyes were closed—with an orange color. The capsize drill faded from memory. Javier started singing.

"Amazing Grace, how sweet the sound, that saved a wretch like me . . ."

Bethany picked it up, much louder: "I once was lost but now I'm found, 'twas blind but now, I see."

"Yeah? I can't see shit!" shouted Tess, which got everyone shrieking. Bianca started dancing. After all my years playing hockey, this was the first time I'd wanted to shower with a team.

Tess and Aubrey were across the room from me, and through the billowing steam I saw Aubrey in her navy-blue swimsuit, stooping a bit to get fully under the shower fixture, letting the water thunder down on the crown of her head, hair plastered to her scalp, eyes closed. Just like when she'd jumped into the icy water, she looked content. An unfamiliar thought jumped into my mind then: I would do anything for her, and I felt insane with the need to keep her all to myself.

Tess danced with Bianca, and Grunewald, who we'd thought was a goner, was smiling.

Tess said, "Are you okay, dude?"

"Fine," he barked.

"I'll personally fire up the motherfucking chopper and get you to shore if you aren't," said Tess.

"I'm fine."

Tess asked him to dance, he shook his head, so we all started chanting, "GRUNEWALD! GRUNEWALD! GRUNEWALD!"

To get us to stop Grunewald shimmied his shoulders, which got the loudest cheers of all.

31. All I Need is a Cigarette

Most of the drive back from Minnesota was tense since I couldn't easily check how my father was faring in the footwell while he slept atop the hospital pillows. But for a few minutes early on, the sun was low in the sky behind me and the fields of soybeans looked golden, flooding me with optimism, allowing me to entertain the possibility of returning to Minnesota at some point under my own steam. It seemed feasible. Getting far away from the coast, disappearing into the verdant intelligence of those rolling fields. After the sun set behind me, I called out to my dad and heard nothing in response which just made me drive faster, and after several minutes of white knuckling at ninety in the school's truck I pulled over, shook my father awake, and gave him a sip of water. He said he was totally okay.

At one anxious moment in western Pennsylvania, I drove to an emergency room, and when I pulled up and told him where we were, he said he wouldn't go in. I stood outside the truck, talking to him through the partially open door, the blanket pulled up over my dad's chin, his head pinned against the side of the grooved footwell. "I'm totally okay. I'm getting to really like it back here," he said.

"Do you want to get out to pee, at least?" I asked. Pee stops had been a challenge.

"All I need is a cigarette."

"If I can't take you in to see a doctor, then you can't have a cigarette."

He was quiet in the footwell. I didn't want to see his face. Finally, he muttered "Fuck this," and I did my best to not take it personally. We kept driving.

32. Pendrick Room (Members Only)

Whaleback Island

We got dressed and gathered again in the lobby, where Grunewald met us and announced the celebration would continue—we were the last to complete the capsize drill. MacLean and Brevard were thrilled. They were inviting some of their friends out to the island for a party in our honor.

He brought us down a hallway past the squash courts to a room that looked similar to the one where convocation had been held, except this one was even fancier, with silver chandeliers, wingback chairs, and a mammoth gleaming table. Beside the double doors into the kitchen was another door, this one stained dark with a brass pull handle. He opened it, revealing maroon-carpeted stairs with a brass handrail. This didn't seem like it fit on the same island we'd been living on. We ascended the stairs together, the tromping of our feet on the treads the only sound, and at the top of the stairs was another locked door, this one with a sign that read: PENDRICK ROOM, MEMBERS ONLY.

Grunewald unlocked the door and let us in.

This room, too, had wingback chairs and a long, shellacked table, and mounted on one wall were club member photos from every year in simple black frames. The early years, 1920s through 1950s, captured only men in suits and hats, two rows, then later the women were included, everyone dressed in their finest, tuxedos and ball gowns, the photos still in black and white, the expressions just as severe. I inspected the photo taken the year I was born, moving my face close to those in the photo. The sharpness of the detail was remarkable. The Club members looked tan, well-rested, well-fed, happy but serious. The photos had probably all been taken around Labor Day. In each of their eyes I could detect an unquestioned sense of belonging and purpose. The moment of the photo was like all moments for them on the island. It was elemental and pure to digest, everyone had an easy relationship with wood and rock and ocean and sky, their expressions were not boastful but calm, part of the island's confidence and vigor. Paul Brevard, back row, third from the left, dark brown hair with a widow's peak, lips thicker than now. The thought of him in a position of power, the thought of him "taking care" of everyone, seeing his pleased, sated face—I remember it made me want to punch him. And he was surrounded by other white faces with symmetrical features, the good hair and the sepia-toned bald heads, the crisp collars and bow ties, the silky, wet-looking dresses, well-fitting but, in my mother's words, "honest." Year to year, one could track the new Club members and old ones who'd died, and this made the life cycle seem organic and dignified. The new ones appeared, toned by Ivy League crew teams, while the old ones drifted off to sleep in immaculate cotton sheets. After death, they'd floated out to sea, maybe torched on a pyre, but they would be long revered on the island with engraved granite benches on the back shore.

There were plate-glass windows on either end of the room: one looking out on the golf course, the other looking out to sea. Between golf and sea were the Club member photos and, on the opposite wall, an ornate, hand-drawn family tree, with the founders at the top:

KEITH · BUCHANAN · MACLEAN · BOYD · BANNERMAN · ABERNATHY · ERSKINE · KINNAIRD

The calligraphy markings filled the wall, and from a distance the pattern of names and dates looked like some kind of cave painting or the stone etchings within an Egyptian tomb. Next to the long table was a sideboard with decanters of brown liquor, crystal tumblers. We floated around the room in the glowing natural light from the windows. The portraits were irresistible. Pouring over that silver archive was the first time since the previous spring I actually felt like I was at school again. They were not dressed as formally as those in the other photos—they wore canvas jackets, shirts without collars, and tall leather boots. Spruce trees filled the background. What was most striking were their burnished, stoic faces and illuminated eyes. All eight were ram-rod frozen, their faces dead serious. Written in ink, in all uppercase letters on the matte within the frame: THE FOUNDERS.

"The kilt-wearing motherfuckers," Corsetti said. "Sans kilts."

"They lived off the land," said Grunewald. "And they answered only to their own consciences. Started this place from nothing." Grunewald stacked tumblers on the table and poured nine tasting portions from a nearly full decanter.

Tess asked, "Where's Awanata?"

"She's cooking those guys their dinner," said Javier.

"Not funny," said Bethany.

Javier said, "B, you're getting more mouthy. I like it."

"Fuck yourself," said Bethany. "And there's Awanata. Right there."

Beside the Founders, within its own frame, was a photo of a woman with long black hair, a gray wool jacket, long wool skirt, and ruffled white blouse, flanked by six children, four boys and two girls, their names written on the matte: *Elizabeth, Cael, Emily, Alec, Skye, Andrew.*

Beside them was another portrait of eight young dirty faces, smiles with missing teeth, sturdy bodies in work clothes, each of them holding a weapon or tool of some kind—an axe, a cudgel, a machete, a shillelagh, a bow, a cutlass. Two of them were wearing kilts and their legs were muscled tree trunks. The photo wasn't labeled with individual names. All it said was GALLOWGLASS.

Corsetti pointed at that frame, his dirty nail clicking against the glass. "Here are the kilts."

"Looks like they're the ones who got shit done," said DeShawn.

"Didn't Davis Keith say something about them on the first day?" asked Bethany.

"No clue," said Corsetti. "But I like the vibe."

"Who'd mess with them?" said Bianca.

"They'd be good at a party," said Tess.

"But they might eat your dog," said Javier.

"Or shit in your closet when you weren't looking," said Bianca.

It seemed to be important to Grunewald that we drink, so we did. We pulled chairs out for ourselves and sat, looked around, holding the glasses like we belonged.

"Look at yourselves," he said. "You've done good."

"Thanks, sir," said Corsetti. He raised his glass to Grunewald and swallowed the liquor in one gulp, crinkled his face up, blasted air from his mouth, and stretched out his tongue.

"This Scotch is like a hundred years old," said Grunewald. "That's the wrong way to drink it, Ohio. Not that I care."

"Shit," wheezed Corsetti. "Just tell me the right way to drink it. Oh God. I should probably burp or puke."

"Go with little sips," said Grunewald, pouring Corsetti another splash. "I don't like the taste of it much, but it warms the cockles."

"Has it gone bad?" asked Bethany. "Are you supposed to kind-of swirl it around in your glass and sniff it first?"

"If you want to be an asshole," said Grunewald.

Across the table sat Tess, DeShawn, Corsetti, and Aubrey. Clean hair, dirty clothes, smiles. By my side were Bethany, Bianca, and Javier. These people seemed capable of saving me from dying in cold water and other hazards. If the Club had unwelcome plans for us, it was these friends, they were the ones I wanted nearby.

Grunewald said, "It would be nice to be in charge, right?"

Aubrey was looking at me, and I looked straight back at her. If she wasn't going to avert her eyes, neither would I. She seemed to be looking through my eyes, past my cornea and into my vitreous gel, and she'd somehow caught a ride on my optic nerve and was hurtling through the synapses in my brain. I tried to reciprocate but couldn't. I looked at her eyes, the green of them, her dark eyebrows, and I could only see her looking at me. I couldn't see past her eyes.

"What do we have to do to be in charge?" asked Corsetti.

"Rule one, don't whine. Whiners are losers. Rule two, don't care too much about anyone else. Rule three, don't follow the rules."

"Really?" asked Tess. "That's your advice?"

"Yes," said Grunewald.

"Don't care too much about anyone else?" asked Tess.

"Outside of your Huddle, that is. Okay, I'll revise that slightly. Take care of yourself. Even if the people in charge have lost their way, there's some great history here. Self-reliance has always been important on this island. Hendrick Boyd and Awanata and their kids, they were survivalists. Those kids grew up, left the island, and ripped capitalism a new asshole. You know what I'm saying? They made a ton of cash," said Grunewald. "The Club, you know they want to use you. You're young and tough. They see you as helpers."

"You're damn right they could use us," said Javier.

"You just have to figure out how, and if you want to be used," said Grunewald.

The whiskey coated my throat and belly, and I looked around at the group photos, the proud posture of all of the members, their platinum eyes. From year to year, I could intuit the gentle passage of time. At the end of the row were the most recent photos, and I took those in, the gratified nonsmiling faces, a few light blazers, a few dark ones, elegant but not-too-fancy dresses. I moved back to the opposite wall where the names of the founders and their descendants were etched in freehand calligraphy from the ceiling to the floor.

We heard the loud crack of gunfire outside. DeShawn was closest to the window. He hopped up, and within seconds everyone else had their noses on the glass.

A Huddle was assembled on the floats of the main pier, all of them in bathing suits, including their leader, Lisa Henshoff, in a red one piece. She held a shotgun and was pointing it toward the dark ocean. It had started to rain. The sky was nearly black. Next to Henshoff was a skinny brown-haired girl I didn't recognize in a green bikini with a hand-held skeet thrower. On Henshoff's command, the girl threw a clay disc up into the air, out over the water, and Henshoff fired. The target exploded, scattering dust and shards into the waves. Next Henshoff handed the shotgun to the kid in the green bikini, and Henshoff manned the skeet thrower. She spoke to Green Bikini, then sent a target high up over the water. Green Bikini fired the gun, which knocked her off balance, and the target kept sailing, unscathed, until it splashed in the blue-black cove. The girl handed the shotgun to West Virginia. Green Bikini dove into the water, swam a full lap around the float, and climbed up the ladder.

Henshoff threw for West Virginia, a hothead in long black shorts who lived in Cook 2. The wind was kicking up, and the rain was heavier. He blasted, missed, and swam a lap. One by one each kid got a shot. None of them hit the target.

"They suck," said Javier.

"You know how to shoot?" asked Bianca.

"No. But I could do better than that."

"In a video game, maybe," said Bianca. "Definitely not in a bathing suit in the rain."

Henshoff Huddle started jogging in place on the float while their leader held the shotgun across her chest. Then the group ran in single file up the ramp and onto the grass, toward the path beside the Athletic Association.

Javier found a latch on one of the long thin panes of glass that flanked the plate-glass window. He swung it open, the cold wet air flooded in, and he stuck his head out and yelled in a booming voice, "You suck!"

Green Bikini, leading their Huddle, stopped. Those behind her bumped into each other. They craned their necks upward.

"*You* suck," she said.

"No, we don't," said Javier. "We just kicked Janowski's ass, and now we're drinking whiskey."

"California, pipe down," Grunewald said. "They're coming in here to celebrate, too."

Tess opened the window at the far end of the room and said, "We're Islanders!"

"To the Islanders!" said Javier, raising his tumbler.

Grunewald yanked Javier away from the window, poked his head out and said, "You guys can hit the showers. They're opening everything up today. We'll see you at dinner. In the nice dining room."

Henshoff yelled at her Huddle to keep moving, and they jogged up the rain-darkened trail toward the building's back door.

33. Banquet Night

Whaleback Island

Somehow they'd gotten a team of wait staff and the summertime cooks out to the island, and they'd gussied up the Bannerman Room—otherwise known as the nice dining room—which was as big as the gym at St. Bart's, but cozier and better lit, with a chandelier in the shape of a whaling boat twinkling above the long rectangular table, which fit all of us, each at an assigned seat. We'd gone from feeling completely abandoned in the late fall island chill to an all-out celebration. Golden and maroon hues throughout the room. For those of us in the program they had party clothes—they put boxes full of white shirts and grey pants for the boys in our locker room, and they had simple white dresses for the girls. They didn't have shoes for us, but we didn't need shoes. We came to dinner barefoot, and the radiators were on—epic heat, way better than the dorms—and two fireplaces added to the ambiance. The warm air smelled like roast beef and gravy. Joey MacLean and Paul Brevard were there with us, as were a few other Club members, maybe eight in all, slightly better dressed than us, the men in blazers, the women in sleeveless dresses, nothing white or cotton like the girls.

It was five-star, all of it—waves of scrumptious food, served in large portions, grilled cedar-plank salmon and pork tenderloin and roast beef, hot baked rolls with butter, spinach salad with bacon. They served us wine, red and white, which not everyone had a taste for, but everyone drank. The atmosphere was so different from how it had been for the last few months that it felt surreal: the warm yellow light from the chandelier, the heat on our faces from the fireplaces and radiators and wine, all of us freshly showered.

MacLean stood. We started shouting and cheering, even those of us who were wary of him, because the mood was so festive and untethered, and it felt good to cheer in the warm room. When we saw he was clinking his glass with a knife, we quieted down and heard the *ding ding ding* of the crystal.

"I have no big speech," he said. "I just want to say thank you for being here with us and for pushing yourselves so hard to succeed. I've asked Joshua Dellahunt, who many of you know as 'Mass,' to say a few words."

Mass stood and smiled with that big mouth of his and said, "Pretty fucking great, right? Can I say that?"

"Of course you can," said MacLean.

"Fuck yeah man, it's an honor, and I'm feeling lucky as hell. Today was hard but now we're here. I don't ever want to leave."

"Hear, hear!" shouted Paul Brevard.

I was sitting between Corsetti and Aubrey, and although Mass was a clown and a bully, what he was saying felt genuine and heartfelt. He said he loved his Huddle and sat down.

I couldn't stop eating and drinking. I'm guessing most of us were getting pretty loaded. It got even louder and hotter in the room, and when I leaned forward to catch eyes with Aubrey, she leaned forward at the same time. She was on the other side of Tess and the fire from the far side of the room reflected in her eyes. Her cheeks were red from the wine. I winked at her, and she stuck out her tongue. Then Corsetti elbowed me and pointed at the taxidermy Arctic Fox on the wall, and he gave it voice, speaking on its behalf. He complained about being stuffed, wished he could keep playing golf, keep fucking his sister and his mother, and I laughed until it felt like mashed potatoes were coming out of my nose.

At some point Bianca stood up, her crooked teeth red from all the wine, and did that dance she'd done in the showers. We cheered her on, even when she stumbled and DeShawn had to help her back to her seat.

I'd just put down my dessert fork—they'd served us blueberry cobbler—when we heard a sharp crack and the tinkling of broken glass. The sound came from behind us. We all craned our necks, and within seconds five tall men holding AR-15s in front of their chests and wearing ski masks ran into the room. They encircled us. At first, we were all just confused. Shouts came from here and there, a scream or two, but then we quieted and one of the gunmen yelled "Stay in your fucking seats!" For a few seconds all we heard was the crackle of the fire.

I think right then a feeling spread throughout the room, from mind to mind, that if we were going to do something it would be best if we did it all together and without delay. When Mass screamed "let's go!" we all jumped from our seats and charged the nearest gunman. Corsetti was the first to get to the guy near our Huddle, putting his shoulder into the guy's gut, wrapping him up, taking him down, and the rest of us piled on top. The room was back at top volume again, all of us screaming, and even when we pulled the guy's ski mask off and he was smiling, telling us it was just a stunt, it was part of the party, we still came very close to ripping his face off.

The fake gunmen turned out to be young Club members. Soon they all had their balaclavas bunched atop their heads, revealing their ecstatic faces. They set their guns down outside the double doors and were ready to party with us. The guy Corsetti tackled was named Sergei. He had a dark-brown goatee and was out of breath from the excitement. He'd flown in from San Francisco for the day, was thrilled to hear how well WILD was going, did we want to have some cocaine? "Oh, shit, I shouldn't be tempting you guys, probably some of you are in recovery?" And he grabbed my empty wine glass from the table, filled it to the brim, and drank half of it. "To the fucking Club!"

Tess, who was still out of breath, said, "We could have snapped your neck. You're lucky."

Some of the Giant Boys on the far side of the room started chanting, "Islanders! Islanders! Islanders!" and then the whole room was yelling it, some of the kids were stamping their feet, and I looked around at our Huddle and sure, we were saying it too, but we all looked more stunned than anything. Corsetti was not chanting, and he looked confused.

When the chanting waned, Sergei drank the rest of the wine from my glass and grabbed a silver knife from the table and dinged it hard against the crystal. "Listen up!" he shouted.

For the fifth time that night the room quieted down.

"When I first heard about the program from MacLean and Brevard, I wasn't really sure what to think. Who would these kids be? How would they change our culture? Holy fuck, people. You're great. I'm a true believer now!"

34. It's Why I'm Here

The party lasted for another hour. We kept eating and drinking, and the room stayed loud. It was hard to get a read on how everyone else was doing, how folks were reacting to the traumatic event. I know Tess and Corsetti actually thought we were going to die, so to then be told it was just a party trick and that we should feel good about ourselves, was a little much for them.

Aubrey and I, though, were in another world. We went outside at one point and peed on the golf course, kissed out there in the cold under the three-quarter moon, and when we came back into the building, most of the adults had cleared out, though Grunewald was still there, putting logs on the fire. Some of the Huddles had gone back to their campsites, others were curled up in the corner on the leather couches. When Corsetti saw Aubrey and I were back, he grabbed us, said he'd been looking for us, said he wanted our whole Huddle to go back up to the Pendrick room. His face looked so different from how it had when he'd been performing the voice of the Arctic Fox. Tess too. We all marched back up the stairs.

"Where's that whiskey," said Bianca.

"Guys," said Corsetti. "We have to focus here for a second."

He was the only one really thinking at all. Most of us were just immersed in the party, or—in the case of me and Aubrey—falling in love. Corsetti had his mind on other things. He stared across the table at Aubrey.

"Brevard told me your mom worked here. Right, Aubrey?"

"Back off, dude," said Tess.

Corsetti pointed at Tess and said, "Hold on. Just let me ask this."

"Don't you fucking point at me," said Tess.

The room was quiet. Aubrey was staring at the table. Apparently Corsetti felt it necessary that everyone know what he knew, because he said, "Her mom died out here."

Grunewald set his drink down. "Your mother?"

"What was she doing out here?" asked Tess.

Tears pooled on the rims of Aubrey's eyes.

Tess turned to Corsetti. "When did you talk to Brevard?"

"The other night," he said.

"You swam out a third fucking time?"

"I'm sorry."

"What the hell is wrong with you?"

"I wanted our Huddle to stay on his radar. I had a bunch of good things to say about each of you. Like, if they're making decisions, they should choose us. He said he couldn't make any promises. And then he just told me about your mom, Aubrey."

Aubrey wiped the tears away and wrote in her notebook that she'd been told not to tell anyone about her mom.

"But then Brevard just goes and tells Corsetti?" said Tess. "That's fucked up. Why don't they want you to talk about your mom?"

"Maybe because she drowned," said Corsetti.

Tess glared at Corsetti. "Why don't you let Aubrey be in charge right now, okay?"

Aubrey took up her pen.

> *They told my mom she was the only living descendent of Awanata and Hendrick. That's why Joey wanted her to come out.*

Grunewald looked irate and confused. "Hold on, hold on. Patty Surette? That's your mom?" he asked.

Aubrey nodded.

"I met her," he said. "She wasn't here long. I'm so sorry, kid."

Again, Aubrey nodded.

Corsetti stood up from the table and began to scan the names on the wall. "Surette. Is that your last name?"

I'm sure we're not on there.

But like Corsetti, she dragged a chair from the table and stood on it so she could see the tiniest names written on the wall above the sideboard.

We all huddled behind Corsetti and Aubrey. I couldn't see much, the names and dates were written so small, but Corsetti conveyed what he was reading, that Awanata had married Hendrick Boyd in 1837. She was seventeen, just a kid, younger than all of us. Boyd was fifty-two. They had their six children. Awanata died in 1858 at the age of 38. All six of her children also died in 1858 at the ages of 12, 14, 15, 18, 20, and 21.

"That couldn't be right," said Grunewald. "You must be reading the dates wrong." He pulled his chair over to the wall, stood on it, and after a few seconds of study said, "Or how the dates are written? Maybe that's wrong?"

"Or 1858 was just a shit year," said Tess.

My mom said all of Awanata's kids were sent off the island to live with families on the mainland. So maybe they weren't dead. Just dead to the Club.

"They were sent off? Well, then, who taught everyone to hunt and forage and protect the island? Wasn't that their thing?" asked Javier.

"We can't depend on what they told us," said Corsetti.

"Maybe it was the Gallowglass," DeShawn. "Maybe they taught everyone."

"You should ask Brevard about that," said Javier.

"Are you fucking high?" said Tess, slamming her hand on the table. "He is *not* going to ask Brevard *anything*. No more swimming over there."

Aubrey leaned against Tess, put her arm around her and wrote:

It's why I'm here.

Everyone sat back down with their whiskey, looking around the room at the photos and calligraphy.

Finally Grunewald said, "Can I just ask you, Maine, what you mean by that?"

"What she means by what?" asked Tess.

Aubrey held her head up and looked squarely at Grunewald. He pointed at the last words she'd written—*It's why I'm here*—and asked, "Can you tell us more?"

Tess seemed ready to interject again, but Aubrey started writing. Everyone was leaning into the table now, heads close together, warm, reading what she wrote. She started with:

My mom cleaned houses on the mainland.

And she continued to write while we all read silently, that her mom didn't know she had anything to do with anyone on the island. She'd had no idea she was related to Hendrick Boyd or Awanata. All she knew was that she was Paul and Danielle Surette's daughter and that they were crap parents who did their best. Or maybe they didn't. Either way, the Club invited Patty out to prove they could be good to poor people, or at least that's how Aubrey understood it. And they hadn't been good to her, not one bit.

And what did it mean for them to be inviting us out, then? What did it mean for them to tell us they wanted us to be Islanders?

"No one wants to do anything good for us," Tess said. "It's not about us. It's about them."

When we all left the Pendrick Room, the weather had changed. The rain fell in sheets and the wind was swirling over the cove.

35. Depending on Undependable Men

Whaleback Island

We marched toward the eighteenth green, toward the Bayberry Trail, and Grunewald whistled at us, had us huddle up. He said, "I gotta talk to Brevard. You all stand by. I'll be back as soon as I can." He reached an arm out, clutching Aubrey, pulled her against his side and squeezed her awkwardly. He released her and before we continued up the trail, Grunewald said, "If you need me and you can't find me, check my cabin."

"Where's your cabin?"

"Backside of the island. You'll find it."

Then he headed back toward the golf course.

On our walk to the dorms, above the whine of the gusts, we heard a loud crack, like a lightning strike, but it was a tree branch snapping and falling to the ground twenty yards behind us. We picked up our pace. Tess was out in front, and we followed her through the rain and the howling wind.

No one said this out loud but it was clear we wanted to stick together, and if we were being given time off, we would spend it eating and resting. So we stuffed our sleeping bags in our plastic-lined canvas rucksacks and went to the galley together, grabbing a two-pound bag of granola, eight plastic bowls and spoons, a ziplock full of powdered milk, and a jug of water. We headed out to the lean-to. Those Club members, the young ones who'd run the banquet and the fake siege, were surely still on the island, and we wanted nothing to do with them. The wind was still screaming, and the rain hit us sideways, but the lean-to was dry. The campsite, situated as it was between a dense pine stand and the rock outcrop, was sheltered from the wind. We tucked our wet rucksacks under the eaves and spread out our eight sleeping bags. Javier divvied the granola into the eight bowls, funneled the powdered milk into the water jug, held his palm over the top and shook it up. He poured the cloudy mixture into the bowls.

I was still a bit dizzy and warm from the whiskey. We all probably were. We shoveled the granola into our mouths, chewing and chomping and making little contented grunting sounds, mixing with the sound of the wind and rain in the trees. Once we were done DeShawn stacked the bowls and tossed them outside. We were then able to do what we'd been looking forward to doing for the last hour, which was to recline with full stomachs.

With all eight of us lined up inside the lean-to, there wasn't a ton of room but there was enough. I used my jacket as a pillow. Tess asked Aubrey if it was okay to ask more about her mom and Aubrey nodded, so Tess asked questions and Aubrey answered them in her notebook. Bethany read her answers aloud as she scribbled them. What we learned then about Aubrey's mom had nothing to do with the Club, it was all about her life before she'd been tracked down by them, that Aubrey and her mom had spent most of Aubrey's life in and around Ellsworth, Maine, where she'd gone to school, and that her mom had bad luck with men but also bad taste in men, including her father who Aubrey had never known, and that her mom apologized for this, and for how many times they'd moved from apartment to apartment, but she never did anything about it. She kept depending on undependable men, and Aubrey had gotten really sick of this. She'd spent weeks at a time living at her friend's house, a friend she ran track with. Track, winter and spring, gave Aubrey something to rely on, the meets and the practices, the work she did on her own behind the fire station, throwing and retrieving the javelin and the discus. She ran the four hundred, too. Her mom supported this when she could, which wasn't always, but at least she never kept Aubrey from staying on the team. It had bothered Aubrey's mom that her daughter was different from her. It had bothered her that Aubrey was driven and focused, or at least it seemed that way to Aubrey.

The rain kept pouring down and the wind was snapping branches, and it continued to feel miraculous that we were all warm and dry. Aubrey got tired of writing, and maybe also of trying to describe her mom to people who would never know her. Her last scribble in the notebook was:

Rambo, Walt?

Because of the whiskey and granola and because we were nestled, safe from the storm, I really didn't want to get up. But I did. Tess said she'd time me.

36. Target Practice

Whaleback Island

The next morning, the sun was shining and the pine branches were covered in frost. We headed back to the dorms and listened for Grunewald to ring the bell in the Cook common room, but he didn't show. Tess suggested we go out on our own and run a half-island. When we assembled on the trail DeShawn said, "Remember on that first day how Bianca asked if she could puke?"

We stopped at the Chapel to stretch. We'd done this before; the Chapel was a mile into the half-island run, and the canopy was thick enough that the ground encircled by the big blocks of granite was relatively dry. Javier had been the one to tell us it was better to stretch after you'd run a few miles, which Grunewald said was stupid, but eventually he'd started going along with it. We put our feet up on blocks of granite to stretch hamstrings, or steadied ourselves against the blocks to stretch quads.

After the run we swam at Osprey Cove. When we swam as a Huddle with Grunewald, we wore suits, but this time we skinny dipped, and we did it quickly and modestly and said nothing about it.

The wind had started to pick up again, even amid the trees, where we gathered to undress. Osprey Cove was a better place to swim than Bridget Point because of the soft grass that grew on the ledge where we jumped. Iron rungs bolted to the granite helped us climb back out as quickly as needed.

One by one we jumped, and those waiting to go next stayed dressed and huddled under the high spruce branches, out of the wind.

When each swimmer came back to the circle, tight-skinned, they'd get their clothes on before the others would smush around them and help them regain their warmth. I went in after DeShawn and was the last to go. I hesitated in the grass above the wind-whipped water. My feet were already numb. The spot by the ladder was one of the places that Aubrey and I had been naked together, and I knew I would soon get warmed up by her and the rest of the group so I stepped out into the air, holding my breath on impact, full-body plunge, hammered by the water that gripped my chest. My blanched hands grabbed the rusted iron rungs drilled into the granite. I pulled myself out into the warm-seeming air, stepped into my shorts, and within seconds the group was gathered around me.

Without Grunewald telling us what to do, we decided to jog back toward the lean-to so we could build a fire.

The rain stopped for a spell, and we were able to get the fire going but it was so smokey because of the wet wood, and we still felt restless so we went out looking for the other Huddles. We came back out the trail we'd cut, which Tess said we should call the Gallowglass Trail. We jogged past Big Rug and the dorms, headed out the Copperthwait Trail. I kept thinking we were going to run into Grunewald, that we'd see him jogging in the other direction out of breath, but we encountered no one. It was at the intersection of the Copperthawait Trail and the Perimeter Trail that we heard gunfire, which got all of our hearts going a bit faster, but instead of running away from the sound, we ran toward it. The booming blasts led us out to the Airport, to the fields where we'd played Forest Takedown, and there was Janowski standing beside a wheelbarrow full of AR-15 cases, and two of his kids were holding the weapons, shooting at targets set up in front of a berm on the far side of the field.

As a group of eight, we approached them slowly, not wanting to startle them. They were wearing earmuffs to protect their hearing, but Janowski seemed like he was on high alert. He noticed us when we were about twenty yards away, and he put his hand up to stop us. He didn't want us anywhere near his shooters. We respected this.

When Feng was done with his round, Janowski had him hand his gun to Kyra from Vermont and when Isabelle from Minnesota was done with her round, he had her hand her gun to Mass. Then he asked the new shooters to hold their fire. He took off his earmuffs and said to us, "You can't be here."

"But we want to try shooting," said Corsetti.

"Where's Grunewald?"

"AWOL."

"AWOL?"

"Not really. We think he's talking to Brevard and MacLean."

"No, no, no. Get out of here. You can't shoot here without Dick. You'll have your turn soon enough."

"Can we at least watch?"

Janowski looked annoyed but after a minute of deliberation he acquiesced. He was softer than Grunewald.

"You stand here," he said, behind Kyra. And then I could tell that he wasn't actually mad in the slightest. He was proud to be teaching his Huddle about this type of target practice. He even said it felt a bit like a graduation ceremony, so in that way, having spectators was fine.

Feng jogged down to the berm to change the targets.

Kyra from Vermont announced that she had to pee.

Janowski said, "You could have done that at any point during the last forty-five minutes."

"I didn't want to miss anything," she said, and she handed her gun to Olivia from South Dakota before jogging off into the woods.

The dense clouds seemed to be hovering there just above our heads. No rain.

"Safety on?" Janowski asked Mass, who nodded, but didn't double check, so Janowski walked over to get a closer look.

Corsetti said quietly to Olivia, "Can I hold it for her?"

Olivia shrugged and passed the gun to Corsetti.

Corsetti held the gun up and looked through its scope.

Janowski turned, and saw that Corsetti had the gun, and said, "For crying out loud."

Mass dropped the gun he was holding and grabbed the gun Corsetti was aiming.

Had Mass not grabbed for the gun, I'm guessing Corsetti would have just placidly handed it back to Janowski. But Corsetti really didn't like that Mass was the one to grab for the gun. So he resisted. And Mass was a lot bigger. And while Mass was ripping the gun out of Corsetti's hands, the gun went off. I guess it would be clearer to say Mass shot the gun, which is true, but afterwards we were all in such a world of hurt that no one was too concerned with the particulars.

The single round was fired in the direction of the berm, and Feng was still down there changing the targets. He got hit square in the thigh, and fell to the ground screaming.

We ran over to him. Both Huddles and Janowski. He was on his back, and I could tell right away that he was trying not to move his leg because of the shockwaves of pain. He had on his canvas pants. We tried to take them off, but this just got Feng screaming louder. The back and sides of the pant leg were blown open and Feng's blood coated the nearby grass. Janowski yelled at us for a belt. No one had a belt but Corsetti unsnapped his rain jacket and pulled off his long-sleeve T-shirt. Janowski twisted it, then wrapped it around Feng's upper thigh. He yanked it tight. Feng screamed again. Then, Feng pulled his breath through his clenched teeth and dropped his head back against the ground.

Janowski said, "I should go get someone."

"I'll go," said Corsetti.

"You stay right goddamn here," said Janowski, nostrils flared, the cords of his neck strained.

Tess said, "He's way faster than you." She was always good at this. She could stay calm and reasonable when we all needed someone to say and do the right thing.

Corsetti took off. We could have carried Feng somewhere, but we needed to wait to hear the directive. We were already right next to the helipad, and Paul Brevard's helicopter was there. We just needed to wait. It was hard to know if the tourniquet was helping. He still bled. You could see it in the pant leg and the grass. Feng kept his head on the ground and was making less noise.

I said to him, "They're going to help you."

"They're going to help you," said Tess.

"They're going to help me," said Feng, quietly, and to hear him say this frightened all of us, because Feng was so smart and cynical and was always two-steps ahead of everyone, and he didn't seem to believe what he was saying even though he must have wanted to believe it. His face was sweaty and pale.

Within minutes Corsetti returned, sprinting up to us shirtless and telling us between heavy breaths that the helicopter was inoperable and that we needed to carry Feng down to the docks by the Athletic Association.

Janowski barked back at him, not understanding what he meant by "inoperable," and Corsetti said it was what Brevard told him, and we were already gathering around Feng, picking him up flat, trying to keep his legs level with his head and his heart. This took six of us. I held his shattered leg. It was awful. It didn't feel like a leg. Feng wasn't yelling in pain anymore. We got him out on the trail and his body was heavy and limp, and we knew he was at least in shock and probably worse at that point, but we kept carrying him, kept winding our way on the wood-chipped trail. Tess kept talking to him, she was up by his head, through tears she said he was going to be okay and that he was strong and fast and young.

When we got to the docks, Paul Brevard was already in his boat with the engine running. He said he'd get Feng to the mainland as fast as he could. We assumed we'd be going with him, but he said no, he needed the boat to be as light as possible, but then he looked up and pointed at Mass and said, "You. Just you." He was moving frantically on the boat, making space for us to stow Feng on the floor in the wheelhouse. Tess asked him why the helicopter wasn't an option, and he said the starter shaft was sheared.

When we lay Feng down at Brevard's feet in the wheelhouse his face was fish-belly white, and he wasn't responding at all. We untied the boat and jumped off and Brevard opened the engine up and they roared out of the cove.

37. A Moment For Feng

We spent the rest of the day doing nothing. A break in the rain allowed us to get a fire going at the campsite, and the warmer I got—my boots were softening on the hot ring of rocks surrounding the burning blowdowns—the more vividly I imagined Feng's limp body at Paul Brevard's feet in the wheelhouse of the boat.

We lay in our sleeping bags, added wood to the fire. We no longer seemed to know how to tell stories.

We went to sleep when the sun went down, which was too early, around four-thirty, but we all slept. We woke at sunrise.

Tess wanted to see the kids from the other Huddles, and she wanted to find a way to communicate with them that didn't involve the all-gather horn. Arizona, another friend of Delaware's, was in Vancouver, so she was easy to find. Bethany knew her well, so she was the first to get a WILDer-to-WILDer invite to the new gathering place, the Chapel, and was told the meeting time, ten in the morning, which was when the Huddle leaders, aside from Grunewald who still hadn't shown his face, gave us a break. We could trust that Arizona would know the right way to get the news of a meeting to the rest of her Huddle, and that she would then tap someone who had a trusted friend in Henshoff Huddle, and so on. Arizona would know who would be sympathetic to having a meeting without any Club members present, and whoever connected with Henshoff Huddle would know, too. No one had seen Mass since he'd left with Brevard on his boat—and New Jersey wasn't gathering with the Janowski

Huddle either. Tess figured many of the giant boys wouldn't be interested in sneaking around behind the Club's back anyway, so the invites weren't extended their way.

At ten, WILDers from all the Huddles sat within the granite slabs of the Chapel. Pretty much everyone, except Mass and New Jersey and Louisiana and Montana and maybe a few others. The wind had died, the air was still and cool, and low-angled sunlight dotted our bodies through the pine needles overhead. The leaves from the few hardwoods on that part of the island had browned and were soaked from the rain.

Tess was the first to speak.

"Okay, so here's the thing. We all have our own reasons for being here on this island and staying here, and I'm not going to try to change any minds. But here's my truth. I believe Brevard didn't try hard enough to get Feng help. I believe Brevard didn't fly Feng in the helicopter because he didn't care if he lived or died. I believe he didn't want to show up on the mainland with a dead kid or a nearly dead kid. And I believe they knew Feng had cut ties with his family and that no one from home knew he was here."

The Chapel was just weathered granite blocks, but with the quiet breathing bodies it felt almost like a building. At the time I thought Tess was right. I still do.

"Whether or not you believe this, I think we should all have a moment of silence for Feng. As a way to say goodbye and good luck no matter what happened."

Clouds passed in front of the sun, and I thought about how far away I felt from my previous life. I'd been holding Aubrey's hand but when the minute of silence started, we both let go and closed our eyes. Sitting there on the damp, hard ground in my rain pants, puffs of raw chilly air came through the underbrush and reached my face. I felt like a tree surrounded by other trees, and my mind felt clear.

There was a decent chance Feng was dead. He'd been bursting with life just one day earlier.

One minute passed quickly. Tess said, "Thank you."

We listened to the wind blow in the trees for another few seconds, waiting to see if others would speak.

Isabelle from Minnesota, with brown roots at the crown of her head and platinum blond hair to her shoulders, said, "Feng scooted himself across that quarry cable and told us dirty jokes the whole way. He was smart and funny and nice."

Little Olivia, from South Dakota, who'd smudged a line of charcoal beneath each eye, said, "He taught me how to play cards. He taught me how to bluff. He was like a brother, and I've never had a good one of those."

Jacob from Nevada, who I'd never seen without his Oakland A's hat, said, "He was the fastest of us, but he always circled back to run with us. I think he just really liked being with us. Sometimes he said things that made it seem like he didn't like us, or was better than us, but the truth was . . . he liked us."

Olivia chimed in, "He loved us and we loved him."

Bianca's friend Delaware, who was really crying hard, asked Tess, "Do you really think he's dead?"

"I know it's awful, and I don't think we'll ever find out if I'm right, but I—for one—will be operating under that assumption. That he died and they won't tell us. You saw him. He'd lost so much blood." She bowed her head. "He was such a good shit. The best thing we can do for him now is be ready for whatever these motherfuckers throw our way next."

I think everyone in the Chapel was crying at that point. We were missing our friend Feng and feeling alone. We didn't know what happened, and it was unclear if we'd ever find out.

"Whatever you believe," said Tess. "Don't let them know. For now anyway."

Again she made space for others to speak, but for the next minute or so we just listened to the wind in the tops of the trees. "All right. Bring it in," said Tess. We stood and mashed together, put our hands in the middle, and those who couldn't reach put their hands on the shoulders of those who could.

38. Eddie Lyon's

New Hampshire

O nce the hospice nurses started their visits, my movements in my dad's house were contained by only two rooms: the living room, where my dad slept in a hospital bed and I slept on the couch, and the kitchen, where I would greet visitors and have conversations out of earshot.

If my mother and I were sitting together on the couch beside my father's bed and the topic of conversation turned to some boring logistical concern, I would just stand up and she'd stand with me, and we'd move to the kitchen. She let me be in charge. All I wanted in the living room were discussions about the spring fishing trips we'd taken on the St. Croix river during middle school; the hamburgers at Gilsboro House of Pizza; the pair of sneakers my father had bought at a yard sale for fifty cents that he wore for fifteen years; camping trips we'd taken in good weather and bad; the silent early morning preseason jogs we'd take before school, my father called them the Lardass Challenge; the butterscotch candies he kept in the left pocket of his parka for outdoor wintertime work; the year my dad and his brother were teenagers, and they were really into jumping from high places including the roof of their two-story house; that time a St. Bart's senior had plucked tulips from the garden by the flagpole to give to his girlfriend for prom, not knowing my dad was nearby, and would own the two kids for a week of "community service"; my dad's secret orders of Girl Scout cookies, which he'd eat three boxes of by himself on the afternoon they were delivered. All of those topics were fine.

During the third week of tending to my dad and not going to school, I started reading aloud the first chapter of my dad's favorite book, *Dune*. As I made way through the story, I underlined any passages that elicited a twitch of an eyebrow, a flutter of an eyelid, a wrinkle in my dad's lips. The cancer had metastasized and was everywhere, including his brain. Before I started the second chapter, my dad opened his eyes a crack and said in the tiniest whisper, "Smokes."

"Just a sec."

"Smokes!"

I left *Dune* with my pen wedged in its pages and went to check a few hiding places—right pocket of parka, never-used salad spinner, fuse box in garage—before I found a few in a soft pack in the top drawer of his dresser. I brought the pack and lighter downstairs, and when I sat back on the bed, my father looked up and whispered, "Walt." I stuck a cigarette in his lips and lit it for him. He couldn't inhale much but I could tell he liked the feeling of the filter on his lips, so I let it just burn there in his mouth. I was ready to catch it if it fell and I held a saucer beneath the ashes. My dad's eyes were tearing up from the smoke and I said, "Enough?" and he just closed his eyes. I plucked the cigarette from his mouth and stubbed it out. Unencumbered by the cigarette, my father said, "Let the nurses do all this shit."

"They're not going to let you smoke."

"Go. Leave. You fucked up. You have to dig yourself out of your hole."

"That's you, Dad. You're the one who fucked up." I wanted this to sound light, but it came out of my mouth raw and too sharp.

"Nope, that's not what we're talking about. We're talking about *you*. Walter McNamara. You need to go."

There was no hesitation in his words. His eyes were still closed but he spoke clearly with full breath.

I didn't heed his advice. I cut myself off from the rest of the world. I wanted no contact with anyone while I tended to him. We'd been back from Minnesota for two weeks, and I'd stopped checking my messages. I knew Alessandra was hoping to talk to me—after I didn't return her calls, she left messages for me in the letterbox on the side porch, and one of them said, "I'm happy to sit with you and your dad if you want." I'd thrown that note in the garbage, along with the others.

But after a few days, Alessandra's offer started to sink in. I was sure there'd be some benefits to having her stop by occasionally. At least she could shift the mood. We could play Scrabble while my dad slept. I didn't reach out to her right away. I didn't trust my impulse to invite her into the house. I also wasn't sure what my father would think, when awake, about having Sarah Shinwell's daughter in the room with us.

The next note arrived two days later:

> *If you need a break, come have dinner with me and my dad tonight. He's in town and wants to take us to Eddie Lyon's. We'll come by at seven and if you want to join us, just come out to the street. Love, Alessandra.*

I remembered what Alessandra had said about her dad, that he'd cheated on her mom, that he was entertaining, that they disagreed about everything but that he was decent company.

After retrieving Alessandra's note from the side door, I sat back down on the couch I'd been sleeping on for weeks. A thin whistling snore came from my dad's nose, his closed eyelids were milky blue. The updates I felt comfortable offering Alessandra were that I was going to do whatever I could to graduate over the summer and that I'd secured work with my mom's brother at the landscaping company. I tugged the blanket up so it covered my father's shoulders. He opened his eyes a crack and said, "Don't you have better things to do?"

"You want something to drink?"

"No."

"A smoke?"

"Okay."

I propped an extra pillow behind my father's head and set him up with his smoke, holding the saucer beneath it. Again, he kept breathing through his nose with the burning cigarette in his lips, then he closed his eyes. After I stubbed out the cigarette, he said, "Now, go."

"You sure you don't want any water?"

"Ice cube."

"Ice cube?"

"Crack."

I brought him half an ice cube, and my father sucked on it until he let it slide out of his lips and onto the blanket.

"You want more?" I asked, plucking the sliver of ice from the pilled blanket.

"No."

"You warm enough?"

He nodded. Then he asked, "What do you need to know?"

It was a lucid question, and I hadn't gotten many of those during the previous week or two. Was there something in particular he wanted to tell me? Or was this truly an open-ended question, an I'll-answer-anything-you-want kind of moment? Maybe, deep inside beneath the hard outer shell, he'd always been willing to talk. I watched him breathe. I realized I'd always wanted my father to ask this question directly and openly. It felt emotional and necessary. I was hungry for it.

I asked him, "What were you like when you were eighteen?"

"Marines."

"How'd you like it?"

"Pumpkins."

"You liked it?"

"Pumpkins."

I tried to smile. "Pumpkins?"

"Muffins."

This was the word my dad had been using instead of "slippers" during the last week. I pulled back the blanket and sheet, exposing his praying-mantis body, put the muffins on his feet, shifted his body to the side of the bed, tilted him up to a sitting position, put an arm around him, and ushered him across the rug to the bathroom.

When I'd gotten him back into bed and pulled up the covers, my father closed his eyes again and exhaled. His body had been a wide tree trunk for as long as I could remember. He was a guy who could lift a full-size snowblower into the back of a truck.

When my mom arrived, I told her I was going out.

"Where?"

"To see friends."

She seemed surprised as she unpacked a bag of groceries, but she clearly didn't want to show this surprise too much and didn't ask any questions.

At precisely seven o'clock, I slipped out the front door and there on the street was an idling silver BMW, Alessandra waving to me from the passenger-side window. She hopped out wearing a yellow sundress with thin straps over her tan shoulders, a cheerier outfit than I'd ever seen her in, and she reached out to hug me, not a bro hug but a real hug, and she offered me the front seat.

I climbed in next to her father, an enormous man—not fat, just thick, with a big head, and a wide smile.

"Paul Brevard," he said.

The handshake was titanic. I'd heard the term "butcher's hands" and now I knew what this meant. Meaty. Paul Brevard seemed like the kind of guy who wanted a handshake to really mean something, continents connecting after eons of drift.

"Thanks for picking me up."

"Glad to have the chance to take you out on the town. Sounds like you've had a rough couple of months."

I wore a blue button-down shirt and corduroys with a brown belt and brown shoes; more put-together than usual, but still underdressed. Alessandra's father wore a blue blazer and pressed slacks.

Eddie Lyon's was the place wealthy kids from St. Bart's would eat with their parents on special occasions—hockey and baseball players especially. The building itself was inconspicuous—plain brick façade, no sign—but inside was all dark wood, green felt, maroon velour, polished brass. When the host saw Brevard, his face softened and he guided us without speaking through a maze of candlelit tables and side rooms with gas fireplaces to a quiet, golden-hued corner booth. Paul Brevard slid into the far spot, his back to the wall, and Alessandra steered me into the bench seat facing her father. She slid in beside me.

A young waiter arrived and showed Brevard a bottle of wine. With quick movements he removed the cork and poured a splash into Brevard's glass, which Brevard sipped and approved. The waiter filled the glass and left the bottle. As Brevard poured some for both of us, Alessandra asked, "When did you order that?"

"Oh, they know me."

The waiter returned with foie gras, bread, olives, little meatballs, and roasted cauliflower.

"So, what has Alessandra told you about our leadership program?"

Confused, I looked at Alessandra, and instead of looking back at me, she just reached for my hand beneath the table and squeezed it, then rested her hand on my leg.

I said I didn't know anything about a leadership program.

"Well, let me tell you. I'm very excited about it. Has she told you about our island?"

"It's not our island," said Alessandra, but she was blushing and smiling, and I could tell she was slightly embarrassed but still excited about the topic.

"Well, Tuckaway's our island, sweetheart, and Whaleback is as much our island as it is the Keiths and the Wheelwrights and the Webbs and the Kimballs and all the others."

"My great-great-grandfather, his great-grandfather, he was one of the guys—"

"One of the founders," Brevard said.

"One of the founders, right," said Alessandra, "of the Club."

"Yes, of the Club, and of the culture out there," her father added, "which really needs a reboot."

She ran her hand along the top of my thigh.

"I think we should both join the program," she said, looking at me, her face and neck still flushed. She had the beginnings of a pimple on her chin. Her hand on my leg was totally distracting.

"No, no, no," Brevard said. "You're not doing it, sweetheart. The program is not for you."

"I mean, it could be. Why couldn't it be?"

"Well, for starters, you already have a plan for next year."

"Walt does, too. But plans can change."

What plan for next year had I told her about? Maybe at some point, I'd said something about college, but those plans were on hold. It wasn't even guaranteed I'd have my high school diploma by the end of the summer.

"So, wait," I said. "What are we talking about?"

She kept stroking my leg, so I put my hand on top of hers and held it there.

"It's a program I'm starting for folks roughly your age from around the country," Brevard said. "We're trying to recruit someone from every state. It's a leadership program. Akin to NOLS or Outward Bound but with a specific purpose. In service of the island and its original spirit. My hope is that the recruits, the WILDers, will really become an integral part of the community. Eventually."

"Self-reliance," said Alessandra. "Wilderness training. I actually think I would be totally into it, and good at it—"

Brevard laughed. "You'd hate it."

"And why would Walt not hate it?"

"Because he doesn't like shopping."

"What the fuck, Dad? I don't like shopping."

"Just . . . relax," said Brevard. "We can talk about this later. I really don't think the program would suit you. And you'd be taking a spot from someone more worthy. We're here to talk with Walt about it. Can we just . . . stick to that for now?"

She pulled her hand off my leg, folded her arms on her chest, and exhaled. "I think the program will be good for the island. Get some new blood out there."

"Thank you," said Brevard.

"I think a lot of my dad's ideas are just mercenary and greedy—"

"What?" he said.

"Hold up, I'm in the middle of complimenting you. I was going to say, a lot of your ideas are mercenary and greedy but *this* idea is pretty wonderful and generous," she said. "And . . . well—" I could tell she really did love her father, despite how much they bickered. The lush brown of their hair and eyes, and the energy of their conversational skills, their willingness to spar, belied their kinship. "—It feels like, finally, the Club is willing to give something back. It's so important! The whole island goes unused for nine months every year."

"You have a cell phone, Walt?"

"No," I said.

"Right, right, of course," he said. "You ever been to summer camp?"

"No, sir."

"Ever had a European vacation?"

"No."

"Dad, what the fuck?"

"And you have a job, right?"

"No, I'm tending to my dad right now."

"Right, exactly my point. You care about family. And about working hard. And God. And our country."

"Dad, you really don't know what you're talking about."

"What I do know is what I see at my companies, new hires coming in and being unwilling to work hard because everything has been given to them."

"What does working hard mean to you, Dad?"

"You know what it means. Putting your head down and staying on task. It's not that old fashioned of an idea."

"I think what you like is the chain of command," said Alessandra. "You want new hires to get hazed by long, monotonous hours of busywork. Like med school or something. The twenty-somethings you hire have a whole set of skills you should be valuing."

"Okay, hold up. Are you arguing *against* the need for the leadership program?"

"No. Camping on the island is a good thing, no matter what."

"This is the problem. You young people. Your bodies are unstoppable, but your minds are made of goo."

"My mind is not made of goo."

"They don't let idiots into Yale," I said.

"Of course they do. I'm not saying Alessandra is an idiot. But you've got to know, Walt, that elite institutions everywhere are full of frauds. Teachers and students. Lifeless, spineless turds."

"That's Yale's motto, isn't it?" asked Alessandra.

"Well, it should be. You'll go into those hallowed halls and be told there's only one way to think, that economic growth is bad, that abortion is good, that eating animals is bad, that letting people out of prison is good."

"Okay, Dad. Put your money where your mouth is. You can save me from Yale if you let me into the program."

"I love this! Finally, there's something my stellar daughter is unqualified for! We're not letting you in, sweetheart!"

"I am not unqualified for your leadership program. You're just being a contrarian ass."

"You've studied history in school, Walt?" Brevard asked, before taking a big sip of wine.

"At, um, St. Bart's. US history."

"You probably think things now are better than they used to be, right?" said Paul Brevard, scratching the side of his clean-shaven face with his pointer finger. Looking at his supple skin, his unwrinkled face, his thick coiffed hair, I thought about the impact money could have on appearance, if quality food and fancy memberships could lead to good looks or if it was all about the right genes. Brevard was benefitting from both factors, surely.

I wasn't convinced Brevard really wanted an answer, but for the hell of it, I said, "I think things are going to hell."

"You do?" asked Alessandra.

"Yup," I said.

"Because of the Clintons?"

"No, Dad!"

"He can speak for himself."

"I don't know much about the Clintons. I don't mind Al Gore, though," I said just for fun. I was barely aware of what was happening in the lead-up to the presidential race, though I'd heard Gore was ahead.

"Gore and Bush are both fools," he said. "But the fate of the world is not in their hands, it's in yours."

"Easy, Dad."

"I give us about twenty-five years, tops. Everything is about to go way, way downhill. On a global scale. Lots of reasons for this. Silicon Valley, globalization, wars in the Middle East and Africa, mass migration. But the one I'm focused on is that young people in our country lack toughness. I know what you're thinking, Walt. *Hey, I'm tough.*"

"I'm actually not thinking that at all," I said.

"Which probably means you *are* tough, if you're judging yourself harshly. Goddamn it, most of these kids who want to work for us are limp cheese. There's no 'there there.' No fight. We need to start over from scratch. We need to show the world, again, how things should be done. Do you know that people your age are having less sex?"

"Oh, great topic," Alessandra said. "Let's definitely talk about sex with my friend you're just meeting for the first time."

He didn't even glance at her. "On its face, it's not a bad thing. It's good that fewer teens are pregnant. And there's less disease. Not a great way to start adulthood, hog-tied by gonorrhea. But *my* takeaway from your generation's disinterest in sex is that you've got a death wish. If you don't want to have sex, you have no real investment in the survival of the human race."

"Ever heard of exponential population growth, Dad?"

Again, her father ignored her.

"Seriously, do you worry about this? The end of humanity?" he asked and poured himself more wine.

"I do, sometimes . . ."

"He's spending time with his dad in hospice," said Alessandra.

"I actually think we have a lot in common, Walt," said Brevard. "Any interest in college?"

"When the time's right."

I'd considered the University of New Hampshire when I'd thought it might be a place where I could play hockey, but UNH was only interested in kids who'd excelled in a good junior league and paid for it in cash.

"You get a scholarship, I can see making that choice," said Brevard. "Anyone paying for college these days, though, is acting foolishly."

"You're paying for my college," said Alessandra.

"Exactly. I'll be giving them six figures over the course of the next four years, and they'll be reinforcing the idea that it's okay to not make any tough decisions. They'll teach you about feelings. I'll pay them, and they'll help you learn how to limit free speech."

After the waiter left, Alessandra leaned over to me and whispered hopefully with her wine breath, "Let's just ignore him. Let's have a good time."

"Hey, no secrets. Tell me about why you got expelled from St. Bartholomew's," Brevard said. "My daughter is biased. All she told me is that you broke some windows. I figure there's more to the story than that. And just so you know, I was expelled from St. George's back in the day, so I know it's not a black mark on one's character."

"It was mostly just the windows, actually," I said.

"Good man, good man. Keep your secrets. But let me just say now, when I'm hiring someone to work at the fund, I'm looking for someone willing to make mistakes. Fail quickly, learn, move on. The squeaky-clean applicants, they're usually disastrous employees. They don't want to take risks, and they need constant direction. All they can think to do is eat what's being fed to them."

"Like the foie gras," said Alessandra.

"No, like the ducks who give us the foie gras. And that's the problem. People believe they'll be taken care of. All those shiny buildings out there and grocery stores and good plumbing, well, all that crap hides the fact we're still cavemen, we still need to kill or else we'll get killed. Knowing the truth is good for you." His large, soft-looking left hand rested next to his silverware on the white tablecloth, while his right hand kept making gestures. "Do you like to take risks?"

"Sometimes."

"We also have that in common, Walt," he said. "I'm going to tell you right now—and this is coming straight from the source—your life is about to change for the better. I will make sure of it."

"Dad," said Alessandra. "How do you know what his life is like now?"

"Not everyone has money like us," Brevard said. "Listen, Walt, my daughter is a brilliant, beautiful, compassionate person. She thinks you're very talented. She thinks you've made some mistakes, but that you'd be a star in our program. What do *you* think?"

"I've kind of got things set up already. I'm going to take care of my dad, and I'm going to work for my uncle's landscaping business."

"Landscaping is kind of a summer thing, right?"

"Yes." I felt a defensiveness creep into my voice.

"And your father probably doesn't have a lot of time left, right?"

"Jesus, Dad. Why would you say that?"

"I don't know how much time he has," I said.

"I'm sensitive to this. I'm just being honest. Why would we need to lie about this? Everyone dies. I'm sure your father deserves your attention. My ex-wife speaks very highly of him. Not that she can be trusted, but—"

"Don't be an asshole, Dad."

"Look, we'll keep a spot for you. No pressure."

"How much does it cost?" I asked.

"*Gratis,*" said Brevard.

"That means free," said Alessandra.

"Don't be an asshole, daughter," said Brevard.

I admitted that I wasn't familiar with the word.

The food arrived. Filet mignon, skirt steak, antipasto, some kind of creamy pasta dish. We all worked on our meals without talking. After a while, Paul Brevard took another sip of wine, wiped his mouth with his napkin, and said, "I know my ex-wife was sleeping with your dad for a while. Good for him. I also know she's bat-shit crazy, and he's lucky they split up."

Alessandra said nothing. She stared at her father, her ears turning red.

"Alessandra knows where I stand," said Brevard.

Alessandra poured us more wine.

My dad had once told me that the Marines had been like the father he'd never had. This leadership program wasn't the Marines, but I knew it could be a stopgap, an adventure, and it was free. It could be something I could say when people—including my father—asked me what I was planning to do in the fall.

Brevard cut himself some more skirt steak and shoveled it into his mouth. He let go of his fork, and it clanged against his plate. He put his right hand on his neck, his eyes bulged, his face brightened. He raised his other hand to his collar.

"Dad?" said Alessandra, reaching across to him, gripping his upper arm.

Brevard made no sound, but he flung back both arms, which seemed his body's way of indicating he needed more room to resolve the blockage in his throat.

"Dad!" screamed Alessandra.

She held onto her father's arm. I stepped out of the booth and tried to pull him out by grabbing one of his wrists, but he had his strong arms pinned to the table, his face purple, veins in his throat bulging. I grabbed him around the shoulders and yanked his man-weight from the booth, then wrapped my arms around him and with all my strength, thrust my balled fist up under his rib cage. Brevard started coughing violently.

As I was letting go of him, I felt his soft belly in my arms, my groin pressed against his backside, which is when Alessandra flung her arms around both of us and started crying.

Brevard took some deep breaths and wiped his mouth with the back of his hand. "Whew," he said.

We all sat back down. Brevard reached down under the table to retrieve his napkin. He drew it across his sweaty forehead.

"Oh, my god," Alessandra said. "That was terrifying."

Brevard's breathing was returning to normal. I grabbed my napkin from beneath the table too, and while I spread it back across my lap I noticed Brevard was laughing. Giggling. His face was red again.

"What, Dad?" asked Alessandra.

"I learned how to do that in college."

"What, Dad? What?" said Alessandra.

"The fake choking routine!" he said, cackling.

"Holy shit," said Alessandra.

"I totally got you!" he said, between gasps of laughter.

Surely Alessandra was convinced I would never join the program after enduring her father's prank, but I was brimming with adrenaline. I was out of breath. I felt angry and excited and alive. Somehow, I thought Brevard was brazen and interesting for having done this and not just cruel and manipulative and awful. I knew my father would never do something like this, and for whatever reason, it won me over. I wanted to understand what would compel someone to act this way.

Brevard wiped his mouth with his napkin.

"Walt, seriously, good job, you passed. Not sure I could have really offered you a spot in our leadership program if you'd done anything differently from what you just did. Terrific. Wonderful. Excellent. Hat's off. You fake-saved my life, kid. If I'd been actually choking, you would have done the right thing. That's how people live and die. With the help of those they can trust."

39. The End of Wait and See

Whaleback Island

In the midafternoon on the same day Tess gathered us in the Chapel, the all-gather horn sounded. When we got to Big Rug, the girl with short red hair in Janowski's Huddle, Bianca's friend Delaware, was at the door, ushering people inside.

Paul Brevard and several other Club members we recognized from Banquet Night were talking by the windows in matching long red parkas.

Nash and his Huddle came in off the porch, having just been in the water. They were wearing bathing suits and shivering, and as the last of them tried to pull the French doors shut, the wind caught one of the doors, whipping it hard against the outside of the building. The sound—like a single rifle shot—quieted the entire room.

I think we were ready to hear whatever they were going to tell us. And we were ready to keep what we knew to ourselves. The building felt like it was tilting in the wind. Nash and a few in his Huddle—Luis from Texas and Angel from Kentucky—went back outside, pulled the doors closed, and locked them with the galvanized bolts at both the top and the bottom. Everyone sat. Paul Brevard stepped forward, cleared his throat.

When I saw Brevard standing confidently in front of us, I thought of my father, and this made me feel a deep, searing sadness about his absence. I wanted him there. I wanted to show my father—to prove to him—that despite his flaws, he was a far better man than Paul Brevard.

"I have some good news to deliver," he said. "Billy Feng made it to the hospital, and he's in stable condition. The round that entered his leg passed straight through. Luckily it missed the femur and the femoral artery. His getting shot was a freak accident for which no one is to blame. His family will pick him up and he'll recover at home in Cleveland. Billy is a good kid, dedicated to the program, and had much promise. He will be missed. We pray for a quick recovery. We will carry on in his honor."

None of us spoke. Not a single peep. Brevard asked if anyone had any questions, and no one raised a hand.

Like Tess earlier in the day, Brevard asked for a moment of silence. We bowed our heads. But this time, Aubrey squeezed my hand so hard that her nails dug into my skin, nearly drawing blood.

"I have one more announcement," Brevard continued. "Mr. Grunewald has resigned."

Wind rattled the windows. I was stunned. We all stayed quiet, waiting to hear more.

"Not the best timing, I know. True to form, Mr. Grunewald actually swam out to Tuckaway Island to tell me this news directly. Apparently there was some urgency."

The spruce branches flailed against the windows.

"Mr. Grunewald was a stellar member of our WILD team. We must not let his resignation shine any negative light on his tenure. He didn't tell us why he was quitting, but we respect his choice. I know this is hard, and it will take time to adjust, but Mr. Grunewald was tough as nails, and he wanted us to succeed. As I'm sure he told you, as I'm sure all the Huddle leaders have told you, much of the work you'll be doing on the island going forward will be in pairs. We will teach you what Mr. Grunewald had hoped to teach you. We must work hard in his honor. And in Feng's honor. Grunewald Huddle, I'd like to speak with you now."

As everyone else exited the building, Brevard walked to the back corner of the room. My hearing felt muffled, and my balance was off. We all seemed jittery. We circled up with Brevard and sat down together on the rug.

"I'm so sorry," he said.

We stared at him, but no one spoke.

He scratched his ear. "I know this is all quite surprising for you. I was surprised myself. He's worked out here for over twenty years. All he told me was that he was tired."

We kept staring.

"Are you okay?" Brevard asked.

"We're upset," said Tess. "But I guess we're okay."

"We need you more than ever. Dick Grunewald wants you to carry on."

"What's the plan for us?" asked Javier.

"Just stick with the training regimen Mr. Grunewald designed for you. Everything can continue. Would it be helpful for me to assign you your pairings?"

We all looked at him blankly.

He pointed at DeShawn and me. Then Corsetti and Javier. Then Aubrey and Bethany. Then Tess and Bianca. "We'll get instruction for you very soon. For now, I'd say you should each create your own two-person campsite. There's more gear if you need it behind the galley in the sheds. We want you to know how to get by without getting minute-by-minute instructions, so this curveball may actually help you along. We'll be in touch. We're with you in spirit."

He stood up, brushed off his slacks.

"Hold up," said Tess. "So we're just on our own?"

"This is just another vote of confidence," said Brevard. "We believe in you." He walked toward the galley where the other Club members were waiting. He came back with four neck straps. "This way, we can help you when you need it. Buddy up. The next phase of training will start really soon."

As he and the other Club members filed out of the room, Tess shook her head and whispered, "What the fuck."

Aubrey looked catatonic, chin tucked against her chest. I put my arm around her, and she didn't budge.

I whispered to her, "Not good."

She nodded.

Javier said to Corsetti, "I'm camping with you?"

Corsetti said, "Camping with me and getting your ass kicked by me."

"In your dreams."

Tess stood up, waving us toward the door. We headed back out into the gusty wind. "Wait and see is over."

40. Fuck Off and Have a Good Life

T ess led our Huddle into the woods, where we collected the four neck straps Brevard had given us, set them atop a trailside boulder, covered them with Corsetti's rain jacket, and smashed them with a fist-sized rock.

"Cleveland," said Corsetti. "Feng would be fucking pissed if he knew Brevard said he was from Cleveland."

"Should we get the guns now?" asked Bianca.

"Not yet," Tess said. She circled us up and said we needed to find Grunewald's cabin. He'd told us to look for him there, and since we had nothing else to do and we didn't believe Paul Brevard, we went looking.

We headed out the perimeter trail to where the island emerged steeply from the water. The trail twisted across the top of the rock cliffs, an open dirt trail. As we walked and held onto each other in the gusts of wind, we peered up into the woods to our left, looking for any signs of Grunewald's spot. He'd described it to us many times. Said it was heaven on earth. Said it was a place to be truly alone. He'd said to us, "When was the last time any of you worthless idiots were actually alone? I mean alone, alone?"

Bethany spotted a thin stainless-steel chimney poking up amid the tops of the spruce trees. The cabin was made of rough-hewn logs, some with flakes of bark still clinging to them, and it was so hemmed in by the surrounding trees that it was invisible from the trail, and probably from the water too. Beside the cabin sat a bench in a tiny, four-foot clearing, where one could sit and look south at the open sweep of ocean. Grunewald had cut down a few more trees to create this vista.

DeShawn said, "Probably locked." But he unlatched the door, and it swung open.

Inside, a tiny, immaculate room—twin bed with sharply creased white sheets and gray wool blanket, a wood stove with a recently cleaned ash tray beneath it, blow-down branches stacked in a tidy wood box, a single chair and a clean wooden table with a candle and a box of blue-tipped strike anywhere matches. Next to the bed, a broom, a chest of drawers. Two hooks on the back of the door: one for hats and one for jackets.

The eight of us barely fit inside. Bethany and DeShawn sat on the pristine bed. Corsetti sat in the chair, Tess and Aubrey and Javier and Bianca and I bumped shoulders standing in the middle of the room. There were windows on three sides of the cabin, but it was still quite dark because of the surrounding trees.

"Check this out," said Tess, and she plucked a small color photo thumbtacked to the side of the chest of drawers—a boy in a little league uniform, kneeling, a bat resting on his shoulder.

Bethany asked, "Is that him?"

The photo didn't seem old enough for it to be him. I said, "Maybe his grandson?"

"Or his son?" said Deshawn.

"He told me he had no family," said Corsetti.

"He did?" asked Tess.

"Jesus, all I did was ask him," said Corsetti. "You could have asked him questions, too."

There in the middle of the woods, surrounded by lichen-covered trees and blowdowns, the place was spotless.

From the front window we could see the narrows between Whaleback and Tuckaway—six-foot swells, waves pummeling the nearby rocks.

On the table under the brass candle holder and beside the box of matches was a small white envelope. Javier snatched it, said, "Dude!" and handed it to me.

Written on the front of the envelope was HUDDLE.

With the letter in my hands, I felt a surge of fear run through my chest. I ripped it open and started reading it aloud as the others stared at me in silence.

> *Hello heathens,*
>
> *If the club ends up firing me and kicking me off the island you can do what you need to do with what I tell you here. Sorry to put it in your hands but you know what, you can handle it. I mean I know you Ohio, you're too impulsive and Maryland you're a fucking handful and New Hampshire you think no one knows exactly what you're thinking because you're not saying much but we do and Alabama and Utah you're too sentimental for your own good and California and Missouri, God bless you fuckers, it takes you a while to understand even the most basic concepts. Maine, I know you're strong but you're also fragile. Or maybe you're not. It's probably a problem I don't know, and you'll need to figure that one out.*
>
> *But as a whole, you're functional and competent. I'm sure about that. You're fine without me.*
>
> *Right now I don't have enough info about this army they're building. It seems like they want you to keep them from being killed. If you want to do this I'm guessing they'll take care of you, which means money and whatever else so you just decide what you want from life. They took pretty good care of me but you can't trust these people. I think they've gotten delusional. They never asked me to do what they're asking you to do. Do all the rich people in the world need their own army? Maybe this is what the world is now.*

I'm not about to offer any life lessons to a bunch of Godless 19 year olds. You'll figure it out.

But I've spent my life taking orders and right now I don't really need to, so I'm going to go talk to them frankly. I knew Maine's mom Patty Surette. Sedgewick is a tiny place, even Ellsworth is. They might have said they wanted her out here because she was a relative and they wanted to be nice. Sure, that might have happened. But most people in town knew she was pregnant when she died. That's the kind of story that gets around, especially if she was knocked up against her will. And if Maine didn't know that, I'm sorry, but there's probably a reason she didn't, and anyway, it just feels criminal to me that they'd have her in the program after her mom died out here even if her death was simply an accident. They shouldn't get away with a "we're just being nice" excuse a second time. I want to find out what happened for Maine's sake.

I've spent enough time with these people to know that when they want to be good to you, they're very very good but I know they're capable of all kinds of bullshit. They're good at changing stories. That's what they do. We're not idiots. I hope this letter is useless, and you won't ever have to read it.

Last thing, I won't get sappy here like Alabama but these months out here with you have been real. Fuck off and have a good life. Look after each other please.

DG

I was crying when I got to the end.

Aubrey grabbed the letter and looked at me the same way she'd looked at me in the bathroom of the clubhouse on the day of Convocation. She scanned the letter herself, turned it over, put it down on the desk, and with Grunewald's pencil wrote on the back:

I should have believed her.

Exhausted by the effort of writing this, she rested her forehead on his desk. We all put a hand on her back. She raised her head again and continued writing.

> *She told me this. She told me that he raped her. I thought she was just being dramatic. I thought she was trying to make something that looked like her fault—getting involved with Joey—into his fault. She always had excuses. But I should have believed her. It's my fault she died.*

Before she could write again, Tess grabbed her by the shoulders, pulled her away from the page, and hugged her.

41. Her Voice

As we were leaving Grunewald's cabin, I unpinned the Little League baseball card and tucked it into my pocket. Outside, we could see the channel between the islands, the bold shores of both, the wind blowing through, and the tide running against the wind, frothing up the waves. Aubrey pointed down at that spot—we were high above it—and she kept her finger pointed, and I knew this had to be the place her mother was found dead. Tess was the one to say it aloud, and Aubrey nodded.

"I mean, Grunewald might be totally fine," said Bianca.

No one responded, we just picked up our pace, ran back to the lean-to. Tess stopped Bethany from putting more wood on the fire—she said it was best to keep our campsite hidden until we could get some guns.

"Guns?" asked Bethany.

"It's time." She said we needed to get to the armory and fill a rucksack or two with handguns and ammo.

"Or just tell them we want to go home?" Bethany said.

"I don't want to go home," said Javier.

"Nope," said Corsetti, who had no home.

Aubrey shook her head.

Bianca asked, "Are we really sure it's as bad as what you're saying? Does that letter really change much? I mean, guns?"

Tess spelled it out for her, that Grunewald had swum to Tuckaway to have a conversation about Aubrey and her mom. He did this for us. He'd revealed what he knew to Brevard or MacLean, or both. He presented himself as a problem. and they removed him. And this could have been the same fate Aubrey's mother, and Feng, had suffered.

"But do we know for sure?" asked Bianca.

"We'll never know for sure."

"It would be better if we knew."

"We know enough!" Tess yelled.

"Don't look at me like that, fuckface!" said Bianca.

"I'll look at you however I want," said Tess.

Bianca took a swing at her, and she ducked. Bethany held Bianca back, and Aubrey grabbed Tess.

"We're gonna to do right by Aubrey," said DeShawn. "And Feng."

If we chose to get the guns, we knew we were officially turning against the Club, refusing what they were offering, saying no to their wealth and their lies. We put it to a vote. We all wanted to get the guns, even Bianca.

Corsetti volunteered to go to the armory, but we decided as a group to wait until dark. We figured we should eat too, and Aubrey put on her coat, quickly wrote in her notebook that she'd grab rations from the galley. She started down the trail and I ran after her. She turned when she heard me and I said to her, "I'll go. You stay put."

In the purple shadows, and faint early-evening light, she flipped me off.

"Seriously, I don't want any of us to get seen by the Club," I said.

She flipped me off with both hands. Then she wrapped her arms around me and squeezed, and with her mouth by my ear she whispered, *"Fuck off, homeboy, I got it."*

Her hot breath on my neck and ear, the timbre of her words clear and soft, I felt like I was drifting up into the trees. She was talking to me.

She didn't say anything more, she let go, spun around, and dashed down the trail with her rucksack.

I returned to the lean-to where Bethany was asking Corsetti to tell the story about cutting his wrestling coach, and Corsetti said there wasn't much to it, his coach had gotten in his face, had pushed him in the chest twice, told him he wasn't training hard enough, was being lazy, so Corsetti pushed him back, the palm of his hand hitting the coach square in the chest.

"And then you cut him?" asked DeShawn.

"Not then."

"When?"

"Actually, I never cut him. That was just something I said to sound tough."

"You lied to us?" asked DeShawn.

"Just that one story."

"So you're not the last Corsetti left?"

"Fuck off. I am. I told you, I only lied once. And I'll never do it again."

I wanted to say something then, wanted to chime in with support for my friend, but I couldn't summon the words, I was still stunned that Aubrey had whispered in my ear. And the further she got away from the lean-to, the more I regretted letting her leave to get food without me.

Bethany then told the circle that she'd never actually gotten caught stealing.

"Did you go to juvie?" asked Corsetti.

"I never told you I did," said Bethany. "The stealing was always a problem, but I never got caught. I should have, but I didn't. The most trouble I got into was for kissing someone."

"You got in trouble for that?" asked Tess.

"Have you been to Columbiana, Alabama?"

"Nope."

"Good place for a lot of things, but not really that great a place for a girl to like a girl."

"Preach," said Tess.

Without a fire, and far from the lights of the Club, the sky was jacked up with stars, millions and millions of glittering pinpricks.

"What do you guys want to do when you get out of here?" asked DeShawn.

"Eat a fucking pizza," said Tess.

"Oh, hell yes. A cheeseburger with fries," said Bethany.

"Supermarket cake," said Bianca.

"I'd watch TV for like three weeks straight. But if we're talking about food, I'll take a burrito," said DeShawn. "Doesn't last year feel like so fucking long ago?"

"What feels like fucking long ago is when Aubrey left to get food," said Corsetti.

I hopped up. "Fuck. I should go check on her."

"Dude, no. Stay here. We don't need two of you gone."

"I'll be right back."

"Shit, no holding back lover boy."

The beam from my headlamp jittered on the overlapping clapboards of Big Rug when I emerged from the trail. I was ten feet from the building when I heard sprinting footsteps in the darkness.

A body struck me from the left, blindsiding me, tackling me to the granite-speckled dirt, sending my hat and headlamp flying. Another body landed on me, pinning my shoulders back before I could get my bearings. The two of them grabbed my wrists, pinching them together with a ziptie. I bucked and twisted, flailing my legs, but they managed to put a hood over my head.

A voice said, "Gotcha."

42. Old Friend

Whaleback Island

The two who'd tackled me each held an arm and marched me down a trail. As soon as I heard them enjoying the way I stumbled on the tree roots I identified them as Mass and New Jersey. I knew the way they laughed. I asked them questions—"What's going on? Where are you taking me?"—and they responded by giggling and shoving me. After ten minutes or so, the terrain changed, we were moving across flat ground, then onto what felt like a wooden walkway, and then down a ramp, the wind gusting at my side, and then from the slight movements I felt in the ground beneath my feet, I knew we were on a float. The possibility of being thrown into the ocean seized me, but I heard a jangling of keys, and one of them was guiding my foot up, then down, and my other foot up, then down. An engine started. I was on a boat.

After less than five minutes of deafening engine sounds, strong wind, violent movements up and down and side to side, the throttle quieted, the boat became relatively still, and once again I was being guided one foot at a time onto new ground.

Another ramp.

Another walkway.

Grass. Steps.

A door.

Another door.

They were giggling again. I felt them cutting the ziptie around my wrists. They shoved me. I stumbled but didn't fall, banged my shoulder into a wall and my shin against something hard. I heard another door close. I ripped the hood off but was surrounded by darkness.

From outside the door, I heard Mass say, "The light switch is on the right side of the door. Change into those swim trunks."

"And if I don't want to?"

"You want to."

I groped my way to the light switch. The small room had a maroon tile floor, ringed by cushioned benches and brass hooks on stained wood. In the middle of the wall facing the door hung a red bathing suit. I took off my boots and my rain jacket and rain pants, stripped down, and put on the suit. I turned off the light and checked the door and was surprised to find it unlocked. Cold wind hit my bare chest as I stepped from the room, and before I knew what was happening, I felt them grabbing me again, one on each arm, pulling me out into the dark night. In front of me was the calm surface of water, moonlight reflected in its stillness. They flung me forward.

I braced for impact and plunged into warm water. It enveloped my body, liquid light and heat. I treaded water, blinked my eyes, looked up at Mass and New Jersey, who wore black watch caps and were cleanly shaven. They each wore a gray track suit and white sneakers. Mass said, "Asshole, swim over to the far corner." He pointed to the left of the diving board, where there was a tray with an ice bucket, a glass, and a bottle of Scotch resting on the poolside tile. I did as I was told. Mass walked on the patio, boots clicking on the tile, and met me in that corner, reached down to the tray, where there was a large mobile phone with an antenna between the bottle and the glass. He placed a call, set it to speakerphone, set it back on the tray and walked into the house with New Jersey.

The call connected.

"Walt?"

"Hello?" My face and my lips were wet with pool water.

"Ha, ha . . . yes! I can't believe it! You're in that corner of the deep end closest to the ocean, right?"

Grass blades in moonlight, fence, cliff, rocks, waves crashing against the rocks, everything in sharp focus. The voice was so recognizable, and as I stared at the stripe of moonlight on the ocean, I felt a chill on the top of my head, despite the incredible heat of the water.

"Alessandra?" I asked.

"I knew this would be fun," she said.

"Where are you?" I felt confused but also genuinely relieved to hear her voice. When I'd put on the bathing suit, I was sure I was going to end up tortured, thrown in the ocean, something awful.

"I'm in New Haven. Is my dad with you?" she asked.

"The guys who tackled me placed the call."

"The guys who—"

"—tackled me."

"Oh, man, I can't wait to hear more about the program! All Dad told me was that you'd be calling me from my favorite spot in the entire world. You're in my corner of the pool, Walt! Are you sitting in the seat?"

I used my knees to feel my way to the grooved underwater platform. I sat on it and let go of the edge of the pool, staying immersed in the water up to my armpits, steam swirling around my face.

"Dad made me that little seat. Now, pour yourself a drink and I'll do the same."

"No thanks," said Walt.

She laughed. "Walt. We're celebrating."

I was quiet on the line.

"Come on, man! My dad said you've absolutely crushed it out there. And I love the idea of you sitting in my little underwater chair, looking out at the ocean. So yes, we are. I'm so glad it's all working out for you."

"I really don't know what's going on, Alessandra. I've been blindfolded for the last half hour."

"Doesn't that mean they have a job for you? And they're surprising you with it? Oh shit. I hope I'm not giving anything away."

"I haven't heard anything about a job."

"You'll find out soon. I mean, I don't know exactly what they have planned, but Dad said it's good, because you've done so well. He said you're incredible, which of course I already knew."

I figured it was time to pour the drink. I put an ice cube in the glass and covered it with Scotch.

"There you go," she said.

I looked around. "Can you see me? Are there cameras?"

"No. Relax. All I heard was you pouring your drink."

I took a big sip. Hot pool, clear night sky, ocean waves crashing and retreating on the rocks, a cold sharp drink. I did my best to dissolve into the moment. Breathe.

"It is *so* good to hear your voice, dude. So many little things at school remind me of you. God, I've been dying to tell you about this mind-blowing class I took this fall. I thought I was going to love Comparative Women's History, or Italian, or Evolutionary Bio, and sure, they were all really good, but I had this dance class called 'The History of Your Body' and it totally made me think of you, and how much smarter you are about your body than I am about mine."

I couldn't even laugh at that, how absurd it was. I didn't understand what she meant by *smarter about your body*, and as if picking up on this, she said, "I mean, like, you're more in touch with how your body works. Probably even more so, now."

I wasn't sure why she thought that, but there didn't seem to be much reason to push back.

"I think I made some progress, though," she continued. "The class had some people thinking it was a dance class, but I think because of distribution requirements it also had a bunch of brainiacs, and they were totally confused by it. They couldn't just study their way through it, they had to be more, you know, intuitive. We spent a lot of time just moving around the dance studio with blindfolds on, running into each other."

"Yeah, you're right, I would have aced that class," I said. It had only taken me about a minute to adjust to the mode of conversation required by Alessandra: an economy of flirtatiousness, flattery, enthusiasm, and not listening too carefully. I took another deep sip of the Scotch. The melting water competed for space in my mouth with the sweet oily booze. I looked around, saw nobody between me and the house, and felt the chilling breeze.

"You really would have. It was very analog. That's what my dad would say. That's maybe the only positive adjective my dad would use to describe the course, if he ever heard about it, which he won't, because he'd have an aneurism if he did."

It felt like a hallucination to be there in that beautiful pool talking with her, smooth Scotch in my mouth. So I said to her, "It's hard to believe I'm really here."

"You're really there. Don't you fucking love that pool?"

"None of this feels real."

"You're living your life, man!"

I whispered, "Do you have any idea? For like three months I've been camping in the cold woods, running around the island, getting trained, and they haven't told us much at all. My instructor is gone. And now I'm here."

"Why are you whispering?"

"Do you—" I started to form the words in my mind. I wanted to confide in her—to tell her I was worried about the fate of my Huddle and Feng and Grunewald, and that I didn't know where Aubrey was—but I stopped before I said anything more.

"What?" she said.

"I don't know. It's weird to hear your voice."

"It's been killing me to not be in touch. Do you wonder what it would have been like if we'd actually gotten together?"

She was so good at this kind of game. I let her words hang in the steamy air above the pool.

"Why are we having this conversation, exactly?" I asked.

"What do you mean?"

"I mean, did your dad put you up to this?"

She was silent.

Finally she said, "That hurts my feelings, Walt."

"Well, it just seems odd that—"

"—the thing is, I *couldn't* call you until he asked me to call you—"

"So he *did* put you up to it. Why?"

"He did, but I was wanting to talk to you. Before he even asked me to talk to you."

"Okay, fine, Alessandra. What did you want to talk about, then?"

"Don't be huffy."

I started whispering again. "Can you just tell me exactly what he said to you? When he asked you to call?"

"Can I just say, first, and this is *me* talking—you're important to me, Walt. I love you, I mean, you know what I mean, you're like my oldest friend. We have all this history together, right?"

"We weren't friends before senior year."

"But we've known each other forever."

"What did your dad say to you?"

"He just told me you needed to calm down. You're an Islander, dude. You're a great story. He asked me to welcome you into the Club."

"That's what he said?"

"He said you'd be overwhelmed, and it would be good to talk to someone who knew you."

"And he thinks you know me."

"Is that a question?"

"No."

"Yes, he thinks this because I do."

"I should probably talk to your dad."

"Yeah, I get that." She was quiet for a few seconds. "But it looks like I'll be seeing you this summer?"

"I really have no idea, Alessandra."

Again, she paused before saying, "I'm feeling a little awkward right now."

"It's okay. Remember, your dad was the one who told you to call me."

"I meant what I said. You're a dear old friend."

"Yeah, you too, Alessandra." I wiped my hand on the towel and clicked the call dead. My heart was racing. I looked at the bottle of Scotch, at the bucket of ice, the tray, and beyond it, the waves in the moonlight, the moon, the stars.

43. Dig Yourself Out of Your Hole

New Hampshire

All I'd wanted were a few more minutes alone with my father. Just the two of us, alone. I crawled into bed with him. I knew I wasn't going to get what I wanted: clarity, understanding, assurance. My father hadn't spoken in days. But being there with him was what I needed. The rest of my life was stripped down, bare to the bone. Right then it was just the two of us on earth. In a silent house. Did I know my father? Did anyone know my father? Could anyone ever really know another person?

I was able to sleep next to him for an hour or so, until the gentlest movement of my father's head woke me up. His brow and his closed eyes showed some disturbance, something other than the perfect dream I was hoping for him, of walking through tall grass on a warm morning.

Or maybe that had been my own dream. I wasn't sure.

I tucked the same dose of morphine I'd been giving him for the past few days into my father's cheek, just as the afternoon sun could be seen through the campus-side windows.

That slight disturbance in my father's brow, the gentle twitch of the muscles around his closed eyes, a sense of something noticed, something changing. And that was all.

What rang in my mind were his words from weeks earlier: *Dig yourself out of your hole, Walt McNamara. Go.*

44. It's Important How We Talk About Things
Whaleback Island

"You must be an absolute prune!" said Paul Brevard, striding barefoot on the poolside tile and shrugging out of his bathrobe. He walked slowly down the stairs into the pool, a big hairless bear of a body in red trunks.

"How about that seat? With a drink in your hand? On a clear night like this?"

Brevard walked in the shallows toward me, dipped beneath the surface of the water, came up for air, then swam a breaststroke toward the corner of the pool.

"How you feeling?" he asked.

"Confused," I said.

"Makes sense. What you need to know is that you're our man, Walt. You're the number one guy. You aced the program, passed with flying colors, and we want to bring you in."

I listened and tried to keep my face neutral.

"To our employ," said Brevard. "I was just talking to Joshua and Brian about this. 'The warm embrace.'"

I asked him who Joshua and Brian were, and he told me they were the ones who'd brought me to Tuckaway. Mass and New Jersey. "So they aced the program, too?"

"Different level, son. Lower level. They'll be great handlers. They're strong. Not super sharp, but they're loyal." Brevard flung a meaty arm over the edge of the pool and rested it on the tile. "And that's an important thing, loyalty."

"You have Aubrey?"

"We have Aubrey, yes."

"You're hiring her, too?"

"Well, she's here. She's a friend of yours, I know, which is good. We need to all be on the same page."

"She's here right now?"

"Indeed she is. I'll bring her out soon."

I stared at Brevard's wet face and neck, not wanting to get rattled, trying to stay focused on the warmth and safety of the pool. "Why'd you fire Grunewald?"

"I'm going to wait until everyone is here so we can have a proper conversation about that," he said.

The light from the house was behind Brevard, but there was enough moonlight on his face for me to see him clearly, his somber eyes. "But no, we didn't fire him."

"Can you just tell me what's going on?" I asked. I could feel the rage building in my own voice.

"Here's what I want. I want you to keep drinking that drink, keep enjoying this pool. And think less. I want you to know what's good for you. That's really all I want, son. You were chosen. I want you to settle down and be real. I think you'll actually have a good time with it."

"Can you at least tell me why you had me talk to your daughter?"

"Don't overthink it. It was nice, right? Just like it was nice for *me* to talk with your mother the other day. She needed to know you were okay. I wanted her to know how you won the program."

I asked him what he meant.

"I'm sorry to say, she seems a bit down on her luck right now. I'd like to help her out."

I was trying hard not to get knocked off balance by Brevard's mixture of extravagant praise and vague threats. I asked him what he'd done to my mom.

"Excuse me? I want to help her, Walt. Calm the fuck down. I'm telling you, I just think she's struggling. With your dad gone."

"You went to my house?"

"Like I said, I wanted to touch base. Let her know how well you'd done. Let her know that you were making a name for yourself on the island, and that you'd really be able to help us." He stretched his arm across the tile and grabbed the Scotch, poured me some more, then poured his own. "Not at your house. She's staying with her friend, the short guy, Dr . . . "

"Dr. Charles?" I'd never been to Dr. Charles's house.

"I felt it was important that she hear from me directly, in person."

I was glad to know she was staying with Dr. Charles. I was sure she had taken on extra shifts, devoting herself to her work, and that it was her exhaustion from working that had led Brevard to believe she was down on her luck. Or maybe he was just flat-out lying.

"You'll see. We *do* take care of each other out here," said Brevard. "Most of the kids in the program have no families, or none to speak of. That kid from Missouri in your group, she'll be able to help us. She was born in a trailer, no hospital, no doctor, no records at all. And none of that is her fault. I know you have your mom, though. She's a lovely woman by the way. She deserves the support you can give her by working for us."

He pushed a hand through his hair, which had stiffened in the cold.

"Look, I know this all must be disorienting. I know you'll be able to figure it all out as we go. You're smart and you're pragmatic and you're careful. I'm glad you're having this drink with me, taking a look around. Joey MacLean really wants to thank you. For your grit and your willingness, we know we can send you anywhere to do any job, take care of any problem, and it'll be like it wasn't done by anyone at all. We'll know it was done by you, we'll be grateful as hell, but no one else will have any fucking clue. Analog help, that's you. And the money, Walt, the money is there. We know how much you're needed. You're worth it to us. And with the way the world is changing, your help is critical." He gestured toward the house. "Let me get them."

He wiped his hand on the towel and picked up his phone. He placed a call and said, "Yeah, it's time."

When Brevard put the phone down, he said, "So, son. How we talk about things. It's important. I want you to be family. I want you to see the world from the same vantage I see it from. I want to help you understand what's coming, and I want us to work together like family."

He seemed to sense that I wasn't convinced. His big face had dried in the cold air, but his eyes were still shining in the moonlight.

I couldn't ask him about Feng or Grunewald or Aubrey's mom, but I mustered the question: "Why do you need an army?"

He laughed. "Army? You're not part of any army. Look, an army, that's government and rules. All we need is to keep what's ours. Stay low profile but be ready to hit back. We can't afford to have anyone fuck with us. And whatever we do, we need it to be untraceable."

"Who would fuck with you?"

"Hey, Walt, be real. It's not our fault what's happening out there, the instability—" he gestured toward the dark waves beyond the crashing surf, "—but it *is* our fault if we don't do something about it."

He said lines needed to be drawn. He said chaos was coming, and there was no changing that. He said we needed to stick together. "It's a lot to take in, son, I get it. And Joey MacLean will talk to you, help make this all the more real," he said. "Just know, you are worthy of what you're being asked to do. We are ready to take you in."

"I didn't really see myself as winning the program."

"Which is yet another reason why you're our number one guy."

"What about the others? Tess? Corsetti?"

"We'll have roles for most of them. We need as many of them as possible. But you could see how it might be a little sensitive. Some of those kids would be a liability to keep, so we'll have to find a way to ship them out, give them something to do that will keep them, you know, happy—and be careful with the info they have."

The door from the house out onto the pool deck opened, and through it came Aubrey, wearing a generic gray tracksuit, black watch cap, white running shoes. Beside her, Mass was in the same attire. He was holding her by the upper part of her left arm, and I could tell she didn't like this—several times she tried to shrug out of his grasp, but he held on. Then came New Jersey, built like a concrete pillar, arms folded on his chest, same gray tracksuit. Finally, Joey MacLean, clean shaven with his hair parted neatly, in a red parka and jeans. "Hey, folks. Pool party's over. Let's talk."

Brevard and I swam to the shallow end and climbed the stairs. From the changing room, New Jersey tossed Brevard a bathrobe and me a towel. I wrapped it around my shoulders and asked Aubrey, "Are you good?"

She nodded curtly.

In the changing room my old clothes had been replaced by a neat stack: the gray tracksuit, briefs and socks, sneakers, watch cap.

When I returned to the group, they were sitting around a patio table in the dim glow of the pool. They'd pulled up a chair for me. I sat between Brevard and MacLean and across from Aubrey, who sat between Mass and New Jersey. I saw the clench in her jaw muscle and the fierceness of her eyes.

MacLean said, "So. Here we all are. This shouldn't take long. I want to talk to you about loyalty, and truth. As far as loyalty goes, either you have it, or you don't."

"Exactly," said Brevard.

"Brian, can you bring that tray over here with the Scotch?" said MacLean.

New Jersey retrieved the tray from the far corner of the pool. MacLean poured six glasses.

"I propose a toast," said MacLean, raising his glass. Aubrey and Brevard and Mass and New Jersey and I all took a glass. "To loyalty." While we were quiet in our sipping, the waves were loud.

"I believe Grunewald thinks he was doing the right thing for you kids by swimming out here during the storm. He sees himself as a loyal person. He wanted to have a talk with us, and we indulged him."

My body felt weak. "Why didn't you tell us that at the meeting?"

"There was too much to explain," said Brevard.

"We gave you what you could handle at the time," said MacLean. "Grunewald swimming out here, asking a bunch of questions, making claims, it was his way of resigning. That's what I believe. He'd brought you to the Pendrick Room. He smashed cameras. He told you we're taking advantage of you, which couldn't be further from the truth."

"We're helping you. Obviously," said Brevard.

"He questioned our reasons for including you in the program, Aubrey," said MacLean. "He didn't think we knew what we were doing. Aubrey, Dick Grunewald didn't even know your mother. You know I was the one who invited her out to the island, gave her a place, gave her everything. I wanted her to be part of our family. I was good to her, and I was doing her a favor by connecting her to her family's story. It's a great story. I wanted to give her room to be here. But she didn't want that. I mean, she wanted some of it."

"It would have been great if it had worked out," said Brevard.

"It would have been," said Joey MacLean.

"We want it to work out with you. To be here."

"It's true, we do."

"But here's what we need from you. From all of you. Joshua, will you please bring Grunewald out here now?"

Mass leapt out of his seat, went into the house, and returned within seconds, pushing Grunewald through the doorway and out onto the patio. His hands were tied behind his back, gray stubble growing on his cheeks and chin, eyes dark from exhaustion. As soon as Mass pushed him out of the foyer, Grunewald starting yelling, "You'll pay for this, motherfuckers!"

"Put the sock back in his mouth," said Brevard.

"No, no," said MacLean, pulling a matte black Glock from the pocket of his parka. "It's fine. He can talk all he wants."

"God sees you, you know. And he's fucking irate." When he caught eyes with me and Aubrey he quieted and seemed genuinely emotional. In nearly a whisper he said, "Oh, Jesus."

"We're just trying to be real, here," said MacLean. "Joshua, what do we do with someone who breaks the rules?"

"Like what?" asked Mass. He was a good six inches taller than Grunewald, and the blonde crewcut he'd had in September had grown out and stuck out of the watch cap over his ears.

"Like, if you're late to swimming," said MacLean.

"Oh right, ha, yeah—*that*," said Mass, but he stood still behind Grunewald, holding on to the rope used to tie his hands.

"We have some rules. We have to follow them. Dick, you broke a swimming rule. And a few other rules, too," said MacLean.

Mass nudged Grunewald toward the pool. He took off his white sneakers and socks and his sweatpants. Grunewald was wearing rain gear and boots. They used the stairs to step together down into the shallow end.

"Fucking criminals," Grunewald said. "This isn't the way things are done."

"Maybe you're right, Paul. Maybe we put the sock back in."

"I should?" asked Mass.

"Well, Joshua, first you need to administer the punishment," said MacLean. "Brian, why don't you give him some backup."

New Jersey took off his sweatpants too, and then stood beside Mass in the pool. Mass kept one hand on Grunewald's wrists, New Jersey put his hand on Grunewald's neck, and Mass pushed the old man's head into the water. Grunewald thrashed against them, but he was no match for the boys.

We could all hear the waves shushing and crashing on the beach again.

Mass was stooped over, the glow of the pool on his face, the cords in his neck straining as he held Grunewald under.

"For how long?" asked Mass.

"It's up to you," said MacLean.

Mass looked at New Jersey. "Like a minute?"

"Your call," said MacLean.

I stood but just as quickly MacLean grabbed my wrist, squeezed it hard, and pulled me back into my chair. Then he waved the barrel of the Glock in my direction and said, "Let them sort this out."

"That seems like enough," said Mass.

Grunewald's legs had stopped kicking.

"If you say so," asked MacLean.

"Let's not kill him, okay?" said New Jersey.

Mass yanked Grunewald out of the water, and the old man pulled a loud gasping breath into his lungs. They dragged him up to the red tile. His knees buckled and they laid him down on his side as he caught his breath.

"Not fun," said MacLean, walking over to Grunewald and nudging his shoulder with his boot.

New Jersey toweled off and put his sweatpants on as Mass stood barefoot on the tile, his chin down on his chest, his hands shaking.

"Bring him here," said MacLean.

Mass helped Grunewald to his feet. Water dripped from the cuffs of his rain gear. When they reached the patio table Grunewald's face looked haggard, depleted. MacLean asked him, "Are we square?"

"Fuck off. You're garbage," said Grunewald, hands still tied behind his back.

"Okay, then," said MacLean.

"You're weak," said Grunewald. "And you don't own me. Never have."

"I didn't ever claim to own you," said MacLean.

"Tell Maine everything. She deserves to know," said Grunewald.

MacLean stood, swung a punch at Grunewald with the gun in his hand, hitting him in the temple, knocking him over. He toppled two of the deck chairs before hitting the patio tile and then lay there, unmoving. I hopped up and went to his side, and this time MacLean said nothing. I put my hand on Grunewald's bald head, felt its heat, and blood from the cut the gun had made. He was breathing but his eyelids, nearly closed, were fluttering.

"Why the fuck did you do that?" I asked.

"Our program is in turmoil right now because of this guy," said MacLean. "We have to start holding people accountable for their actions and for the things they say. Sit down, please. He'll be fine."

I put a seat cushion under Grunewald's head and left him on his side. I returned to the table.

"Joshua and Brian, I have another loyalty test for you," he said. "You have one hour. Swim back to Whaleback. Each of you select the member of your Huddle that no longer deserves to be in the program. Completely your choice. Bring them back here."

"An hour?" asked Mass.

MacLean turned his hand that held the Glock, looking at his watch. "Fifty-nine minutes and fifty-five seconds."

Mass and New Jersey jumped the fence and began running down the blueberry field to the channel separating the islands.

MacLean turned his attention to Aubrey and me. "I don't know guys. Seriously, it's no longer enough to just quietly believe in something. You have to act on your beliefs. I do this every day of my fucking life. It's hard but it's the way we have to be."

"Yeah," said Brevard. "It's not easy."

"So. Aubrey and Walt. Can we revisit some common understandings? When we leave this table for the night, I want to make sure we all have the same clarity. The same truth. You can bring this understanding back to your Huddle."

"This is extremely important," said Brevard, pouring himself more Scotch.

"You go first, Walt," said MacLean. "Tell us what happened here tonight. What can you tell your Huddle when you return to them, when you select the person that no longer deserves to be here."

"You mean, what will I tell them?"

"Yeah, what will you say. About what happened here, and what will you say about the person you choose."

I wanted to be strong, but I felt nervousness and weakness spreading through my body. I felt it in my voice, too, when I said, "I'll tell them that you guys demand loyalty."

"No, you don't need to say that," said MacLean, waving the gun casually. "Let's start with Grunewald. What do you say about him?"

"Maybe nothing?"

"Probably right," said MacLean.

My mind was racing. "How about that you want us all to work together on a common goal that will help everyone?"

"Pretty good," said MacLean. "That sounds okay to me."

Grunewald was stirring. He lifted his head off the seat cushion and rolled onto his knees.

Joey MacLean craned his neck to the side of the table to see Grunewald, who was struggling to right himself with his hands tied. "Welcome back, Dick. I'm glad you're awake to hear this. Your turn, Aubrey."

Aubrey's face was dark blue from the glow of the pool. She stared at the glass of Scotch in front of her.

I wanted to know what was in her mind. I was struggling to think clearly. My body was shaking. I asked, "What do you want her to—"

"I know what he's asking," said Aubrey, her voice clear and steady. When I'd heard her speak in a whisper earlier that evening, it had been just for me. This was a bigger, full-toned, direct voice, and she was sitting up straight in her deck chair. "You're asking about my mom. You want me to tell her story."

"Yes," said MacLean.

When she spoke, the waves seemed to quiet for her and the light from the pool glowed on her face "You knew her well, Joey. She liked drugs and guys. And you helped her. You gave her stability. You offered her a place out here and told her about relatives she'd never known. You were drawn to her because she was beautiful and strong. Everyone here on the island, all the Islanders, they know their ancestors. We didn't. She'd lost her way. You loved her. You respected her. You gave her a purpose. You propped her up. But she couldn't handle it. My mom was loud and impulsive, and she was an addict. She wasn't capable of being with just one guy. You did everything you could. You just couldn't save her from herself. You are someone who wants to help needy people. That makes you a good guy. But sometimes us poor people just can't get out of our own way."

Aubrey kept looking calmly at MacLean, whose eyes were brimming with tears. He took a sip of his Scotch, cleared his throat, and said, "It's just not fucking easy to do what I did. You got it right. Thank you."

"You saved her," said Aubrey. "As much as she could be saved."

"Thank you."

Aubrey said, "You're welcome." She raised her glass.

Joey MacLean raised his.

"To my mom, Patty Surette," said Aubrey. Brevard and I raised our glasses, too.

MacLean tilted his glass all the way up, getting the last drops before setting it down. Finally, a tear traveled out his left eye and ran down his cheek. Aubrey picked up the bottle and gestured to him, *more?*, and he nodded.

She stretched her arm across the table, but he didn't move his glass toward her, so she pushed herself up from her chair. Holding the bottle, she walked around Brevard's deck chair toward MacLean.

45. Life Beyond

Minnesota

Thank God there's been life beyond that moment.

Just recently, Aubrey and I were together on a warm summer evening in a new city where no one knew us.

Minneapolis.

I had a job as a day laborer—a member of the grounds crew for the parks department, on my knees in the dirt planting flowers, weeding, and mowing lawns. Aubrey had a gig pedaling a bicycle taxi from seven to three, not the best shift but not bad for a rookie.

We had all the time we wanted to walk and tell stories. One about the guy in the Twins hat, her last ride of the day, who'd hailed her and asked her to head toward the river, and fast, like she was some kind of harness pony. He had no real place to be . . . but also a story about her mom, that time they'd driven together to Montreal to see Bad Penny.

We picked up sandwiches and walked through the park to watch the ducks. We pretended the ducks were the main event, but the main event was really that we could walk anywhere and be together.

46. Listen to the Waves

Whaleback Island

hen Aubrey reached MacLean's side, ready to pour more Scotch into his glass, she was moving slowly, deliberately, politely, until she whistled the two notes from "Heigh Ho," reared back, and swung the bottle, cracking it against his head.

MacLean's gun clattered to the tile. I sprang from my chair and went to him without thinking. Shafts of dim light from the windows of the house filtered through the table and chair legs. I spotted the gun and stretched my arms out with my belly on the tile to reach for it, but it was Aubrey who managed to grab it from the other side of the table. When I stood back up, she was holding the gun in both jittering hands, pointing it at MacLean and breathing hard.

Paul Brevard yelled, "Stop this right now!"

She steered the barrel over in Paul Brevard's direction, and he shielded his face with his hands. Grunewald had gotten up to his knees, blood smeared on his cheek and chin. Aubrey moved the shaking gun back toward MacLean.

The ocean rolled in and out, the swells pummeling the rocks.

MacLean was holding his head, cuts from the bottle on his cheek and forehead.

He said "You hit me in the fucking face—"

"Here's another story I'd like you to hear," she said, louder. "And this one's true. My mom would be alive right now if it hadn't been for you. She drowned herself because you raped her. That's the truth. That's the truth. That's the truth!"

She breathed deeply, in and out.

MacLean said, "Please—"

She fired the gun four times, ear-splittingly loud retorts filling the night sky, MacLean and his chair knocked backward in the shadows. On the tile in the darkness, he raked his hands at his chest.

I had been helping Grunewald to his feet, untying the rope around his wrists, but the sound of the blasts made me grab Grunewald around the chest. We nearly fell over again, but I regained my balance and tore open the knots.

MacLean's hands stopped moving, as did the rest of him. We couldn't see his face clearly in the shadows but the dark blood from his body spread on the tile. Aubrey kept the wobbly gun pointed at him, her shoulders and chest rising and falling.

It's hard to say what Paul Brevard whispered in that moment. It may have been "holy fuck" but it also might have been "save me."

Aubrey had the gun pointed at him, and again Brevard tried to shield his face with his hands.

Standing beside me, Grunewald yelled, "No!"

For a breath, maybe two, we were all frozen, listening to the waves. Grunewald said, much quieter, "Don't shoot him. Hand the gun to me."

He moved slowly to Aubrey and opened his palms. She kept the gun pointed at Brevard but looked at Grunewald.

"Oh. My. God," said Brevard. "Thank you. This is the right thing. I knew I could count on you."

Aubrey surrendered the gun to Grunewald. He took it into his gnarled hands and in one fluid motion brought the barrel to Brevard's right temple.

"Me? It's me, Dick. Please."

Grunewald was holding the gun, but Aubrey was the one to talk. "Feng didn't make it to the hospital, did he."

"Why does that matter?" stuttered Brevard.

"He was dead in the boat, wasn't he."

"I wasn't the one who shot him, for fuck's sake. It was an accident."

"You didn't bring him to the hospital, did you."

"He was already dead."

Grunewald pulled the trigger.

The single shot felt even louder than the others, echoing off the granite cliffs on Whaleback.

Brevard toppled in his chair and was resting sideways on the patio, his head unrecognizable on the tile.

Grunewald used my towel to wipe the gun. He knelt down and placed it in Brevard's lifeless hand.

47. The Islanders

When we got to the water's edge, the tide and wind were moving in opposite directions, kicking up the waves. I was the first to wade into the dark water. Aubrey was right behind me and yelled, "Careful!" and I wheeled around and grabbed her arm and pulled her into the surge, which is when Grunewald dove in, too.

We pulled ourselves up onto Whaleback's far shore, our hands torn by the barnacles, our breath short in our frigid bodies, and once on the round boulders above the churn, I grabbed onto Aubrey, gripping more tightly than we had on Pickett Island or any other time. Grunewald said nothing, he jogged in place waiting for us in his waterlogged clothes.

Aubrey's chest shuddered, and I let go and took her hand, pulling her into the woods. We bushwhacked through the thicket, tree branches slashing our bodies. I was momentarily grateful to be numb from the swim. I couldn't see how bloody my hands were in the dark. We reached the perimeter trail, and then we were sprinting, charging through the dark. I stayed right behind Aubrey. We stopped twice on the trail to make sure Grunewald was close enough to follow.

The lean-to was silent, no fire, and I was terrified our Huddle had already been found by Mass or New Jersey or any of the young Club members, until I saw the tops of their heads poking out of their sleeping bags.

No one clicked on a headlamp to see who'd walked in under the eaves.

"It's Aubrey," Aubrey said. "And Walt. And Grunewald."

A tick of silence before Javier whispered, "Aubrey and Walt and Grunewald!" and the quiet frenetic celebration began. Tess acknowledged hearing Aubrey's voice for the first time by leaping up and saying, "What the fuck is going on?"

"We can't stay," Aubrey said, flinging clothes out of her rucksack, looking for dry ones. I unearthed a pair of wool socks and pulled them onto my bleeding feet.

"We heard gunshots," said Bianca.

"We need to get off the island," I said. "Now."

We tied up our boots, and I led the group to the Bayberry Trail, still without headlamps.

"There aren't any boats," said Corsetti.

"Capsize Drill," I said.

When we got within view of the floats, I had us get our bellies in the wet dying grass, wriggle to a spot where we could see if anyone was on the floats. We moved from shadow to shadow outside the Athletic Association to the little sandy beach. We silently pulled the canvas tarp off the boat and stepped the fully rigged mast while the boat was still in the seagrass. Getting that tall mast in the right hole took longer than it should have, but once it was up, we untied the boat from the tree and pushed it through the sand to the lapping shallows, and then into waist-deep water before climbing aboard.

We used oars to pole the boat further away from the beach and point it toward the mouth of the harbor. I found the line to raise the sail, and DeShawn got the gaff in place to make it square. We all needed to help get the boat moving, and we each remembered just barely enough. The flapping of the raised sail was loud, so I scrambled to the foredeck and pulled the canvas across the bow of the boat to fill it with wind. Aubrey brought the tiller all the way over to the same side of the boat. I felt the greasy pull of the boat through the water and could see the lights on the island shifting as we moved.

But it wasn't until we were outside the cove, the cold December wind pressing hard against our flat sail, that Aubrey pointed the boat downwind toward the twinkling lights of the mainland.

Bethany was on bow watch but everyone else crammed in the cockpit, even Grunewald, who'd been quiet since we'd set sail, offering no instruction. I told everyone exactly what had happened on Tuckaway.

"Joey and Paul," Grunewald said. "They had reason to be worried."

No one said anything in response, but we knew this was true. Water sluiced against the hull. When the wind gusted, we'd glide up and down a swell while the smaller waves kissed the boat, pitter-patter.

Amid our stunned quiet and the smooth fullness of the sail arose a faint buzz, like an electric toothbrush. Our eyes searched the boat for the source of the sound until the buzz grew into the unmistakable drone of a helicopter.

The roar of the helicopter's engine got louder and louder and we could see its lights brightening, heading straight for us. In the boat we were all silent. We just stayed on course. Some of us probably prayed.

I held my breath, and the aircraft zoomed overhead and kept on toward Whaleback. Word must have already gotten to the mainland.

Then it felt as though the whole world was tipping us toward the other side of the channel, every line taut, the boat really flying along.

Bethany sat on the bow, scanning the sea in front of us. Deshawn was on the main sheet, ready to pull it in or let it out. Javier checked the sweep of ocean on either side of us, and sometimes looked aft.

"Bowwatch! How we looking?" I yelled. I trusted Bethany up there.

"All clear," she said. "No rocks, no breakers, no other boats. Seems like we'll be clear for a while."

I called her back to the cockpit to warm up and we all huddled together, the pattern of waves sharp in the light from the moon. It got quiet among us again. Grunewald spoke. "You stuck together. For fuck's sake, you did. That's why we made it this far."

Javier put an arm around him.

Later, after we'd reached the mainland, Grunewald would point us toward where we needed to go. Our plan as a group would be to stay quiet about what had happened. We figured the Club members who found the bodies on Tuckaway would want to bury the story, too. We had no idea how the other WILDers on the island would fare.

Aubrey and I went to see my mom in Headfield first. Corsetti had some money squirreled in his backpack, enough for bus tickets for him and Tess to get back to Ohio. All nine of us scattered. Grunewald, too. We vowed to stay in contact over the years, and even if that wasn't possible, we knew we'd always be a Huddle.

When Aubrey and I got to Headfield, we told my mom enough that she could understand why we needed to keep moving. We didn't tell her about our plans to go to Minnesota, but we promised to keep her posted whenever we could. We cried together, all three of us.

It's the life we've made for ourselves. Sometimes it's hard to see how our choices have gotten us to where we are. We try to remain grateful. I still feel like an Islander even now, sixteen hundred miles away. Aubrey and I help each other, remind each other that to survive we must be self-reliant, and we also know we are just as vulnerable as everyone else in the world.

But there in the cockpit on the night we left Whaleback, Aubrey unearthed my paperback copy of Rimbaud from the inside pocket of her parka. Moonlight was enough for her to read the one we'd read together several times—"Drunken Boat"—in a clear and steady voice:

> "No longer can I, bathed in your languor, o waves
> Follow in the wake of the cotton boats
> Nor cross through the pride of flags and flames
> Nor swim under the terrible eyes of prison ships."

"Hell yeah," said Tess. "Fuck the prison ships."

Above the dark waves, even with that moon, the Milky Way was crazy bright, like a sunlit cloud.

THE END.

About the Author

Lewis Robinson is the author of *Officer Friendly and Other Stories* and *Water Dogs*, and he is the winner of a Whiting Award, the PEN Oakland/Josephine Miles Award, and a Fellowship from the National Endowment for the Arts. His writing has appeared in *Sports Illustrated*, The *New York Times Book Review*, and on the National Public Radio program *Selected Shorts*. He teaches at the University of Maine at Farmington and lives in Portland, Maine with his family.

Acknowledgments

This book, in its earliest conception, was inspired by the bravery of the student activists who survived the Marjorie Stoneman Douglas High School shooting in Parkland, Florida.

Thank you, Arthur Rimbaud and Emily Dickinson, for your poems.

Thank you to my brilliant and good-humored literary agent, Emily Forland. Your steadfast support means the world to me.

Thank you to my editor, Ron Currie, for asking the right questions, and for being willing to talk shop while we walked George and Lyle.

Thank you, Islandport Press, for your devotion to Maine stories, and to bringing those stories to readers: Shannon Butler, Marion Fearing, Dean Lunt, Emily Lunt, and Genevieve Morgan.

Thank you to the band, for your love and support and close reading: Sarah Braunstein, Kate Christensen, Bill Roorbach, and Monica Wood.

Thank you, Asa Tussing, for making Whaleback Island less fictional with your computations, and Cate Marvin, for the use of your typewriter, and Tori Oliveira, for your careful proofreading, and Kris Rosado, for teaching me how to shoot a semi-automatic rifle, and Paul Tortorella, for telling me stories about your days as a hockey goalie, and Bruce Robertson, for offering me a peek into the world of venture capital.

I wrote the first draft of this book while working for the Adamantine Spine Moving Company, based in Iowa City. Thank you, Eric Jones, for letting me estimate moves from my backyard shed in Maine, and for your friendship.

For your keen eyes and encouragement, thank you to these early readers: Zach Brockhouse, Nathan Conroy, Brock Clarke, Susan Conley, Alex Coppola, Theo Emery, Meghan Gilliss, Tasha Graff, Bill Lundgren, Meredith McCarroll, Aaron McCollough, Sean Mewshaw, Kevin O'Connor, John Ryder, and Curtis Sittenfeld.

Thank you to my amazing siblings. And thank you to my late father, Sam Robinson, for living so fully, and for loving us unconditionally. And my mother, Mimo Riley, for showing me what it means to be a "pluggah" and for prioritizing the making of art.

Thank you, Maisie, for giving Tess her name, and thank you, Leo, for naming my book *Nature Machine,* which, I grant you, is objectively a better title.

And finally: thank you CC, for believing in me and this book, and for being my favorite person.